I0728605

UNDER A SOUTHERN SKY

ACROSS THE SEAS
BOOK 4

CLARE FLYNN

For my Australian family - Sebastian, Hermina, Davina (plus Carlo, Mateo and Rodrigo), Roland, Daniel and Richmond. With love x

Under the wide and starry sky,
Dig the grave and let me lie.
Glad did I live and gladly die,
And I laid me down with a will
This be the verse you grave for me:
Here he lies where he longed to be;
Home is the sailor, home from sea,
And the hunter home from the hill.

Requiem, Robert Louis Stevenson

UNDER A SOUTHERN SKY

Copyright © 2025 Clare Flynn

All rights reserved. No parts of this publication may be reproduced, or used in any manner without the copyright holder's prior written consent.

Use of this work to train generative AI technologies is expressly prohibited and the author reserves all rights to license uses of the work for generative AI training and development.

ISBN 978-1-914479-41-0

Print ISBN 978-1-914479-42-7

This is a work of fiction. Any similarity between the characters and situations within its pages and places or persons, living or dead, is unintentional and coincidental.

Cover design JD Smith Designs

Published by Cranbrook Press, London, England.

1

SYDNEY DECEMBER 1941

Hannah couldn't believe she'd been in Australia for two months. She'd left her sister Judith and Judith's baby daughter in Tatura, in Victoria, where Judith's Italian husband was imprisoned as an enemy alien. It was time for Judith to stand on her own feet, break free of her dependence on her older sister and build a life for her small family.

And Hannah now needed to carve out a future for herself. It wouldn't be the one she'd dreamt of – living on a small farm in Australia with her husband, Will. Instead, she was in Australia alone as a widow at only twenty-two, thousands of miles from home in Liverpool. Tatura was a backwater where the best she could hope for would be a job in a café or a bar. Work so tedious it would be as much a prison sentence as the one poor Paolo was serving simply for the crime of being born Italian. And so Hannah had come to the decision to head off to Sydney, alone.

She found a room with half board in a small terraced house in Darlinghurst, near the centre of Sydney. The place was shabby but spotlessly clean. The landlady, Mrs Hodges, was a widow in her late fifties, and Hannah was her only lodger.

'You're my first paying guest,' she confided to Hannah. 'But since my son left home I've missed the company and having someone to look after.'

Hannah wasn't sure she liked the sound of being looked after but it would make a change to reverse the role she'd always played with her sister.

After days of anxious job-seeking, she had landed a post in a solicitors' office. Her previous experience and references from working in the Map Room of Western Approaches Command in Liverpool, plotting the movements of allied and enemy shipping, had impressed her employers. The work wasn't demanding, or even terribly interesting – just filing, a little typing, making tea for the partners and carrying documents and messages to and from the courts and barristers' chambers. But at least it would pay the rent.

Despite the friendliness of her new colleagues and Mrs Hodges, Hannah was cautious about revealing too much of herself. Telling anyone about the death of her husband was to be avoided at all costs. The inevitable sympathy would break her. She could only keep going by trying not to think about Will and his terrible death in the icy waters of the Atlantic after an attack on his ship by a German bomber. Talking about it was unimaginable.

She filled her evenings and weekends by walking around the city, strolling through the parks and the harbour, and going to the pictures. With Mrs Hodges, she was always polite but guarded and presented a cheerful face to the world whilst giving nothing away.

But alone in bed at night, Hannah couldn't keep her loss and loneliness at bay. Even after nearly a year, it was unbearable to think she would never see Will again, never experience the warmth of his body beside her, to wake up in a tangle of limbs, never again hear his laughter, listen to his stories or feel the tenderness of his lips on hers.

Unable to sleep, she would take out the only photograph of herself and Will, well-thumbed and grainy. It had been taken on a rare day spent together soon after the war began. They were hand in hand on the Mersey ferry to New Brighton. She studied the image now, scarcely able to recognise the young woman with the shining eyes and the huge smile. She was wearing a winter coat and a beret, her hair tumbling over her collar as she leant against the railings, her head on Will's shoulder. He was wearing his usual old battered cap and pea jacket, and his gaze was fixed on her.

She thought of the recording of a French song Will had bought for her the day before they were married. That was when he told her that instead of them going to Australia, he was going to stay in the merchant navy for the duration of the war. She couldn't remember the French words of the song but knew what they meant: I will always wait for you to come back. The record had been destroyed along with the gramophone player when their Liverpool home was bombed.

And Will was never coming back.

A WEEK after she started work, the war Hannah believed she'd left behind in the blitzed ruins of Liverpool encroached on her life again with a suddenness she could not have foreseen. She came downstairs to find her landlady in a state of anxiety. Mrs Hodges, pale as a bowl of cream, sloshed the tea over the tray as she carried it to the table.

'The Prime Minister's just been on the wireless. We're at

war with Japan!' Mrs Hodges put down the tray and ran her fingers through her usually immaculately groomed hair. 'They've gone and bombed the American navy.'

Stunned, Hannah pulled out a chair and sat down, gratefully accepting a cup of tea.

'I can't remember the name of the blooming place.' Mrs Hodges fiddled with the dial on the radio set and she kept up a running commentary. 'That was it – Pearl Harbour! Never heard of it. Have you?'

Hannah hadn't.

The disembodied voice on the radio said, 'There have been surprise attacks all around the Pacific. The Japanese have invaded Malaya and bombed Singapore. In a shock raid on the United States Naval base at Pearl Harbour, Hawaii, hundreds of Japanese planes attacked and destroyed the American fleet.'

The two women listened in disbelief.

Mrs Hodges' hand shook as she cracked eggs into a frying pan. 'Those poor Yanks didn't stand a chance. Sitting ducks! On a Sunday morning too.' She clutched the front of her blouse, then folded her ample arms and shook her head. 'I'm worried sick. My son's serving with the RAAF up in Darwin. He's a maintenance engineer.'

'I'm sorry. That must be a worry. Have you had news of him?'

'Nothing in more than a fortnight. I usually hear from him every week. Just a postcard but it's better than nothing.' She glanced towards a framed portrait on the sideboard of a young man in military uniform. 'Suppose there's not much time for letter-writing when you're fighting a war.'

Since Hannah had been in Australia, there had been much talk and mounting worry about the Japanese threat in the Pacific. Understandably, Australia feared it would be targeted. Those fears must be mounting now.

Hannah closed her eyes. Was she going to go through it all over again? She'd believed she'd escaped the horrors of air raids – the terror of nighttime bombing, the scramble – cold and half asleep – for the Anderson shelter, the death and destruction rained down from German planes. Was she going to face it over again, this time on the other side of the world and from the Japanese?

'Does it mean America will join the war? Surely, they'll have to get involved now.' She sipped her tea, her appetite for breakfast deserting her.

Mrs Hodges huffed as she put down a plate of bacon and eggs on the table in front of Hannah. 'I blooming well hope so. They can't possibly stay out after that. Bloody Yanks – always late to the party. They sat the last war out until it was almost over.' She pulled up a chair, sat at the table and poured herself a cup of tea. 'Still, better late than never. It's good news for Australia as otherwise we'd only have Singapore to keep the Japs at bay. We're at the back of the queue here as far as Mr Churchill's concerned. With the Americans getting stuck in, we'll have a better chance of keeping the Japs out of Australia.'

Hannah hoped she was right, imagining Sydney Harbour being strafed by Japanese planes with bombs raining down on this beautiful sun-drenched city.

Mrs Hodges stood up. 'Mind if I turn the wireless off? It's setting my nerves jangling.'

Hannah nodded assent and struggled to eat her breakfast.

.   .   .

WHEN HANNAH ARRIVED AT THE SOLICITORS' office in Castlereagh Street, a short tram ride from her digs, it was abuzz with talk of the Japanese attacks and their implications. Clerks and solicitors alike were gathered in the scullery dissecting the news. While the Americans' entry into the war was likely to change its course, any form of escalation filled Hannah with horror. When would it all end? The addition of the United States would create a massive upgrade in numbers and capabilities, but the range and ferocity of the Japanese attacks showed they were in deadly earnest and planned to make this an all-out world war.

Apparently, the Japanese army had landed at Kota Bharu in northern Malaya and had also attacked Manila in the Philippines and the US naval base on Guam. Thailand had been invaded and had already surrendered. The words of the Australian Prime Minister, John Curtin, saying, 'This is the gravest hour of our history,' sent a chill down Hannah's spine.

The senior partner called the staff to order and told them to get back to work and stop speculating. Hannah was relieved to shut it all out and focus on the routine of her job. She picked up a pile of completed briefs from her in-tray and set about filing them alphabetically in the wall of wooden cabinets.

After Will's death, she hadn't wanted to come to Australia. What was the point of being here in his homeland without him? She'd given in to Judith's pleas that they come to Australia to find Paolo after he was deported. Reluctantly, Hannah had bowed to the pressure. She was happy to have played her part in reuniting the couple, but being in Australia was a constant reminder of her loss. Yet she told herself it was what Will would have wanted her to do. As soon as the bombing started in Liverpool, he'd begged her to go with Judith and sail to Australia until he could join her there after the war. At the time, she'd refused. It was important to her to be there on the dockside waiting for him every time he came home from sea.

How different it would have been to discover this country with Will to guide her. Now everywhere she went she couldn't help wondering whether he had been there himself. But he would have wanted her to be strong, so she put on a brave face and had tried to get on with building a life for herself.

During her lunch break, Hannah walked over to Dymock's Book Arcade in George Street to consult a world atlas. As she passed through the streets, there were already signs of the changing conditions caused by the war. Instead of window displays of Santa Claus and his reindeer – a sight she'd found incongruous in the height of the Australian summer – workmen were up ladders attaching loud-speakers to buildings for air raid warning sirens, brown paper was being taped to shop windows to act as blackout, and wooden blast reinforcements were being erected around the stone façade of the general post office in Pitt Street. *Dear Lord, please don't let me go through all that again.*

Inside Dymocks, she studied the map of the Pacific region. Manila and Malaya were closer to Australia than she'd thought. If the Japanese established bases there, it would be easy to launch an attack. She looked at where Hawaii sat in the middle of the Pacific far from Japan – Australia was no greater distance. Consulting the scale on the map she calculated that Pearl Harbour was about four thousand miles from Tokyo, whereas Darwin was about six hundred miles nearer.

THAT EVENING, when she returned to her lodgings, Mrs Hodges handed her an envelope.

'I hope you don't mind me asking, darl, but I see your letter's from Victoria. Do you have relatives there?'

Bowing to the inevitable, Hannah nodded. 'My sister and her family.' She didn't want to reveal that Paolo was a prisoner of war.

But Mrs Hodges was not so easily satisfied. 'Your sister? What's she doing there?'

It was none of Mrs Hodge's business, so Hannah stretched the truth. 'She met her husband before the war, and they moved to Australia after the invasion of Poland. When the bombing got bad back home, they invited me to join them.'

'Your sis married an Aussie? He a farmer?'

'Yes.' It was partly true. The inmates of the camp were put to work as farm labourers.

'Let's hope he doesn't have to serve. They got kids?'

'Just one. A baby girl.'

Mrs Hodge nodded. 'Can't say I'm surprised you didn't stick it out there in Victoria, ducky. Not much going for a young girl like you.'

Eager to end the interrogation, Hannah said she was going to her room until dinner, and clutching the letter, she escaped from her nosy landlady.

Her bedroom at the back of the house was small – just space for a narrow bed, a wooden chair and a chest of drawers, with a couple of hooks on the wall to hang up her few clothes. Since Mrs Hodges insisted that she keep the window shut when out at work, it was hot and stuffy, even now in the early evening. Hannah opened the window and flung herself on the bed to read Judith's letter.

It was short. A single sheet. Judith wasn't proving to be much of a correspondent.

Dear Hannah,

Hope you're well. Sarah has two new teeth and has been keeping me awake half the night. It's hard to be cross as she's such an adorable baby when she's not teething!

Paolo has been singing with the camp choir again, and they are practising for a concert at Christmas. I can't wait. You've no idea how awful it is only being able to see him through a wire fence.

Hannah flung the letter down. Judith was so insensitive. No idea? She would give anything to see Will through a barbed wire fence. She bit her lip and swallowed her anger. Judith would never change. She was unthinking but there was no malice in her, and she certainly didn't intend to be hurtful. Hannah picked the letter up again.

Good news that you have found a job at last. I hope it's not too boring. Have you done anything yet about finding Aunt Elizabeth? It was the main reason you went to Sydney, so you should jolly well get on with it!

Hannah sighed. Judith was right. Finding their long-lost aunt mattered now more than ever. She'd been using her search for a job as a reason for prevaricating, but there was no longer an excuse. With her sister nearly five hundred miles away, Hannah longed to connect with someone else who had known Will.

Indirectly and unknowingly, it was Aunt Elizabeth who had brought Hannah and Will together. Elizabeth had left

Liverpool for Australia in 1920, and Hannah bore a close resemblance to her. She was Will's stepmother, and a chance sighting of Hannah on the Liverpool waterfront had almost convinced Will he was seeing his stepmother herself. It was what caused him to speak to her and, in doing so, to change the course of their lives. Now Will was gone and Elizabeth was one of the few connections Hannah had to her husband.

When it came to tracing her aunt, Hannah had very little information to go on. The only link with Elizabeth she knew of was a woman called Verity Radley, a schoolteacher in McDonald Falls, the small town in the Blue Mountains where Will came from and where Elizabeth lived when married to Will's father. But Verity Radley was dead – the letter Will had written to her had been returned to them unopened. Hannah would need to go to McDonald Falls and try to pick up the trail from there.

She carried on reading Judith's letter.

The Clancys have asked me to invite you to join us for Christmas. I do hope you aren't going to make excuses. Little Sarah is growing up fast and you're missing out. You can come to the concert at the camp - the locals have all been invited. It will be fun. Much better than staying on your own in the city. I can't imagine why you want to be there anyway. You'd be much better off here with us.

The Clancys were the couple with whom Judith lodged. Terry Clancy worked as a warder at the Tatura internment camp and had befriended Paolo. Hannah had become fond of Terry and his wife, Sal, during her brief stay there. Tempting as it was to accept the invitation, Judith would never break out of her dependency on Hannah until she had no choice. If Hannah wanted to build a life in Australia, it had to be on her own, even if the thought of spending Christmas alone was a miserable one.

Her decision was made the next day when the firm needed someone to support the duty solicitor over the holiday period. It would mean overtime pay, so Hannah volunteered. With a heavy heart, she picked up her pen and wrote her reply to her sister.

2

MID DECEMBER 1941

Sydney's Central Station was an impressive Edwardian structure built from buttery sandstone with colonnades and a clock tower. Hannah stepped onto the wide concourse with its vast arched ceiling. She bought a ticket for McDonald Falls, the town in the Blue Mountains where Will lived until he ran away to sea.

The trip would take about two and a half hours. It was early morning, so she'd have a full day to explore the town and make inquiries about her aunt. Already the day was getting hot, and Hannah was glad that her destination was likely to be much cooler than the city.

As the train chugged towards the mountains, she thought about the tragic history of her family. After her Aunt Elizabeth had been forced out of the family home more than twenty years ago, her name had never again been mentioned in the household. Hannah had forgotten her aunt's very existence until she happened upon a photograph. When her father saw the picture, he'd flown into a violent rage. He'd beaten Hannah and destroyed the precious photograph, setting in train the events that led to his brutal murder of Hannah and Judith's mother, Sarah. He paid the price on the gallows.

Although he was her father, Hannah felt only loathing for Charles Dawson. She would never forgive him for the savage killing of her mother or for what she found out he had done to Elizabeth, her mother's sister. He had raped her then thrown her out.

As the train left the city behind, Hannah wondered whether she'd ever find her aunt. Even if she did, would Elizabeth be ready to accept her after what her father had done? The ties that bound them were not only the familial links – she was related to her aunt also by marriage – Elizabeth was Will's stepmother.

Will had regarded Elizabeth as his only friend when he was a lonely adolescent with a troubled relationship with his father, Jack. Finding Elizabeth had mattered as much to Will as it did to Hannah. She was doing this for both of them.

Would she even recognise Elizabeth were she to find her? She no longer had that old photograph, and more than twenty years had passed since it had been taken. Her aunt must be around fifty now.

THE DAY WAS warm even here in the mountains when Hannah emerged from the station at McDonald Falls. Above, in a eucalyptus tree, white cockatoos were screeching. She walked towards what she presumed was the main street. The place had the feel and appearance of a small frontier town. On one side, set back from the road, was a large colonnaded Victorian building, with formal gardens in front, and prominently signed as The Queen Alexandra Hotel. Strolling under the canvas shop canopies that provided shade from the summer sunshine, Hannah wondered where to start. After so long, the likelihood of finding anyone who had known Elizabeth Kidd, let alone knew her present whereabouts, was remote.

Tears threatened and she swallowed them down. She was retracing Will's footsteps in his old hometown. How many times had he walked along this stretch of pavement, looked in this shop window, paused to greet a familiar face? She walked aimlessly until the sadness ebbed away, replaced by curiosity. The place was small enough not to be intimidating, but large enough that she didn't feel too conspicuous.

A plan was needed – she only had a day in the town. It would be foolish to waste it. Having missed breakfast to make the early train, she was hungry, so she went into a tearoom and ordered morning tea with a toasted teacake. It came dripping with butter, and as she ate, she savoured the taste. It was only a matter of time before rationing would be introduced in Australia too.

A discarded newspaper lay on the next table. She reached across, and scanned the headline, which was about anger and frustration in Canberra that Britain wasn't doing enough to support the Pacific region. Hope was pinned on the supposedly impregnable Singapore, but since the sinking of the *Prince of Wales* and *Repulse* warships soon after Pearl Harbour in early December, there was no longer any significant defensive presence there. Apparently, the British strategy rested on the impregnability of Singapore itself – and the fact that to reach it, the Japanese army would have to travel the length of Malaya through impassable jungle and roads too narrow to allow the mass transportation of an invading army.

It was all too depressing. Hannah pushed the paper

aside, opened her handbag and took out a notebook and pencil. When in doubt, make a list.

She chewed the end of the pencil. Where to start? Here in this tea shop was as good a place as any.

- *Tearoom (are there other cafés too?)*
- *Post Office*
- *School – did Verity Radley have friends?*
- *Pub or bar*
- *Shops*
- *The Queen Alexandra Hotel*

Things to ask
- *Where did the Kidds live?*
- *Did Elizabeth Kidd have any friends other than Verity?*
- *How far is McDonald Creek?*

Would the Kidds' former smallholding at McDonald Creek be close enough for her to visit the place where Will had spent most of his young life?

Slipping the notebook back into her bag, she summoned the young waitress and asked to settle the bill. The girl was clearly too young to have known the Kidds, so Hannah asked whether the owner or manager was in.

The girl's face fell. 'You making a complaint?'

Hannah rushed to reassure. 'No. Quite the contrary. That toasted teacake was delicious, and your service was faultless. I just want to inquire about someone who used to live around here.'

The girl grinned with relief. 'Mrs Taylor's in the kitchen. I'll see if she's free.' She vanished behind a curtain at the rear, emerging soon after, accompanied by a portly woman in her fifties.

'G'day. How can I help?'

Hannah started by repeating the words of praise she'd used with the waitress.

'The baked goods are all made on the premises with my own hands. Glad ya liked them.' The proprietor turned to go back to the kitchen.

'Please. Just a moment. I imagine this place has been open some time?'

'More 'n twenty years.' The woman wiped her hands on her apron.

'So you must know most people in the town. I was wondering if you knew my late husband's family, the Kidds?'

The woman frowned. 'Who was your husband?'

'William Kidd. Called himself Will.'

'You're Will Kidd's wife? He's passed away?'

Hannah bit her lip. 'Last year. Will was a sailor on the Atlantic convoys. He was killed in a German aerial attack.'

The woman's expression softened. 'I'm truly sorry to hear that, Mrs Kidd. Will was a nice boy. Always a smile for everyone. Used to come into town selling rabbit skins. Must be fifteen, twenty years since he left the Falls. That was the last I heard of him.' She frowned again. 'So what can I help you with? I presume you know about his old man and how he got what was coming to him at the end of a rope? Killed his own son, Will's older brother. Nat Kidd was a wrong 'un but nothing justifies a man killing his own child.' She jutted out her lower lip and shook her head. 'Now if that's all, I'll be getting back to my kitchen.'

Hannah wanted to protest that Nat's death had been an accident. Manslaughter at worst. According to Will, his father had been defending Will and Elizabeth from Nat who had already stabbed Will in the stomach. Will always believed the hanging of his father had been a grave miscarriage of justice. But Jack Kidd had accepted his fate and refused to lodge an appeal against the murder verdict.

Hannah needed to stay focussed on finding out about Elizabeth.

'Please, just one more thing. I'm actually interested in Jack Kidd's widow, Mrs Elizabeth Kidd. She's my aunt and I don't know where she is.'

'Best keep it that way then.' The woman folded her arms, the smile fading from her face. I'm sorry to say it, as you look a decent, respectable lady, but your aunt was no good.'

3

———

Burning with indignation, Hannah left the tearoom. Why did the proprietor think so badly of Elizabeth? It was unjust and unfair after all her aunt had gone through. If everyone in this town felt the same way about Elizabeth, her trip was likely to prove fruitless.

She stood in the shade under the canopy of a hardware shop and looked at her list. Finding someone who had known Verity Radley might be her best bet – the teacher had remained a loyal friend to Elizabeth until she'd died. The school would be the best place to start, but it was a Saturday. Although Miss Radley had lived on the premises, there was no guarantee her successor did.

After asking directions, Hannah found the school, but as expected, it was closed. Based on the cluster of modern buildings, it had expanded significantly since the days when Will lived in the town. Hannah walked on past the locked gates and came upon a stone-built cottage set back from the road and bearing a sign: The Old Schoolhouse. She took a deep breath and knocked on the door.

A young woman emerged almost immediately. She looked Hannah up and down, her expression curious. 'Yes?'

'I'm looking for information about Miss Verity Radley. She used to be the schoolteacher here.'

'Sorry. The school's nothing to do with us. We just own the house.' The woman started to close the door.

'Please. May I ask you a couple of questions? I've come up from Sydney, and I'm trying to trace my aunt, who once lived in the town and was a friend of Miss Radley.'

'You're from England, aren't you?' The woman smiled.

'From Liverpool. I moved to Australia a few months ago. My family lost touch with my aunt and I'm trying to trace her.'

The woman cocked her head to one side. 'You wrote to Miss Radley about a year ago, didn't you? I remember a letter from England. I marked the envelope to be returned to sender.'

'That's right.'

'Apparently, she died suddenly. We bought this place after her death and never met her. Sorry but I'm afraid there's nothing more I can tell you.'

Desperate, Hannah said, 'Just one more question, please. Who handled the sale of the house?'

The woman shrugged. 'Presume it would have been the lady's lawyers. My husband dealt with all that.' She looked over her shoulder. Somewhere inside the house, a baby was crying.

'May I speak to your husband? It's really important that I find my aunt. Miss Radley was probably the only person who would have known her whereabouts. I imagine she left some papers, letters. Something with my aunt's address on.'

The woman snapped, 'My husband's not here. He's an

airman serving with the RAAF in Singapore and I haven't heard from him in weeks. Now I need to feed the baby. G'day.' She closed the door, leaving Hannah standing on the step.

She turned away and walked back down the path, her spirits low. Across the road was a post office and general store. Hannah crossed over and went inside.

The postmistress told her there were three firms of solicitors in McDonald Falls but she didn't know which one had been Miss Radley's. She wrote down the addresses, pointing out that they would all be closed for the weekend. At least this woman was being helpful.

Encouraged, Hannah asked, 'Can you tell me anything about Mrs Elizabeth Kidd? She lived here about twenty years ago. I'm her niece and I'm trying to trace her.'

The woman's expression hardened. 'Everyone in the Falls knew the Kidds. They used to live in Kinross House, the fancy mansion at the end of this street. Overlooking the canyon. She sold up when Jack Kidd was condemned to death for murder. Sold the coal mine too. After that, I can't tell you since she left no forwarding address, but my guess is she went to Sydney.'

'Miss Radley stayed in touch with her. Didn't she mention where Elizabeth had gone?'

The postmistress shrugged. 'Miss Radley kept to herself after what happened. People round here didn't take kindly to the Kidd family or anyone who took their side. If she stayed close to Mrs Kidd, she kept it quiet. After all, she had a school to run and a reputation to uphold.'

A customer entered the shop, and the woman turned to serve her. Murmuring her thanks, Elizabeth left.

Another dead end. The journey had been a waste of time and effort. Disheartened, Hannah decided to take a look at Elizabeth's former home before getting the train back to Sydney. On Monday, she would contact each of the three law firms, and if that produced nothing, she would seek the advice of one of the solicitors in her own office. Somewhere, there must be a record of who handled the sale of Miss Radley's property.

Hannah straightened her shoulders as she walked to the end of the street. There were some concrete leads to follow and her employment at a law firm fortuitously put her in an excellent position to pursue them. The air was fresh with the scent of flowers, and the shops had given way to pretty weather-boarded bungalows with porches, small verandas and well-tended gardens.

The last house in the street was different. A polished brass plaque on the gatepost bore the words Kinross House. Hannah stood at the foot of the drive, amazed at the scale and grandeur of the place. Unlike most of the properties in the town, this was a dwelling of two or three storeys. It was encircled with a wide veranda, and a long driveway swept up to the substantial front door. So this had been her aunt's home. Will's home too – although he'd told her that until he was sixteen, he'd lived in a tumbledown cottage at his father's smallholding out at McDonald's Creek, without even knowing his father owned this grand house. Jack Kidd had won the property, along with the coal mining business and a substantial sum of cash, when playing cards for high stakes.

Curious, Hannah walked up the driveway, drawn towards the splendid house and gardens. The crunch of her feet on the gravel was muffled by the hum from sprinklers watering the lawn. She kept close to the boundary and walked past a garage or stable block to the rear of the house. Here she gasped again – this time at the sheer beauty of the panorama in front of her. Lush lawns ran down to a picket fence that bordered a sheer cliff edge. Beyond the fence, the ground gave way to a vast chasm with rocky sandstone crags, waterfalls, and ferns, surrounded by a forest of eucalyptus trees with their ghostly white trunks covering the valleys and mountains as far as her eye could see. In the bright sunlight there was a bluey haze above the trees. That must have been the source of the Blue Mountains' name. She moved across the grass and stood in front of the fence, gazing out over the canyon, entranced.

Hannah shivered and her eyes welled with tears. How often had Will spoken to her of the beauty of these mountains? He should be here with her now, holding her hand or placing a protective arm around her shoulders. So much beauty. Too much pain.

Lost in her thoughts, she didn't hear the approaching footsteps behind her.

'What are you doing here? This is private property.'

Hannah spun round, embarrassed at being caught trespassing. The woman, who had a lilting Irish accent, was plump in build but held herself with her shoulders pulled back and a rigid bearing that gave the illusion of height. She was wearing an apron over her dress.

'I'm so sorry. My husband used to live in this house and I wanted to satisfy my curiosity.'

'Your husband?' The woman's brows knitted.

'William Kidd. His father once owned this house, I believe.'

The woman's face broke into smiles. 'You're Master Will's wife? I'm delighted to meet you. How *is* Will? I've so often wondered what happened to him. Why isn't he with you?' She glanced back towards the house. 'I was that fond of him.

I'm so pleased he's married and to such a pretty girl.' The words flowed out of her in an excited flood.

Hannah hesitated before replying. 'I'm afraid Will died. At the beginning of this year. His ship was sunk in the Atlantic by a German bomber.'

The woman's face crumpled and she burst into tears. She dabbed at her eyes with a handkerchief, blew her nose loudly, then pulled herself together. 'You poor wee thing. Come inside and I'll make us both a nice cup of tea. The owners are visiting their son in Canberra so we won't be disturbed.'

As they walked towards the house, the woman asked Hannah how she and Will had met.

'He was a merchant seaman and was in port in Liverpool where I lived.'

'Ah! I should have guessed. He always wanted to go to sea. Poor lad was forced by his daddy to work in the coal mine and hated it. Used to tell me that one day he was going to become a sailor and travel the world.'

Hannah smiled sadly. 'He certainly did that. He went all over the place. At least until the war began and he joined the Atlantic convoys.'

The woman said her name was Mary O'Hara. 'I used to be the maid here for the Kidds when Mrs Oates was the housekeeper and Mr Oates was the chauffeur. Then when Mrs Kidd sold Kinross House the new owners kept the staff on. The Oates retired two years ago and I was promoted to housekeeper.'

She showed Hannah into a spacious kitchen and invited her to sit at a large deal table while she prepared a pot of tea.

'So you knew Mrs Kidd? Elizabeth Kidd?' Hope surged inside Hannah's chest.

'I did indeed.' The woman grinned. 'The loveliest of ladies. I was in the room when she was delivered of her two babies. First, little Mikey and then poor wee Susanna. God bless their souls.' She made a hurried sign of the cross. 'A terrible thing to happen. The diphtheria took them both at the same time. It was heart breaking. That Mikey was a scamp. Cute as a button, and Susanna only a wee babby. I thought Mrs Kidd would lose her mind with grief but she's a strong woman.'

Mary O'Hara sighed and stared into the middle distance, remembering. 'After Mrs Kidd sold this place to Dr and Mrs Sullivan, I went to live with her as housekeeper in a little house she rented in town. When she moved to Sydney the Sullivans took me back here.'

Hannah felt a suffusion of warmth inside her. At last, someone who had known Elizabeth well – and had actually liked her. She wanted to hug Mary O'Hara.

'You're the first person I've met who's has a good word to say about Elizabeth.' She hesitated then added, 'She's my aunt.'

Mary clasped her hands together. 'Your aunt! Mrs Kidd's niece married to Master Will. Heavens above! God works in mysterious ways.' She poured the tea and handed a cup to Hannah. 'Are you in Australia to visit your aunty then? I imagine she was devastated about Will too. She loved that lad as though he were her own. Now I think about it, you're the living image of her.'

Hannah sipped her tea. 'I'm trying to find out where Aunt Elizabeth is. All I know is that she and her husband live in the north of New South Wales and he's a sheep farmer.' She told Mary O'Hara about the correspondence with Verity Radley and how Hannah's last letter had been returned after Miss Radley's death. 'My husband had written to her to enquire about Elizabeth. She replied to us, delighted that we'd got in touch and promised to forward Will's letter to Elizabeth. But we heard nothing after that, so I was afraid Elizabeth didn't want to have anything to do with us. I wondered if she wanted to put the past behind her. There'd been so much sadness in it. But Will was adamant that she would have wanted to hear from us.'

'Will was right.' Mary O'Hara folded her arms. 'Elizabeth told me she had nieces – you've a sister, haven't you?'

Hannah beamed. 'Yes. Her name's Judith.' Hannah explained her sister's circumstances. The warm, friendly manner of the Irish housekeeper and her evident close knowledge of the family made Hannah relax. At last, here was someone who spoke highly of the Kidds. 'Mrs Kidd told me she was sad she'd lost contact with her family.'

'She did?' Hannah felt a rush of emotion. 'Do you have her address?'

The housekeeper's lips formed a tight line. 'I'm afraid I don't. After what happened to Mr Kidd, she moved to Sydney. She was expecting another baby and I think she wanted to put the past behind her. Who can blame her? She offered to take me with her but I'm not a city girl so I chose to say here in the Falls.' The housekeeper took another sip of her tea. 'You say she married again? I'm truly happy for her.'

'She married my late husband's friend, Michael Winterbourne.'

Mary O'Hara gasped and clasped her hands together. 'Mrs Kidd married Mr Winterbourne? Well I never.' She gave a long sigh. 'Such a handsome man. Most of the women in the Falls were sweet on him.' She blushed, chuckling. 'I was no exception.' She stared into space, clearly conjuring memories. 'Master Will hero-worshipped him.

Anyone could see that. Poor Will hated working in the mine and going underground but Mr Winterbourne looked out for him. Then all of a sudden he went and married Miss Harriet.' The housekeeper shook her head, her bottom lip jutting out, indicating her disapproval of Harriet Kidd.

Will had rarely spoken about his sister Harriet. Hannah had the feeling their relationship was too sensitive a subject. Perhaps she oughtn't to be sitting here gossiping about the dead with the housekeeper. But it wasn't gossiping. She was trying to piece together a puzzle.

Either way, Mary O'Hara was keen to talk. 'Miss Harriet was a holy terror. Used to getting her own way all the time. Spoilt. Forgive me, but she was a little madam. I remember when she got all her hair chopped off and her father went mad.' She grimaced. 'Your aunt went out of her way to be kind to the girl, but Harriet threw it all back in her face.'

She made the sign of the cross. 'Then, after what happened with her father, she threw herself into Sydney Harbour and drowned.' The housekeeper lowered her voice into a whisper. 'They say that she and Mr Winterbourne had a very unhappy marriage.'

Hannah listened as the woman's memories flooded out.

'Miss Harriet was what they call a party girl. Champagne and drugs.' She lowered her voice to barely a whisper, signifying her disapproval. 'And *other men*.' The woman looked about her as though afraid of being overheard. 'Not wanting to speak ill of the dead – you've a right to know all the facts – but I think the lassie also had a guilty conscience about what she'd said in court.' She paused, weighing her words. 'I suppose Master Will told you about his father's trial?'

Hannah nodded. It had been a strange and terrible bond between Will and herself that they had both had fathers executed for murdering a family member. 'Will told me his brother Nat was a bad egg, and their father shot him only to defend both Will and my aunt when he attacked them.'

Mary closed her eyes and mumbled an unintelligible prayer. 'I was in the court. It was all going well for Jack Kidd. Everyone believed he only shot Nat to stop him killing Will. The poor lad was unconscious on the ground, and his brother was all set to finish him.'

Hannah listened intently.

'I was sure the worst possible verdict would be manslaughter. Honestly, Mrs Kidd, until the point when Miss Harriet – or I should say Mrs Harriet Winterbourne – turned up in court, we all thought he'd get off altogether. She was all togged up in her finery like one of those drama queens in the pictures and demanded to say her piece.'

Hannah leant forward, fascinated. Will had never told her any of the details of his father's trial. Presumably he'd found it too painful or was mindful of sparing Hannah after she'd gone through her own father's murder trial.

'It seemed to me she was only interested in trashing your aunty's reputation. But in accusing Mrs Kidd of carrying on with Mr Winterbourne and with Nat too, she was giving her father a motive for murder.' The housekeeper refilled their cups of tea. 'She went white as a sheet when the judge put his little black cap on. I'll never forget it. After that, she went back to the city and drank herself to death and ended up floating in the harbour.' Mary O'Hara raised her eyes in silent prayer and swallowed another slug of tea.

'Will's sister took her own life?' Will had said nothing of this. It must have been too painful.

The housekeeper crossed herself again. 'I hope not. I'd hate to think of the poor girl going to hell for all eternity for committing a mortal sin. But she had clearly lost the will to live by giving herself up to drink, drugs and – so they say –

debauchery. It seems to me she let her dislike of your aunt cloud her judgement. She never gave a thought to what her words would mean to her father's situation. When he was condemned to death she couldn't live with the guilt.' The woman released a long sigh. 'Mrs Oates said at the time she also thought Miss Harriet couldn't face the disgrace of having a father who was hanged. She used to go round with the cream of Sydney society. They would have dropped her like a hot potato after poor Mr Kidd was put to death.'

Hannah took a deep breath. It was such a horrible story. The parallel between her own situation and Will's in both having fathers condemned to death was extraordinary. But she wasn't going to tell Mary O'Hara about that.

The housekeeper reached over and patted Hannah's hand. 'I'm so happy to have met you, Mrs Kidd. I can see why Will fell for you. And you're so like your aunty. The living image of her.'

Hannah sensed Mary had reached the end of her revelations. But she was desperate to find out more information about Elizabeth. 'Did Miss Radley have any other friends who might know where my aunt is now?'

'Miss Radley kept her own company. Mrs Kidd was her only friend. Otherwise she was completely dedicated to her pupils. A very private person.'

'Did she die suddenly?'

'To be sure it was very sad. A heart attack. Dropped dead in the schoolyard on her way home at the end of a day's teaching.'

'I'm sorry to her that. Might Mr and Mrs Oates know my aunt's address?'

'I doubt it. By the time Mrs Kidd left the Falls, the Oateses were working for the Sullivans here. They'd no contact with her after she moved to the city. But I'll ask them anyway should I see them in the town. We're not in touch, though they're still in the area.'

It was time to go. Hannah got to her feet. 'Thank you so much, Mrs O'Hara. For the tea and for filling in so many blanks for me.'

'It's Mary. Miss not Mrs – I've no husband so I've no claim to that title.' The Irishwoman smoothed her apron down. 'It's been an honour meeting you and hearing about Master Will. I'm very sorry about what happened to him. God bless his immortal soul.'

Hannah delved into her handbag and pulled out her precious photograph. 'Would you like to see the only snap I have of Will?' She held out the photograph to Mary.

'Oh! Jesus, Mary and Joseph! What a gorgeous picture! Such a big, tall, handsome man he turned into. And the two of you so lovely together.' She placed a hand on Hannah's arm. 'I can see from the look on his face that he loved the bones of you.'

Tears pricked Hannah's eyes. 'And I him.'

'God bless you, Mrs Kidd. He'll be looking down on you from heaven and watching over you. I'll ask the priest to say a Mass for him.'

Hannah reached again into her handbag to find her little notepad. Tearing out a sheet, she scribbled her address on it. 'This is my address in Sydney. If you should come across my aunt, please give this to her.'

'Of course, but don't get your hopes up, Mrs Kidd, it must be more than fifteen years since she left the Falls.'

Hannah took her hand. 'Just in case.' She smiled. 'Thank you. I'm so happy I met you. Now I must get my train back to Sydney.'

She was halfway down the drive when the housekeeper ran after her. 'I think you should have this, Mrs Kidd. Master

Will made it for me with his own hands.' She pressed a little wooden carving into Hannah's hand. 'It's a wee kangaroo. He loved whittling wood. He'd have wanted you to have it.'

Hannah's tears could no longer be kept at bay. She hugged the Irishwoman. Clutching the wooden figure in her hand, she hurried down the drive and onto the street. She walked back to the railway station through a sea of tears.

4

———

Back in Sydney, Hannah's letters to the three McDonald Falls law firms had, after a week, elicited no response. Christmas – the summer holiday season – was days away, so Hannah resigned herself that she was unlikely to hear anything until well into January. Most Australians would be off work for the holiday season as it was rumoured that next year because of the war, holidays would be severely curtailed by law.

When she told Mrs Hodges she'd be staying in Sydney over Christmas, the landlady said, 'I thought you'd be heading to Victoria to join your sister and her family.'

Hannah explained that she'd been asked to provide holiday cover at the office. 'I'll have Christmas Day and Boxing Day as leave, but most of the staff will be off work between then and New Year so there'll just be the duty solicitor and me. Apparently, there won't be much to do.'

'So, you'll be here for your Christmas dinner?' Mrs Hodges looked concerned.

Hannah's spirits sank. Was she going to ask her to leave over the holiday period? She tried to keep her voice light when she replied. 'If you're going away for Christmas I'm happy to fend for myself – or if you're expecting guests I can find a hotel for a few days.'

The landlady stretched out a hand and gave Hannah's arm a reassuring pat. 'I'm going nowhere. I'll be glad of your company, Miss Kidd.'

She always referred to Hannah as Miss, having assumed that she was unmarried, and Hannah had chosen not to correct her.

A quiet Christmas would be fine. After a childhood where Christmas had been viewed by her extreme funda-mentalist father as a pagan Bacchanalia, Hannah wasn't used to the festivities celebrated by most people. Growing up, first in Northport, and then in a small, terraced house in Bootle, near the Liverpool docks, Christmas had been a miserable affair, unacknowledged as a time of festivity. Bible readings and prayers had taken the place of Christmas carols and plum pudding. It was only after her father's death and her marriage to Will that she'd experienced the joyous side of Christmas. In the big old house on Moss Lane that she, Will, and Judith had shared with their landlord Sam and his late father's mistress, Nance, they'd all tried to make it a jolly occasion, despite the war. Sam had bought a gramophone player, and there had been party games and dancing. Now Hannah struggled to imagine ever being joyful at this time of year again.

She spent Christmas morning helping her landlady prepare their dinner, peeling potatoes and making the stuffing for the chicken. As they worked, Mrs Hodges had the wireless on, so they were accompanied by carols and seasonal music. It seemed bizarre to be cooking a roast with all the trimmings when the temperature was in the high eighties.

They had sat down for the meal and Mrs Hodges beamed across the table at Hannah. 'Tell me something about yourself, Miss Kidd. You've been lodging here a few weeks now, yet I barely know you.'

Hannah hesitated for a moment, then remembered Mrs Hodges was a widow too. She had shown her kindness and Hannah hated keeping secrets.

'Actually, It's not actually *Miss* Kidd. It's *Mrs.* My husband died eleven months ago.'

Mrs Hodges clamped a hand over her mouth. 'I'm so sorry, darl. I'd no idea. You're so young.'

'That's what war does. It takes no account of age. Will was in the merchant navy. His ship was bombed on what was meant to be his last Atlantic crossing before he was due to start a shore-based job.'

'You poor thing, that's heart breaking. How long had you been married?'

'Our wedding was the day after Hitler invaded Poland. Will was killed in January this year, so we were married just over a year.' She gave a rueful smile. 'And most of that he was at sea.'

Mrs Hodges put down her knife and fork. 'It isn't fair. What I'd like to do to that Adolf Hitler. I can't tell you how sorry I am, Mrs Kidd.'

Hannah bit her lip. That was the worst bit. The sympathy. It always set her off. 'It's why I don't like to talk about it. It's still too fresh and painful.'

'I hate to tell you this, darl, but it always will be. Doesn't get any easier. My Stan was taken from me ten years ago and barely a moment goes by when I don't think of him. Lung cancer. Horrible disease.'

Hannah expressed her condolences, then they ate in silence.

Eventually Hannah broke it. 'You have just the one son?'

'Our Billy, yes.' Mrs Hodges glanced towards the framed photograph of the uniformed young man on the sideboard. 'Up in Darwin. I thought they'd send him to Malaya but thank God they didn't. A friend of mine has just lost her son in Malaya. Stationed at the Butterworth base. He was killed during the invasion of Penang last week.' She sighed. 'Cath's distraught. She's got another son in Singapore. They say it will hold out, but I've learned to believe nothing where war's concerned. And ships full of women and children from there are arriving in Perth all the time according to the papers.'

She shook her head, her eyes full of sadness and probably fear. Spearing a roast potato with her fork, she popped it in her mouth. 'We don't hold much with formality down under so why don't you call me Dot?'

'In that case, Dot, I'm Hannah.'

After the meal they washed up and when Dot retired to the parlour for a snooze, Hannah went out for a walk.

She'd bought a wide-brimmed straw hat soon after arriving in Sydney. The sun here was so much stronger than back in Liverpool, where she more often wore a beret with a thick woolly scarf round her neck as she walked in the dunes on Crosby sands.

Today, she headed for the Domain, strolling past the art gallery and into the botanic gardens. Not only beautiful in their own right, the gardens offered the best views of the city and its breathtaking harbour. The blue waters sparkled under a cloudless sky. Hannah wandered between the trees: sprawling giant figs, lush ferns, spiky palms and cacti, pine trees and spreading cedars, past ponds bright with colourful waterlilies. Above her head, flying foxes hung, Dracula-like, from the trees, and possums ran up the trunks and along the branches.

She was not alone as she wandered. Numerous city dwellers had headed to the Domain to enjoy the sunshine and fresh air. Strains of a melody were coming from somewhere beyond the trees – violins and cellos. The music filled her with nostalgia – her earliest childhood memory was listening to her aunt playing her violin. Elizabeth had taught the instrument to children and, in those long-gone days, the house in Northport had echoed with the sounds of music, until Elizabeth vanished from their lives.

Hannah wondered whether her aunt had walked through these botanic gardens, had stood gazing out over the harbour, thinking about the life she'd left behind in England. Will had told Hannah that Elizabeth had come to Australia in the expectation of joining her father – only to find he'd died a day or two before her arrival. If Hannah felt alone, it must have been even worse for Elizabeth. Penniless, and with no choice but to marry Jack Kidd, after discovering she was pregnant.

Kidd had been a widower, over twenty years older than Elizabeth, and according to Will, brusque and cold in manner. The marriage had been her only means of surviving financially and of having a home for her unborn child. Hannah couldn't imagine how tough that must have been.

Tired and hot, she settled on a bench under some trees, with a view towards the Harbour Bridge. She'd brought a book to read but was so entranced by the scenery and the people passing by that she placed it unopened on the seat beside her. All this was a world away from Liverpool, battered and blitzed by enemy aircraft. She thought of the iron-grey skies, the watery sun so often blocked out by heavy cloud, the dark murky water of the Mersey estuary, and the smell of salt in the air – which had recently given way to the choking stench of cordite, dust and rubble.

It was unimaginable that all that destruction might be heading Sydney's way. Hannah prayed that the Americans would counter the advance and ambition of the Japanese army and its ultra-modern air force.

She looked around. Children playing, couples strolling hand in hand, families picnicking on the lawns. Why did men choose war over peace? It had always been thus since the dawn of time, for whatever reason – greed, lust for power, hunger, ambition – often religious differences. It all seemed so cruel and pointless to inflict harm on oneself in order to inflict greater harm on another. Surely there was enough beauty and bounty in this world for everyone – if men only took time to see it. And yes – it was mostly men. Women didn't start wars. They got to deal with the consequences. Women like her, sitting here thousands of miles from home, her heart ravaged by grief at the cruel death of the man she would love for the rest of her life.

Tears threatened again, so she dug her fingernails into her palms to staunch them. She reached into her handbag for a handkerchief, and her fingers closed around the little wood carving Mary O'Hara had given her. She took the kangaroo out and looked at it, running her fingers over the roughly carved shape. Will would have been a boy when he made this. It was unvarnished but smooth. The kangaroo had large ears and was sitting on its haunches with its long fat tail stretched out behind. Hannah smiled, trying to picture how Will would have looked as a lad, sitting on the porch chipping away with a penknife.

He wouldn't want her to be trapped in her grief like this. He wouldn't want her brooding. All these dark thoughts were futile. Nothing was ever going to bring him back to her, so she must snap out of it and make the best of life.

She picked up the book that lay beside her on the bench and began to read.

On the Monday after Christmas, Hannah went into work. The duty solicitor didn't appear until after ten, shutting himself away in his office, so she was left alone to catch up on her filing and answer any telephone calls.

After about forty minutes, he emerged and walked over to where she was sitting, putting folders in alphabetical order ready for filing in the bank of cabinets that lined the walls of the office. A tall man in his mid to late twenties, he'd never spoken to Hannah before now. He perched on the edge of her desk and looked her up and down.

'So you're the one who drew the short straw? You're new, aren't you?' He stretched out a hand for her to shake. 'Roger Wallace, but everyone calls me Wally. What's your name?'

Hannah told him. The easy intimacy of Australians still surprised her. She couldn't imagine a solicitor being on first-name terms with a junior clerk back in England.

She was a little nonplussed when he asked if she'd had a good Chrissie, then realised he meant Christmas.

'Very nice thank you.'

'Here's the deal. I can't see any reason for me to hang around here all day. No one's likely to want to instruct a solicitor until after the holidays. So, I'm going to head to the beach for the rest of the day. In the remote possibility that anyone asks for me, tell them I'm out on urgent business and leave a note on my desk. I'll stop by on the way home this evening.' He gave her a wide grin. 'Same drill tomorrow if it's as quiet as this. I'll come in for an hour in the morning to check the post. Then as long as you don't dob me in to old Finlay, how about I take you for a nice lunch on Friday?'

Hannah gaped at him, unsure whether she was more shocked by him skiving off or by his offering to buy her silence. Before she could shape a suitable response, he bounced off the desk and gave her a mock salute. 'There's a good girl.' Then he was gone, leaving her staring after him, dumbfounded.

5

———

The following day, Wally arrived again around ten o'clock.

'Morning, Hannie,' he called, as he went into his office and closed the door.

Hannah cringed, wondering how she was going to tell him politely that she couldn't abide this adaptation of her name. Judith occasionally called her Han – but she was her sister – and Hannie sounded ridiculous, especially the way he pronounced it with the first syllable protracted – *Haarnie*. Why did the Australians have this tendency to infantilise people's names?

The previous day, she'd cleared her backlog of filing, tidied her desk, completed the copy typing one of the partners had left for her, and read the entire *Sydney Morning Post* including the sports pages. Today, during her lunch break, she joined the library. If she were to get through this week, she'd need some reading matter to sustain her. It was clear Wally wasn't going to keep her supplied with work.

She chose only titles by Australian authors. It was time to stop feeling nostalgic and cut herself free from the mental ties to England. Australia was home now, and she needed to learn more about it. She picked a volume about the history of Australia and a selection of novels by Eleanor Dark, Nevil Shute and Miles Franklin – later discovering the latter was a woman.

The pattern of Wally arriving, shutting himself in his office for half an hour or so, then disappearing for the rest of the day continued until Friday. That day, he stayed longer in his room, so Hannah had almost forgotten he was there.

She was reading Franklin's saga *All That Swagger*, when he emerged from his office. Moving aside the pile of library books, he sat on the edge of her desk, picked up the top volume and flicked through the pages. 'Glad to see you're keeping busy, Hannie.'

Blushing, she swept the pile of books off the desk and into the straw bag she used to carry them, tucking it underneath her desk. 'They're only on the desk because I'm going to exchange them at the library during my lunch break.' She wondered why she was bothering to lie to him when he was so unashamedly going to the beach every day.

Wally laughed. 'Only joking.' He folded his arms. 'Can I blame you for reading when there's nothing else to do here?' He looked around the office. 'I said it was pointless staying open, but old Finlay insisted on it. I promised you lunch today so let's go.' He flourished an arm, indicating the door.

Hannah was in awe of Roger Wallace. He wasn't a partner in the firm, but he was a solicitor – even if a relatively junior one – and as such required her respect. Unused to dining out, she had no wish to join him for a meal – indeed she'd never been in a restaurant before, even back in Liverpool.

Wally clapped his hands. 'Crack the whip! We haven't got all day.'

It was pointless to protest, so Hannah followed him through the door and locked it behind them. She was nervous. It felt like a test – one she wasn't qualified to pass.

He took her to a place called Cahill's next to the Theatre Royal, a five-minute walk from the office. The windows onto the street showcased a sumptuous display of the restaurant's homemade chocolates.

Wally pushed open the door and gestured for her to enter. Inside, the place was panelled in wood and had a cosy, inviting atmosphere. Hannah tried to relax and let the tension leave her, telling herself Australians were not stuffy and snobbish like British people could be.

It was clearly a favourite haunt of Roger Wallace's. He acknowledged the waitress by her name. Turning to Hannah, he said, 'The chef's from Switzerland. His Wiener schnitzel is famous.'

Hannah gulped. 'I've never actually been to a restaurant before.'

Wally laughed, but not unkindly. 'Well, I reckon it's time you made a start. Aren't I the lucky one then, to help you break your duck?'

'Break my duck?' She frowned.

'Cricketing term.' Seeing she still looked puzzled, he added, 'It's called a duck if you score no runs. Then when you finally hit one, it's breaking the duck.'

Hannah smiled. 'I see. I'm afraid I don't know anything about cricket.'

Wally chuckled. 'Like the England team, if you ask me.'

The waitress brought them each a menu. Hannah ran her eyes over it. 'Gosh. I doubt I can manage anything on here. I have my meal in the evening and usually skip lunch or just have a piece of fruit and a biscuit.'

'Not a good idea for a growing girl to skip meals. I

recommend the mixed grill. They have a lady's version if you're not that hungry.'

Hannah studied the menu again. The lady's grill consisted of a lamb chop, pork sausage, grilled pineapple, vegetables and potatoes. More than she could cope with on a hot day like today. 'What are you having?'

'Full mixed grill. It's like the lady's only bigger. It comes with kidneys, bacon and chips as well. And no pineapple. To tell you the truth, Hannie, I think slices of pineapple have no business being on a plate of meat.'

She would not disagree. Back in England she'd never eaten pineapple. 'I think I'll just have a ham sandwich.' It was one of the cheapest items on the menu at ninepence, whereas Wally's mixed grill was two and nine. The plentiful availability of fresh meat and tropical fruits was taking some getting used to after the privations of British rationing.

'If you're only having a sanga, you'd better choose the special club. Comes with chicken and tomato, as well as ham.' He turned to the waitress, who had appeared again. 'Club sandwich for the lady and the usual for me. Make sure there's plenty of chips, Sal.'

As they waited for their food, Hannah studied her companion. She was still nervous in his company. She didn't really want to spend the two shillings the special club sandwich cost but felt uncomfortable about the idea of him treating her. When they'd met on Monday, he'd implied he was buying her discretion about his trips to the beach, but now she wasn't so sure. He was quite a handsome man, tall, lean and with a shock of fair hair. His well-cut trousers and brilliant white shirt looked professionally laundered – or brand new. She hoped he didn't have designs on her.

The waitress brought their food. The club special sandwich was a surprise to Hannah as it had three layers held together by a cocktail stick and was so big she didn't know how she was going to get her mouth round it. She picked it up and took an experimental bite from one corner, deciding she'd have to nibble her way around it.

Wally, who was tucking in with gusto to his enormous mixed grill, looked at Hannah appraisingly. 'Tell me about yourself,' he said. 'What brings a girl like you to Sydney?'

'I'm from Liverpool. It's been heavily bombed. It's one of the most important ports and the hub for transatlantic shipping, so naturally the Germans targeted it.' She bit her lip, thinking of Will. 'The house where my sister and I lived was hit and the side of the building was blown off. My sister and her husband have a small baby – they're now living in Victoria but I wanted to come to Sydney.'

To her relief, he asked nothing else about her background, and the conversation moved to a general discussion of the war. Gradually Hannah relaxed. Wally was easy to talk to – mainly because he was happy to do most of the talking.

'No beach today?' she asked.

'Back to work after this. Old Finlay is likely to drop in sometime this afternoon before accompanying his missus to the theatre, so I need to be on parade. He told me you used to work in a top-secret government job. Must be quite a comedown working for Tibbetts and Finlay.'

Hannah nibbled her sandwich. 'The department I worked in was secret, but my work wasn't all that different from what I'm doing here.' She didn't want to get drawn into a discussion about the workings of the map room at Western Approaches. Changing the subject, she asked how long he'd worked at the firm.

'Since graduating from uni. Seven years ago. I wanted to be a barrister, but I like an easy life, so I settled for being a solicitor. Routine stuff. Conveyancing when I started out, matrimonial, adoptions, a bit of probate. That type of thing.'

'Perhaps I can ask your advice about something?' She looked up at him as he speared a piece of kidney with his fork.

'Fire away.'

'I'm trying to trace somebody, and the only person who might have known her whereabouts died this year or last. She was unmarried and, as far as I know, had no living relatives. Her house has been sold, and the new owners claim to know nothing.'

'Have you checked the probate records?'

She gave him a blank look.

'Did she leave a will?'

'I don't know.'

'If she did, and the estate was over a certain threshold, the executors would have applied for probate. If not, then Letters of Administration.'

Hannah looked at him blankly.

Wally smiled. 'Give me her name and her last known address and I'll look into it. I could do with a stroll this afternoon to get me out of the office and away from the old boy.'

'Where will you go?'

'The probate records are kept at the Supreme Court of New South Wales. Leave it to me, Hannie. I'll see what I can find out.' He grinned at her again, revealing a set of perfect white teeth.

As they walked back towards the office, Wally said, 'If I'm not back when Old Finlay shows up, tell him I've gone to the court to research something for the Potterton case.' He turned off in the direction of the Supreme Court while Hannah went back to work.

Alone in the empty office, she admitted she was in a

quandary. She was enormously grateful for Roger Wallace's offer to help but worried he may have designs on her. Whilst he was undeniably a good-looking man, Hannah had no interest in any form of romantic relationship. Not now. Not ever.

6

To Hannah's relief, the senior partner, Mr Finlay, put in only a brief appearance at the office and accepted without question her explanation for Wally's absence. She was about to lock up and return to her lodgings for her evening meal when Roger Wallace came back from the court.

He offered a broad grin to Hannah, ran the palms of his hands over the sides of his head with an expression of satisfaction and perched in his favourite spot on the edge of her desk. 'I thought I was going to come away empty-handed. The probate packet hadn't been filed yet but I managed to track it down,' he said.

Hannah's heart jumped with excitement. Was this going to be the lead she needed?

Wally opened his briefcase, took out his legal notepad and read from the notes he'd made there. 'Your Miss Radley bequeathed her entire estate in a charitable trust to the McDonald Falls School to fund a library and an annual student bursary. Seems she'd accumulated quite the nest egg. Including the proceeds from selling her house, her estate was almost five thousand pounds.'

'No mention of my aunt?' Hannah was disappointed. She had pinned her hopes on Verity mentioning Elizabeth – perhaps leaving her a small bequest so that her address would be included.

Wally placed a hand on her arm. 'Don't look so glum, Hannie. I haven't finished yet.' He wagged a finger at her. 'I've found out who handled the probate.'

'Which firm was it? I wrote to all three lawyers in McDonald Falls but haven't had any replies yet.'

'None of them. Her estate was handled by Hardcastle, Wainwright and Struthers. They're just around the corner from here, in Pitt Street. As it happens, Eddie Greenbank, a good mate of mine from uni works there. Your Miss Radley was bound to have left some paperwork. It may take a while to dig it out but if there's anything pertinent relating to the person you're looking for, it could be there. I'll take you over on Monday and introduce you to Eddie.'

Hannah clasped her hands together. 'Thank you, Wally. I can't tell you how grateful I am.'

'No worries.' He gave her a huge grin and leaned towards her. 'Have you made any plans for the weekend?'

Hannah's cheeks burned. Her fears were materialising. Scrambling around for an excuse she blurted, 'I'm going to be very busy. I've letters to write. Washing to do.' How lame it sounded.

He studied her, smiling, his head on one side, clearly amused. 'You think I'm trying to crack onto you, don't you?'

Her cheeks were on fire now. 'I don't know what you mean.'

'You thought I was going to ask you out. On a date.' He

grinned impishly. 'I'm only trying to be friendly, Hannie. Do you even know anyone in Sydney?'

Her face must be scarlet by now. 'Only my landlady.'

'Strewth, woman. That's no good. You need to meet some people. Some of us are going to the beach tomorrow. Why don't you join us?'

Desperate to find an excuse – although tempted by the thought of a day at the seaside, she said lamely, 'I'm afraid I can't. I don't even own a bathing suit.'

He chuckled. 'A bathing suit, eh?' He mimicked her British accent. 'That's easily fixed.' He reached for the telephone on the desk of Mr Finlay's secretary and spoke to the operator. A few moments later he was connected. 'It's me. About tomorrow. I've invited that new girl I told you about from the office. Dig out a spare cozzie will you.' He turned to look at Hannah, his eyes skimming her up and down. 'She's about your size.' He listened for a moment then laughed. 'You know me too well. See you in half an hour.'

He put the receiver back in the cradle. 'All sorted. Shirl's bringing a spare. Now give me your address and we'll call for you at around ten tomorrow.'

'Shirl?'

'My girlfriend.' He winked at her.

Mortified that she'd jumped to the wrong conclusion, Hannah wasn't sure whether to be relieved or embarrassed.

THE FOLLOWING MORNING, Hannah waited in the front parlour as the clock ticked by. Just as she'd convinced herself that Wally and his girlfriend weren't turning up, there was a loud knock at the door. Hannah grabbed her straw bag and called a goodbye to her landlady.

'Have a good time, darl,' Dot shouted back from the kitchen.

Hannah stepped onto the sunlit street. Wally had a large flat wooden board propped on one shoulder. He introduced her to the suntanned blonde beside him. 'G'day, Hannee. Meet Shirl.'

'Hello, Hannee.' The young woman gave her a warm smile. 'Good to meet you.' She was dressed in a pair of slacks with a crisp linen blouse. Her lips were carefully painted in red, and she was wearing a pair of sunglasses. Hannah felt like a frump in her old-fashioned cotton frock.

'We're going to Bronte. The rest of the gang will meet us there.' Wally headed off at a brisk pace. leaving the two women to follow.

'Are you a strong swimmer, Hannie?' Shirl asked.

Hannah decided to put Shirl right about her name from the start. Apologetically, she said, 'Actually, Shirl, if you don't mind, I prefer to be called by my proper name – Hannah. And I'm afraid I can't swim at all.'

'That's fine, Hannah. To tell you the truth I prefer Shirley to Shirl.' She stretched out a hand for Hannah to shake. 'Deal?'

Hannah shook her hand and smiled. 'I didn't like to tell Wally.'

'He wouldn't take any notice anyway. Believe me. I've been going out with him since school. He won't be told about anything.' Shirley laughed and Hannah decided she liked her already.

'How come you don't know how to swim?'

'No one taught me. I lived close to the Mersey estuary but I suppose we don't have the weather for it.' She didn't mention that her authoritarian father would never have condoned the wearing of swimsuits and would have been outraged by the idea of either of his daughters bathing – or being in the company of men. Her visits to the beach at Crosby had been frequent, but clandestine, and consisted of hiding herself in the dunes and reading library books.

'Righto. The surf can be brutal at Bronte – and there are dangerous riptides so we'd better stick to the baths.'

Imagining something akin to municipal baths, Hannah's face fell. 'Don't worry about me. I'll be happy just sitting in the sunshine. I don't want to spoil it for everyone else by us having to go to the swimming baths.'

Shirley grinned. 'Wait till you see Bronte Baths. It's a big tidal rock pool just above the beach. The boys will be surfing so we can enjoy ourselves without them.'

'Surfing?' Hannah had never been so conscious of her own ignorance.

'Riding the waves on wooden boards. You'll see. They paddle out on top of the boards until they find the wave they want to catch, then they stand up on the board and balance while the wave carries them to the shore. It's all the rage in America and is getting hugely popular here.'

'It sounds terrifying.'

'You wouldn't catch me doing it. I'm more than happy swimming up and down in the baths and lying on the beach catching the rays.' Shirley linked Hannah's arm. 'We can find a spot near the bogey hole. If the tide's out it's calm as a millpond in there so you can have a splash quite safely.' Seeing the puzzled look on Hannah's face, she added, 'The bogey hole is an area of the shore ringed by rocks. You wouldn't know it was there at high tide. But as the tide goes out the rocks protect it from the waves and it's a nice safe place to swim.'

They had reached the tram stop. A tram appeared almost immediately and the three of them boarded.

Wally propped up his surfboard and sat beside it, in front of the two women, twisting round in the seat to talk to Hannah. 'We change at Bondi Junction and get another tram to Bronte.'

'Who else is coming?' asked Hannah.

'Eddie, the mate I told you about from the firm that handled that old girl's will. But no work talk on the weekend. Eddie's younger brother, Mark, will be there too. Oh, and Shirl's cousin, Brenda.'

Hannah began to feel nervous again. Would she be the only non-swimmer?

Shirley smiled at her. 'Brenda and I let the boys get on with their surfing. We like to lie in the sun and chat. Brenda's great. You're going to love her.'

'What do you do for work, Shirley?'

'I'm a nurse and Brenda's an operator in a telephone exchange. Did you work in a solicitors' firm back in England?'

'No. In shipping,' Hannah said, skating over the truth.

'She can't talk about it, Shirl.' Wally tapped the side of his nose. 'Top secret work for the navy.'

'Crikey. That sounds important, Hannah.'

'I can assure you it wasn't that interesting.'

'Now Japan's at war with us as well as Hitler, everything's come closer to home. Maybe you can get some similar work here. Perhaps you could join the WRANS or the WAAAC.'

They were approaching Bondi and, in the rush to get off, Hannah didn't have time to answer. Besides, the last thing she wanted to do was go back to her old life.

Shirley's cousin Brenda was waiting for them at the tram interchange. A small, freckled blonde in her early twenties, her eyes were also shaded by sunglasses. She and Shirley greeted each other with hugs and much hilarity, then

Shirley introduced Hannah. Brenda gave her a quick smile and a hello, then continued her excited chatter to her cousin.

The tram to Bronte took about twenty minutes. It was crowded and they all had to stand. When they alighted at their destination, Hannah looked around in awe. A crescent-shaped beach stretched out below grassy lawns, edged on each side by sandstone cliffs. The southernmost cliffs cradled the Bronte Baths, where the swimming pool edged straight onto the ocean and was accessed from the beach by steps carved into the rocks.

The tide was going out, and Shirley pointed out the tops of the rocks that formed the bogey hole, which were just beginning to be visible above the water. 'Let's set up here,' she said, dropping her bag onto the sand. 'Once the tide goes out a bit more, the bogey hole will be calm as a billabong.'

'Why do they call it the bogey hole?'

Shirley shrugged. 'No idea. Never really thought about it.'

Brenda interjected, 'It's from an old Aboriginal word for bathing hole.'

Shirley rummaged in her holdall and pulled out a blue swimsuit which she tossed to Hannah. 'Spare cozzie. You can get changed over there.' She jerked her head towards a row of white-painted wooden huts. 'I've already got mine on under my clothes.' Shirley pulled her shirt over her head and unfastened her trousers, letting them fall to her ankles. Underneath she was wearing a two-piece swimming costume that revealed a taut, tanned midriff. Meanwhile, Brenda had also stripped off and was wearing a sleek black one-piece swimsuit.

Hannah went to get changed. The bathing costume was a reasonable fit and she pulled it on, self-conscious at revealing so much of herself. Her father would have been apoplectic at her appearing in public half naked. Anything that Charles Dawson would have hated was good as far as she was concerned. She pushed the thought of him to the back of her mind. Draping her towel over her shoulders, she returned to join the two women, who were now sitting on their towels chatting. Wally and two other men were each standing with a wooden surfboard held upright beside them.

'Here she is!' cried Shirley. 'Come and meet the boys, Hannah. This is Eddie Greenbank and his brother, Mark.'

Like Wally, the brothers were above averagely tall and good-looking. They were both wearing tight-fitting swimming trunks. Hannah, embarrassed, fixed her eyes on their faces, which were remarkably similar.

'G'day, Hannah,' said Mark, the younger of the two by a year or so, stretching out a hand.

Eddie meanwhile stood, arms folded, studying her intently but he said nothing.

'Surf's up, let's go.' Wally raised his surfboard onto his shoulder and trotted off over the golden sand to the ocean, followed by the brothers.

'Well?' Shirl asked her cousin, pointedly.

'Drop it, Shirl.' Brenda stared after the men as they moved through the shallows, her face set in a grim expression.

'You're going to have to make the first move, Bren. If you wait for Eddie, you'll wait for ever.'

Brenda scowled. 'I said, drop it, cuz.'

Ignoring her, Shirley turned to Hannah. 'Brenda's got a massive crush on Eddie. I keep telling her, there are some fellas who need a bit of a push and Eddie Greenbank's one of them.'

'Bloody hell, Shirley. Tell the whole world while you're at it,' Brenda snapped. 'I'm going up to the Baths.' She pulled on her rubber swimming cap and waded across the bogey hole towards the stone steps which led up to the tidal pool that was Bronte Baths.

'She's in a foul mood,' said Shirley, smiling sadly. 'Poor thing has a crush on Eddie but he's oblivious. I've tried dropping hints and asked Wally to give him a nudge, but you know what men are like. Sometimes you need to bang them over the head to make them see what's under their noses.' She chuckled. 'He'll get there in the end. Brenda's a great catch.'

Hannah thought it was possible that Eddie didn't feel attracted to Brenda but she wasn't about to voice that. Brenda was a pretty girl, but looks weren't everything. The conversation made her think about Will. He hadn't needed to be banged on the head. He claimed he'd fallen in love the moment he set eyes on her when she walked past him on the dockside. Maybe Will was unusual and Shirley was right that most men needed help to know what was good for them. Hannah wasn't exactly experienced in the ways of men in general. 'I'm sure you're right,' she said.

Shirley sighed and looked over to the cliff-side swimming pool. 'I do hope so. Bren's even wondering if he's – you know – one of *them* – not interested in girls. But I don't think that's the case.' Shirley rummaged in her bag. 'You got some zinc cream for your nose?' She tossed a tub to Hannah. 'A dab stops it going red and peeling. The sun's powerful. Go to the chemist on Monday and get yourself some. And a pair of sunnies while you're at it, unless you want to damage your eyesight.'

Sunglasses and a bathing suit were going to make a dent in her wages. But that was the price of living here in Australia.

The day passed in a haze of sunshine and chatter. The men returned in the late afternoon and Shirl passed around sandwiches – or sangas as they all called them. Hannah was grateful that Dot Hodges had insisted on giving her some slices of ham and a bag of tomatoes, along with a packet of biscuits and some oranges, so Hannah was able to contribute to the picnic.

There was no sign of Brenda, so Shirley pointedly asked Eddie to run up to the Baths and fetch her for the picnic. He returned soon after with a smiling Brenda beside him. Her smile vanished when Eddie sat down between his brother and Hannah, leaving Brenda to sit beside her cousin. She ate next to nothing and said even less.

Eddie didn't say much either, leaving his brother and Wally to supply the conversation. Unsurprisingly, it centred on the war and the surrender of the British colony of Hong Kong to the Japanese on Christmas Day.

As they ate, Hannah became increasingly aware of Eddie's presence beside her. He said nothing to her, but she could sense his eyes on her. It made her self-conscious. Should she try to talk to him? Based on the dirty looks Brenda was sending in her direction, probably not.

While the three men continued talking on the beach, Shirley and Hannah went to cool off in the bogey hole. Brenda stayed with the men.

Hannah's nervousness about the sea abated when she realised how calm and refreshing the water was, protected inside the bogey hole from the waves crashing onto the open part of the beach. She waded in to waist height then bent her knees, dipping down to immerse her top half and soothe the heat from her skin. Shirley tried to get her to try floating on her back, but she was content to splash around and enjoy the unfamiliar but pleasant sensation of the salty water on her skin. Shirley was right about the sunglasses though – the sun reflecting on the surface of the ocean was painfully bright.

After a while, Brenda, Mark and Wally went up the steps to the Bronte Baths while Eddie went back into the sea, this time without his surfboard.

Shirley said, 'Brenda's happiest when she's swimming. Good at it too. Wins competitions.'

'What about you?'

Shirley gave a snort. 'Me? Far too idle. I like a bit of a swim but mostly to cool off. And I'm not the least bit competitive. Not like Brenda. But as for you, Hannah, I reckon you ought to sort yourself out with some swimming lessons.'

More expense.

Shirley returned to the subject of her cousin. 'Brenda's in a bad mood because Eddie's giving her the cold shoulder.' She hesitated. 'Actually, she's probably sulking because it's clear as day what's going on with him.'

'And what's that?'

'Come on, Hannah. You must have noticed Eddie's keen on you. He's hardly taken his eyes off you from the moment you appeared.'

Hannah didn't know what to say. A rogue cloud blotted out the sun for a few moments. She shivered. A man being keen on her was the last thing she wanted. 'I didn't notice. I expect he was just curious as I'm the new girl.' She tried to laugh it off. Uncomfortable now, she told Shirley she was going back to the beach. 'I'm going to read my book for a while.'

Settling back on the sand, Hannah glanced up and saw Shirley climbing the steps to the Bronte Baths to join the others.

A few minutes later, Eddie emerged from the surf, ran up the beach and flopped down beside her on the sand. He draped a towel round his shoulders. 'You're not swimming,' he said, stating the obvious.

'I've never learnt how to. I was in the bogey hole just now though. It was nice to cool off.'

'I'll teach you.'

She stared down at her feet, not knowing how to respond. 'Teach me?' she echoed, lamely.

'We could start now. Over in the bogey hole. It's calm. You'll be quite safe.'

She looked around, desperate to find an excuse.

'Or tomorrow,' he suggested. 'There's another place I could take you, another ocean pool. Much smaller and not too busy. The Fairy Bower in Manly. Mark and Wally won't be around as they're both swimming in a competition at Bondi Icebergs.'

Quickly, she said, 'I can't tomorrow.'

'Next weekend then?'

It wasn't just the timing. How to make it clear the thought of letting a man she barely knew teach her to swim terrified her? 'No. I can't.' She turned away.

Eddie's voice was flat. 'Righto, some other time.' He sprang to his feet, dropped his towel and ran back down the beach into the sea.

Hannah turned and looked towards the ocean baths and saw Brenda on the rock wall that circled the swimming pool, staring down at her.

7

JANUARY 1942

Hannah spent a quiet Sunday at her lodgings. She had the house to herself as Dot was visiting a friend on the North Shore. There was a small backyard where she settled under the shade of a wattle tree, since the temperature was hotter than she'd ever experienced – over one hundred degrees with no breeze. Trying to read the volume on Australian history she'd borrowed from the library, she found it hard to concentrate and her mind kept drifting back to the previous day at the beach.

Hannah couldn't stop thinking about Eddie Greenbank's unexpected offer. Even though she'd been aware of him looking at her while they were on the beach, he hadn't said a word to her until he suggested teaching her to swim. When she'd been in the bogey hole, there were parents teaching their children to swim – supporting them under the chin or with a hand placed under their tummies. It was a level of intimacy she couldn't contemplate with a virtual stranger. Eddie being such an attractive man made it even more uncomfortable.

Brenda had been silent and scowling after she and

Shirley returned from their swim. Hannah had wanted to tell her she had no designs on Eddie, but it would have felt presumptuous and intrusive.

When Shirley invited her to accompany her and Brenda to watch Wally and Mark race in the swimming competition at the Bondi Icebergs swimming club, another of Sydney's tidal swimming pools, she'd declined politely. If Eddie were to turn up at the club and approach her again, it would likely upset Brenda even more.

But avoiding Eddie today would not help her tomorrow. If she wanted to track down her aunt's address, she had to go to the offices of Hardcastle, Wainwright and Struthers and seek the assistance of Eddie Greenbank. Why was life so complicated? Then she thought of what Will would have said: 'That's what makes it so interesting.'

She turned her attention back to the book on her lap and with grim concentration immersed herself in the tragic plight of the explorers, Burke and Wills in 1860. It was just after three when she heard rapping on the front door. Thinking perhaps Dot had forgotten her key, she went to open it. Standing on the threshold was Eddie Greenbank. Unsmiling, he ran his fingers through his hair and fixed his eyes on her. There were beads of perspiration on his brow and damp marks on his shirt.

'May I come in?' he said.

Hannah hesitated, then stepped aside to let him into the hall. He must have got her address from Wally or Shirl. 'I'm out in the back garden. Would you like something to drink?'

'Just a glass of water, please.'

She led him to the kitchen and poured some water. 'Do you want to bring that chair to sit on? There's plenty of shade, but I'm afraid there's no breeze.'

Eddie picked up the wooden chair and followed her outside.

They sat in silence for a few moments, then both spoke at once.

Eddie gave way.

Hannah said, 'Sorry, I was only going to ask whether you'd been to watch the swimming contest today.'

He looked down. 'No, I didn't.'

She waited. The silence was oppressive, but she was uncertain what to say.

Eventually he spoke again. 'Look, I meant what I said about teaching you to swim. It's a crime to live in Sydney without being able to swim.'

'Actually, I probably won't be here for long.' She realised this was something she hadn't articulated before, even to herself. 'I have long-lost relatives in Australia. An aunt, uncle and cousin. I'm hoping to join them.'

'Where do they live?'

'That's just it. I don't know exactly. I believe it's some-where north of Sydney. On a sheep station.'

'You want to live on a sheep station?' He looked horri-fied. 'Do you have any idea what that's like? The isolation? The heat? You'd die of boredom.'

Affronted, she said, 'Well, I won't know until I try but unless I find out exactly where they are, I won't know at all.' She fixed her eyes on him. 'That's where I need your help.'

Eddie's brow furrowed. 'My help? How?'

'I thought perhaps Wally would have mentioned it to you. The only hope I have of finding my aunt's location is among any papers that may have been left by her late friend. Wally checked the probate documents, and it turns out your firm handled her estate.'

Eddie shrugged. 'I don't handle probate. I deal with commercial law.'

She bit her lip. 'But you must know someone there who can help me.'

'I suppose I can ask.' He sounded reluctant.

They lapsed again into silence, broken by the squeaky chatter of a pair of galahs in a neighbouring tree. Hannah looked up, distracted by the sound, and saw the flash of rose pink around their necks and breasts as they squawked away. The sight made her feel impossibly far from Liverpool where the birds were uniformly dull grey or brown. She swallowed, a wave of sadness engulfing her for everything that was lost.

Eventually, Eddie spoke again. 'Look, Hannah. I think we've got off on the wrong foot, so can we start again, please? I really like you.' He looked away, his expression troubled. 'I'd like to get to know you better.' He ran his fingers through his damp hair again. 'I'm not very good at this. I shouldn't have suggested the swimming lessons. How about instead I take you to the pictures or to a concert?' His eyes looked at her pleadingly.

Hannah felt cornered. How was she going to say no without hurting his feelings? Honesty was the best policy – much as it pained her. 'Look, Eddie, I'm sorry, but I don't want to go out with anyone. It's not about you.'

He looked wounded. She'd have to tell him the truth. 'I'd be grateful if you wouldn't mention this to the others, but I was widowed less than a year ago. My husband was killed at sea, and I can't get over it. No offence to you, Eddie, but seeing anyone is out of the question.'

He stared at her in shock. 'You're a widow? But you're so young. Bloody hell, Hannah, you've certainly had the rough end of the pineapple. I'm sorry. And don't worry. I won't breathe a word to the others.'

She smiled. 'Thank you.'

He stood up. 'I'll leave you to it then. Pop into the office sometime. I'll do what I can to help you find your aunt, but no promises.'

She thanked him again, then blurted, 'You know Brenda really likes you.'

He gave a half-laugh and shook his head. 'Don't I know it. Look, I can't pretend to like her that way when I don't.' He gave a sad smile. 'Just like I can't pretend not to like you, Hannah.'

Before she could muster a response, he was gone, striding down the street, his retreating outline distorted by the heat haze off the pavement.

Hannah returned to the garden. Eddie's intensity had shaken her.

Before she had time to dwell on it, she heard the front door open, and Dot called out a greeting. She appeared at the back door, fanning herself with her hat. 'Strewth, Hannah, what a scorcher.' She glanced at the empty chair left by Eddie, then settled herself on it.

'I see you've had company. I presume it was that handsome fella I saw just now. I was at the end of the street and could have sworn he was coming out of my house.'

Hannah winced. 'I'm sorry, Dot. I would have asked your permission, but he turned up out of the blue – and it's so hot, I felt I had to invite him in for a glass of water.'

'That's all right, darl. And no need to ask permission. He was a looker, a right bobby dazzler. Are you stepping out with him then?'

'No. Of course not. I wouldn't. I couldn't.' She wiped her brow with her handkerchief then scrunched it in her hand.

'Is that because of your late husband? Maybe it's time to move on. Good-looking fellas like that one don't come along too often and you're still a young woman. No harm in having a bit of fun.'

Hannah said nothing, twisting the hankie in her hands.

'Athletic too. I could tell that from the way he walked. And so tall. He'd a face like a film star.'

'Please stop. I've no intention of going out with him. I only met him yesterday. He's a friend of a friend. That's all. Now I think I'm going for a walk before we eat, if that's all right?'

'Course it is, darl. Take care though. It's like a furnace out there.'

The following day, the fifth of January, most people were back at work, since wartime regulations had already tightened the amount of holiday time. The Christmas decorations had been replaced by posters listing precautionary measures in case of enemy action, and there was a sombre atmosphere in the office.

Hannah was kept busy all morning taking documents to and from the courts and answering the telephone. Wally, along with all the firm's solicitors, was in a meeting with the senior partners for almost two hours. When he emerged, he went off to lunch with three of his colleagues, having apparently forgotten his promise to take her to Hardcastle, Wainwright and Struthers.

She wondered whether to go on her own and decided she would. Since Eddie was a friend of Wally's, she was bound to run into him from time to time, and besides, he'd said she should call at the office, so he'd probably be expecting her. She didn't want any awkwardness between them, and her reason for seeing him was entirely professional.

When she arrived at the nearby firm's premises, she was told by a secretary that Mr Greenbank was out of the office and she didn't know when he would be back. 'Would you like to leave your name and a number if you have one?'

Hannah hesitated then said, 'No, thank you. I'm working round the corner at Tibbetts and Finlay, so I'll pop in again next time I'm passing.'

She didn't see Wally for the rest of the day. When she asked where he was, she was told he was briefing counsel in chambers.

The return after the Christmas and New Year break meant there was a rush of work, and Hannah was last to leave that evening. After tidying her desk, she locked the office and set off down Castlereagh Street, choosing to walk home through Hyde Park rather than take the tram.

She'd just entered the park when she heard footsteps behind her. Turning, she saw Eddie Greenbank hurrying towards her. He looked different in his work clothes: a shirt that was crisp and white despite the heat of the day, his suit jacket slung casually over one shoulder.

'Was it you who came looking for me today?' His eyes were bright with hope. 'I'm sorry I wasn't there.'

'Yes, it was. I was hoping you might help track down my aunt's address.'

'Oh right.' His voice slumped. 'So you haven't changed your mind about going out with me?'

She stretched her lips into a smile and gave a slight shake of her head.

'Right. You said something about us holding some papers of your aunt's.'

'No, it's papers belonging to her friend. Miss Verity

Radley of McDonald Falls. She left her estate to the school she used to teach at. She had no relatives and no one else was mentioned in the will. I'm hoping your firm might hold her personal papers, if there are any. It's possible my aunt might be mentioned in them.'

Eddie shrugged. 'We're the oldest solicitors office in Sydney. We have paperwork dating back to the First Fleet. It's impossible to store it in the Sydney office, so it all gets sent to a storage place – if there's nothing of importance, it's disposed of after five years. We just hang on to deeds and certificates and that type of thing.'

'She only died last year. Where's the storage? Are you able to access it?'

'I'm not sure.' He looked irritated, clearly unused to dealing with such trivial matters as document storage. 'Possibly in a warehouse in Parramatta.'

'Is there a record of what's there?'

He tilted his head to one side, his face softening a little. 'I haven't a clue, Hannah. I imagine there's some kind of index system. But I doubt there'll be an inventory if there's nothing there of consequence. It'll probably be listed under miscellaneous personal papers. What exactly are you looking for?'

'Correspondence probably. Anything relating to my aunt.'

He nodded. 'What's her name?'

'Elizabeth Winterbourne – Mrs Michael Winterbourne.'

He led her over to a bench near the Archibald Fountain, took a notepad out of his briefcase and wrote down Elizabeth's name. 'Give me the name of the dead woman again. God knows how I'll explain why I want to check her files, but I'll see what I can do.'

She repeated Verity Radley's name. 'Thank you. I really appreciate it.'

'Look, even if I find your aunt's address – which is going to take a bit of time – I can't just hand it over to you, Hannah. I'd get struck off for professional misconduct. While I'm sure your aunt will be delighted to hear from you, we can't make that assumption and breach her privacy.'

Hannah's shoulders slumped.

His tone softened. 'You could write a letter to her and we'll forward it, but it's up to her to reply or not.'

'That was exactly what Miss Radley said she was going to do when my husband and I wrote to her last year but she died suddenly. We never found out if she'd forwarded our letter.'

Hannah felt a chill of disappointment. If Verity Radley had sent the letter on, why hadn't Elizabeth replied? Perhaps she wanted to keep the door to her past firmly shut.

Eddie closed his briefcase. 'I'm really sorry I can't make things happen any faster, Hannah.'

'No. I understand. There's no hurry except my impatience.' She decided to tell him a little more. 'There was a family quarrel. No one's heard from my aunt for over twenty years. My parents are both dead now, so I want to heal the rift.'

'You really are all alone in the world, aren't you?' He looked concerned, sympathetic.

'I have a sister in Victoria – Tatura, near Shepparton. But she has a husband and a baby, and they live in the middle of nowhere, so that's why I came to Sydney. I knew it would be easier for me to find work here.'

He smiled. 'Yet you're considering going to live with your aunt and uncle on a remote sheep station?'

She gave a sigh. 'To tell you the truth, I left Victoria

because my sister was too dependent on me. Now that she has her own family, she needs to build a life of her own. My aunt is older and...'

'And what?' His voice was kind.

'She also happened to be my husband's stepmother. My husband was Australian. From McDonald Falls. He and my aunt were close. She's a link to him.'

Eddie said nothing. After a few moments, he got to his feet. 'Come on. I'll walk you home.'

'There's no need.' Hannah didn't want to feel any more beholden to him than she already did.

'I want to. Indulge me.'

It was pointless to argue, so she fell into step beside him as they walked in silence out of the park and into Darlinghurst. Eventually, to make conversation, she asked him if he'd heard how Mark and Wally had got on in the swimming competition.

'As expected: Mark won, Wally came third.' He didn't sound very enthusiastic.

'That's super. Mark must be thrilled.'

'He always wins. My brother lives for swimming. Surfing too.'

'And you don't?'

'For me, it's a fun thing to do at the weekend and a good way to stay fit. For Mark, it's all-consuming.'

'And for Wally?'

'Somewhere in between. He's incredibly talented. He'd be the best swimmer in the club if he put the effort in. But his career matters more to him – and Shirl. You probably know they're planning on getting married but the war's got in the way.'

She didn't know but wasn't surprised. 'That's wonderful – I mean that they're getting married, not that they have to wait. Hitler and Hirohito have a lot to answer for. My late husband and I married the day after war was declared. No honeymoon. He was straight back on board.'

'He was in the navy?'

'Merchant navy.'

'That must have been hard. I expect he was at sea a lot.'

'Most of our marriage. He was killed on what would have been his final voyage before taking up a land-based job.' Her voice trembled. She hadn't planned on talking about Will but Eddie's quiet understanding and sympathy had broken through her defences.

'I'm sorry. It must be painful talking about it. I shouldn't have asked you.'

She smiled, pulling herself together. 'No need to apologise. It's just that it's still raw.'

'It must be.' They walked on in silence for a few minutes then Eddie spoke again. 'I know it's not the same as losing your spouse, but I do understand about loss and grief. My twin sister died two years ago.'

She stopped and turned to look at him. 'I'm so sorry, Eddie. That's terrible.'

'We were very close. It's as though I've lost part of myself.' He swallowed, looking into the distance. 'It hit Mark hard too, of course – I think that's why he's so driven. Why he keeps pushing himself. But I don't know for certain since we never talk about June.' He fumbled in his jacket pocket and pulled out a pack of cigarettes and lit one after offering one to Hannah, which she declined. She hadn't seen him smoke before. He took a long deep draw, exhaling slowly.

He looked away, and Hannah sensed he was close to tears. She felt a surge of sympathy for him.

They had reached the top of her street and walked on in a newly companionable silence. It surprised Hannah how easy he was to be with. As they approached Hannah's lodgings, a curtain twitched, the door swung open, and Dot appeared on the pavement, her face lit by the broadest of grins.

'Unless I'm mistaken, you're the fella who called on Hannah yesterday. I saw you leave.' She stretched out a hand in greeting. 'Dot Hodges. And you are...?'

Eddie shook her hand and told her his name.

'Kind of you to walk Hannah home. Would you like to stay for your tea? I've made shepherd's pie. There's plenty to spare.' She winked at Eddie. 'I may even have a couple of cold beers in the fridge.'

Eddie looked at Hannah, who nodded, helpless.

He smiled disarmingly. 'How can a man resist a shepherd's pie, Mrs Hodges?'

'Dot, please. Any friend of Hannah's is a friend of mine.

It was pointless protesting. Dot was clearly taken with Eddie. Hannah would have to explain to her later that he was just a friend.

8

To Hannah's surprise, that evening, Eddie in contrast to his silence and reticence two days ago on the beach, was talkative. Over the shepherd's pie, he chatted happily to Dot, telling her about his love of surfing.

Dot clasped her hands together. 'My Billy always wanted to learn how to surfboard. But when war was declared he volunteered and got sent up to Darwin. Too many crocs up there so he's never got round to it. He's in the Airforce,' she said proudly. 'What about you?'

'Only the three-month compulsory military training in '39.' Eddie paused to take another mouthful of pie. 'I thought of joining up back then but we had illness in the family and the war seemed very far away.' He glanced at Hannah then looked back at Dot. 'Now it's a lot closer. Uncomfortably close.'

'You're telling me.' Dot got up from the table and fetched the framed photograph of her uniformed son, Billy. 'Here's my boy. He's a maintenance engineer. Keeps the planes flying.' Her voice was proud but her eyes betrayed her anxiety. In a quiet tone she added, 'Even though he's on Australian soil, I don't get to hear from him often. They don't have the telephone up in Darwin – not that I have one myself. So we rely on letters. I expect he's very busy. And they keep all the troop movements secret.' She chuckled. 'I have a suspicion there's a girlfriend up there in Darwin.' She gave a sad smile. 'Not that he'd tell his old mother.' Her eyes went from Eddie to Hannah and back again, then she turned away and replaced the picture on the sideboard.

She settled back at the table. 'I can't believe how many Yanks there are in Sydney. Every day there are more of them pouring into the place. Just this morning, I was saying to Val next door, that soon there'll be more blooming American soldiers than there are Aussies here.' She shook her head. 'You hear the accents everywhere. Still, it's good for business. They have plenty of money, I gather.'

'The war will be over a lot sooner with the Yanks in it.' Eddie frowned. 'Otherwise we wouldn't stand a chance against the Japanese with the rest of us stretched on so many fronts and most of our own troops stuck in the Middle East.'

Dot leaned forward. 'They say the Americans have the best equipment and armaments.'

'True,' said Eddie. 'Not to mention the resources to replenish them.'

'It sounds awful to say it but those Japs did us a favour when they bombed Pearl Harbour.' Dot gathered up the plates. 'I know it's terrible to think of all those young men who lost their lives, but otherwise I can't see how America would've ever got into the war. And without them, we don't stand a chance.'

Hannah didn't want to talk about it. Any illusions she'd

nursed about escaping the war when she left Liverpool were being confounded every day.

'Why don't you two go and sit outside and I'll make you both a nice cup of tea while I get on with the dishes.' Dot gave Eddie a sly grin. 'Unless you'd like another beer?'

'A cup of tea will do nicely, thanks. I've a big case to deal with tomorrow. I'm hoping to reach a settlement before it goes to court next week.'

Hannah and Eddie carried their chairs outside into the small back garden. Hannah had long since given up offering to help her landlady with the washing up – Dot always insisted it was her job. 'You don't work hard all day in that office only to come home and help me scrub the pans and dry the dishes. That's what you pay rent for,' she'd said.

The evening was cooler now and the stars twinkled in an inky sky. Hannah leant back and looked up at them, feeling small and insignificant.

'My brother's thinking of joining up.' Eddie's voice was quiet, flat.

Hannah jerked her head round to look at him. 'I thought Mark was still at university.'

'He is. About to start his final year. But he's talking about postponing until after the war.'

'Goodness. Did that come out of the blue?'

'Not really. I think he's wanted to join up since the beginning but with June being sick, it was out of the question.'

Hannah hesitated then asked, 'What was wrong with your sister?'

'Leukaemia.'

'That must have been awful for her and for all of you.'

'It was.' Eddie's mouth set in a hard line, and Hannah sensed he didn't want to go into more details.

She was about to steer the subject onto safer ground

when Dot knocked on the window and signalled for her to come and collect the tray of tea.

A few minutes later they were settled again, sipping the hot brew.

'Do you really think Mark will volunteer?'

'Not if our father has his way. Dad fought in the last war. He was at Gallipoli. Lost both his brothers there. He never got over it and has tried to instil pacifist sentiments in Mark and me.' Eddie looked thoughtful. 'In the last war there was no choice. Conscription. This time there is – at least so far.'

'How do you feel about it?' Hannah slapped her hand to squash a mosquito on her wrist.

Eddie thought for a moment. 'Don't get me wrong. I'm a patriot. But I hate the very thought of war. What's the bloody point of all that killing? Men like your husband dying. How does that help anything? Carrying on until one side can't sustain it any longer because so many are dead? Cities flattened by bombing. It's attrition. Kill everything and the spoils to the last man standing...' He stopped and glanced over at her. 'I'm sorry. I shouldn't have said any of that.'

Hannah bit her lip. 'No. You're right. It's how I feel. The men who make the plans, who hold the power, have no conception of the sacrifices the men who serve make.' She released a long breath. 'And they give even less thought to the men they kill. They don't seem to have any awareness that the dead had wives, mothers, children, hopes and dreams. But I suppose we have to make a stand against Hitler and everything he stands for.'

He looked at her intently. Eventually, he spoke again. 'The last war was about aggression and hubris on Germany's part – but there was little difference between the warring countries' world view. Germany and Britain had monarchies that were related to each other. They had the same views about morality, religion, culture, even politics.' He fumbled in his shirt pocket. 'Mind if I have another smoke?'

Hannah shook her head. 'It might keep the mosquitoes at bay.'

Eddie lit his cigarette, inhaled and continued. 'This war's different. It's a clash of civilisations and belief systems. Back then, people had ingrained views about duty and empire and a sense of derring do. This time it's about standing up for democracy, fairness, culture, and an entire way of life.'

Hannah listened, surprised that he'd clearly thought so much about this. She thought of Hitler, his hatred for the Jews, for what he defined as degenerate art and literature, his crazed political rants to packed stadiums. Eddie was right. She despised everything Hitler stood for.

'As to the Japanese, they see their emperor as godlike. They're militaristic, and driven by a desire to spread their imperial fascistic vision throughout the east. And that includes Australia. So it's hard to stand by and let that happen.'

'Do you think your father will manage to dissuade Mark from joining up?'

Eddie exhaled a puff of smoke, watching it rise. 'No. He won't be able to stop him. And that means I'll have to go too.'

'Really?' She twisted round to look at him. His face was illuminated by the light from the kitchen window. He was frowning, his eyes distant, as though he was picturing himself uniformed and primed for action. 'When you don't believe in it?'

'I can't let him go alone. Just like my father couldn't

stand by and watch his brothers go. They were all volunteers, not conscripts. Keen to serve King and empire.'

'When will this happen?'

His mouth stretched into a thin line. 'I don't know but I imagine sooner rather than later.'

'Have you tried to talk him out of it?'

'Of course I have. But I haven't a leg to stand on. The Japanese are knocking on our door. It's only a matter of time before they try to batter it down. And all the Americans in town makes it more pressing. I can't watch from the sidelines while they defend our country. I'm a proud Aussie. It's my duty.'

A wave of desolation washed over Hannah. She stretched out a hand and took his. It was instinctive. A reflex reaction to what he'd said.

But it had an electric effect on Eddie. He snatched his hand away as if from a fire, put his cup back on the tray and stood. 'I need to get home. I've papers to go through tonight ready for tomorrow.' He went back into the house.

Hannah, stunned, heard him call out his thanks and a goodnight to Dot, before the sound of the front door closing.

Why had he fled? All she'd done was take his hand. Keen to avoid questions from her landlady, she carried the tray back inside and, after telling Dot she had a raging headache, fled to the safety of her bedroom.

She lay on top of the bed, asking herself over and over again what had happened. Why had her taking his hand provoked such a sudden violent reaction? Earlier that evening and the previous day, he had professed his desire to go out with her, yet now he had reacted as though her touch was repellent.

Then it occurred to her. Eddie thought she felt sorry for him. He must think she believed he was afraid to fight. He was a proud man and tonight he'd probably revealed more of himself than he'd intended. Or perhaps he thought she was mocking him, patronising him – refusing to go out with him but offering that touch of her hand as a consolation prize.

Whatever the reason, it left Hannah in an awkward position. She depended on Eddie to trace Aunt Elizabeth, so she couldn't afford to upset or alienate him. He was clearly prickly, and she didn't want this evening to come between them. While she didn't want to consider him romantically, she was beginning to value him as a friend. Had she ruined their fragile relationship?

She drew the curtains but left her window open to allow what little breeze there was to enter, then began to undress and ready herself for bed. In the half light from the moon, she could see the dark outline of the little wooden kangaroo Will had made for Mary O'Hara. Oh, Will, why were you taken from me?

9

A couple of weeks passed with no sign of Eddie Greenbank. Hannah thought of calling at his office but sensed it wouldn't be wise. Better to leave him some time and space. She decided to give it to the end of the month then call in and ask whether he'd had any luck tracing Miss Radley's paperwork.

Wally had tried to encourage her to join them at the beach, but each time he asked, she was ready with an excuse. She spent her free time walking in the parks and gardens, visiting the Art Gallery of New South Wales or taking the ferry across the harbour to explore the North Shore. Were these pursuits shallow when there was a war raging? Reading books from an earlier, more innocent age, standing in a gallery looking at landscapes and portraits of long-dead people, and wandering aimlessly along the ravishingly beautiful shoreline of Sydney Harbour all seemed selfish things to do. Yet she needed this time alone – a period of quiet reflection away from the hurly-burly of the office and the kindly chatter of Dot Hodges.

There was nothing she could do to prevent the world's

misery, solve the crisis of displaced people, stop the guns and the bombs and the devastation that was tearing the globe apart. There was no way she could bring back what was lost – her husband, her country, her old way of life – and, most of all, peace. The simple pleasure she took from her visits to parks and galleries was a way to nurture hope. It was a reminder that there might one day be a better world. Meanwhile, it offered some distraction from the complex present.

Everywhere she went, she heard American accents. At work she'd overheard Wally and some of the other solicitors talking about how the Eastern beaches had become crowded with Yankees – some of them showing their prowess on a surfboard, all of them flashing their money around. But surely it was wrong to begrudge them that, when they were thousands of miles from home and could face the enemy in a matter of days.

On a Friday morning late in January, Wally cornered her in the scullery when she was making a cup of tea for Mr Finlay. 'Hello, stranger. I have the distinct impression you've been avoiding me.'

She blushed. 'Not at all. Just very busy.'

'Well, I want no excuses now, Hanee. Some of us are going to Cahill's after work for a bite, then on to a concert in the Domain. It'll be relaxed – sitting on the grass and listening to the music. There's an American military swing band playing and they're meant to be very good.'

Hannah poured milk into the cup. 'I can't come for a meal. My landlady cooks for me, and I haven't given her any warning. It wouldn't be fair.'

Wally pushed his lower lip out. 'Come to the park later. The music starts at seven-thirty. We'll be there about seven. Phillip Precinct – you know – it's the area right opposite the art gallery. We'll keep a lookout for you.' He paused. 'After what happened yesterday, we all need some cheering up.'

He was referring to the Japanese invasion of the Australian territory of New Guinea. Hannah had heard the news on the wireless that morning. The small but strategic port of Rabaul in eastern New Guinea housed a battalion of the Australian Imperial Force to defend the naval base and airfields from potential enemy attack. Japanese bombing began in early January, but in the early hours of the 23rd, around five thousand Japanese troops invaded. Within hours, the airfield had been captured, and the Australians faced a hopeless situation. Their commander had no alternative other than surrender, and declared it was every man for himself.

'What will happen to those men now?' she asked Wally.

'God knows,' he said, looking grim. 'I suppose they'll hide in the jungle and try to do as much damage to the Japs as they can. But without provisions and supplies of ammunition it's pretty hopeless.'

'Won't there be a counterattack? Can't the Americans take the base back?'

His expression was solemn. 'I'm no expert. But I do know that New Guinea is all jungle and mountain. Those poor bastards were there to defend the base, not to conduct jungle warfare or survive in hostile conditions without food and water supplies. I doubt they've had the training for that.'

Hannah poured the tea. 'It doesn't seem right to sit in a park listening to a band while those poor souls are suffering.'

Wally shrugged. 'Nothing we can do though. It's important for morale to stay high. We all have to keep our spirits up.'

· · ·

WHEN HANNAH GOT BACK to her lodgings, Dot was pacing up and down the kitchen. 'I've been chewing my nails off all day, terrified my Billy might have been involved up in New Guinea yesterday.' She pressed her hands against the edge of the kitchen sink and stared out of the window into the small garden area. 'In the end, I went to my friend Lil's and she came to the post office with me and we sent a telegram to the base. We eventually got a reply, and thank heavens he's safe. I still can't help worrying. Now that the Japs are in New Guinea, he'll be in danger, but he's not allowed to tell me a blessed thing. I suppose it's the same for all our young men, and I'll have to get used to it. He said I can't send a telegram to the airbase every time I'm anxious. I hope I haven't got him into trouble.'

'I'm glad he's safe, Dot. It must be a weight off your mind.'

'It is. For the moment.' She shook her head. 'I don't think I'll ever get used to this war.' She stretched out a hand and touched Hannah's arm. 'Listen to me telling you – when you know better than I do, with all you've gone through.'

Changing the subject, Hannah said, 'Can I do anything to help with the meal?'

'All done. I'm afraid it's just cold meat and salad tonight as I was at Lil's most of the afternoon waiting for an answer to the telegram.' Dot put the plates on the table and signalled to Hannah to sit down.

'That sounds perfect. I'm going out with some friends from work this evening, so I'll be back late. No need to wait up for me.'

Dot settled her ample form into her chair. Her face lit up with a wide grin. 'Will that Eddie be there?' She raised her brows, eyes twinkling. 'Such a charming young man. So handsome. I reckon he really likes you.'

'I told you, Dot, he's just one of the gang.' She made her voice as nonchalant as possible.

HANNAH SET off for the Domain, walking past the cathedral and towards the art gallery. The temperature had dropped that day, with this evening down to sixty-three according to the thermometer Mrs Hodges had fixed to the back wall in the tiny garden. It felt odd to be wearing a cardigan, and Hannah wondered whether she ought to have brought a jacket too as it would probably be cold sitting on the grass. Not for the first time she told herself to be thankful that she was here in this beautiful city where open-air concerts were the norm and there were no bombs raining down from cold dark skies.

When she reached the Phillip Precinct, the crowd was larger than she'd expected, and Hannah doubted she'd be able to find her friends among the throng gathered on the lawns waiting for the band to start. Wally had told her they'd be somewhere directly opposite the Art Gallery of New South Wales, so she walked along the road skirting the park until she got to the gallery, then went to the top of the steps to gain the best vantage point as she surveyed the crowd.

'Hello, Hannah.'

The voice made her jump. She turned around.

'I thought I'd wait for you here,' Eddie said. 'It's been a while.' He nodded in greeting but didn't smile. 'How's Dot? That was a great shepherd's pie.'

Hannah smiled at him. 'She's fine. Relieved that her son wasn't involved in the fighting in Rabaul.'

'Of course. She must be.' He looked at her, his eyes lingering on her face. 'I'm sorry I left so abruptly the other night. I wasn't myself.' He looked at the ground, shuffling awkwardly. 'And I had to get back to prepare for my case.'

Hannah was unconvinced, but glad he'd acknowledged it. 'How did it go? The case?'

'They settled.'

Hannah scanned the people sitting on the lawns. 'Where is everyone? I thought I'd be able to spot them from here, but there's a massive crowd.'

Eddie pointed to where Wally, Mark, Shirley and Brenda were gathered close to the stage but he showed no sign of wanting to join them. 'I've traced Miss Radley's papers. Apparently, there are boxes of the stuff. It won't be practical to get it all sent here to Sydney as there's nowhere to store it in the office.'

Hannah's face fell.

'Instead, I thought we could go over to Parramatta and have a look.'

She stared at him. 'Won't you get into trouble?'

He gave a little laugh. 'Hardly. I've told them truthfully that you work for Tibbetts & Finlay and – less truthfully – that you believe there may be something pertinent to a commercial case your firm and mine are both involved in for different litigants.'

Hannah's eyes widened. 'Gosh. It sounds complicated. I hope no one will ask me any questions.'

'That's why we'll go at the weekend when no one's about.' He looked at her intently. 'If you're free, we could go tomorrow or the weekend after.'

'You'd do that? Give up your Saturday? When you could be at the beach?'

He tilted his head in a little shrug. 'I've kept you waiting a long time. It's the least I can do.'

She smiled. 'I'm enormously grateful, Eddie.'

He gave her a curt nod and suggested they join the others. 'The band's due to start in a few minutes.'

Hannah followed him as he wove his way between the people gathered on the grass – American servicemen and a variety of Sydneysiders. There was a mix of anticipation and the usual Australian easygoing atmosphere. It seemed everyone tonight wanted to forget about the war and the losses in New Guinea. She took a slow breath, filling her lungs with the scent of freshly mown grass.

She didn't know what to make of Eddie Greenbank. He had professed a wish to go out with her but had acted like a scalded cat when she'd taken his hand, and he'd avoided her since – yet now he was ready to give up half his weekend for her.

Shirley jumped to her feet when they arrived. She gave Hannah an enthusiastic hug. 'We've missed you, Hannah. I've been hoping you'd come to the beach again. So pleased you made it tonight.'

Mark gave her an easy grin and a mock salute, but Brenda ignored her, fixing her eyes on Eddie. Hannah sat down on the grass beside Shirley and Wally. Eddie was about to join her when Brenda jumped up, linked her arm through his and steered him onto the rug between herself and Mark. Eddie looked annoyed but did nothing as a uniformed lineup of musicians took to the stage and a saxophone burst into the opening arpeggios of 'In the Mood'.

Hannah was entranced by the music. She'd never been to a concert before – music was one of the many pleasures her bigoted father had banned in their household when she was growing up. After she'd married Will, they'd enjoyed listening to records on the gramophone but had never experienced live music – other than a piano player in the local pub. She nodded to the rhythm as the band worked their way through popular swing jazz numbers. 'In the Mood' was followed by 'Take the A Train' and Hannah leant back on her hands, as the music washed over her. A trio of women in American military uniforms stepped onto the stage in front of the band and started to sing 'The Boogie Woogie Bugle Boy'. As the music swelled, people jumped to their feet and swayed and danced to the music.

Out of the corner of her eye, Hannah saw Brenda grab Eddie's hand and jerk it towards her in an effort to coax him to dance with her. All around them couples were dancing, and the evening had become a vibrant celebratory party in defiance of the bad news that had struck that day. Hannah had no choice but to get to her feet as the entire crowd danced, clapped and sang along. Eddie detached himself from Brenda's grip and moved to stand next to his brother. Hannah felt sorry for Brenda, whose face crumpled in disappointment.

The band reached the climax and the three women on stage, in synchronisation, ended their song with a perfectly timed salute. The crowd roared.

The encore of 'Moonlight Cocktail' served to calm the crowd and set a more mellow mood. As it finished, people gathered their things and began to disperse. Hannah walked out of the Domain onto Art Gallery Road beside Shirley and Wally, while the Greenbank brothers and Brenda brought up the rear. As they reached the road, a tram heading towards Double Bay drew up and the group piled on. Hannah's lodgings were in the opposite direction, so she waved goodbye. Just as the tram moved away Eddie jumped off it.

Hannah looked at him in astonishment.

'I can't let you walk home alone,' he said. 'Besides, we haven't made the arrangements for Parramatta. I've remembered it can't be tomorrow as I have a family thing. How about next Saturday?'

He fell into step beside her. The crowds from the concert had thinned rapidly with people heading in different directions. As they passed into Darlinghurst, the streets were quiet.

'Are you happy to take the train to Parramatta? Only they've got much stricter about petrol rationing.'

'Of course.' She remembered passing through Parramatta when she'd taken the train to McDonald Falls. 'Are you sure you don't mind doing this, Eddie?'

He brushed away her concern with a wave of his hand. 'Did you enjoy the show?'

Hannah grinned. 'I loved it. I'd never been to a concert before.'

He twisted his head to look at with incredulity. 'Never been to a concert? Don't they have them in Liverpool?'

'There's the Liverpool Philharmonic. The oldest symphony orchestra in the country. Lots of concert halls too. And jazz clubs. But my father never permitted us to listen to music. Then there was the war and with my husband at sea...' She let her voice trail away as she didn't want to get into the details of her miserable childhood and the terrible circumstances of her parents' deaths. 'We don't have the reliable weather to allow outdoor concerts. It's one of the most wonderful things about Sydney.'

'So why do you want to leave? Are you still set on finding your aunty and living on a sheep station?'

Hannah didn't really know what she wanted. Why was finding Elizabeth so important to her? Yes, she was family –

but so was Judith. She'd left the little town of Tatura where Judith was living near to the detention camp, because it had nothing to offer her – would a remote sheep station be any different? If she were to be honest with herself, it was the connection between Elizabeth and Will that was driving her. But hadn't she decided she needed to get on with her life? Here in Sydney, she had a job, friends, things to do. Did she really want to give all that up?

She realised Eddie was waiting for an answer. 'I don't know. I'm desperate to find my aunt but perhaps I'm less sure about going to live there.'

A flicker of a smile crossed his face.

'Besides,' she added. 'Aunt Elizabeth may not have room for me or want me to live with her.'

They had reached the end of her street. Hannah stopped. 'I'll be fine from here. Thank you. Now get home yourself.' She didn't want to risk Dot twitching the curtains and seeing Eddie, as that would lead to an inquisition over breakfast the following morning. 'What time shall we leave next Saturday? No need to pick me up. I'll meet you at the station.'

He looked about to protest but nodded. 'Okay. In the booking hall. Nine-thirty? It takes about half an hour.'

Hannah smiled up at him, grateful. 'Thank you for seeing me home. And thanks again for helping me like this. It's so kind of you to give up your free time.'

His mouth stretched into a tight line and he nodded, then turned on his heels and walked away.

As Hannah went down the road to her lodgings, she continued to puzzle over Eddie. She wasn't convinced about the reason he'd given for reacting so badly when she'd taken his hand.

10

There was a crowd of American soldiers sitting on their packs, chewing gum, when Hannah arrived at Central Station the following week. She spotted Eddie at the kiosk buying their tickets, skirted the Yanks and went into the booking hall, mortified by the wolf whistles as she passed. Eddie turned his head, frowned and gave her a curt nod.

Hannah was bemused by his reaction. Surely, he wasn't blaming her for the behaviour of the American soldiers?

The train was already at the platform. Without bothering to speak to her, Eddie escorted her through the barrier and into a carriage. When they were seated, facing each other next to a window, Hannah tackled him.

'Look, Eddie, I'm sorry to be wrecking your weekend. You clearly don't want to be doing this.'

His jaw dropped, and that frown appeared again. 'What do you mean? I can't think of anything I'd like to do more than spend the day with you.'

She stared at him, confused. 'But you were frowning when you saw me. You're frowning now. And then when you came to the house for your tea you left abruptly. I don't believe it was because you suddenly remembered you had a case the next day.' It was hard saying this, and she could feel the blood rushing to her face. 'When I took your hand, it was as though you'd been stung. You couldn't get away fast enough. Then you appear to have avoided me for days, until the concert last week. Did I say something to upset you?'

His lips stretched into a taut line. 'I haven't been avoiding you. I'd hoped to see you at the beach, but Wally said you've been making excuses. I thought it was because of me.' He leant forward, and she could feel the touch of his knees against her own. 'I've told you how much I like you, Hannah. But I don't want your pity.' He sat back, running a hand through his hair. 'When I told you about trying to dissuade Mark from volunteering for the army, you looked at me as though you felt sorry for me. I got the impression you think I'm looking for excuses not to join up. That's why you took my hand.' He looked away from her. 'I could see it in your eyes. I could tell you were thinking I'm a coward.'

Hannah gasped. 'You're putting things inside my head that aren't there. I wasn't thinking any such thing. I reached for your hand instinctively. The war is making us all do things we don't want to do.' She struggled to find the right words. 'If I hadn't been bombed out of my home, I wouldn't even be in Australia. I was simply trying to convey that we're all having to make difficult choices we don't want to make. But I most definitely wasn't thinking you're a coward because you hate war.'

He said nothing at first, gazing out of the window. After a few moments, he spoke without turning around. 'I promised June I wouldn't go into the forces. She was already ill when war was declared. We knew she was dying. I shouldn't have promised, but it seemed easy when the war was so far away.

But how can I stand by and let Mark go without me? June wouldn't have wanted me to let him go alone.' He thumped his fist into his open palm. 'I'm damned if I do and damned if I don't.'

Hannah resisted the urge to reach out and touch him. It wouldn't help and could be misinterpreted again.

'And there's you too now.'

'Me?'

He turned away from the window and looked her in the eyes. 'I know it's hopeless. You've made that clear, but I can't help hoping that in time you'll give me a chance and, when you know me better, you'll change your mind. If I go to fight this war, I'm absolutely certain I won't come back. So that makes me want to stay. Not because I'm afraid of dying but because I want to stay and work on convincing you to give me a chance.'

Hannah stared at his handsome face. His words were a tortured logic. How could she tell him it wasn't a question of her needing time? No matter how much she might like Eddie Greenbank, she'd never be able to love him. He deserved much better.

If only she hadn't pressured him to do this search with her. She would have been better submitting a formal request for the information to Hardcastle, Wainwright and Struthers and being prepared to wait a long time for them to get around to answering it. Now she felt guilty at dragging him on this errand, forcing him to give up his free time, and subjecting him to her presence when it was clearly a source of pain. Was she taking advantage of his feelings for her?

He turned to stare out of the window again. Outwardly he presented the image of a confident, strong and successful man, yet under the polished surface, she could see the rawness of his emotions and the brokenness of his spirit.

Losing his twin sister must have knocked him for six. It doubtless explained his protectiveness towards his younger brother – but that put him in conflict with his promise to June before she died. And now Hannah was making matters worse.

She cleared her throat. 'I know how you feel about that promise to your sister. But people change their minds as circumstances change. Were June alive now she might feel differently. We the living can't be held to promises we once made to the dead.'

As soon as the words were out, she wanted to take them back. If she'd made a promise to Will, she'd never break it. And saying June might have changed her mind sounded as though Hannah was encouraging him to join the army. Quickly, she added, 'Only you can decide what's right for you, Eddie. Not June, not Mark and not your father. And certainly not me. What do *you* want to do?'

He looked at her, then absently out of the window before returning his gaze to her. 'I want to stay here in Sydney, continue with my career, and keep trying to get you to go out with me.' He breathed a sigh. 'But I can't let my brother go into battle alone.'

Hannah was unsure whether she felt sorry for him or annoyed. 'Have you talked to Mark about this? I don't mean about trying to stop him going. But about how you feel obliged to go with him.' She bit her lip. He wouldn't like what she was about to say. 'Isn't it a bit patronising of you? Mark's an adult. It's his life. He can make his own decisions without you supervising him.'

His eyes narrowed as he opened his mouth to reply but he must have thought better of it. His gaze turned again to the window as the train clattered on between factories and houses. Hannah stared at the red brick buildings, chainlink fencing and telegraph poles. A few minutes later, the train braked and drew into Parramatta station.

The legal storage facility was five minutes from the station, close to Parramatta Park, a walk they undertook in silence. The building was fronted by a branch of the law firm, closed today for the weekend. Eddie took a key from his trouser pocket and unlocked the door. Hannah followed him inside and through a doorway at the rear of the small office into a corridor at the end of which was a narrow staircase.

'Afraid it's on the third floor and there's no lift. There were plans to relocate to a more modern facility but the war's put them on hold.'

They climbed the stairs and entered a large room that covered the whole footprint of the building and was filled with rows of numbered filing cabinets and cupboards. Still uncomfortable after their conversation on the train, Hannah now felt that the entire venture was a mistake. She walked behind him feeling miserable. Eddie stopped in front of a grey metal cupboard and opened the doors. Inside were several cardboard boxes, as well as bundles of documents tied up with ribbons.

'I think we can safely ignore the legal stuff,' he said, pointing at the ribboned bundles. They'll be documents relating to the sale of her property and the liquidation of assets. Since you already know how the estate was distributed, it's unlikely there'll be anything there relating to your aunt.'

Hannah nodded. Eddie took down two of the large boxes and led her to a table in the centre of the room. He pushed one of the boxes towards her. 'You go through this one. If you find anything, tell me. As I explained, any approach to your aunt must be through the firm or I'll be in hot water.'

'Of course.'

They pulled out chairs and unpacked each box, piling the contents on the table and working through them.

Hannah started with a bundle of letters. She untied the satin ribbon that bound them – not the legal office kind, but a haberdashery ribbon in a tartan pattern. On the top were cards and letters addressed to Miss Radley at a Melbourne address. The postmarks were decades ago – before the turn of the century, long before Elizabeth would have arrived in Australia. Before setting them aside, Hannah fed her curiosity by opening the first envelope. It was a Valentine's card, with an illustration of a pair of turtle doves and a red rose. The writing was neat and cursive. *To my dearest girl on Saint Valentine's Day. I count the days until we are married and I can bring you to our new home in the Blue Mountains. Your ever loving Bernard.*

So, Miss Radley once had a fiancé. Hannah wondered why they never married. Her question was answered by the next items in the pile – an order of service for the funeral of Bernard Evans and an announcement of his death from diphtheria, cut from the classified columns of the *Melbourne Herald*.

'This is sad,' she said. 'Miss Radley was engaged to be married and her husband-to-be died.' She shook her head. 'It must have been just before the wedding. There's even a booking confirmation for the wedding breakfast.'

Eddie looked up, shook his head, but said nothing.

Hannah felt a sudden affinity for the late schoolteacher. At least Hannah had enjoyed a short but happy marriage before her own bereavement. Diphtheria was the same horrible disease that had taken Elizabeth's two children, according to Will. Hannah squeezed her eyes shut. This was something she didn't like to think about. Elizabeth's first child, Mikey, had been Hannah's half-brother, thanks to the rape by Charles Dawson that had precipitated her aunt's flight to Australia in 1920. The second child, Susanna, a baby girl, was Will's half-sister. Tears pricked at her eyes. How closely entangled her life and Will's had been before they'd even met. She swallowed back the tears, determined not to show emotion in front of Eddie. After retying the bow, she put the first bundle back into the cardboard box.

The next item she unearthed was a gold-embossed invitation to the wedding of Miss Harriet Kidd and Mr Michael Winterbourne. Will's sister had married the man Elizabeth had fallen in love with on the voyage out to Australia – the man that she was apparently now happily married to at last.

The next item she unfolded was a newspaper cutting – reporting that a body found in Sydney Harbour had been identified as Harriet Winterbourne, née Kidd. Hannah remembered Will telling her that Miss Radley had virtually brought his sister up after the death of their mother. Harriet's death must have been a bitter blow.

There were more cuttings from the *Sydney Morning Herald* about the trial and execution of William Kidd for the murder of his eldest son, Nathanial Kidd, as well as notices of the death from diphtheria of Elizabeth's two children, Michael John, and Susanna. What complicated stories were captured on these scraps of yellowing paper? What a catalogue of tragic deaths – to which now Hannah's own husband's could be added.

Hours passed as they worked their way through recipes torn from magazines, school reports, lesson notes and articles cut from newspapers about Australian flora and fauna. Miss Radley had evidently been a nature lover, as well as a dedicated teacher. There was a collection of Christmas cards from her parents in Doncaster, England, and one or two from what must have been Bernard Evans's parents in Wales.

It was scorchingly hot and the ceiling fan slow and ineffective – or, if sped up, noisy and blowing the papers about – but the pair pressed on, mostly in silence.

A woman's voice broke into their concentration, and they looked up.

'Mr Greenbank. I heard the noise of the fan and thought someone had left it on last night. What on earth are you doing here on a Saturday, and who is this?'

So absorbed in the task were they that neither Hannah nor Eddie had heard the woman approach.

Eddie got to his feet. 'Miss Kelly. I'm trying to find some information for a case I'm working on. This is Miss Kidd from Tibbetts and Finlay. She's working on the same case.'

The woman, tall, stout and wearing enormous horn-rimmed spectacles, looked Hannah up and down and appeared unimpressed. 'No one advised me of your visit. Have you signed these papers out?'

'No, we're not taking them anywhere. Just going through them here.'

'According to protocol, you have to sign them out even if they aren't removed from the building. Otherwise, how do we know who's been looking at them if something goes missing?'

Eddie folded his arms, clearly irritated. 'You wouldn't know, anyway. There's no inventory. They're just described as miscellaneous papers.'

'If that's so, what do they have to do with your case?' She moved closer and looked at the label on one of the boxes. 'This isn't Corporate. It's Probate. What does that have to do with you, Mr Greenbank? As for this woman, she has no business being here at all if she's from Tibbetts and Finlay.'

She gathered the papers up and returned them to the boxes. 'If you wish to submit a formal request, Mr Greenbank, I'll be happy to consider it. *In normal working hours.* Now I'd like to lock up and must ask you both to leave.' She swept an arm in the direction of the stairs.

Hannah and Eddie had no choice but to comply.

When they were outside on the street, Eddie apologised to Hannah. 'I knew it was a risk, but I didn't think the librarian would be around at the weekend.'

'Will you be in trouble?' Hannah felt bad.

'No, Miss Kelly's bark's worse than her bite. She enjoys throwing her weight around, but I'll send her some flowers on Monday, and that will restore her good humour.'

'I'm sorry. It's been a wild-goose chase,' Hannah said.

He gave a rare smile. 'We can go to Parramatta Park. I've brought us some sangies.' He held up the canvas holdall he'd been carrying. 'Unless you're keen to get back to Sydney.'

Hannah could hardly refuse when he'd gone to so much trouble for her.

'Thank you. I'd like that.'

They went through the impressive brick gatehouse and into the park, following the path towards Old Government House.

'How come there's a government house here as well as in the Sydney Domain?' Hannah was trying to keep the conversation light.

'It was built as a country retreat for the governor back in 1799. Sydney was a penal colony then and wasn't the most savoury of places. Hard to imagine Parramatta being seen as the countryside as it's so close to Sydney.' He pointed at the pale Georgian building. 'Built by convicts. As far as I know, it's Australia's oldest building. Used as a school residence now.'

They walked past the house towards the Parramatta River, which wound through the park. Finding a pleasant spot, they sat on the grass under some trees where there was shade from the punishingly hot sun, to partake of the food Eddie had brought. It was more than a couple of sandwiches. There was fruit, a flask of cold lemonade, hard boiled eggs, cold meat and tomatoes and lamington cakes covered in chocolate and desiccated coconut that Hannah knew were beloved by Australians. She was hungrier than she'd realised and thanked Eddie for his thoughtfulness.

'No need to thank me. Mrs Golding, our housekeeper, has a life mission to fatten me up.' He grinned, his eyes squeezed against the brightness of the sun, seeming relaxed now.

After they'd finished the meal, they strolled in the park before heading to the station for the trip back to central Sydney. In contrast to the outbound journey, Eddie smiled and chatted happily. Hannah wished she could understand what was behind the strange swings in his mood. There was no mention of the war, his dilemma about joining up, or about their abortive search that day.

As they drew into Central Station, Hannah didn't want to spend more time with him that afternoon. Refusing his suggestion that they go for tea by the harbour, she told him she had some shopping to do. It was obvious she was making excuses. After all, they had originally planned to spend the whole day in Parramatta. But Hannah felt uncomfortable in Eddie's presence. The tension in him. The intensity. The swings from cheerfulness to brooding misery.

As she turned to walk away, he called after her. 'Hannah,

wait! Tonight. I thought I might go along to the Troc to hear some more jazz. Would you like to come too?' His expression was hopeful.

She was taken by surprise with no ready-prepared excuse. 'The Troc?' she repeated.

'The Trocadero. It's on George Street. Next to the Regent Theatre. They have the best band music in Sydney, and you seemed to enjoy that concert in the park.' Seeing her hesitation, he quickly added, 'Not a date. Just as friends. It would be nice for me not to go alone.'

Feeling cornered and grateful for his kindness that day, Hannah said yes.

'I'll pick you up at seven-thirty then.'

She was about to protest that it wasn't necessary, when he added, 'I'll have the car tonight.'

'Thank you. I'll look forward to it.'

As she walked away, Hannah hoped he meant what he'd said about it not being a date. When he was in a light-hearted mood, she enjoyed Eddie's company. He was intelligent, interesting and good-looking. But there were those strange dark moods. Most of all she felt guilty in his presence, knowing he harboured romantic feelings for her. Feelings she would never reciprocate.

11

———

Eddie arrived punctually, drawing up outside the house in a shiny red car. Dot Hodges had been thrilled when Hannah mentioned she was going to the Trocadero with Eddie. Hannah had swiftly disabused her of any expectations on the romantic front, but it seemed her landlady shared Eddie's optimism that she would eventually succumb. Hannah was uncomfortably aware that she had to make her feelings clearer to him. It would be unfair to string him along when there was no hope.

He was ready at the kerb, holding the passenger door open when she emerged from the house. She settled onto the leather bench seat and looked around at the interior. 'Very smart car. What sort is it?'

'A Ford Deluxe Coupé. You know about motors?' His voice was cheerful, and she inwardly relaxed.

'Absolutely not.' She gave him a sheepish smile. 'Don't laugh, but this is the first time I've been in one.'

Eddie's head jerked in surprise. 'Really? Aren't there many cars in England?'

'There are plenty. Just that I didn't know anybody who had one. I went everywhere on the bus.'

'It's my pride and joy,' he said proudly. 'A birthday gift from my parents. It even has a clock on the dashboard.'

Hannah struggled to imagine what it must be like to have parents who bought one a motorcar as a birthday present. Eddie had mentioned that his father was a judge. They lived in Double Bay, which, according to Dot, was the most affluent area of the city.

Eddie parked the car around the corner from the impressive Art Deco building that was the Trocadero. Topped with a floodlit sandstone tower, it was impossible to miss.

As they crossed the road, Hannah noticed the words 'Dancing Every Night' in lights above the Trocadero sign. Her heart contracted. She hadn't known the Troc was a dance hall.

Oblivious to her anxiety, Eddie said, 'We used to have formal dances here when I was at uni. It's huge. The music's terrific. Frank Coughlan, the bandleader, is a fantastic jazz musician.'

He ushered her through the doors, into the marble-floored foyer. Among the excited crowd were uniformed American soldiers. Most of the women were dressed up to the nines, and Hannah felt out of place in her simple cotton frock.

Eddie steered her by the elbow into the vast auditorium, where the band was already in full swing, and the dance floor crowded with couples. They were playing a catchy song – according to Eddie, a classic called 'Jeepers Creepers'.

The bandstand was in front of an illuminated arc, which gave the impression the musicians were contained inside a giant shell lit up with coloured lights. The other walls were ornamented with Art Deco murals of dancers. Hannah was in awe but her insides clenched. She had assumed this would be a regular concert, like the event in the Domain. She wouldn't have agreed to come had she known it was a dance. Dancing was another life experience outlawed by her bigoted father. What if Eddie asked her to dance? How would she explain that she hadn't a clue how?

He steered her to the bar – not a liquor bar but a milk bar, serving only soft drinks and ice cream sundaes. That was one thing that had surprised her about Australia. Whilst there was no shortage of pubs in Sydney, by law no alcohol was served after six p.m., a stricture that had led to the 'six o'clock swill,' where men would rush to consume as much beer as possible in the hour after finishing work. It struck her as strange in a country that otherwise appeared relaxed and easy-going – particularly as it led to binge drinking.

They sat with their ginger beers at a table towards the rear of the dance floor, where they could watch both the band and the dancers. The American servicemen were skilled at what Eddie said was jitterbugging – an energetic dance that consisted of the man throwing his partner as vigorously as possible around the floor. Hannah watched in awe as the dancers executed their moves, relieved that Eddie showed no inclination to dance. Gradually, she relaxed and focused her attention on the music.

About an hour had passed when the tune shifted to a slow tempo. Eddie turned to her and asked her to dance. Before she could decline, he took her hand and drew her onto the floor.

'I don't know how to dance,' she said with a quiet despair.

'Just hold on and I'll shuffle you around.' He gave a rare smile.

Mortified, Hannah let herself be steered into the throng. At least the place was too crowded to permit any critical inspection of her performance, and her fellow dancers were all too caught up in the moment to bother looking at anyone else. She relaxed and realised she was enjoying herself.

Later, in the ladies' room, she was combing her hair in front of the mirror when she became conscious of someone standing next to her. She turned and saw Shirley's cousin, Brenda, skewering her with narrowed eyes.

Hannah stiffened. 'Hello, Brenda.'

'So, you're seeing Eddie?' Brenda's voice was clipped, icy. 'You got what you wanted then. Explains why he's never around anymore.'

Not knowing how to deal with Brenda's palpable hostility, Hannah said, 'I'm here to enjoy the band. I've never been to the Troc before. Eddie told me the music was wonderful, and he was quite right. Are the others here?' She plastered on a cheery smile and hoped Brenda would drop her antagonism.

'You deliberately set out to steal him from me. Just as everything was going well between him and me, you came along and flung yourself at him.'

The two other occupants of the ladies' room turned and looked at them.

Hannah put her comb back in her handbag and gave a sigh. 'Look, Brenda, he's all yours, as far as I'm concerned. Eddie and I are just friends. He was helping me out with a legal matter today and offered to bring me along tonight as he knew I'd enjoyed the concert at the Domain last week.'

Brenda's eyes narrowed. 'Don't expect me to believe that. I saw you dancing with him.' She folded her arms, scowling.

'It's not fair. Eddie and I were becoming closer. I'm certain he was about to ask me out – until the day you turned up at the beach and ruined everything.'

Hannah sighed again, knowing this to be untrue. 'What do you want me to do, Brenda? I'll happily leave now if it makes you happy. I'm not "seeing" Eddie, as you put it. It's nothing like that.' She wasn't prepared to tell Brenda about Will. It was none of her business and shouldn't be necessary anyway.

Her words had no effect on Brenda. 'It's worse if you don't even want him yourself.' Her shoulders slumped, and her voice turned into a whine. 'I hope you're happy that you've spoilt everything.' She swung around and left the powder room, slamming the door behind her.

As Hannah made her way back to her seat, she looked around for Brenda but there was no sign of her. Perhaps she'd gone. Hannah hoped so.

When she rejoined Eddie, she mentioned that she'd bumped into Brenda in the ladies' room, but he appeared indifferent. She didn't want to be caught in a drama, so she told him what had happened.

Eddie gave a laugh that was nearer a snort. 'So she thinks you came between me and her? Nothing could be further from the truth. I wouldn't have anything to do with Brenda Mulligan if she were the last woman in Sydney.'

Hannah hadn't expected that.

Eddie scowled. 'I'll never forgive her for what she did to my sister.'

She waited for him to elaborate.

'They were at school together, then college. Brenda was seeing a fellow called Ollie in the year above at college, but he finished with her. A couple of months later, he asked June out. She and Ollie were going strong when Brenda spread the false and malicious rumour that June was sleeping with Ollie. Our parents were summoned by the principal. June was distraught. Under pressure from his own parents, Ollie finished with her and then a couple of months later, she was diagnosed with leukaemia.'

Shocked, Hannah murmured her sympathy.

'Obviously, Ollie ending it had nothing to do with her illness, but all the drama added to her stress. I don't care what anyone says. The gossip Brenda stirred up contributed to June's illness or to her ability and determination to fight it. June was humiliated, unhappy. It was as if she saw her diagnosis as her fate. I blame Brenda for that. She must know that I feel that way, and if she doesn't, she's stupid as well as nasty.'

Hannah was taken aback by the strength of his reaction. Instinctively, she reached out and touched his wrist. 'I'm so sorry to hear June went through all that.'

'Thank you. Anyone who hurt my twin sister will never be a friend of mine.' He drained his glass of ginger beer. 'Not long before June died, I overheard Brenda complaining that June being sick had derailed the summer. She resented us spending time with her rather than going to the beach.' He frowned. 'I'd spend every living moment I have with June if it could bring her back. I'll never understand why Brenda couldn't see that.'

'Why do you go round with her then?'

His mouth formed a hard line. 'Wally's my best friend. We've known each other since kindy. Our families are close. He was a rock when June died. Shirley's a good egg and they'll probably get married as soon as the war's over. Unfortunately, Brenda, being Shirl's cousin, is part of the package.'

'Do Wally and Shirley know how you feel about Brenda?'

'Probably, although we've never discussed it. I'm not good at talking about that kind of thing.' He gave her a wry grin. 'But Wally knows how much I miss June and how lonely I feel without her – that's why they're keen on you and me getting together.'

The blood rushed to Hannah's face. But before she could frame a response, the band launched into a lively rendition of 'Chattanooga Choo Choo' and they both turned to watch the Yanks displaying their skills on the dance floor.

12

Hannah sat, knees drawn up, gazing at the harbour, imagining Will as a young man in 1926, sitting here on the grass, dreaming of going to sea. When he left Australia, he hadn't known he'd never return. His time as a sailor took him up and down the coast of East Africa on a tramp steamer, then carrying cargo through Suez and into the port of Liverpool. At that time, his hopes and dreams didn't include meeting her. He'd had no expectations, certainly no plans to fall in love and settle in England. All he'd wanted back then was to escape from Australia, the country that had wrongly found his father, Jack Kidd, guilty of murder and sentenced him to death.

Hannah's thoughts drifted back to the book she was reading about the settlement of Australia by the eleven ships of the First Fleet. Six ships full of convicts – fourteen hundred of them – found guilty of a variety of crimes deemed worthy of the death sentence, commuted to transportation. How must they have felt, emerging from the dark stench of the wooden ship's hold, after over eight months at sea? The convicts included women and children, more of whom were born on the voyage. The new arrivals would doubtless have been lice-ridden, blinking in the blinding light of the Australian sun as they looked upon Port Jackson, as Sydney was then known. Would they have appreciated the beauty of the natural landscape, the rocky outcrops, the trees, the sparkling blue waters, and been filled with hope? Would they have shared Captain Philip's opinion that it was 'the finest harbour in the world'? More likely they would have seen it as a hostile alien land, barren, cruel and empty. For them no frolics on the beach at Bondi, Bronte or Balmoral. It was their prison. Inescapable, for what remained of their natural lives.

This was probably Hannah's fate too. The likelihood of her ever returning to Britain was remote. The voyage was too long, and even were she to undertake it when eventually the war was over, there was nobody there for her, apart from her friend and former landlord, Sam. Her only relatives were in Australia. It made it even more important that she find her aunt Elizabeth – though the prospect of doing so via the assistance of Hardcastle, Wainwright and Struthers was now looking remote. Eddie had made a formal request to Miss Kelly at Parramatta to go through the papers herself. She'd agreed but said only when she had some spare time – Hannah thought this likely to be never.

What else could she do? An advertisement in the newspaper? There was no national one. If she covered only New South Wales, there were still numerous publications, not to mention a plethora of small local papers. And if her aunt was living in a remote area, they may not bother with a paper at all. The population of Australia was only around seven million, but that was still a big number if you didn't know where to start. And the country was vast. It was hopeless.

Hannah racked her brain, searching for a solution to what seemed an insurmountable problem. According to that letter from Miss Radley, Elizabeth's husband, Michael, was a sheep farmer. Perhaps that could be a lead. Presumably, he must produce either meat or wool, and there was surely some way of tracing where they would be marketed. From her time working for her father's coffee business, Hannah knew commodities were often traded through a central exchange. It was a remote hope, but better than nothing. Her only other option would be to pay for a private detective to undertake a search, but that was likely to be expensive and she didn't have the money to fund it.

Dispirited, she made her way back to her digs in Darlinghurst.

OVER THEIR SUPPER, Dot quizzed her about the previous evening at the Trocadero – Hannah had been spared at breakfast by her landlady's rush to get to church.

She squirmed under the inquisition and attempted deflection. 'Have you been to the Troc? It's enormous. I didn't realise beforehand that it was a dance hall – I was imagining a concert hall. I'd never seen such a massive space. And the band was terrific. There were lots of Americans there. Such good dancers. Tossing their partners in the air and under their legs. Jitterbugging, they call it. I've never seen anything like it.' She paused for breath, hoping that would suffice, but knowing it probably wouldn't. She forked a potato into her mouth.

Dot folded her arms. 'You know I wasn't asking about the latest dance craze. I'm far too old for that kind of nonsense. But not too old to appreciate hearing about a blossoming romance.' She gave Hannah a cheeky grin. 'Come on, young lady, what's the go with Eddie?'

Hannah swallowed her spud. 'The go?'

Dot rolled her eyes. 'Don't play the Pommie fresh off the boat with me. You know exactly what I mean.'

Hannah put down her knife and fork, biting back the temptation to tell her landlady to mind her own business. 'I told you before, Dot. Eddie's just a friend. I'm not interested in finding a husband or having a boyfriend. No one can ever replace Will for me. If you don't mind, I'd prefer it if you didn't suggest there could be something between me and Eddie, because there isn't now and there never will be. He's a nice chap and has been extremely kind, but that's as far as it goes.'

Dot pursed her lips and leant back in her chair. 'That's me told.'

Seeing that she was offended, Hannah softened. 'Look, I could do with some advice. I think he's still keen on me. I've tried to clarify that I'm not interested in pursuing a romance with anyone – not just him. On top of that, there's a girl in our little gang who's keen on Eddie, and she's convinced I'm the reason he's not interested in her.'

'She's probably right.'

'As it happens, she's not. It's all down to things that happened before I was even in Australia.'

'So what advice do you want?'

Hannah took a sip of water. 'I'm caught in a dilemma. I like Eddie as a friend and don't want to cut him off altogether, particularly as he's the best pal of one of my bosses. He's also been generous in giving up his time and expertise to help me trace my aunt. But the more I rely on him for that, the more he seems to hope we'll eventually get together. I'm still desperately in need of his help and support in tracing Aunt Elizabeth, but doesn't that mean I'm taking advantage of him and his interest in me?'

Dot considered for a moment. 'You've told him you don't want a romantic relationship?'

Hannah nodded.

'Then you've done the right thing. If he continues supporting your crazy hunt for your aunty – which, if you ask me is like hunting for a ha'penny on Lady Robinson's Beach, then that's his choice.' She gave a sigh, closed her eyes for a moment and shook her head. 'But I reckon, chook, you need to get your head tested.'

Hannah looked straight back at her. 'Since you lost your Stan, Dot, have you ever thought of marrying again?'

Dot jerked upright in her chair, visibly bristling. 'I wouldn't even think about it. Not for a moment. Not after eighteen years married.'

'Then why do you think I would?' Hannah leant forward, elbow on table, chin on fist, keen to hear the response.

'It's different. Completely different. You were only married for five minutes and you've no children. Me and my Stan had our Billy. That's what makes a marriage.'

Hannah pushed her plate forward to show she'd finished eating. There was no need to justify herself to Dot Hodges. She wasn't going to tell her how the grief she felt at the loss of Will could not be any more profound, and the love she still felt for him wasn't any less because of the brevity of their marriage. If anything, it was all the more intense.

She stood, pushing back her chair. 'I can't even respond to that comment or tell you how much it's hurt me. I'm going to bed. Goodnight, Dot.'

As she left the room, she ignored Dot's apologies and pleas that she return.

Safe in the sanctuary of her bedroom, Hannah flung herself on the bed. Dot's comment about her childlessness had cut her to the quick. She and Will had longed for a baby. After his death, it had taken all of Hannah's fortitude to support her sister when Judith fell pregnant. Judith had conceived Sarah so effortlessly – indeed accidentally, because of a single afternoon when she and Paolo had gone to Formby for a picnic. For Dot to imply that a marriage wasn't really a marriage if it was without children, and that grief wasn't really grief if the marriage had been short-lived, was a dagger through Hannah's heart.

The grief at losing Will might have been bearable if there had been a child to tether her more firmly to him. A child whose features and character as it grew up might have offered her echoes of her husband.

Having endured a fanatical father whose bigotry and zealotry had turned her against religion altogether, Hannah wasn't even sure she believed in God. Charles Dawson's God had been a cruel vengeful one, eager to smite, to punish and destroy everything in His path. But while she would have liked to subscribe to a kinder, gentler God, the way Will had been taken from her made Hannah think that if there was a God at all, He would be closer to her father's version. Either way, she struggled to imagine Will at peace in some celestial paradise, watching protectively over her as she struggled to get by without him.

For it was a struggle. No matter how brave a face she put on. No matter how hard she worked at being positive. No matter that she sometimes smiled or laughed, passed a pleasant day, enjoyed a new experience. Underneath it all was the dull ache of loss, emptiness and heartbreak.

Not knowing many details about the circumstances of Will's death made matters worse. All she knew was that he must have known he was about to die. According to the survivors of the *Shelbourne*, watching helplessly from a safe distance on life rafts, he and the captain were on deck when the vessel went down, tending to a dying man. They were sucked under with the ship itself, sinking down into the icy depths and never seen again. Hannah's fevered mind saw Will whirled like a corkscrew, drawn down into the vortex created by the ship.

People say drowning is the best way to die, but how do they know? Surely, nothing could be worse than the embrace of the ice-cold waters of the Atlantic. How long would he have been conscious? How afraid? She'd been told of his bravery in staying on board to help the dying man, but she thought it was madness. It made her angry that he'd done that – put a man who was already doomed ahead of himself – and ahead of her. Yet, at the same time, it made her love him more for his courage, loyalty and optimism.

She punched the pillow. How could Dot Hodges be so brutal? How dare she assume she could quantify another person's grief?

THE FOLLOWING MORNING, Hannah awoke early. Although reluctant to face Dot, she had to do so. Better to get it over with quickly. When she went down for her breakfast, the landlady was sitting at the table, nursing a cup of tea. Dot jumped up, evidently nervous. 'You're early this morning, Hannah. Oh my lord, you've been crying, haven't you? Your eyes are all puffed up. Look, I'm sorry for what I said last night. It was wrong of me. I went too far, but it's just that I want you to be happy and not throw your life away brooding.'

Hannah bit her lip, wishing Dot would shut up. She was making her feel pitied, which was worse. It was judgmental and bossy and, frankly, none of her business.

'Apology accepted, but I don't want to talk about it, Dot. And I don't want to hear anything else about Eddie Greenbank.'

Dot looked relieved. Muttering about getting the eggs on, she hurried into the kitchen. Hannah glanced in the mirror that hung over the sideboard. Her eyes were puffy. She took her compact out of her handbag and applied some powder in a botched attempt to cover the redness. It would have to do. She was glad she and Dot had cleared the air, but it had coloured her view of the woman and made her feel less comfortable being under her roof.

AFTER SPENDING her lunch breaks checking the wool storage and meat warehouses to find out if anyone knew of Michael Winterbourne, Hannah was disheartened. The best response she'd had was a shake of the head; most gave her short shrift, saying even if they knew, they wouldn't hand out information about their clients. She'd now exhausted all the places in the telephone directory and had to conclude she'd reached a dead end.

To cheer herself up, and avoid spending her evenings with Dot, she often went to the pictures. One evening, sitting alone in the darkened cinema she watched as a news-reel played. The urgent voice of the commentator described the activities of the Australian army in Malaya. The footage showed shirtless Aussie soldiers grinning at the camera as they loaded guns or packed into boats to float down jungle-lined rivers. The commentator spoke of how the 'yellow men' stood no chance against these plucky Australian troops – yet the same reel pointed out that the Airforce was severely hampered by its reliance on under-powered, under-equipped, out-of-date American Brewster Buffalo airplanes and could do with some Spitfires or Hurricanes.

'No more Penangs!' declared the newsreader with conviction but. to Hannah, the claim rang hollow and was belied by virtually every recent attack by the Japanese.

The newsreel finished, and the main feature began. The film, *High Sierra*, starred Ida Lupino and Humphrey Bogart, a B-movie actor Hannah had never heard of. It was a gangster film about a bank heist. At first, she let it wash over her but as the film progressed, she was drawn into the drama and captivated by the doomed Bogart character. Any hope that the film might lift her spirits was dashed when he was shot dead after a last-ditch shootout with the cops, his presence betrayed by his little dog.

Leaving the picture house, Hannah tried to buck herself up. Instead of being saddened by the end of the film, she ought to enjoy the movie for its own sake and for the performances of the cast. If every little thing, every setback in the war, every disagreement with her landlady was going to send her into a funk, she might as well give up now. She was stronger than that. Better to count her blessings: a good job, comfortable lodgings, in a beautiful city surrounded by stunning beaches. Her sister was safe and happy. They were away from the bombing. Even though there was justifiable fear about the threat from the Japanese, it was still a far cry from the intensive bombing she'd lived through in Liverpool. Inevitably, rationing would be introduced before long, but life in Australia was a vast improvement on the conditions back in Britain. Even meat was still plentiful here.

Despite the chirpy optimism of the newsreels, things in Malaya were not going well. In early February, the battle of Singapore began, and two weeks later, the British colony fell to the Japanese. Now Japan was poised to sweep all before it throughout the Pacific, unless America could block its progress.

A few days later, fears were realised when the Japanese bombed the city of Darwin, the capital of the Northern Territory, in the first strike on Australian soil. Hannah didn't know whether the government was heavily censoring the news or if the attack was a minor one. The report in the *Sydney Morning Herald* was brief and sparse on details, and she suspected the decision had been taken to downplay matters. According to the paper, ninety-three enemy aircraft had attacked in two heavy air raids and four Japanese planes had been brought down. No details were given regarding loss of life on the ground.

Prime Minister Curtin's words managed to be both vague and ominous: '... information does not disclose details of casualties but it must be obvious we have suffered.'

Inevitably, it was more than enough to propel Dot Hodges into a state of fevered anxiety as she awaited news from her son. When a letter eventually arrived – one side of a sheet of paper heavily redacted by the military censors – it offered little in the way of consolation or reassurance. But Billy was alive.

Hannah said nothing. Staying alive was all that mattered.

13

———

The day after the news broke of the bombing of Darwin, Hannah was finishing up some work after most of the staff had gone home. Wally emerged from his office and perched, as was his custom, on the edge of her desk.

'I'm under instructions from Shirl to persuade you to come to the beach with us tomorrow. We haven't seen you in ages. We're going over to Manly on the ferry. You been there yet?'

She admitted she hadn't.

'You'll love it. You've got to make the most of the summer, Hannie. I'm hoping it'll be quieter in Manly since the Yanks have taken over Bondi. Shirl wants to see you get some wear out of that cozzie she gave you. She made it clear that she'll blame me if you don't turn up.' He gave her a disarming grin. 'I can tell you that will be no fun. Our Shirl has ways of making her displeasure felt that'd make your hair curl.' He winked at Hannah. 'Not that your hair needs curling, with those pretty waves.'

'Stop it, Wally, I give in!' she protested, laughing, glad

that there was no one else in the office to hear this little exchange. 'As long as you're sure? I don't want to intrude.' She was thinking about Eddie and dreading any repercussions if he talked to her and ignored Brenda.

'Intrude? Course you wouldn't be intruding. You're one of the gang.'

Hannah was backed into a corner and didn't want to tell Wally about her recent conversation with Brenda. Remembering her resolution to stay positive and try to make the most of being in Sydney, she agreed to go. Why should she let Brenda's ill humour and unfounded accusations ruin things for her?

'Meet you tomorrow morning at the Manly ferry terminal at Circular Quay. Let's say ten o'clock. Don't forget your cozzie! Time you were heading home now, Hannie. No point in doing unpaid overtime.'

She glanced up at the clock. He was right. She'd better get moving, or she'd be late for the meal Dot would have prepared. The atmosphere between them was still tense and Hannah didn't want to give her landlady any cause for complaint.

It was another glorious sunny Sydney morning when Hannah arrived at Circular Quay. Wally and Shirley were standing with their arms wrapped around each other, eyes locked. Hannah paused before approaching, not wanting to interrupt an intimate moment.

'Here she is,' cried Shirley, breaking away from Wally, running over and flinging her arms round Hannah. 'So pleased you decided to come. We've missed you, chookie.'

They boarded the green and cream twin-funnelled steam ferry for the harbour crossing and went to sit on the outside deck. As the boat moved away from the wharf,

Hannah spotted the Greenbanks and Brenda. Mark called and waved and the three of them crossed the deck to join them.

'It's Hannah's first trip to Manly,' announced Shirley. She swept her arm out towards the Sydney Harbour Bridge and the boats bobbing on the water. 'Best view in the whole world.'

'How do you know?' Wally grinned at her. You've never been anywhere but Sydney.'

'Well, best view in Sydney then. Although I can't believe there's better anywhere. What do you think, Hannah? How does it compare to Liverpool?'

Hannah thought of the Mersey overlooked by its three landmark waterfront buildings at the Pier Head, and the long stretches of warehouses and docks lining the estuary. The Luftwaffe had devastated the city, and her thoughts turned to the sands at Crosby, where she and Will had walked together when they first met and had their first kiss.

'Liverpool has its charms and some fine buildings,' she said evenly. 'Although the German bombing has wreaked havoc. But I must admit, for the beauty of the setting, it can't compare to this.' She looked about her at the coves and inlets, the rocks and trees and the sparkling water. 'Shirley's right. I can't imagine a better view.'

Shirley grinned and gave Wally a playful punch. 'There! See?'

Eddie had edged his way to stand beside Hannah as she leant against the railings at the side of the boat. He pointed to a circular stone tower that appeared to float in the harbour. 'That's Fort Denison. When the First Fleet came, they called it Rock Island and used it as a place to punish convicts who'd misbehaved. Solitary confinement – stuck them there in chains for a week on bread and water.'

'Sounds grim – not even the stunning view would make up for that.'

'The place became known as Pinchgut. The convicts were brought there to level it, and the sandstone was used to make what's now Circular Quay. One of the poor devils found guilty of some heinous crime in the penal colony was condemned to death and hanged there, then slung up in chains as a warning to others. The story goes that his last words to the hangman were that the view from the gallows was beautiful. They left his skeleton dangling on the gibbet for four years.'

'Plenty of time to enjoy the scenery then,' said Wally. Shirley rolled her eyes.

'Is it still a prison?' asked Hannah.

'No. It was turned into a fort in the mid-nineteenth century to defend the harbour and renamed Denison after the governor of the time. It's a lighthouse now.'

Eddie was evidently in one of his more talkative moods. On the other side of him, Brenda was staring into the distance, her expression inscrutable.

Hannah was keen to avoid further conflict with her, so moved away to join Shirley on the other side of the boat. The water was calm with virtually no waves until they reached The Heads, the rocky promontories that marked the entrance to the harbour from the Tasman Sea. There, despite the calm conditions, the boat rose up and down on the swell.

Eddie appeared next to her again. 'The crossing's always choppy between The Heads. You can imagine what it's like when the weather's bad. Even these big old ferries bounce around like flotsam. Terrifying in a storm.'

They docked at Manly Wharf in a churn of peppermint-coloured wash. The group walked along the Corso to the opposite side of the isthmus, where a long sandy beach lay in front of them. Hannah noticed the men hadn't brought their surfboards. 'Isn't Manly suitable for surfing?'

Mark answered. 'It's fantastic. We're just giving it a miss today.'

They found a spot and set up camp, piling up bags and baskets and laying out towels. This time, Hannah had put on her swimming costume under her dress before leaving home so she wouldn't have to worry about changing. The sandy beach spread in a gentle crescent, edged with Norfolk pines and stretching for more than a mile beside the crashing surf of the Tasman Sea.

Hannah didn't like to admit it, even to herself, but the sea made her nervous. She'd coped with the rock pool at Bronte but this wild open sea with nothing between here and Tasmania terrified her and made her think of Will's body lying at the bottom of the Atlantic.

'Last one in buys the ice creams!' Mark dashed towards the water, followed by his brother, Wally and Shirley, leaving Hannah, to her dismay, with Brenda.

Brenda turned to look at her, but Hannah couldn't read her expression as her eyes were concealed by her sunglasses.

'We haven't seen you in a while,' Brenda said. 'Things didn't work out with Eddie, then?' Her mouth formed a smile, and she tilted her face towards the azure sky as she leant back, propped up on her elbows.

Hannah decided not to let Brenda darken her mood. She simply wouldn't engage with the hostility. 'It's not really been that long. I've had quite a lot to do. And, as I told you at the Troc, there's nothing between Eddie and me. He'd been helping me with a legal matter and I haven't seen him since.'

Brenda smirked. 'As I say, things haven't worked out for you.'

Hannah bit her tongue knowing any response would antagonise Brenda further. She reached into her straw bag and pulled out her library book. Better to ignore her.

But Brenda was evidently in the mood for conversation. 'What are you reading?'

When Hannah held the book out for her to see the jacket, Brenda pulled a face. '*Shadows over Rangoon*. It was serialised on the wireless. I switched off after ten minutes. Utter tosh. Sentimental nonsense. What made you choose that?'

'I'm trying to read only Australian books, and the librarian recommended this author. She said whenever he brings out a new book, there's a waiting list.'

'There must be a lot of idiots using the library services then.' Brenda stretched her hands out in front of her, admiring her red varnished fingernails.

'Are you a keen reader?' Hannah attempted being friendly.

Brenda snorted. 'Not of books like that. In fact, I'm not terribly impressed by Australian literature at all. I prefer American novels. Steinbeck, Faulkner and Fitzgerald.' She gave Hannah a supercilious look.

Hannah felt on more solid ground. 'I loved *The Grapes of Wrath*. Awfully depressing, but so powerful. *The Great Gatsby* is one of my favourite books. I haven't read any Faulkner yet.'

Brenda frowned, clearly irritated that Hannah seemed to be as well informed about American literature as she was. 'If you're an admirer of Steinbeck and Fitzgerald you shouldn't be wasting your time on FJ Thwaites.' She nodded disparagingly at the book in Hannah's hands as she scrambled onto her feet. 'I'll leave you to your trashy novel. I'm off for a swim.' With that, she ran across the sand and splashed into the sea.

Hannah stared after her. At least she'd been talking to her about something other than Eddie. She opened *Shadows over Rangoon* but before she'd finished the first page she had to acknowledge Brenda had a point. Consigning it to her bag, she lay back on her towel and decided to top up her suntan instead.

She must have dozed off as it was only when a drip of water landed on her cheek that she realised a soaking wet Eddie was standing beside her.

He reached for a towel. 'Water's beautiful today. How about a stroll along to the Fairy Bower rock pool where you can bathe in complete safety? My offer about the swimming lesson is still open if you change your mind.'

She pushed her cheap sunglasses up on top of her head so she could see him more clearly. 'I don't want to upset Brenda. I told you how she was at the Troc when she cornered me in the ladies' room. She seemed to think we were going out together—'

'Not for want of trying on my part.' He grinned and shrugged. 'But I got the message, Hannah. I'm not trying to lure you away. It's just that it would be a shame for you not to enjoy a dip, and the rock pool is much safer than the open sea. As for Brenda, it's none of her business. She ought to know by now that I'll never think of her that way.' He stared towards the sea. 'I'm civil to her because she's Shirley's cousin, but that's as far as it goes. And if she persists in questioning your behaviour, I won't even bother to be civil.'

'She was quite friendly just now. Talking about her favourite books.'

Eddie appeared to be already bored with the topic of Brenda. He jumped up, reached for her hand and pulled her up. 'Fairy Bower? You never know; we may see some little penguins.'

Reluctantly, but curiosity piqued, she followed him. 'Penguins? Here?'

'Yes. Little penguins. They nest in the coves around Manly. They're only about a foot tall. It's highly unlikely we'll see any in the height of the day as that's when they're out swimming. You can see them after dusk when they return to their burrows.'

Australia never ceased to surprise Hannah. She still remembered the thrill of seeing her first grazing kangaroo when travelling by train between Melbourne and the internment camp at Tatura where Paolo was held. Even the birds were colourful, strange and exotic – the noisy parrots, the vibrantly plumaged rainbow lorikeets and the ridiculous laughing kookaburra.

It was a ten-minute walk to the Fairy Bower, a triangular rock pool accessed by a stair from the promenade. Nervously, she followed Eddie down the steps as he held out a hand to steady her. The water was warm and sparkled under the sun. Hannah was relieved to find they were at the shallow end, where the water lapped gently around her knees.

She began to relax and, with Eddie's encouragement, walked through the pool, gradually immersing herself up to the waist, refusing to go any deeper. Eddie was patient, coaxing her gently, until eventually he got her to hang on to the side of the pool and kick with her legs, feeling the sensation of the salty water buoying her up. The time passed, and before long he had helped her to let go, ease away the tension and give herself up to the water. She still had her feet on the bottom but little by little she began to feel more at home in the water. Eventually, he persuaded her to let her feet drift up so that she was floating on her back, supported by Eddie with one hand lightly positioned under her spine, barely making contact. She looked up at the little puffy clouds scudding across the blue sky and gave herself up to the sensation. His hand underneath her back made her feel secure. He wouldn't let anything happen to her. She could trust him. Then she realised his hand was gone, and she was floating unsupported.

A few moments later, another swimmer jumped in at the far end and began splashing about. All Hannah's fears returned in an instant as her legs thrashed until she found her footing.

'You did well,' Eddie said. 'It's about letting go and not stiffening or trying too hard. Let the water do the work to hold you up. It's actually harder to go under than to float, especially in seawater.' He pulled himself out of the pool onto the seaward wall and reached his hand down to help her up beside him. They sat side-by-side, facing out to the sea in a companionable silence, letting the sun dry them.

Hannah's thoughts returned, as they always did, to Will. Eddie's comment about it being harder to go under than to float rang hollow when she thought of how her husband had died. He'd been a strong swimmer. He'd told her how he used to swim in a nearby billabong when he'd lived out at McDonald Creek. But the undertow of a huge ship sinking would have been an irresistible force. Will would have been dragged down so deep and so rapidly that he'd have been powerless to resist.

Her daydreaming was interrupted when Eddie spoke at last. 'I've made up my mind. I'm going to join the forces.'

'My goodness. That's a sudden change of heart.' Hannah was shocked. 'What made you decide?'

'Darwin was the last straw. I can't stand by any longer while the enemy attacks my country.'

'I'm sorry to hear that, but I understand why.' She bit her lip. 'Which service will it be?'

'The AIF I imagine – just a humble foot soldier.' He stared into the distance.

'When will you go?'

'I told the firm yesterday. I'll go to the recruiting office on Monday. There'll be a few of us from the firm. I expect they'll do some background checks, and I'll have to have a medical. I've done my basic training but there'll probably be some more before I see action.'

'Where do you think they'll deploy you?'

'Somewhere in the Pacific region. They need all the men they can get as most of our boys are in Europe. And the Yanks are still building up troops and resources. Since Rabaul was invaded, New Guinea and Papua are probably the biggest area of threat.'

All these place names were alien to Hannah. Before she'd arrived in Australia she'd never heard of New Guinea and now she was always consulting the atlas in the library, trying to familiarise herself with the regional geography. 'I presume Mark will join up with you?'

He gave a dry laugh. 'As it happens, no, he won't. Dad read him the riot act and Mum turned on the tears, so he's agreed to finish up at uni first.'

'But he was the reason you were thinking about joining up in the first place.' She looked at him, puzzled.

'I know. But once I got my head around it, it all made sense. There's nothing to keep me here.' He looked away. 'I can't stand by and watch the Japs take over.'

'You think they'll try to invade Australia?'

'Not yet, but if we let them take the rest of the Pacific, they will. Too much mineral wealth here for them to ignore. And in the meantime, they'll do as much damage as they can because they know we and the Americans will launch our attacks from here. That's what Darwin was about. At least, I assume it was, because no one's telling us anything.' He frowned. 'Didn't your landlady have a son up there? Is he all right?'

She nodded. 'As far as we know. Dot got in touch, but he's given her strict orders not to contact him there anymore. I think he got his knuckles rapped.'

'Can't have every anxious mother calling the bases.' His brows knitted despite the effort at levity.

Hannah hesitated and then plunged in. 'What about your promise to June?'

He gave her a sad smile. 'You put me right on that, Hannah, when you said we can't be held to promises we made to people who are dead.'

She gasped. 'Look, you shouldn't listen to me. It's nothing to do with me.'

'But it is, Hannah. It very much is. You're the only person whose advice I'd trust right now. In fact, apart from Mark and my parents, you're the only person I really care about.'

Her stomach contracted with fear. 'You barely know me, Eddie.'

He reached out and took her hand. 'That's not how it feels.' This time she let him hold it but avoided looking at him, fixing her gaze on the far horizon. Before she realised it, he had turned his head and drawn her closer to him. He reached a hand up and gently turned her face towards him and kissed her.

It had been so long since Hannah had been kissed. The

sensation was warm and comforting, and she could taste the salt from the seawater on his lips. She found herself responding, slowly at first, then more urgently. His lips were soft, and the kiss sent an unexpected charge through her body.

What was she doing? This was madness. She broke away.

He gave her a slow lazy smile. 'You've no idea how much I've wanted to do that. Ever since I first set eyes on you at Bronte. You're in my head all the time. I can't concentrate.'

She was aghast. What was she doing? Why had she responded? Why had her body betrayed her when her head was clear that she didn't want to have anything to do with this man? With any man.

'Look, Eddie. I can't—'

'I think you've just shown that you can.' He gave her a smile but didn't touch her.

She put her head in her hands. 'I'm married.'

He took her hand again, gently stroking it. 'What did you tell me about not keeping promises made to the dead?'

'That's not fair.'

'Look, I know it's hopeless. I'll be gone very soon. And I told you already, I have a feeling I won't be coming back.'

'Don't say that.'

'Why not? I'm being realistic. I've had a recurrent dream and a strong sense that I'm not going to make it. Just like my sister did when she was first ill before the diagnosis was confirmed.'

She stared at him, horrified. 'A recurring dream?'

'Yes. I'm up to my ankles in mud. Trying to run, to get away from something or someone, but my legs are paralysed. I keep struggling and there's a blinding light and an explosion, then darkness. I have the same dream, night after night.'

'Dreaming about your legs not moving is really common.'

'Perhaps. But the mud? The blinding light? The explosion? The sudden total darkness?'

'Have you talked to anyone? A doctor?'

He laughed. 'How can I tell something like that to a doctor? He'd think I was mad. "Doctor, I've been having a bad dream" – he'd laugh me out of the surgery.'

Hannah looked around. The sun had moved low in the sky and there was a cool breeze that made her shiver. Eddie put his arm around her, and the next thing she was kissing him again. This was not supposed to happen. When the kiss ended, she took a long, slow breath. Where was the harm? Eddie would be gone away soon. Who knew when they'd meet again? If he was right, it could be never. She was still a young woman, who for a long time had tried to suppress that side of herself. Kissing Eddie had unearthed something she'd thought was buried forever.

She didn't love him. He could never replace Will in her heart, but surely there was no harm in her experiencing some physical pleasure. She'd been clear to Eddie that she could never be with him, and none of that had changed – but perhaps they could steal some pleasure and a little joy in the midst of this terrible war. Didn't they deserve that much? She curled her hands into tight fists so that her fingernails left deep red indentations when she opened them again.

Eddie's voice in her ear was reassuring. 'It's getting late. We should get back to the others.' But contrary to his words, he took her hand and pulled her into another kiss.

When it was over she drew her hand away. 'You know

this will never lead to anything, Eddie? Much as I like you –
and I do like you – I can never love you.'

'I know.' His voice was soft. 'I'll settle for what I can get.
I'll be gone soon. Having memories to draw on will make all
the difference.'

'I don't want the others to know about this.'

'Of course.' He smiled at her. It was a sad smile. Then he
drew an imaginary zip across his mouth.

They walked back to Manly Beach in silence, Hannah
still churning over whether she'd done the right thing.

Wally was the first to spot them as they headed to the
group. 'Hey! you must be ready to enter the Ladies Sprint at
Icebergs by now, Hanee. Eddie will have you on a surfboard
next.' He slapped Eddie on the back. 'We were thinking we
might have to go without you. Shirl and I are going to the
theatre with her parents tonight. Bren's already gone as she's
going to the pictures.'

'Sorry. It's my fault,' said Hannah. 'I'm a slow learner. I
certainly won't be sprinting any time soon. I only managed
to get my feet off the bottom once – for about ten seconds.
And I've just remembered I was meant to buy the ice
creams...' She was talking too much. Everyone could surely
see the guilt written all over her face.

'Ready to head back?' Shirley asked. 'Or are you two
staying longer?'

Before Eddie could answer, Hannah said, 'I have to be
back for my evening meal. I don't want to incur the wrath of
my landlady.'

They made their way back along the Corso to the ferry
wharf, Hannah falling into step beside Shirley, determined
to be as far as possible from Eddie – but wishing that wasn't
the case.

14

———

In bed on Sunday night, Hannah was still reflecting on the events of the previous day at the beach. She'd been over and over her time with Eddie but was no nearer a resolution, other than admitting to herself that she'd actually enjoyed the swimming lesson. Eddie had been kind and thoughtful. What happened later when they'd sat together on the edge of the pool was the real cause for concern. Had she been right to let herself be kissed? Was she leading Eddie on and being unfair to him? But hadn't he said he'd settle for whatever she could give? It felt wrong – like scattering crumbs from the rich man's table. It troubled her because Eddie was a decent man who deserved to be loved in return. But no matter how much she might want to, she had no feelings for him, other than friendship and, to her surprise, a strong physical attraction. She couldn't risk the possibility of getting close to Eddie and losing him to the war. She couldn't afford to let herself care.

Until now, she'd assumed physical attraction depended entirely on love. With Will, it had been impossible to differentiate between love and desire. With Eddie there was no love, yet he had aroused an undeniable desire in her.

The source of her anxiety now was that Eddie could assume that love would bloom eventually. Having experienced that all-consuming feeling in her marriage, she knew that what she felt for him was just a physical response, without the overwhelming joy, deep affection and trust that had characterised her feelings for Will.

It would be all too easy to settle for what Eddie offered. He was intelligent, kind, interesting, successful, attractive. He would make someone a wonderful husband. Just not her.

She lay on her back, staring at the pattern of light made by the street lamp on the ceiling, as she tried to reconcile the problem. Eddie had made it clear that he wanted her on any terms. He'd even said being with her would furnish him with memories to draw upon when he was away at war. How could she deny him that? And if she were wholly honest and listened to her body rather than her head, *she* wanted it too. But was it right? Was it fair?

Eventually she drifted off to sleep, her problem still unresolved.

THE FOLLOWING morning she woke with her head clearer. She had to stop second-guessing Eddie. He was a grown man, capable of making his own decisions. As long as she made it clear that there was no future for them, it was up to him to decide if he was willing to accept those conditions.

As for Will, he was gone forever, but while she would always love him and hold his memory sacred, she was still in her early twenties and not prepared to live like a nun. It was understandable to want to grab whatever pleasure one could; after all, who was to say whether they'd even survive the war? Hannah had seen enough death and sadness back in Liverpool. What was wrong with making the most of what she had in the here and now? They were in the midst of a world war. Who knew what lay ahead? There was something about wartime that seemed to excuse behaviour she wouldn't allow herself in peace.

Having arrived at a decision, she washed and dressed hurriedly then went down to her breakfast.

'You look pleased with yourself this morning.' Over the top of the *Sydney Morning Herald*, Mrs Hodges peered at Hannah through her reading glasses. 'Like the cat that got the cream.'

'Probably because I slept like a top last night.' She pulled out a chair and sat down, as Dot folded the paper and got to her feet.

'I'll get your brekkie. Nothing like a nice fry up to set you up for the day. My Stan used to say there was no problem that a good night's sleep and a plate of eggs and bacon couldn't cure.' She shook her head, lips tight.

Hannah didn't say that it hadn't cured the cancer that took him from her.

Dot crossed to the sideboard. 'I almost forgot. There's a letter from your sister.' She handed it to Hannah.

Hannah ripped it open. She hadn't heard a peep from Judith in weeks. Sarah had just had her first birthday and Hannah had sent her a little dress – which had presumably been the spur for Judith to write at last.

If only I had a camera I'd take a photograph of Sarah in her new dress. She looks like a princess, so thank you very much. She's spoken her first words. It had to be Pappa of course! For some reason she hasn't yet managed Mummy. I expect it's because I'm here all the time whereas we mostly see Paolo through the fence and she seems to find that exciting. He blows kisses at her through the wire and plays Peekaboo – it's called cucù *in Italian. Which reminds me,* cucù *is another word she knows! At least under the new camp commandant we get to go inside for half an hour to see him once a month. He asked me to send you his love. He's playing lots of football or* calcio *as the Italians call it.*

Hannah felt a wave of sadness that she was missing Sarah growing up. She also missed Judith and Will's best friend, the warm and funny Paolo.

Paolo is working in the camp kitchens. They get good food, he says – lots of lamb and fresh vegetables. There's plenty of pumpkins coming into season so he made big batches of pasta con la zucca. As you can imagine, he's very popular in the camp!

The letter continued in a similar vein. Hannah was relieved that Judith had settled in well to her strange new life. She had proved more resilient than in the past – no doubt having a husband and child depending on her had forced her to become stronger and able to break her reliance on her older sister.

Judith's letter took up one and a half sides of paper. At the end, Judith's landlady, Sal Clancy, the wife of one of Paolo's guards at the Tatura camp, had added a message.

Judy lets me read your lovely letters. I'm so pleased you're settled well in Sydney and have a nice place to live and a good solid job. Your life there sounds wonderful – far more exciting than here in sleepy Tatura. We were disappointed not to see you at Christmas but it's a long old journey and the train trip would have eaten up all your leave. If you do manage to get more time off (fat chance in this war!) we'd love to have you come and stay. Your sister's doing great and so's the bub. Lots of love from me. My Terry sends his best too.

Hannah folded the letter back into the envelope, smiling

to herself. Sal Clancy had shown more interest in Hannah's news than her own sister. Judith was doubtless preoccupied by Sarah and Paolo – but Hannah couldn't help feeling a twinge of sadness that Judith was so wrapped up in her own affairs that she couldn't spare much thought for her sister. Hannah had given up her life in Liverpool, her interesting job at Western Approaches, where she was making a real contribution to the war effort – all because Judith insisted on her coming to Australia too. Judith was never going to change and Hannah loved her anyway. Besides – she was all she'd got.

A FEW DAYS LATER, as she was walking home through Hyde Park, Eddie appeared out of nowhere.

'Hello,' she said. 'Are you following me?'

He tilted his head in affirmation. 'I couldn't come to the office or your digs since you said you wanted to keep us quiet.'

'Us?' Hannah felt immediately uncomfortable. 'There is no *us*, Eddie.'

'I know, I know. What I meant was you wanted to keep our friendship from the others.'

Hannah had a sinking feeling this would not work. All her resolution from a few days ago melted away. It would be wrong to enter into such an unbalanced friendship. It wasn't fair on Eddie.

He fell into step beside her and, without words, they settled on a bench near the Archibald Fountain. The fountains were a spectacular feature of the park, dominated by a huge bronze sculpture of Apollo on a plinth in the centre, with bronze water-spouting tortoises, dolphins and classical figures around the basin. Hannah often sat there with a book during her lunch break. Eddie reached for her hand, but she drew it away.

'I'm not sure about this,' she said. 'It seems wrong. I don't think you've understood that while I won't deny I find you attractive, I can't feel any more than that. And I know I never will. Sorry to be so blunt, but I can't help thinking you still have a hope – or even a belief – that a physical relationship will blossom into something more.'

His expression was forlorn, his mouth turned down 'I'd be deluding myself if I thought that, Hannah. You've been brutally honest. As I said last weekend, I'll take whatever you're prepared to give.'

It was proving hard to hold her resolve as his hand had moved back again. It was now laid over hers and the pad of his thumb moved gently back and forth across her palm, sending shivers up her arm.

'I have no time left,' he said.

'You signed up?'

'Yes. I'll be heading to training camp in North Queensland in a few days.'

'I see.' Hannah bit her lip, cursing this endless war. 'What will you be doing? Where will you be going?'

'I can't tell you that. I don't know myself.'

She nodded. Her time at Western Approaches Command had conditioned her to the need for secrecy. 'So this is goodbye.'

'Not yet!' His hand tightened over hers. 'That's why I wanted to talk to you. Will you come to Double Bay tomorrow evening? My parents are in Canberra. Dad's involved in some governmental inquiry and Mum's gone with him. Mark's back at uni in Melbourne.' He fixed his eyes on hers. 'Please, Hannah. It's all I ask of you. Then I'll be gone.'

She hesitated, then made up her mind and nodded, her heart pounding. 'What time?'

'After your evening meal. I'll come in the car.' She was about to protest when he added, 'Don't worry. I'll park out of sight at the end of the street so your nosy landlady won't spot me. What time?'

'About seven?'

'I'll be there.'

HANNAH HAD NEVER BEEN ANYWHERE like Eddie's home before. They drove up through open metal gates onto a driveway in front of a large Victorian house. The gabled building was red brick and decorated with the ornate wrought-iron balconies that were characteristic of the Eastern suburbs of Sydney. After parking the car on the driveway, Eddie led her around to the rear of the property to a paved terrace, where she gasped at the panoramic view over Sydney Harbour. The property boasted a tennis court and a swimming pool, as well as extensive lawns and shrubberies. Hannah immediately felt out of place. She didn't belong here. Never would. Never could.

'Is there anyone else here? Servants?'

'Only the housekeeper and gardener. They're a married couple and they live over there in the cottage,' He pointed to a small white rendered building tucked away in a far corner of the grounds. 'The rest of the staff, what's left of them since the war began, are all day workers.'

All? Hannah was already wishing she'd never agreed to come. The house and grounds were gorgeous, the view of the harbour more so. But these affluent surroundings were alien to her. Then she reminded herself – it didn't matter that she couldn't picture herself here – she'd never need to.

If anything, the grandeur helped reinforce how unsuited she and Eddie were.

He took her hand. 'Let's go inside. I'll get you something to drink and we can sit on the terrace for a while.'

She let him lead her into the house, through an impressive entrance hall with a wide wooden stairway. Her shoes clattered on the parquet floors as they passed through the hall where stained-glass windows threw coloured patterns onto the walls and floor. When they reached the kitchen, he asked what she wanted to drink.

'Just water, please.'

'Come on, Hannah, have a glass of wine. I'm having a beer.'

She didn't want wine. She wasn't used to drinking, but maybe it would make her feel less on edge, so she nodded. They took their drinks through a pair of French windows onto the terrace. The harbour was spread in front of them in all its splendour, and her breath hitched at the beauty of it.

The wine tasted surprisingly good. Hannah took some satisfaction – as she always did – from the knowledge that this was another thing that would be regarded as an unforgivable transgression by her late father. As was what she was about to do that night. She could imagine all too clearly what Charles Dawson would have said. *Whore of Babylon! Adulteress!* he would have cried, his face contorted with anger and hatred. She pushed the image away and stared at the beauty of the harbour as the light faded into dusk.

The wine was going to her head. It was also loosening her inhibitions. Before she knew it she was walking up the wide wooden staircase, hand-in-hand with Eddie.

15

Hannah agreed to spend the weekend with Eddie in the big Victorian house.

She made the decision with mixed emotions. It was like a betrayal of Will, even though she knew he himself would never have thought so. He'd have wanted to her to live life to the full. There was guilt about Eddie and the risk he was falling more deeply in love with her. Could she bear losing someone else to the war? All these reasons ought to have held her back but in the end her body wouldn't be denied. The sex was a release, a pleasure, a joy. And she needed some joy in her life again, however fleeting.

Eddie drove her back to Darlinghurst, parking discreetly a street away, while she gathered some things together and left a note for Dot, who was out at her weekly canasta game. She told her she was going for a last-minute weekend break with friends. Hannah felt bad lying but it was basically true – Eddie was a friend. Anyway, it was none of her landlady's business. It probably wouldn't convince Dot – but what did that matter? Hadn't Dot encouraged her to spend time with Eddie – even phrasing it as 'having some fun'? She was unlikely to criticise her on moral grounds. But Hannah didn't want to share her private life.

They spent the weekend in bed, as well as swimming in the pool – where Eddie continued his patient coaching of her until by Sunday afternoon she could float, do a few strokes on her back, and was mastering the breaststroke as he supported her under the chin. They walked on the private beach at the bottom of the extensive garden. She couldn't help wondering why Eddie and Mark went to the public beach when they had this on the doorstep, but realised it was for the surf as the water was calm here within the Harbour, protected from the open sea by the Heads.

As they walked, they talked about the war. Hannah said she couldn't understand why the Japanese had bombed Pearl Harbour. 'Surely, they must have known the Americans would immediately declare war?'

'They miscalculated. They probably convinced themselves that America's isolationism was immutable, and they'd negotiate.'

'Yes, but what purpose did it serve?'

'They timed their invasions across the region simultaneously, and knowing America would retaliate, they crippled their navy to prevent that.' He looked thoughtful. 'I reckon they expected the Yanks to do a deal and lift the oil embargo. It was all about the oil. Japan imported most of it from the USA until the Americans blocked it. That's what's behind all the Japanese invasions – they're grabbing the resources they need to become a great imperial power like Britain, the USA, and the Soviet Union. They need the rubber, metals and oil from Malaya and the Dutch East Indies.'

It all made deadly sense to Hannah. 'Until I came to Australia, I hadn't paid attention to what was happening with Japan. I was aware of the war with China and all the atrocities but I'd never understood the bigger picture. Thanks for explaining.'

Eddie nodded. 'If the Chinese hadn't put up such a fight, the Japs would have got what they needed from there and probably wouldn't have moved south.' He reached for her hand. 'Enough about war and politics. Let's just enjoy the weekend. Come on, I'm hungry. It must be time for lunch.'

Hannah saw the Greenbank's housekeeper, Mrs Golding, crossing the lawn on the way to and from the kitchen to prepare their meals but otherwise the woman kept out of sight in the cottage concealed behind a line of oak trees at the side of the lawn. Perhaps Eddie had warned her in advance as she was the soul of discretion and Hannah never got the chance to meet her.

Over the weekend, Hannah got to know Eddie better. While he was sporty and focused on his career, like his brother and Wally, they had a lust for life he lacked. He was more measured, quiet, introspective, serious. His twin sister's death had clearly taken a toll on him, and there was an aura of sadness that hovered about him all the time. She felt sorry for him, but a relationship based on pity – albeit with a strong physical attraction – was not enough.

'Do you have a photograph of June?' she asked. There wasn't one among the cluster of framed family photographs on top of the grand piano in what he referred to as the music room.

'Mum won't have any on display. She finds it too painful. Come, I'll show you.' He led her back upstairs to the end of the landing and unlocked a door with a key he took from his trouser pocket. 'I keep it with me all the time. Mum, Dad and Mark never go in here. Mum wanted to clear all June's things out, but I put my foot down.' He opened the door.

The room was dark, curtains drawn, and Eddie pulled them open. The windows looked over the garden to the private beach fringing the harbour. June's room was like a shrine. The walls were covered with framed certificates – music examinations, prizes for swimming and diving, photographs of netball and swimming teams and a shelf full of trophies.

'She was sporty, like you and Mark.' Hannah smiled.

'Runs in the family.' He went over to the bedside table and handed Hannah a framed photograph. June was smiling, radiant, full of life. It looked like a portrait taken to mark a birthday or a special party.

'She was beautiful.' Hannah looked up at Eddie. 'I can see a resemblance. She has your eyes.'

'Hers were darker.' His mouth twitched, and he looked away, clearly finding being in June's room with someone else difficult.

'Sorry, I shouldn't have asked you to show me this. It must be painful for you.'

'No more painful than anywhere else. I think about her all the time, no matter where I am.' He placed the picture back on the cabinet. 'I talk to her too.'

Hannah moved towards the door, Eddie's raw grief too painful to handle. 'Thank you for trusting me enough to show me. I think I'd like to go home now. It's almost five, and I told Dot I'd be back for Sunday tea.' She turned and took hold of his hand. 'I've really enjoyed being here, being with you, seeing your home. Thank you. And for teaching me to swim.' She tilted her head and reached up to kiss him lightly.

'Must you go? Already?'

'I've been here since Friday!'

'It seems only five minutes. But I've loved every moment.'

She smiled, wishing she could feel more for this man. 'When do you leave for Queensland?'

'Tuesday morning. First thing. I've already finished up at work. Tomorrow morning I'll be sorting kit and packing.'

A thought suddenly occurred to her. 'So you've already said your goodbyes to Mark and your parents?'

He looked away. 'No. They don't know I've volunteered. No one does except my boss and you, Hannah. My father would have tried to talk me out of it. Mum would have cried, and I couldn't stand that. Mark would have insisted on coming too. I haven't even told Wally. I'm rather hoping you'll do it for me.'

She wasn't comfortable with that. It would make it beyond doubt that there was something between her and Eddie, and she didn't want to be cast into the role of the girl-friend. 'You ought to tell him yourself, or he'll be hurt. I presume you'll be writing to Mark and your parents?'

'On the list for tomorrow. You're right. I should tell Wally myself. I'll call his office and ask him to meet me for a farewell beer tomorrow after work.' He drew her towards him and kissed her. 'Let's go back to bed.'

Hannah eased herself away. 'No, Eddie, I have to go. I'll get a tram or a bus home as I can't stand long goodbyes.' She was about to add that she'd had enough of them in the short time she was married to Will but she didn't want to compare this present parting to the agonies she went through every time Will set off to sea.

His jaw set hard, and his mouth stretched into a thin line. Grasping her hands between his, he said, 'Thank you, Hannah. I can't tell you how much these past two days have meant to me.'

She gave him a tight smile. 'Thank you for your hospitality.' Then realising she sounded like a municipal functionary, she added, 'I had a wonderful time,' and gave him a last lingering kiss. 'I'll miss you.'

It would have been all too easy to go back to bed with him. She'd enjoyed the sex – a welcome release from the tension that had been building up inside her ever since Will was killed. But she needed to get away from Eddie. He was dangerously close to declaring his love for her.

'I don't suppose there's any point in asking if you'll write to me?'

She shook her head. 'It's better like this. We've had a beautiful, magical weekend, which I'll remember fondly.' She raised a hand and stroked his cheek. 'Stay safe and good luck. I hope when this beastly war is over you'll find the woman you deserve.'

He looked at her, his eyes full of sadness. 'I'm glad I have this to remember.' He held her shoulders. 'I won't see you again, Hannah. I'm certain I won't be coming back.'

'Don't say that, Eddie. Please don't tempt fate.'

He gave a little shake of his head then watched her as she walked away down the drive. When she reached the gate she forced herself not to look back.

16

───────

After she'd said goodbye to Eddie and gone back to Darlinghurst, Hannah mulled over what had happened that weekend. Her feelings veered between conviction that she'd done the right thing – lived life in the moment, given some happiness to a man about to go to war – and guilt. The latter gained momentum as the days passed and the memory of the weekend receded, replaced by a nagging concern that she'd taken advantage of Eddie's feelings for her – not to mention a belief that she had been unfaithful to Will. It made no difference how often she told herself that infidelity was meaningless when her husband was dead. She saw it as a weakness, a lack of resolve and a betrayal of the only man she could ever love.

It was impossible not to make comparisons. The sex with Eddie was just that. A physical release, pleasurable, but missing one essential ingredient – intense emotion.

She tried telling herself she'd done nothing to be ashamed of. The war had changed everything. It was inevitable one would challenge what had been rigid morals, when death could come in a moment. Life was to be lived.

Sitting in darkened cinemas, watching the newsreels, she couldn't help but feel anxious about Eddie and what he would soon be facing. She might not love him, but she definitely cared for him.

News of the war offered little comfort. Twenty-one Australian nurses had been massacred on Banka Island in the Dutch East Indies when the Japanese opened fire on them. The Americans evacuated the Philippines and General MacArthur moved from there to Australia. The Japanese army invaded Java, and Rangoon in Burma. News from Europe was no better. More rationing in Britain. The Mediterranean island of Malta under siege. More bombing.

The war was relentless – no matter how positive a slant the newsreels tried to put on it.

NOT LONG AFTER Eddie had departed for Queensland, Hannah left the house early one Monday morning, avoiding breakfast and the usual chatter from Dot. She walked to work instead of taking the tram, hoping the exercise would clear her head. There had been no more excursions to Bronte Beach, so Hannah wasn't required to conceal what had passed between her and Eddie.

As soon as she arrived at Tibbetts and Finlay, Mr Finlay's secretary, Dilly, pounced on her. 'Mr Finlay would like a word with you, Mrs Kidd. In his office at ten sharp.'

Hannah, nervous, wondered why the senior partner wanted to see her. She'd barely exchanged a word with the man and until now had had few direct dealings with him. At ten, she knocked on the door of his corner office.

Mr Finlay looked up. 'Ah, Mrs Kidd. Come in and take a seat.'

He cleared his throat and shuffled some papers needlessly on his desk, avoiding her eyes. 'As you're aware I'm sure, since we took you on here, the war has escalated. After the attacks on New Guinea and the Northern Territory, it's looking more likely that Australia itself is facing serious risk of further Japanese attacks. The volume of work passing through the firm has significantly diminished since Pearl Harbour.' He fiddled with his fountain pen. 'People don't often buy houses or get divorced in wartime. Several of the younger partners and junior solicitors have volunteered for the services or expressed the wish to do so.' He put down the pen and looked at her for the first time.

Hannah knew what was coming. 'You're dismissing me.'

He gave a little cough. 'I wouldn't put it so bluntly, Mrs Kidd, but yes there is going to be a significant decline in the number of billed hours for the firm and we can't keep staff on when there's insufficient work for them to do. I'm afraid it's a case of last in, first out.'

'When do you want me to leave?' Her stomach clenched. How was she to afford her rent? She'd have to use her paltry savings until she could find another job, and it would mean looking for somewhere cheaper to live.

'The terms of your employment contract provide for a week's notice but we could allow a little flexibility on that. Shall we say two weeks?'

His words hit her like a battering ram.

'Dilly has the relevant paperwork to go over with you. Good luck Mrs Kidd, I'm sure you'll find a suitable position quickly.' He held out his hand for her to shake.

As she opened the door, he spoke again. 'By all reports, your work here has been exemplary. Indeed, once the war is over and things pick up again, don't hesitate to enquire whether we have a vacancy.'

Dilly looked up as Hannah went back to her desk, giving

her a sympathetic smile. Hannah sat down, shaking, trying to make Mr Finlay's words sink in. She opened a manila folder and blindly went through the pages, playacting that everything was normal while she waited until she could escape at lunchtime.

As she went through the door into the street she almost crashed into Wally.

'You've seen the old man, then?' He gave her a knowing look, one eyebrow lifted.

'How did you know?'

'It was discussed in the partners' meeting. Sally Tyler in Accounts is getting the chop too. I'm truly sorry. I put in a word for you. But it's strictly based on length of service. How do you feel, Hannie?'

'Not exactly wonderful. I have rent to pay. And I liked the job. It took me ages to find it.'

His expression was rueful. 'I'll keep my ear to the ground. So will Shirl. Someone will snap you up in no time.'

That evening, Hannah debated whether to tell Dot the bad news now or wait and see how her job hunt went. She scoured the situations vacant columns but found nothing comparable. There was demand for women to join the land army, or to work in a factory. Hannah wanted to stay in Sydney – and factory work wasn't appealing. In the end, she chose to postpone telling her landlady.

HER ANXIETY WAS GROWING when a few days later, Wally approached her and took up his perch on her desk.

'You worked in some role with the navy back in England, didn't you? I remember you had a glowing reference. Some kind of secret work?'

'I was with Western Approaches Command. Plotting shipping movements.' She kept it vague.

'This may be a long shot, but would you consider something like that here?'

Her heart leapt in her chest. 'Definitely.'

'My old law professor is now in the RAAF and I ran into him in Cahill's the other night. They're recruiting women to do something similar. How about I have a word with him? See if I can get you an interview. Sounds like you'd be more qualified than anyone else.'

Hannah jumped up and flung her arms around him. 'Would you, Wally? That would be utterly marvellous.'

'Obviously, the set up would be different here and the Americans will likely be in charge. No promises but I'll see what I can do.'

She thanked him and could hardly contain herself as she waited for more news.

THE FOLLOWING DAY, Wally approached her again, a broad grin on his face. 'Uncle Wally delivers the goods, Hanee! I've got you an interview. Now it's up to you.'

She grasped his hands between hers, squeezing them. 'You're my guardian angel.'

'There's one drawback I've since discovered.'

Hannah held her breath.

'Most of the women recruited are being drawn from outside Sydney. The idea is to reduce the risk of them running home every night and spilling the beans about what they've been working on. They're being put up in dormitory accommodation. The wages reflect the fact that bed and board are provided.'

She hadn't expected that. But beggars can't be choosers,

and she really wanted this job. It would mean breaking the news to Dot. 'That's not a problem.'

He reached into his trouser pocket and pulled out a piece of paper. 'Go to this address and ask for Sergeant Prendergast. She'll be able to answer your questions better than I can.'

'When?'

'No time like the present. She's expecting you.'

Still stunned, Hannah picked up her handbag and slipped on her jacket.

'Hit it for six, Hanee!' he called after her as she left the office.

OUTSIDE ON THE PAVEMENT, she looked at the piece of paper Wally had given her. Hotel Metropole, at the intersection of Bent, Phillip and Young Streets. Hannah went into a cafeteria where she consulted her pocket-sized map of Sydney. The Hotel Metropole was less than ten minutes' walk away.

A stern and imposing Victorian building, capped with French-style turrets and fronted by an enormous canopy, it overawed her as she entered. Inside, she went up to the reception desk, introduced herself and asked the clerk for Sergeant Prendergast.

'Take the lift. Third floor. She'll meet you there.'

When Hannah emerged from the lift, she was greeted by a tall, angular woman in her forties, wearing what looked like a man's uniform. 'Follow me, Mrs Kidd,' she said, and walked briskly down the corridor to a room which she unlocked. 'I'm hunkering down in here to conduct the interviews,' she said in explanation. 'We're only here because the Yanks have based themselves in this hotel. Bit grander than we'd have chosen'

Hannah looked about her. It was a single bedroom with a desk and two chairs squeezed into the space next to the window.

'Not very roomy, but needs must. Take a seat.' Miss Prendergast waved at one chair and sat down in the other.

'I understand you're an old hand at plotting work. Tell me what you did back in Britain.'

So, it was to be straight in, no messing about.

'I was a Wren working in the map room at Western Approaches Command, gathering information about movements of allied and enemy shipping and putting markers on a map. There were WAAFs doing the same for aircraft.' She went on to describe in some detail the set up at Derby House – or The Citadel as the inmates of Western Approaches Command called it, and how she had spent her time up a ladder, putting pins in a gigantic map of the Atlantic.

'We do things a bit differently here. The Women's Army Corps do the naval plotting over in Manly, while we're set up here in the city in a railway tunnel. Very cramped and not enough height to have the maps on the walls. They're on big map tables but the principle's the same.' She scratched her head. 'There'll be training first – we have a training school for all aircraft personnel near Newcastle.'

'Aircraft? But I worked on shipping.' Her heart sank.

'They're fully staffed at Manly and we have a big need here. I imagine it's much the same except the planes move faster.' The woman gave a guffaw. 'Obviously, the training will cover things like aircraft identification, coding and suchlike. To be honest, I don't know much about it as I only deal with recruitment and staff management. I presume you want to stick to doing what you've already done rather than try out something else like telephony or transcription?'

'I enjoyed it, and it probably makes sense to stick to what I know.'

Sergeant Prendergast stuck out her bottom lip. 'Maybe. As long as you're not going to keep on all the time about the way they did things back in Britain if we're doing them differently here. That won't go down well. Perhaps it might be better to try you on something new.' She scratched her head again, causing a little shower of dandruff onto her collar. 'But I suppose if you enjoyed doing it, it makes sense to keep you on it. I always reckon people work best and hardest when they enjoy their work.'

The sergeant ran through a checklist of points before saying that Hannah would have to move into the Metropole.

'Here?' Hannah gasped. It was very grand.

'The Yanks are using this place as their HQ and we have a floor here, although you'll be up at the training school first. Where do you live now?'

'In lodgings in Darlinghurst.'

'Better warn the landlord you'll be moving out soon. The training takes three months but as we're desperate for staff and you already know the ropes, I'll see if we can make it shorter in your case – we'll need you to know the identification codes for aircraft since you've only worked on shipping. Once I've sorted things with HQ, we'll be in touch, and you'll be off for whatever training is deemed appropriate. I want to stress the importance of the strictest confidentiality about the work you'll be doing. Any questions?'

'What about uniform?'

'I don't suppose you still have your Wrens one?'

'I'm afraid not. I didn't foresee a use for it over here after I was discharged.'

'Why were you discharged? There's no information here.' The sergeant tapped the slim file in front of her.

'I was bombed out of my home. My sister too. She had a new baby, and her husband was here in Australia.'

The sergeant frowned. 'But why did you come?'

Hannah hesitated, then decided the truth was her best option. 'My late husband and my sister's husband both served under Commodore Palmer. They were all close. My brother-in-law is Italian and was deported as an enemy alien to Australia. He's in a camp at Tatura in Victoria. When we lost our home, Judith was desperate for her and the baby to be close to her husband and the commodore pulled some strings to get her a passage out here. She was afraid of U-boats and refused to go without me. She's the only family I have left so, with the commodore's permission, I agreed to go with her.'

'I see.' The woman frowned. 'Is she here in Sydney?'

'No, she's living close to the camp.'

'What happened to your husband?'

'His ship was sunk by an enemy aircraft over the Atlantic.'

'Rotten luck.' She shook her head. 'My husband was based in Singapore so he's a POW now. God knows what he's going through. Bloody damned war.' She closed the file in front of her. 'Leave your current address with Patsy in the room opposite the lift. She'll oversee your IQ test then you'll have a medical. After that, we'll be in touch.'

'You didn't say about the uniform.'

'Bit of a shortage.' She looked down at her own apparel. 'At the moment we're making do with the men's. No one foresaw we'd be recruiting so many women. When you report for duty, you'll be kitted out with whatever's available.' She slung the file onto a pile on top of a metal cabinet behind her. 'Now I've others to see. Busy day. Dismissed.'

Hannah made her way along the hotel corridor and

found Patsy, who was installed behind a desk in an open-doored room opposite the lift.

'How did you get on with the sarge?' Patsy, a petite blonde, with overlarge spectacles and a broad smile, greeted her.

'Very well, I think.'

She filled in her name and address on the index card Patsy passed her.

'She's all right, is Sarge. Used to be the staff manageress at Mark Foy's, so she's used to bossing lots of girls about. I know, as I was one of them. Ladies lingerie. Bit different here.' She added the card to a box on the desk in front of her. 'You'll like living here at the Met. The food's fantastic. I hear it's not so good at training camp, but you'll survive.' She took a printed booklet from a box on the desk and handed it to Hannah. 'Your IQ test.' She glanced at her watch and wrote the time down. 'You can complete it next door. I'll come and collect your answers in forty minutes. Don't worry, it's not that difficult – but there are a couple of other girls in there, so no conferring. I'll be able to hear any whispering.' She gave her a friendly wink.

Hannah found the test relatively basic and easy. She glanced at the two other women completing the forms – one was chewing the end of her pencil and the other had her head bent over the test and didn't even look up. The first one was about Hannah's age, the other older. After a while, Patsy appeared and liberated the pencil chewer and a few minutes later, another woman appeared and took her place, looking as though this was the worst thing that had ever happened to her.

After the test was over, Patsy witnessed Hannah make the oath of allegiance, then she told Hannah to go to another room where the doctor would conduct her medical.

'Once he's done with you, you're free to go. Nice to meet you, Mrs Kidd, and see you again when you've been through training.'

The medical examination was fairly cursory, and Hannah left the Metropole and went to sit in the Botanical Garden. So much had happened since she'd arrived in Australia the previous October. She was still trying to take in the week's unexpected developments. Her entire world had been transformed in a matter of days.

She settled down to finish the book she was reading so she could return it to the library before being fined. Goodness knew how soon she might be heading for training camp.

Back at her digs, she broke the news to Dot that she had lost her job but had been recruited into the WAAAFs because of her experience in a similar role in Britain. 'They insist I move into barracks with the other girls. We'll be sent away for training first, but back in Sydney, I'll be billeted in the Metropole. The pay isn't great because it includes bed and board.'

Dot took it better than expected. 'I'll be sorry to see you go, darl, and I hope you'll drop by to say hello now and again when you have a bit of time. I can't really complain, what with me having a son in the services too. We all have to do our bit, don't we?'

THE TRAINING CAMP was at a place called New Lambton, about a hundred miles north of Sydney. It was based within Number 2 RAAF Fighter Sector Headquarters – or 2FSHQ as it was known. The operations were housed in school buildings, the pupils having been dispersed around various other schools in the district. Hannah was issued with a uniform jacket, cap, shoes, stockings and underwear – as well as a pair of men's trousers which she was told would be replaced with a skirt when there was one available. In the meantime, she had to turn up the legs and roll the waist over and pin it, as they were far too big.

The sleeping conditions were basic. They were issued with blankets and sheets and had to make up their own beds according to a strict method. The mattresses were straw palliasses, lumpy and uncomfortable. The WAAAFs were required to be in class at eight each morning, having queued to wash in the shared facilities, cleaned the dormitory, made the beds, and breakfasted, so her days began at six. In the evening, the lights were out at ten. The food was awful, cooked out in the schoolyard in three-gallon dixies and big copper pots, making her think wistfully of Dot's home cooking. She told herself it was no worse than being on rations back in Liverpool – and at least it was more plentiful.

There were two other recruits from Sydney – one of whom was the pencil chewer she'd seen at the Metropole. The other WAAAF trainees came from other sectors. The school also trained male servicemen, including Americans. Hannah didn't know what kind of training they were going through.

The filter room, the nerve centre of operations, was in what had been the school assembly hall, now housing an enormous map table covering the whole of Australia, the Coral Sea, and the South Pacific. There were WAAAFs and RAAF officers, the former armed with wooden cues to move aircraft markers around the table or with headphones to pass on messages from the Home Chain radar stations and the observation corps – the VAOCs – to the plotters. The male RAAF officers oversaw everything, analysed the information, assessed threat levels and issued orders for aircraft to scramble, or antiaircraft guns to deploy, via the teleprinter operators and over the telephone. There was a buzz of activity that immediately took Hannah back to her time in the map room at The Citadel.

By the end of her training period, Hannah was exhausted. The training had included everything from aircraft identification and basic communication codes, to interpreting radar signals. She couldn't wait to get back to Sydney and put it all into practice.

17

SYDNEY, APRIL 1942

As soon as she got back to Sydney, Hannah went to see Dot Hodges. She wanted to collect the possessions she'd left at her lodgings while up at New Lambton – only a few items of civilian clothing, her letters from Judith and a trinket box from Zanzibar that Will had given her on their wedding day, as well as the little kangaroo wood carving Mary O'Hara had given to her.

It was colder now, and today was overcast and raining, so Dot made a pot of tea and they sat in the front room to drink it. Now that she no longer lived with Dot, Hannah was more forgiving.

Dot looked Hannah up and down critically, noting the cobbled-together uniform with the baggy trousers. 'You want me to take those in for you, darl? I can run up a few darts on the Singer to make the waist sit more snugly. It'll only take a few minutes. You look like a sack tied in the middle.'

Hannah smiled. 'Not very flattering, are they? We're supposed to be getting skirts, but the supplies have been delayed again. They hadn't anticipated the demand.'

'Can't say I approve of women in the forces. Nursing, of course, but not the army and air force.' Dot pursed her lips. 'You won't actually be flying planes, will you?'

Hannah smiled. 'Sadly not.' Conscious of the need for secrecy, she lied, saying, 'It's basically just clerical work, similar to what I was doing at Tibbets and Finlay, but for the air force. Not terribly interesting but it frees up men to go to the front.'

'Oh well. Somebody has to do it, so why not you? What's it like in that posh hotel?'

'Full of Yanks. They have one floor, we have another and a third is the mess and kitchens.'

'Do they feed you well?'

'I'll find out this evening. If it's anything like the training camp, it won't be a patch on your cooking. I'll be sharing a room with three other girls.'

Dot pulled a face. 'You won't like that.'

'Actually, it'll be rather fun. At least we get proper beds and mattresses – better than at training camp where we were in a big dormitory sleeping on straw ones.'

Dot pulled a long face. 'It's quiet here without you. I've had no takers yet for your room. So many chaps away with the forces and then girls like you getting their accommodation provided. No one wants to rent a room. Good thing I have some savings to keep me going. And my Billy sends me money each month. He's a good boy, is Billy.'

Hannah felt bad for Dot, but there was nothing she could do about it. The war was hard for everyone and would likely get harder. They chatted on, Hannah in her dressing gown, while Dot worked away at the sewing machine taking in the seams of her trousers.

Alterations complete, Hannah was taking her leave, when Dot clapped a hand to her head. 'Strewth! I almost forgot. There's a letter for you.' She went into the back room and returned moments later, brandishing it. 'Postmarked New South Wales, so it's not from your Judith. Who else do you know in Australia?'

Hannah suppressed her irritation at Dot's curiosity and examined the envelope. The handwriting was unfamiliar. Her heart raced. She didn't want to open it and read in front of Dot. She stuffed it into her handbag.

'Aren't you going to read it, darl?'

Hannah gave her a smile. 'Nothing interesting. It's from a girl I met at training camp. She promised to send me a knitting pattern.'

AFTER LEAVING DOT'S, Hannah made her way to her favourite spot beside the Archibald Fountain. She wanted to be alone to read the letter, even though she hadn't a clue who it was from.

Hunter's Down,
Hazelton, NSW

My dearest Hannah,

I can't tell you how happy I was to hear news of you after all this time. I am overjoyed, shocked and in disbelief that you are here in Australia and living in Sydney.

I return to McDonald Falls every year to visit the grave of my children and lay flowers. Afterwards, I used to call on my dear friend Verity, but poor Verity died this year, so I had the sad task of laying flowers for her too. Afterwards, having some time before the train back to Sydney, and anxious to avoid the centre of town, on a whim I called at Kinross House to see Mary O'Hara, and she told me about meeting you and gave me your address.

Oh, Hannah, I wept tears of joy and of sorrow. She told me the astonishing news that you had met and married dear William and that he was killed in enemy action last year. I went through a whole gamut of emotions on hearing that tragic news. I was so fond of Will. From the moment I met him when I first arrived at McDonald Creek, he was my firm friend. He stole my heart, and I loved him as though he were my own son. Michael, my husband, was a great friend of his and is as devastated as I am on hearing of his death.

When I got back to Sydney, I went immediately to your lodgings in Darlinghurst, but there was no one at home. Running a farm makes trips to the city rare and my husband and I couldn't stay in Sydney any longer, so I have had to settle for writing this letter.

I don't know where to begin. I have so many questions. Please, please write as soon as you can. Nothing would make me happier than for you to come here to stay with us. We don't have a telephone. So please write. Tell me what you're doing, but I so want to see you.

We have such a lot to catch up. So many years. Mary said there was much more you had to tell me but that it would be better coming from you, now that she has put us in touch. I need to know it all. Your mother, little Judith – and your mother had another baby on the way when I left. Don't delay, dear girl. Please write soon.

Your loving aunt, Elizabeth

P.S. You have a cousin. Harry will soon turn sixteen. He'll be excited to meet you, as will Michael.

Hannah's hands were shaking. After reading the letter through three or four times, she folded it back into the envelope. How ironic that after all her efforts to find Elizabeth, she should do at the point when it was impossible to visit her. The address was somewhere up in the Hunter Valley.

Possibly it was close to where she'd been doing her training. How frustrating! Still, no point in bemoaning fate. At last, after giving up hope, she was in touch with her aunt.

She wanted to tell Eddie the good news, but she'd no means of contacting him. Then she remembered that he'd promised to have the librarian at Parramatta continue the search. She'd better call that off. So she got up from the bench by the fountain and went to Hardcastle, Wainwright and Struthers, where she left a note to be passed onto Miss Kelly at the document depository, then made her way to the Metropole Hotel.

There was no time to write her reply to Elizabeth that evening as she was summoned immediately to a briefing meeting, where the dos and don'ts of 1FSHQ were spelled out to them. Fraternising with the Americans was frowned upon, if unavoidable. The women were told that anyone found on the American floor of the hotel would be discharged – but mixing at meal times was accepted. She studied her fellow WAAAFs in the lineup. One young woman who was new to Hannah winked at the girl next to her.

Hannah was sharing a room with a woman who had joined the service in January when her husband went missing in New Guinea. Betty, a Queenslander, with film star looks, was a stoic, determined to do her bit for the war effort – even though she didn't know whether her husband was alive, dead or a captive of the Japanese. The other two occupants were Joyce – the pencil chewer – from Wagga Wagga, and Phyllis, a miner's daughter from Mudgee. Joyce was the daydreamer, while Phyllis was the comedian with an endless supply of terrible jokes. Hannah soon discovered that Phyllis, a habituée of the Troc, was going out with an American flight sergeant from Detroit. Being the last to arrive, Hannah had no choice but to take the upper tier of one of the bunk beds. All the girls were friendly, and Hannah had an immediate sense of camaraderie. Lying in her bed that night, she had a chance to take stock. The requisitioned hotel was a major improvement on life at New Lambton. The beds were comfortable, and the hotel food plentiful and delicious.

The following day, Hannah and her room-mates were introduced to the place where they were to work. Like The Citadel in Liverpool, it was underground, but rather than a purpose-built bunker, it used a section of the St James railway tunnel under the city. To Hannah's surprise, it was accessed by a set of stairs in an area she had walked past frequently. How many times had she passed them without even registering? Going underground via the steep stairway was like a descent to the Underworld. She clung to the hand rail and counted the steps. Eighty-seven. It was going to be a trial getting up and down at the beginning and end of each shift. At least it should keep her fit.

The conditions down in the tunnels were not pleasant. As soon as she went into the plotting room where she was to spend her working hours, the stale, fuggy air, heavy with cigarette smoke, hit Hannah and she wrinkled her nose. There was a lack of ventilation, making it an extremely unpleasant place to work. Over the coming weeks, the airless condition of the tunnels would cause the WAAAFs frequently to be unwell.

The operations were not as efficient and effective as the equivalent back in Liverpool. It became clear to Hannah on that first day that the radar systems were inferior to those back in Britain and there was heavy reliance on manual forms of communication. Whereas information flowed into The Citadel from a large network of Home Chain radar stations across the country, Australia had only a few radar towers close to the coast. Identification of aircraft seemed very hit and miss, the plotting equipment below par and the map table always contained many unidentified plots.

As well as the unsavoury airless conditions in the tunnel, there was a lack of proper office equipment beyond a few tables and chairs. After the efficient operations at The Citadel, Hannah found the setup at 1FSHQ far from satisfactory. The American officer in charge appeared to be bewildered by the conditions he was expected to work in and had little or no prior experience of running a filter room. It seemed to Hannah that Australia, perhaps because of the longstanding assumption that Singapore would provide a stronghold of protection against any Japanese threat, was singularly under-prepared and insufficiently equipped to manage a credible early warning defence system.

The best thing about the work was the camaraderie between the WAAAFs. They outnumbered the male officers in 1FSHQ. There were about sixty WAAAFs to just seventeen RAAF officers.

After her first day in the tunnel, Hannah sat in the mess room at the Metropole, exhausted and nauseous because of the airless atmosphere she'd endured all day. She wrote her reply to her aunt, expressing delight that at last they'd found each other when she'd been at the point of giving up hope, and explaining that she had joined the WAAAFs.

Sadly, I have no idea when I'll be able to visit you, as I only get one day off a week. The work involves long hours working in shifts. Back in Liverpool, I was doing something similar but for the navy, so it should be relatively easy for me to adapt.

She put down her pen and hesitated, wondering how she was going to tell Elizabeth that Charles Dawson had murdered her mother, Elizabeth's sister Sarah, and had paid the ultimate penalty. It would be so much better to be face to face, but that could be months or years away. She had to do it now. She picked up her pen and told her Sarah was dead at her husband's hand.

It's only thanks to Will that Judith and I survived. If he hadn't intervened, my father would have killed us both in his rage. My mother had told Will she believed Dawson (I cannot call him father) was the father of your son Mikey. I can think of him only as the most evil of men. I'm so sorry I have to be the bearer of such bad news. I know my mother was filled with regret and sadness about her estrangement from you – entirely at Dawson's behest. In your letter, you mentioned her pregnancy at the time you left England. Sadly, I have nothing good to recount there either. My brother, Peter, died of whooping cough in infancy.

She went on to recount Judith's situation and to pass on her sister's address.

I am so happy to have found you at last. It makes me feel less alone – especially knowing we are in the same state, even if about a hundred miles apart. Life in Sydney is hectic and I am enjoying it. During the summer months, I often went to the beaches, and I love going to the pictures and have made some friends. Of course, I miss Will every single day, but life must go on. I am enclosing a recent photograph. I had to have it taken for my I.D. and asked for a spare. Please send one of yourself, Michael and Harry if you have one.

As soon as I am entitled to some leave I will come and visit you as I can't wait to see you and to meet Michael and Harry.

Your loving niece, Hannah.

WALKING BACK to the Metropole one evening a couple of days later at the end of her shift, Hannah bumped into

Shirley, who looked at her in astonishment, taking in her uniform – which now included a regulation skirt.

'Hannah! You're in the forces!' She wrapped her arms around Hannah. 'What are you doing? That's Airforce uniform. Gosh, Brenda's a dark horse – you must be working with her out at the Bankstown aerodrome. She never said a word.'

Hannah looked at her blankly. 'Brenda's a WAAAF?'

'Yes. She operates the switchboard at the RAAF station there.'

Hannah gave a sigh of relief. 'I'm based here in the city. Clerical work.'

'Why haven't you been in touch, chookie?'

'I only got back to Sydney last week – I was training up near Newcastle. And to be honest, Shirley, I've been exhausted.'

'Well, at least we're in touch now.' Shirley clutched at her sleeve. 'Are you free on Saturday evening?'

'Yes, I think so.'

Shirley squeezed her hands into tight fists. 'Wally and I are having a little party. It's supposed to be a secret, but we're getting engaged.'

Hannah grinned. 'Congratulations, that's terrific news. Although I can't say I'm surprised.'

'It's a bit sooner than we'd intended.' She looked sheepish. 'Actually, the reason it's meant to be a secret is we've had to speed things up.' She pointed both index fingers at her stomach.

'You're not!'

'Are you shocked? I know I was. We thought we were being careful – but not careful enough. But now it's sunk in, its bonzer. I'm really excited about becoming a mum.'

Hannah squeezed her hand. 'Congratulations.'

'The wedding's going to be just our parents. So, the engagement party will be the main celebration. We'll have a couple of days honeymoon, up on the coast in Queensland where the weather's still warm.'

'When's the baby due?' Hannah was stunned at Shirley's news.

'I'm nearly five months. It's not showing much yet. End of August to early September. My parents aren't happy about it. But Wally's mum and dad have been great. I'm living at Rose Bay with them.' She looked at her wristwatch. 'I have to dash. Promised to meet Mum for supper at Cahill's. Another attempt by me at a reconciliation. No doubt it will turn into a long lecture about me having the morals of an alley cat. She'll come round once we've tied the knot.'

'When's the wedding?'

'Next week.' She glanced at her watch. 'Righto, Saturday from seven. At Wally's place – at Rose Bay.' She scribbled the address inside the little notebook Hannah passed to her. 'Now I must dash. See you on Saturday.'

She hurried away towards Castlereagh Street, leaving Hannah gazing after her. It was then she realised she hadn't asked if Shirley had heard any news of Eddie.

18

———

The gathering at the Wallace's home in Rose Bay was small and hosted by Wally's parents. Shirley had evidently won over her mother, as both her parents were present and chatting happily to Wally's. There were about two dozen guests: nurses Shirley worked with, family members including Brenda and her parents and younger sister, a couple of old university friends of Wally's, and Dilly, Mr Finlay's secretary from Tibbetts & Finlay. The rest were middle-aged friends of the Wallaces. It seemed to Hannah that this was more a party for the parents than the bride and groom. But they were the hosts, after all.

Hannah looked about her – Wally's home was less grand than Eddie's but nonetheless impressive, with expensive-looking artworks on the wall and good quality furniture. Not for the first time, she felt this was a world where she didn't belong.

She talked for a while with Dilly, who told her that since the staff cuts, she was now handling work for Wally and another partner, as well as Mr Finlay. Hannah was running out of small talk when Eddie's brother, Mark, appeared at her side and Dilly went off to inspect the buffet.

'I didn't expect to see you here, Mark,' Hannah said, smiling. 'Back from university for the weekend?'

'I've left uni completely.' Mark returned her smile. 'I went to the army recruiting office in Melbourne and did the deed. I'm only back in Sydney to say goodbye to my parents before I head off to camp on Sunday evening.'

Hannah was stunned. Eddie had been sure his brother would not volunteer until after his degree. 'I thought your father was set against you volunteering?'

'He is. That's why I did it in Victoria. Just as Eddie did it when Dad was in Canberra. Dad carries on like we're still schoolboys. It's been a bit of a rough show today – much wailing and gnashing of teeth from Mum. She's convinced herself she's going to be childless before the year's out.' He gave a hollow laugh. 'She's certain both Eddie and I are doomed.' He gave Hannah an exaggerated eye roll. 'I gather from Shirl that you're in the WAAAFs yourself. When did that happen?'

Surprised by his flippancy, she said, 'A couple of months ago. I've been at training camp, and now I've been billeted in the Metropole, along with a big contingent of Americans.'

Mark whistled. 'Beats being in barracks, I imagine?'

'Definitely. Proper beds and decent food.'

'Then long may it last.' He chinked his glass of beer against her fruit juice.

There was a moment's awkward silence, then Hannah swallowed and asked if he'd had any news of Eddie. Her cheeks were burning, and he looked at her curiously.

'He was posted into the combat zone a few days ago.'

'Where?'

'Don't know, but my guess is New Guinea. I reckon

there'll be a counterattack soon, now that the Japs have taken New Britain. We'll need to pull out all the stops to prevent them taking Port Moresby. Lord knows how though. The terrain is awful – no roads, steep mountain ranges, dense jungle and lots and lots of rain.'

'Sounds grim.' She bit her lip, trying to imagine Eddie hacking through the jungle. It was hard to picture him wading through mud, completely out of his natural element as a suntanned surfer.

'It will be. But then so will every theatre of the Pacific. The Japs can't possibly win this war, but they're going to make life hell for us and the Americans in the meantime.'

Hannah knew more about the current situation than he did. She was all too aware that over the past week the Americans had intercepted signals that Japanese aircraft carriers and warships were heading for Port Moresby. As a result, a combined US and Australian fleet had been engaged with the Japanese navy and air force in the Coral Sea, causing the Japanese to retreat and halt their planned invasion of Port Moresby. Mark was right though – the Japanese would be unlikely to give up, so another attack on Port Moresby was likely.

She wanted to know about Eddie though. 'How *is* Eddie? I mean, do you know if he's liking life in the army and glad he joined up?'

Mark looked at her steadily. 'I don't think my brother has been glad about anything for a long time.' He took a sip of his beer. 'I'm wondering why you even care. I hoped for a while that things would have gone differently with you, Hannah.'

The blood rushed to her face again. How much did Mark know? She didn't want to get drawn into a post-mortem, nor did she want Mark to know about the weekend she'd spent with his brother. She cast about for a change of subject. 'Wonderful news about Shirley and Wally.'

Mark shrugged. 'Not sure I'd call a shotgun wedding great news.'

Hannah bristled on Shirley's behalf. 'They'd planned to marry anyway, I gather. This just brought it forward.'

He shrugged again. Mark appeared to have lost his sense of fun and energy. Perhaps it was concern over Eddie going into combat, or maybe he was exhausted after the arguments with his parents.

Mark studied her, his head tilted on one side. It made her uncomfortable. 'My brother had it bad over you, Hannah. I've never seen him like that over a girl before. Eddie's always had a host of female admirers and doesn't pay any of them much attention.' He jerked his head at the other side of the room where Brenda was in conversation with Shirley and Wally's mother. 'Bren's been throwing herself at him for months. I've never known him to fall hard for a girl until you appeared. You broke his heart, Hannah.' He fixed his eyes on her – it was a penetrating look.

She put her glass down, unable to form a suitable response. The words in her head scrambled and she looked at him, open-mouthed. Eventually, she said, 'That's not fair, Mark. I made it clear to Eddie from the beginning I don't want a relationship with anyone.'

He studied her for a moment. 'I know. I'm sorry. I shouldn't have said that. It's just that I hated seeing him unhappy. And I'm still sore about him joining up and heading off for camp without saying goodbye. I understand why he didn't tell Mum and Dad, but he and I are tight.' He took a slug of his beer, his eyes assessing her. 'He said goodbye to you though, didn't he?'

She blushed again and nodded. This felt like an inquisition.

Mark reached into his trouser pocket and pulled out a little tortoiseshell hair slide, a birthday present Judith had given to Hannah. He held it out in the palm of his hand. 'Yours, I reckon.'

She fixed her eyes on him as she took the slide but said nothing.

'I found it in the pool house.' He picked up a handful of peanuts and tipped them into his mouth, his eyes still on her. 'Did you spend the weekend with him? Were you sleeping with him? When Mum and Dad were in Canberra?'

Hannah was appalled. It was such a deeply personal question, and she barely knew Mark. She struggled to imagine being asked a question like that back in England. Realising he would take her silence as an affirmative, she straightened her shoulders. 'I find that question offensive. I was there because Eddie was teaching me how to swim.'

His eyes were cold. 'Like he was doing at Fairy Bower.' He gave a little snort. 'Brenda saw you. She reckoned there wasn't a lot of swimming tuition going on. Said you were sitting side by side on the seawall, kissing. That doesn't sound like avoiding a relationship, Hannah. Sounds more like leading a man on.'

A jolt of defiance burst through her. 'It's none of your business, Mark.'

'He's my brother. It *is* my business. We're a close family. He didn't want to join up until you turned him down. I was the one who wanted to go. He was always trying to talk me out of it. I actually listened to him. It's why I agreed to go back to uni. Nothing to do with Dad. I did it because of Eddie. And I'm convinced he joined up because of you.'

She stared at him, not knowing what to say. He was articulating her own worst concerns.

'If you didn't want him, you shouldn't have led him on. Shouldn't have agreed to the swimming lessons. Definitely shouldn't have come to the house.'

Hannah looked about her, desperate to escape, but all she could see was Brenda's cold gaze from across the room. 'I don't feel comfortable talking about Eddie when he's not here. And you're speaking of him as though he's a child, as though he has no capacity to make his own decisions. It's patronising. Eddie's an adult. He's older than both of us. You've no right to say what you're saying. You've no idea what passed between us.'

'It doesn't take a lot of imagination.'

'I think that's the point, Mark. You have too much imagination. Now I need to introduce myself to our hosts.' With that she picked up her drink and went to join Shirley and Wally and their respective parents. She spent a few minutes conveying her best wishes, then made polite apologies about having a six a.m. shift and needing an early night and left the party.

AFTER THE ENGAGEMENT PARTY, Hannah avoided seeing 'the gang'. Mark's words had cut her to the quick. He had implied that she had trifled with Eddie, treated him shabbily, led him along only to dash his hopes. But she'd been clear from the start. Eddie had gone into that weekend with his eyes open.

She thought back to those days in Double Bay. Eddie had been happy, even relaxed. They'd enjoyed the time they spent together, including the time in bed – but she had never given him hope that it was anything more than two people enjoying each other's company. There had been no emotion, as far as she was concerned, no intensity of feeling – just shared physical pleasure.

But then she remembered how he'd taken her into June's room, how he'd talked about his sister, about his family. She had to admit their friendship was based on more than just a physical attraction, and she would be wrong to deny that. But it wasn't love. She could say that with the certainty of knowing what love was.

A few days later, she spotted the announcement of the marriage of Shirley Emsworth to Roger Wallace in the *Sydney Morning Herald,* so she supposed the couple must be honeymooning in Queensland by now. All three men were in, or about to be in, the army, Shirley would soon be preoccupied with being a mother, and Brenda had never been a friend. Winter was here, Hannah was working round the clock and there would be no more beach trips for a while. She resolved to put them all out of her mind and concentrate on her new job and making friends with her fellow WAAAFs.

As soon as she qualified for some leave, she would visit the sheep station and meet her aunt and uncle. Meanwhile, she had work to do and a war to help win, no matter how insignificant her own part was.

WORKING in the tunnel under the Domain was often hellish. The unventilated conditions made many of the WAAAFs ill, so the number of shifts was increased and the duration of each reduced. Joyce, the girl from Wagga Wagga, found the conditions particularly hard and twice passed out while working and had to be sent back to the hotel. Hannah herself felt below par, lacking energy and often listless, but managed to make it through her shifts.

What they most appreciated were the five-course meals served to them at the Metropole. Even the breakfasts were exceptional, with fresh fruit, various different cereals some of which she'd never seen before – thanks to the Americans, eggs, bacon, tomatoes and toast – even doughnuts, doubtless also a concession to the Yanks. All of the WAAAFs, Hannah included, were putting on weight. After having to take in the ill-fitting men's uniforms of their early days, the WAAAFs were now letting out the seams of their skirts.

On May 31st, Hannah was due to work a night shift. It was cold, and the air crisp as she walked the short distance between the Met and the tunnels. As she neared the entrance to the tunnels, there were sirens sounding. She presumed it was a practice air raid warning, a frequent occurrence these days. When she came on duty at ten p.m., Betty, who was handing over to her, flapped her hands in front of her face signalling that something was up. The two stood on one side for their handover briefing.

'Something's been going on in the harbour,' said Betty. 'All kinds of contradictory messages. Most of them probably false alarms. But there's definitely something strange.'

'You think it's enemy action?' Hannah shivered. 'Where are the planes?'

'Not planes. Nothing we've picked up in the air. It's submarines. Messages from North Fort in Manly. We're getting updates and the boys at Bankstown and Richmond are on standby, but they haven't confirmed anything yet.'

'There are enemy submarines in the harbour?' Hannah's jaw dropped.

'The official consensus is not but, surely, it's no coincidence that there have been strange sightings from different sources according to the teleprinters. And the Americans are very jumpy. They seem to think the Japs are about to chuck a bomb down here.' Betty rolled her eyes then put her coat on. 'Remember last week when they got themselves worked up over a radar reading that showed a huge Japanese fleet off Wollongong and it turned out to be the steelworks?'

Hannah suppressed her laughter. The WAAAFs kept themselves sane by indulging in dumb Yankee jokes – most of which were unjustified.

Betty yawned. 'Good luck. I'm off to bed.'

Hannah studied the logs. A report of an unidentified craft from South Head Loop had been dismissed by their naval colleagues. Another report mentioned an earlier sighting of a submarine temporarily caught in the anti-submarine net.

Conflicting reports reached 1FSHQ. As Hannah took her place at the plotting table, there was no cohesive picture of what was happening in the harbour – other than a general impression of chaos. The airspace was quiet. Over the next hour there were further incidents, as naval patrol vessels confirmed the presence of a what they described as 'a baby submarine'. They released two depth charges which failed to detonate.

In the filter room, Hannah watched as the RAAF and US officers struggled to build up a coherent picture of what was taking place. The American duty officer seemed edgy during a flurry of phone calls. Orders given earlier in the evening had been countermanded. Instead of closing the harbour to traffic, the British admiral in charge of Sydney Harbour decided the ferries could continue running, as their presence would discourage any submarines from surfacing to attack. Hannah found this decision puzzling, but she was a humble air force plotter, not an admiral of the fleet with a Distinguished Service Cross and the French *Légion d'Honneur.*

While they waited for more news, Hannah checked the logs for the previous week. She thought it unlikely that a submarine attack on a strategic port would take place without prior reconnaissance. Sure enough, just two days earlier the radar had picked up a floatplane over the harbour, but the authorities had assumed it to be an American naval Seagull seaplane. There had been no special defensive measures taken since. Hannah wondered if the mysterious floatplane had been reconnoitring the position of naval vessels in the harbour. She reported her suspicions to the officer in charge who listened but gave nothing away. Sometimes it was unsatisfying and frustrating to show initiative and receive no feedback in return. But she reminded herself that it was all about winning the war not personal gratification.

Before the night was over, two of the three Japanese midget submarines had been sunk – scuttled by their own two-man crews to avoid capture. A third could not be traced, possibly also scuppered when its batteries were exhausted. Hannah shuddered, thinking about the way the Japanese code of honour appeared to demand suicide as the honourable alternative to surrender.

The enemy mission, although it had not gone to plan, took the lives of twenty-one Australian sailors aboard the dormitory vessel, *Kuttabul* which was broken in half by a misfired Japanese torpedo aimed at the USS *Chicago.*

As she headed back to the hotel the next morning, Hannah concluded that the events of that night demonstrated the poor standard of radar intelligence and the lack of efficient cross-communication between the services. Not for the first time, she thought nostalgically of The Citadel, which had surveilled the entire western approaches to Britain from the Atlantic, and where the RAF and Royal Navy worked side-by-side in the same building. Australia only shouldered part of the blame – there were British officers present, including the man in charge of the harbour's defences. Indeed, Hannah couldn't help wondering how much more smoothly things might operate were the different nationalities more trusting and collaborative.

In the days that followed, there were further attacks on Sydney's eastern suburbs, on Newcastle and on shipping in the area, but with no lives lost.

Nothing appeared in the papers for a couple of days. Hannah read the heavily censored report, which merely stated that the Allies had destroyed three enemy submarines in Sydney Harbour. The article dismissed the sinking of the *Kuttabul* and its twenty-one lost lives as the loss of 'one small harbour vessel of no military value'.

But the attacks made it clear to its citizens that Sydney wasn't safe from the threat of the Japanese. The affluent homes, such as that of Eddie's family and of Wally's, lost some of their cachet when they proved to be in an area vulnerable to enemy action.

Whilst the bombing of the eastern suburbs seemed minor to Hannah after the heavy nightly raids which had flattened so much of Liverpool's docks, city centre and residential areas – including her own home – it had an impact on Australian resolve. The war was no longer far away in Europe and the North Pacific; it had reached the leafy streets of East Sydney.

After the attacks, barbed wire was installed on the beaches, and security heightened. For Hannah, it was all too familiar.

19

For the WAAAFs working in the tunnels, the conditions didn't become any easier. Nothing was done to remediate the lack of freely circulating air. To make matters worse, the consolation of being billeted in the Metropole came to an abrupt end when the Americans relocated to Queensland. It was decided by the powers that be that there was no justification in the WAAAFs continuing to use the hotel, so they were transferred to alternative, cheaper accommodation. Their new home was the Labrador building, a three-storey tenement block opposite the hospital in Macquarie Street.

It was quite a comedown. The place was in a filthy condition, so their first task was to scrub out the entire building. Then it was back to straw mattresses and wire beds, with improvised dressing tables made from wooden fruit boxes, garnered from local greengrocers. No more five-course meals and doughnuts for breakfast; their food was prepared and served in the basement off metal plates. Stewed meat and soggy vegetables.

The reduced diet and the fact that they were not

permitted to eat while on duty in the tunnel, led to the WAAAFs and RAAF officers sustaining themselves by drinking cans of condensed milk mixed with coffee and diluted with boiling water. This habit led to the sordid practice of stacking the foul-smelling, discarded cans in the tunnels so that the women had to run the gauntlet of hundreds of sticky tins every time they came on duty. But the coffee helped them stay awake and alert in the airless environment, so everyone accepted it.

Despite the absence of doughnuts and multiple courses, Hannah was unable to shake off the weight she'd put on while staying in the Metropole. She put it down to the cans of sugary condensed milk which Betty told her were death to the waistline. Over the months since joining 1FSHQ she had become close friends with Betty. Perhaps it was the fact that, unlike most of the girls, they were both married – albeit Hannah a widow and Betty not knowing whether her husband was dead or alive. Their shared experience of loss created a bond between them. Like Hannah, Betty enjoyed going to the pictures and wasn't keen on dancing, which the other WAAAFs loved. Whenever their shifts coincided, they spent time in picture houses, watching the mostly depressing newsreels about the war and then cheering themselves up with the feature film. They avoided war movies, preferring the escapism of zany comedies.

One afternoon, emerging from a matinée after watching a Hope and Crosby picture, the two women braved the blustery showers of the Sydney winter and went to a café for a cup of tea. Whenever possible, they avoided the confines of the Labrador, which, despite the cleanup, was a depressing place to spend time in. Almost as bad as the tunnels. Hannah found herself longing for the end of the mild

Sydney winter and the return of days of heat, sunshine and being outdoors.

'Any news from Singapore?' Hannah asked, knowing it was unlikely Betty would have heard from her husband.

Betty gave her a sad smile. 'Nothing. But thanks for asking.' She took a sip of tea, pulled a face then added a spoonful of sugar. 'You're the only one who understands what I'm going through.'

Hannah gave her a sympathetic smile. 'I don't know what's worse: the knowledge that someone's gone forever or the awful uncertainty where you swing from hope to despair. That's how it used to be every time Will was late returning from a voyage. I'll never forget Dunkirk. I'd had no idea he was even involved. His ship was days overdue in port. It turned out they'd been diverted into the Channel to help with the evacuation.' She paused and reached over the table to squeeze Betty's hand. 'At least you have hope. You must keep hoping and believing.'

She reached into her coat pocket and pulled out her purse, taking out the photograph of Will she carried with her everywhere. 'This was Will.'

Betty looked at it. 'A handsome man. Older than you though?'

'Yes. He was thirty-seven. Quite an age gap but it never mattered. It hit her then. One day, she would reach the same age he'd been when he died – and from then on she would always be older than Will. She bit her lip. It hadn't occurred to her before.

'Do you have a photograph of your husband? I don't think you've ever told me his name.'

Betty hesitated and then pulled out a grainy image and handed it to Hannah. 'Jimmie. His name's Jimmie.'

Hannah looked at the picture and was taken aback. Her

face must have registered her surprise as Betty said, 'Yes. He's a blackfella. I'm aboriginal too. Didn't you realise?'

'Hannah blushed. 'No. I didn't. Not that it makes any difference to me.'

'Most of the time I pass as a white woman. But for Jimmie it's different. He joined the army right at the beginning of the war before they brought in the ban.'

'The ban?'

'You must know about the White Australia policy. They'd like us to disappear. Even though we were here for millennia before the First Fleet sailed in. They banned us from serving in the military. It's all changed since Pearl Harbour and the Sydney attacks. Now they're desperate for anyone they can get.' Her voice was understandably bitter.

'Why did Jimmie want to serve?'

'It's a steady job. Decent pay. At least on that score, they don't discriminate. Once you're in, the wages are equal. And at the beginning of the war, things were quiet. He thought it was unlikely he'd see much action. No one expected Singapore to fall. Jimmie loved being out there.' She gave a little sob – it was rare to see Betty crumble. 'I can't bear to think about what he must be going through in captivity.'

Hannah placed her hand over Betty's. 'If he's a POW, there are international rules and regulations for how prisoners are treated.'

Betty gave a snort. 'You think the Japs will abide by the Geneva Convention?'

'We have to hope they will.' Hannah squeezed her lips together tightly then took another sip of tea. 'How long have you been married?'

'Since January '38. We met when we were kids. In an orphanage.'

'You're both orphans?'

Betty sighed. 'I doubt it. But we don't know who or where our parents are. We were put in the orphanage for the nuns to educate us. Knock the blackness out of us.'

'That's appalling. Utterly dreadful.'

'You don't know much about Aboriginal people, do you? Did you realise we don't even get to vote?'

Hannah stared at her in disbelief. 'I'm so sorry. I had no idea. No vote, and yet your husband is expected to fight for his country.'

'No need for you to apologise. It's not your fault. Look, Hannah, I'd be grateful if you wouldn't mention any of this to the other girls. You're from England and maybe it's different over there, but I know some of them wouldn't be happy working alongside me if they find out I'm black.' She tapped her fingers on the tabletop. 'Specially Phyllis. I've heard some of her remarks about "dirty Abos". White Australians can be an intolerant lot.'

'I'm afraid the British can be too. It's where the Australians got it from.'

After that, they changed the subject, but Hannah was honoured that her friend had felt able to confide in her. It had drawn them closer together.

THE NEWS ARRIVED that 1FSHQ was to relocate from the tunnels to the aerodrome at Bankstone, where they were to occupy a requisitioned local cinema until permanent bunkers were constructed. Hannah was relieved to know they would be escaping the cramped, stuffy conditions of the railway tunnel, although that was tempered by the knowledge that Bankstown was outside Sydney, with no regular public transport from the base.

During her last days at the Labrador, Hannah received a

rare letter from Judith. This time she enclosed a photograph of herself and Sarah.

Paolo insisted I got the picture taken as he wanted a copy to pin up by his bed. We had a long talk last week when I was able to visit him inside the camp. He's never going back to sea and has decided he no longer wants us to go to Italy after the war. I can't tell you what a relief that is. He loves working in the kitchen and wants to open a restaurant with one of the other cooks in Melbourne when the war's over. He has such plans. I think that's all he does these days – think up names for the place and what the menu will be and how many staff they'll need. At least it keeps him cheerful. It makes me angry though, the way they are all locked up when they've done nothing wrong and none of them have an ounce of sympathy for Mussolini. That's why most of them were living in Britain – trying to get away from the blooming fascists.

I'm glad you finally tracked down our aunt. Give her my good wishes if you see her. I hope this doesn't mean you'll be traipsing off to see her instead of coming to Tatura to see us. Don't you miss Sarah? She's growing up so fast. It would be awful to let her grow up not knowing you. I sometimes think it was rather selfish of you to go gadding off to Sydney.

That was it. The limit to her sister's interest. No questions about Elizabeth. Not even any questions about Hannah herself. No curiosity about her new job – she'd told Judith she had joined the WAAAFs but obviously gave no details of the nature of the work. It was as though the war were happening on another planet as far as Judith was concerned – and Hannah might as well be there too.

TWO WEEKS before the planned relocation to Bankstown, Hannah paid a visit to Dot. She was feeling guilty that she hadn't been in touch for weeks and wanted to let her former landlady know she would be moving outside the city soon.

Dot took her coat from her and hung it behind the kitchen door. Before putting the kettle on, she looked Hannah up and down, frowning, then gestured for her to sit at the table.

Tea made, Dot sat down opposite her. 'I can't get used to tea being on the rations. It was bad enough with butter. It's meant to be enough for three cups a day. You know me, darl. I drink that much in a couple of hours.' She chuckled, then her frown returned. 'Right, young lady. You'd better tell me everything. How far gone are you? And why didn't come to see me before now.'

Hannah, puzzled, said, 'We've been very busy and with the short shift system I never seem to have any free time. I presume you mean moving to Bankstone? How did you know?'

Dot leaned forward. 'Not that. Whatever that is. I mean *that.*' She pointed at Hannah's stomach.

Hannah jerked her head back in surprise. 'Oh, we've all put weight on. It was the food at the Metropole and now I'm horsing down cans of condensed milk during my shifts as they don't feed us well. It's frightfully fattening.'

Dot folded her arms. 'You can't fool me, darl. You're having a baby.'

It took a moment to sink in. Hannah's jaw dropped and she stared at the older woman. 'I'm not. I can't be.'

'Before I was married, I was training to be a midwife. I didn't finish the training as my Stan didn't want me working, but I learned enough to know what a pregnancy looks like. Even when it hardly shows, like yours.' She frowned. 'Don't tell me you didn't realise.'

Hannah's chest constricted and she struggled to breathe.

This couldn't be happening. Dot had to be wrong. Her hands moved down to the small swelling. 'I can't be. I've had periods. Not heavy but then I'm always light... Actually, now I think about it, I've had little more than spotting.'

Dot gave her a meaningful look.

'Oh, my goodness, Dot, surely not?'

Dot shook her head, a sad expression on her face. 'If I were you, I'd go and see a doctor at the earliest opportunity.' She folded her arms. 'What about the father? Don't tell me it's one of those Yanks.' She looked about to say something else but clamped her lips shut.

'Not a Yank.' Hannah put her head in her hands.

'You'll have to tell whoever it is. He needs to stand by you. Or are you going to get rid of it?'

'I can't tell him. He's been posted. I've no idea where.' She swallowed. 'I don't know what to do.'

'Do you have any idea how long you've been pregnant? When was your last period?' Dot asked.

'It's only been light spotting, so I'm not even sure. But if I'm pregnant it must have happened over a weekend at the end of February. That was the only time.' Her voice trembled. 'Just before he was posted.'

'You silly girl. Don't you know about birth control?'

'Of course I do.' But as she said the words she was aware that she'd never even thought about it. After all the unsuccessful trying for a baby with Will, she had simply assumed she couldn't get pregnant. But in all honesty, she hadn't consciously considered the possibility at all.

Dot got up and moved round the table to put her arms round Hannah. 'It's not the end of the world, you know. There'll be news of the father, I'm sure, before long, and he'll come back, eventually. Meanwhile, you won't be the first or the last young woman to find herself in the family way thanks to a soldier. You have a choice. There's getting rid of it...' Dot looked up at the ceiling as she did the mental arithmetic. 'Probably too late for that. And too risky. You'll have to have it. So, it's down to either giving it up for adoption or keeping it and hoping the fellow will do the right thing when he hears about it.'

'It's Eddie Greenbank's.' The words were out before she could stop them.

'Strewth! I thought you said you didn't fancy him.'

'Well I changed my mind. But not about marrying him. Not that it's even on the cards. I got a glimpse into his life when I spent that weekend with him. It's another world, Dot. Not mine at all. And I'm certain his parents would move heaven and earth to stop us marrying.'

'Maybe you should go and talk to them. They may be able to help you.'

That was the last thing Hannah wanted. 'No. It's out of the question. I've never even met them. How could I possibly turn up out of the blue and accuse their son of being the father of my unborn baby?'

'Because he is.' Dot folded her arms again. 'Bloody men. They get away with murder.' She thought for a moment. 'But that Eddie is a decent fellow. He'll do the right thing. Do you love him?'

Her response was instant. 'No. Definitely not.'

'So why did you sleep with him?' Dot was frowning.

In a sudden fit of weary defiance, Hannah said, 'I find him attractive. He wanted it. I wanted it. So, I thought, why not?'

Dot shook her head, frowning. 'At least you're honest. You know they'll discharge you from the WAAAFs as soon as they find out. And if you ask me, it's a bloody miracle they haven't noticed already. Will your sister take you in?'

The thought of crawling back to Tatura and throwing herself on the mercy of Judith was unthinkable. Besides, how could she expect Sal and Terry Clancy to take her and a baby in, when they were already housing Judith and Sarah?

'No,' she said, 'That's out of the question. I have an aunt up in the Hunter Valley. I'll write to her.'

Dot's eyebrows shot up. 'You're a dark horse. You've never mentioned her.'

'That's because I didn't know where she was. I was searching for her address. Eddie was helping me look. In the end she found me. But we haven't met yet.'

Dot raised her eyebrows again. 'She's in for a surprise then. What does she do up there? Is she married?'

'Yes. She and her husband have a sheep station.'

Dot gave a whistle. 'That's fortunate. Plenty of room for you then. Well, young lady, you've certainly brought some interest into my dull old life today. You'd better stay and have some supper. It's lamb chops.'

'Thank you, Dot. It will be a joy to have some well-cooked food. Whenever we have lamb chops at the Labrador, they stew them in a dixie can till they taste like damp cardboard.'

'Righto! After all you're eating for two now, darl.'

Back at the Labrador that night, Hannah tossed and turned on her uncomfortable bed, unable to sleep and unable to believe that she was expecting a baby. It was bitterly ironic. She and Will had longed in vain for a child and now, after a mere weekend with Eddie, she was in this condition.

The following morning, she decided to go to see the RAAF doctor. She'd met the man only once, when he'd given her the cursory medical when she'd joined the service. Straight after breakfast, she went to his clinic across the street in the hospital and explained her situation.

She was asked by the attendant nurse to provide a urine sample and told to return the following day. This time she was shown into the presence of the doctor who was wearing RAAF uniform under his white medical coat.

'Aircraftwoman Kidd,' he greeted her, as he flipped through a buff folder with her name on the outside. 'According to this you are a widow.'

She nodded.

He frowned, eyes narrowed in a gimlet stare. 'Well, it appears from the test on your sample, you are indeed pregnant.'

She felt his hostility as he went on to ask about the date of her last menstruation. Hannah explained that she'd always had irregular periods and the last two or three were extremely light.

'It's common to have light spotting over the first few months. When was your last full period?'

'I can't remember. As I said, it's irregular - and worse since we work all kinds of shifts. But the only time I could have become pregnant was at the end of February.'

He directed her to undress behind the curtain.

As he felt her abdomen and listened with a stethoscope, he said, 'Yes, you are about eighteen weeks pregnant. Get dressed.'

When she emerged from behind the screen, he was writing in the file. He didn't even look at her as he spoke. 'I will inform the staff sergeant of your condition. You realise this means immediate discharge.' He looked up. 'You can go now.'

Rather than waiting to be summoned, Hannah chose to

take the initiative and go straight to see Flight Sergeant Prendergast.

The sergeant took the news of her pregnancy phlegmatically. 'Bad luck. One of the Yanks, I presume?'

Hannah said nothing but looked down.

'Didn't I warn you girls? They're only after one thing. You're the last one I expected this to happen to. Robson or Moffatt, yes. They'd have their knickers round their ankles as soon as a Yank looked at them. But you?' She opened a drawer of the steel cabinet behind her and took out a file. 'You'll be discharged, of course. Immediately, I'm afraid.' She looked over the top of her glasses. 'You've seen the doc? He's confirmed it?'

Hannah nodded, feeling miserable. 'Eighteen weeks.'

'Yes, you're beginning to show, aren't you? I'll be sorry to see you go, Aircraftwoman Kidd.' She wrote something in the file. 'Damn. We can ill afford to lose good women.'

The sergeant put down her pen, got up and stretched out her hand to shake Hannah's. 'Best of luck, old girl. Do you have somewhere to go?'

Hannah nodded. It was all happening faster than she'd expected. She hadn't written to Elizabeth. It would have to be a telegram. She decided to throw herself on the mercy of Dot for a couple of days while she thought things through.

Back in the dormitory, she packed her things quickly. Fortunately, no one else was about. Betty was on an early shift, so she left her a quick note.

In haste. Need to speak urgently. Meet me after your shift at the usual café. Will explain then.

SHE SENT the telegram to Elizabeth, then went straight to

Dot's and asked if she could stay with her for a couple of days until she'd heard back from her aunt.

'Your old room is made up and you're welcome to stay as long as you like. I'll be glad of your company.'

'Can I pay you tomorrow when my wages are due?'

'Keep your money, darl. You need it more than I do. Two can live as cheaply as one.' Dot grinned. 'Even two and a half. As far as I'm concerned, you're a guest not a lodger now.'

'It's just for one or two nights.'

Dot flapped a hand in dismissal.

That settled, Hannah hurried into the centre and arrived at the café just as Betty got there.

'What's going on?' Betty frowned at her. 'I thought you were on straight after me. Did you swap shifts with Phyllis?'

'I've been discharged.'

Betty's mouth dropped open. 'Why?'

'I'm having a baby. I hadn't a clue, but it explains why I've been putting on weight. My old landlady noticed at once.'

'Have you seen a doctor?'

Hannah nodded. 'I'm eighteen weeks gone. That means it's due in late November. She put her hands over her belly. There was a fluttering sensation, like small bubbles inside her. 'And I can feel it myself now.'

Betty frowned. 'But how did it happen, Hannah? I didn't know you'd been seeing anyone.'

'It was before I joined up. Back at the end of February. I spent a weekend with a friend before he went off to join the army.' Anticipating Betty's question, she added, 'And no, I don't want to marry him. I didn't anyway, and I still don't now. It wouldn't be right. I don't love him.'

Betty gave a long sigh and shook her head. 'Never mind

whether you love him or not. Face facts, Hannah. Your husband's dead and another man's put you in the family way. You must think of your child now. Else how will you live? You can't work with a baby. People will frown on you as an unmarried mother.' She paused, a sudden look of dismay on her face. 'And please don't tell me you'll put the kid in an orphanage. Having gone through that myself, I wouldn't wish it on my worst enemy.'

Hannah buried her head in her hands. Betty was talking sense, just as Dot had.

'Besides, doesn't he have the right to know?' Betty picked up the cardboard menu and tapped it on the edge of the table. She muttered something that Hannah suspected was a swear-word in her native tongue. 'Second thoughts. He doesn't. He should have thought about that before he slept with you. He should have taken precautions. He's foregone any rights.' She rapped the menu card again, 'But looking at it from your point of view, it would be so much easier for you if you married him. Don't you like him at all? Surely, if you slept with him— Oh no— don't tell me. He didn't? Didn't force himself on you?'

Hannah closed her eyes for a moment, suddenly weary. 'No, he didn't. I wanted to do it. If I'm being honest, I was longing for some affection and I missed sex. He was going away. I thought there'd be no harm. I never even considered pregnancy as a possibility. My husband and I tried hard enough.' For the first time since discovering her condition, Hannah began to cry. Furious with herself, she rubbed her eyes with the back of her hands.

Betty handed her a clean handkerchief. 'What will you do? Surely the sarge won't throw you out immediately.'

'She already has. Rules are rules. I'm staying for a couple of nights at my old lodgings. My landlady is being very kind.

Then I'm hoping I can stay with my aunt and uncle in the Hunter Valley.'

'So this is goodbye?'

Hannah nodded.

'What shall I tell the others?'

'Whatever you like. Knowing the sarge, she'll no doubt use it as an excuse to give you all a lecture on morality, so no point hiding it.'

'No one's going to believe it. You're the least likely of us all, Hannah.'

Hannah gave her a wry smile. 'I don't know whether to take that as a compliment or an insult.'

AFTER LEAVING THE CAFÉ, rather than returning straight to Dot's, Hannah diverted to enjoy a last visit to the fountain in Hyde Park. It was an unseasonably warm day and she sat on a bench, thinking about the future. It was pointless trying to make any plans until she'd seen her aunt. She took Elizabeth's last letter out of her bag and read through it. There was so much affection, a repeated wish that Hannah visit them.

Elizabeth's words made her feel optimistic about her aunt's reaction to the pregnancy. Hoping Elizabeth still played her violin, Hannah decided to go to a music shop and buy some sheet music as a gift. Not musical herself, she sought the advice of an assistant and finally chose a collection of sonatas by different composers. She found a detective book she hoped would find favour with Harry and decided to play safe by buying some handkerchiefs for the uncle she'd never met. The purchases made a dent in her pot of savings. Her wages were due today, but Sergeant Prendergast hadn't mentioned them. Reluctantly, she made her way back to the Labrador to collect them.

Wages in her pocket, Hannah started to walk back to Dot's, exploring the possibility of telling Eddie about her predicament. A baby changed everything. Even though she didn't love him, she liked him a lot. They were from different worlds, but did that really matter? She'd give it more thought. It would be foolish to jump to a decision. But first, she had to find out how to contact him. Calling on his parents was out of the question – she'd never met them and they might refuse to pass his details to her.

The obvious answer was Wally. She didn't want him to know about the baby before she told Eddie, so she put on her coat, despite the warmth of the day, and positioned her shopping bags strategically in front of her stomach, then headed for Tibbetts and Finlay.

Wally wasn't his usual ebullient self. His face was drawn and he didn't look pleased to see her when she was shown into his office.

He stood to greet her. 'We haven't heard from you since the engagement party, Hanee. Shirl went to the Metropole to tell you the news about Eddie, but they said the WAAAFs had moved from there and the hotel receptionist didn't know where.'

'What news?' The blood pounded in her temples. 'What about Eddie?'

He looked at her, his face solemn. 'He's dead, Hannie. Didn't you see it in the paper? There was a memorial service last week.'

Her legs buckled under her. Jumping up, Wally pulled out a chair and she collapsed onto it, letting the shopping bags fall to the floor.

'You didn't know? Oh, Hanee, I'm sorry to be the bearer of bad news.'

Hannah slumped in her chair, gathering her coat around her like protective armour. 'How did it happen?' Her voice was faint as she tried to absorb the shock.

'Killed in fighting in Papua. End of last month. We're all devastated. Shirl's been very depressed. Everyone's cut up about it – especially Brenda. And you can imagine how the Greenbanks feel, after losing June too. Eddie's father is trying to pull strings to make sure Mark doesn't see active service. I doubt he'll succeed though. Mark wants to fight. At the moment, he's still at training camp. But he's even more determined since Eddie died.'

Wally got up from behind his desk and went to stand by the window. 'To be honest, I'd be tempted to join up myself if it weren't for the baby. I still may once it's here.' His voice had an undercurrent of anger. 'Right now, I'd like to mow down as many Japs as possible.'

Hannah couldn't speak.

Wally turned to look at her. 'I often thought you and Eddie might get together. He was crazy for you.'

'I liked him very much. It's why I'm here. I told him not to write to me but I'd changed my mind. I came to ask you for his details so I could get in touch.' She looked down, twisting her hands together. 'Too late now.'

'Yes,' he said, his voice flat. 'It's too late.' He cleared his throat and glanced at his watch. 'Still with the WAAAFs?'

She didn't want him to suggest she see Shirl. She didn't want to see any of them. 'I'm being posted out of Sydney. New assignment.'

'You're going away? Where? When?'

'Can't say where, I'm afraid. It's immediately. So this is goodbye.'

He crossed the room and took her hands in his. 'I'll tell Shirl I saw you. She'll be sorry to have missed you.'

'Give her my love and best of luck with the baby.'

'Thanks. Not long to go now.'

She fought back the tears, desperate to get out of this office and be alone. Muttering goodbye, she gathered up her shopping and left.

Out on the street, she walked in a daze, barely aware of where she was going. She made for the first bench she came to in the park, sat down, and stared blankly into space, trying to make sense of the turmoil of emotions coursing through her.

20

―――――

Back at Dot's, Hannah wanted to go straight to her room. She told her landlady she was tired and wanted to lie down for a while.

Dot pointed at the shopping bags Hannah was carrying. 'I'm not surprised, darl. You need to take it easy. Go and put your feet up. I'll have your tea ready for six o'clock. Sausage and mash tonight and a rice pudding afterwards.'

Hannah sat on the edge of the bed, trying to process the news about Eddie. To lose his life so soon after joining up was shocking. During their weekend together, he'd told her he was certain he wouldn't return from the war. She couldn't help wondering if he'd had a death wish. A weariness with life and a longing to be reunited with his twin sister. How much had Hannah been to blame for that? If she'd given him even a scintilla of hope, mightn't he have gained the will to carry on, to keep fighting, to stay alive? If only he'd known he was going to be a father.

All it would have taken was a well-aimed sniper's bullet, or being on the wrong end of a Japanese shell. Even a relatively minor wound could lead to infection and rapid death in jungle conditions. Then there were all the tropical diseases. Malaria, dengue fever, dysentery, cholera. But Wally had said he'd been killed. That must mean enemy action. Why hadn't she asked him more questions? When he'd told her Eddie was dead, all she'd wanted was to get away as quickly as possible so he couldn't see her reaction. But she'd had no reaction. Just shock and a terrible empty numbness.

All this agonising was pointless. Nothing was going to bring him back. And now she was going to have a child who would never know their father. If she'd had any doubts about telling Eddie she was pregnant, it was impossible now.

Just before six, she went downstairs and joined Dot. She had already decided to say nothing about Eddie.

Two days later, Hannah's life was about to change. Her aunt's telegram had instructed her to take the Armidale line and alight at a place called Hazelton, where Elizabeth would be waiting to meet her.

Dot insisted on accompanying her to Central Station to carry her small suitcase. The older woman hugged her warmly as they said their goodbyes. 'Don't forget to write, darl. And the best of luck with the bub. Remember, you're always welcome at my place.'

It was a long journey. Almost seven hours. The train chugged its way up the coast to Newcastle before swinging inland towards Tamworth. Hannah stared blankly out of the window, scarcely taking in the scenery beyond. She was weary but sleep eluded her.

All the way there, she agonised about telling her aunt about her pregnancy, afraid of Elizabeth's reaction. Might she view it as a betrayal of Will's memory and assume that Hannah had loose morals? Might she refuse to help her? Elizabeth had conceived her own first child out of wedlock but in very different circumstances – rape by Charles Dawson, Hannah's father. She could well be horrified at Hannah's laxity. As the hours ticked by, her anxiety grew.

Hazelton Station was a single platform with a simple wooden station building. Hannah was the only person alighting from the train. The afternoon sunshine was hot, so she was glad of the canopy shading the platform as she watched the train pull away. She felt a tap on her shoulder then she was gathered up into Elizabeth's arms.

'Let me look at you, Hannah! I can't believe at last I'm seeing you and you're real.' She stroked her hand along her niece's cheek and gazed fondly into her eyes then took one hand, swept up the suitcase with her other hand, and steered Hannah into the station waiting room.

Elizabeth looked exactly like the photograph Hannah had discovered and treasured – until her father had destroyed it. There were now traces of grey around her temples, but she still wore her hair in a loose bun. She was an older version of Hannah.

'We still look alike.' Hannah grinned at her aunt. 'That's why Will first approached me. He thought he was seeing a ghost.'

Elizabeth held her again. 'Poor dear Will. Life can be unbearably cruel.'

Hannah bit her lip. She didn't want to cry. 'Even though losing him has broken my heart I wouldn't change meeting him. Every minute we spent together was precious.'

Elizabeth looked at her with love and understanding. 'I'm so happy we've found each other. I can't wait for you to meet Michael and Harry. They've had to go into Tamworth, so they took the car, and Ray drove me here in the pony and trap. Ray's worked with Michael for a long time. He's at the hardware store. We can stroll round there in a few minutes and I'll introduce you. He should be done by then. Not that there's much to see in Hazelton.'

'Is your home nearby?'

Elizabeth smiled. 'About half an hour away.'

Hannah was tired and her heart sank. She was desperate to use the toilet and told her aunt, who directed her to the one in the station. When she returned, Elizabeth looked at her quizzically. 'I did wonder when I hugged you, but I didn't like to ask in case you were just a bit plump, but it looks like you're going to have a baby. Is that why you're suddenly able to be here? Were you discharged from the WAAAF?'

Hannah nodded, feeling ashamed.

Elizabeth took both her hands in hers and drew her into another embrace. 'Oh, my darling girl, you must be terrified. I remember how that felt. The father?'

Hannah put her hand up to her mouth. 'I heard the day before yesterday he was killed on active service.'

'Oh Lord!' Elizabeth, eyes welling, held her close. Hannah struggled to hold back her own tears.

'Come on. Let's get you home. We can talk properly then. Ray's a good man but I imagine you won't want to discuss your private life in front of a stranger. Damn. I should have come alone and let him do the trip to the hardware store tomorrow. But with this war and petrol being rationed, we have to be careful. And Michael needed the ute to go to Tamworth.'

They walked into the small settlement of Hazelton. The hardware store, like the grocery store, was basically just part of the pub and the pub was the only part of the settlement that offered any sign of life. Hannah could hear the faint murmur of voices from inside. Elizabeth pointed out Ray, who was outside, watering the pony. As they approached, Hannah noticed he was missing his left arm from the elbow. When Elizabeth introduced them, he managed only a laconic, 'G'day,' as he took her suitcase and swung it effortlessly into the rear of the pony trap with his remaining arm. He was short and stocky in build, his face – or what Hannah could see of it under the large bush hat that was pulled low on his brows – was lined and leathery, presumably from years working in all weathers, with a firm jaw. It was hard to tell his age but she guessed he was in his late thirties. After Elizabeth had enquired whether he'd got what he needed at the store, they all climbed into the cart and with a flick of the rein and a click of the jaw, Ray signalled the pony to move off.

Ray maintained his silence throughout the journey to the farm. Elizabeth, who sat in the middle, talked about the district to Hannah, pointing out landmarks as they drove. The scenery was beautiful – gentle rolling hills with grazing horses, sheep and cattle, vineyards, occasional gum trees and rich green grass. As they made their progress at a stately pace, Hannah spotted a mob of wallabies, grazing in the shade of some distant trees.

'It's so beautiful,' she said. 'Calm and quiet. So different from the city. How big is your sheep station?'

'It's small – too small to be called a station. Hunter's Down is small by Australian standards but we have quite a big farm for this region. About five hundred acres.'

'Do you like living here?'

'I love it, Hannah.' Elizabeth swept out an arm. 'I love the openness, the beautiful skies, the hills. I'd feel differently if we were on a huge station in the outback, reliant on short wave radios and the flying doctor, and terribly isolated from the rest of the world. This region is idyllic.'

As they rattled along the dirt track, Hannah had to agree it was indeed a bucolic paradise.

The homestead was a single-storey, weatherboarded building with a veranda wrapped around it. Bougainvillea was growing up the front of the house. In the yard, kangaroo paws and a colourful bottle brush tree had started to bloom. Hannah found it delightful. They got down from the trap, and Ray handed the suitcase down to Elizabeth, then tipped his wide-brimmed hat to Hannah before picking up the reins and trotting off to unhitch the pony and cart.

'Where does Ray live?' Hannah wondered if he shared the house with the Winterbournes.

'Over in the shearers' quarters. Next to the shearing sheds. He's the only permanent help, so he lives there on his own. There used to be two other hands but they're both serving overseas. We hire seasonal shearers but there's a shortage of them too at the moment. We've been using girls from the Women's Land Army. They live in a camp nearby and are brought in each morning. They've been a tremendous help, but Michael is reluctant to let them loose in the shearing sheds.' Elizabeth smiled. 'Don't worry we'll give you the full tour. The shearing will be starting soon, so we can get their coats off before the heat of the summer.'

Once in the kitchen, Elizabeth filled the kettle and set it on the hob. 'You must be exhausted. Let's get you something to eat and drink. But first, I'll show you your room.' She led Hannah along a passage to the rear of the building. 'Bathroom's here. Your room's next door. It's not huge, but it's cosy. And there should be enough space to put a cot in too when the time comes.'

Hannah felt a clutch of fear. The mention of a cot was a

stark reminder of what lay ahead for her. It felt like a trap, changing and limiting her future.

In the bedroom, a colourful patchwork quilt was spread over the single bed, a little bookcase was stacked with books and a vase of flowers stood on the chest of drawers.

'What a delightful room,' Hannah cried. She moved to look out of the window. The view was over green pastures where there were sheep grazing, including a number of lambs, and a paddock with several horses. Beyond was the outline of distant hills. She could see Ray leading the pony that had transported them into the paddock, where he unbridled it, gave it a slap on its haunch and it trotted away towards the shade of a tree. The sky was flushed with a rosy pink above the hills. It was almost sunset.

'What a beautiful place,' Hannah murmured.

Over a pot of tea with a plateful of Lamingtons, Elizabeth began by asking Hannah about Judith.

Hannah rummaged in her bag and drew out the photo of her sister holding baby Sarah. 'Your younger niece and great niece,' she said smiling.

Elizabeth looked greedily at it, then gave a sigh. 'Judith is the living image of her mother. I still can't take in that Sarah is dead. I'm sorry that we parted on such bad terms all those years ago. And she must have been heartbroken to lose your brother. Whooping cough, you said in your letter.'

Hannah nodded knowing what was coming next.

'You told me Charles Dawson killed your mother but gave no details. I understand telling me is painful but I would like to know everything.' Elizabeth fixed her eyes upon her.

She couldn't put it off any longer. She reached for Elizabeth's hand. 'I'm afraid it was brutal.' She stared straight ahead, her heart thumping so strongly that she thought it would burst through her chest.

'How?' Elizabeth's face was a mask but Hannah could see she was trembling. 'Tell me exactly how he killed her.'

Hannah swallowed. 'He struck her over the head with an iron.'

'An iron?' Elizabeth's face contorted as she digested this.

'Then he tried to strangle Judith. Will managed to break into the house and Dawson ran away.'

'Thank God for William.' Elizabeth's voice was quiet. Barely a whisper. 'Did Sarah suffer? Did she die at once?'

'According to the coroner, the single blow from the iron was enough to kill her. Mama had been washing the dishes while Judith was ironing his shirts. He grabbed the iron, swung it and struck Mama. Judith ran upstairs and managed to lock herself in her bedroom but he broke the door down and tried to strangle her.'

Elizabeth's hands were covering her face. She lowered them and said, 'The man was a monster. Why weren't you at home too, Hannah?'

'I no longer lived there.' She realised she'd have to tell her aunt the whole sordid story. 'After you left, and Dawson was running the family coffee import business, he mismanaged it and defrauded his clients. His debts forced him to sell the house in Northport and we moved to a small, terraced house in Bootle. His religious mania grew more extreme. He made all our lives a misery. Mama was powerless against him. Eventually he forced me into marriage to Sam, the son of his crony. Will and I were planning to run away together but he was out of port when it happened. It turned out to be a sham wedding with no legal standing, but neither Sam nor I knew that.'

Elizabeth was shaking her head in disbelief. 'So, you had to move in with this Sam?'

Hannah nodded. It was hard having to live all this again in the telling. 'The marriage was never consummated. It turned out Sam likes men not women. He became a good friend to us all after the murder. In fact he was our landlord, sharing his home with us. We still write to each other. But when Will found out, he thought I'd married Sam voluntarily and legally, so he re-joined his old ship heading for Africa. It was a miracle that he came back. While he was away at sea, he decided he had to fight for me, regardless of the marriage.' She looked up. Neither of them had touched the cakes. 'Thank goodness he came back. Otherwise, I'd be dead. My poor mother died because she tried to help Will and me. The day Dawson killed her she'd told him she'd found evidence that he'd been defrauding his clients and that my marriage was illegal. She was going to tell the police. That's why he killed her.' Hannah squeezed her hands into fists and pressed them against her cheeks. It was terrible reliving all this, but Elizabeth had a right to know all the details.

'He couldn't have thought he'd get away with it. Surely?'

'When he was in one of his rages he was a man possessed. There was no reason. Just blind hatred and anger.'

Elizabeth dropped her head into her hands again.

Hannah explained how Will had taken a taxi and got to Hannah, just before her father turned up with a knife. 'The police arrived just in time. Dawson was arrested, tried, found guilty, and executed at Walton Jail. Will and I married a few days later, on the day before war was declared.'

Elizabeth made a little choking sound.

Hannah nodded. 'I will never find it in my heart to

forgive him. He was an evil man. But you know that as well as I do.'

Elizabeth closed her eyes for a moment. 'You know then. What he did to me?'

Hannah nodded. 'Yes, and how my mother took his side after he attacked you. Something she came to bitterly regret. She never forgave herself for what she did. But she was under his control. At first, she believed she loved him but after my baby brother died his cruelty was directed at her too. He blamed her for Peter's death, beat her, belittled her, made all our lives a misery.'

Speaking about her father was reopening the wounds, but it had to be done. 'Poor Mama blamed herself for what happened to me, for not standing up to him when he compelled me to marry Sam. But mostly she blamed herself for not believing you. She said that if she had supported you instead of him, all our lives would have taken a different course.'

Elizabeth took Hannah's hand. 'I have no regrets about the course my life took. If your mother hadn't thrown me out, I'd never have come to Australia, never met Michael, never had Harry. I forgave her long ago. I'm devastated about what happened to her – but so thankful that you and Judith are safe.' She stroked Hannah's hand and gave her a broad smile. 'And I'm overjoyed that you're here in Australia with us.' She glanced at Hannah's swollen belly. 'In case you're worried about the future, don't be. You'll always have a home here with us. You and your baby.'

Tears coursed down Hannah's cheeks. 'Thank you, thank you.' She pressed the heel of her hand into her eyes, then found her handkerchief and wiped the tears away. 'The father of the baby was a nice man, but I didn't love him.'

'When was he killed?'

'Last month but I only heard a couple of days ago. We weren't in touch.'

'Oh Hannah, I'm so sorry. You've had a rotten time.'

'I never dreamt I could be pregnant. I didn't even think I could have children.' Another sob burst from her. 'Will and I tried. It never happened. I slept with Eddie only over one weekend. He was about to go to war.' She looked at Elizabeth, her face tear-stained. 'I should never have done it. It wasn't fair. He had feelings for me and I took advantage because I was lonely.' She wiped her eyes again. 'You'll think I'm some kind of...of...slut. That I couldn't have truly loved Will. But I did. I loved him so much.' Her voice broke. 'Eddie told me it would give him some happy memories to draw on when things got tough overseas. I thought he deserved that.' She told her aunt about June's death. 'Eddie wasn't a happy man. But that weekend he was happier – I know it was wrong of me, but it felt right.'

Elizabeth got up from the table and wrapped her arms around Hannah. 'You poor dear girl. I could never think badly of you. I'd probably have done the same in your place. Did Eddie know about the baby?'

'No. I discovered I was pregnant only the day before I found out he'd been killed.'

'What about his family?'

'I've never met his parents. They're very wealthy. His father's a judge. They live in an enormous house on the harbour. It's a different world. Not my world. And his brother was angry with me when he suspected I'd slept with Eddie. Please don't ask me to tell them. My landlady said they have a right to know – but I can't – I just can't.'

'Why does she think they have a right to know? Just because he's their son? Perhaps one day you may decide you want to tell them, but you have no obligation to do so. You must do what's right for you and right for the baby.'

Elizabeth got up and collected vegetables from a rack. 'I'll just give these a rinse, and then you can help me chop. We're having slow-roasted lamb shoulder. I put it in the oven before I went to meet you.'

Hannah felt a surge of relief that she'd got the hard conversations out of the way. She didn't want to talk about her parents anymore. She didn't want to think about Eddie either. At some point, she'd have to face up to thinking and planning for her baby's future. Right now, though, she was grateful for the chance to chop vegetables mindlessly.

'I wondered what that heavenly smell was as soon as we walked in. The idea of a whole joint of meat is still a great novelty to me. The rationing back in Britain is much more stringent than here.'

Elizabeth stood at the sink, peeling potatoes and carrots. She passed a bunch of parsnips to Hannah to prepare. At first, they worked silently, Hannah sensing that her aunt needed time to absorb everything she'd told her.

Eventually, Elizabeth spoke. 'I know how it feels to be alone and expecting a baby. Finding out I was pregnant after I'd arrived in Australia was utterly terrifying. I'd never felt so alone or so desperate.' She set a pair of pans to boil on the stove. 'But things worked out in the end, as I'm sure they will for you. Then, years later, I was alone again and expecting Harry. I had thirteen years with just him and me in Sydney. We got by. I scraped a living teaching the violin. We were very happy, just the two of us, although I worried about him growing up without a father. And then, out of the blue, four years ago, Michael and I found each other again and here we are.'

She wiped her hands on her apron. 'None of us can

predict the future, Hannah, but you've suffered so much, I have to believe it's time for the universe to smile on you. You may think having this baby is the worst thing that can happen, but I'm certain he or she will bring you great joy and happiness. As I said before, and I speak for Michael and Harry too, you will always have a home with us.' She looked out of the window. 'Speak of the devil. I can see the car coming down the track.'

She took both Hannah's hands in hers. 'Don't worry. You won't have to go through all that again with Michael. I'll tell him what you've told me. He may want to talk to you about William though. But only when you're ready.' She smiled. 'Now we have a roast lamb to eat.'

21

Hannah immediately warmed to Michael Winterbourne – and to her initially shy, sixteen-year-old cousin, Harry. Father and son looked alike: Michael taller and broader and Harry a younger version, with an Aussie accent in contrast to Michael's British North Country burr. As soon as he set foot inside the homestead Michael rushed to embrace, his eyes beaming.

'Delighted to meet you, Hannah. Yer aunt's been too excited to sleep knowing you were on the way.' Then he paused, eyes sad. 'I were right sorry to hear about Will. He were a good man and a great friend to me. I loved that lad like a brother. A gentle soul. Sensitive. You couldn't have found anyone more different from his old man.' He gave her shoulders a quick squeeze then stepped back. 'Come and say hello to yer cousin, Harry.'

Harry, who had hung back, gave Hannah a shy grin and submitted to a hug from her.

Elizabeth ushered them all to the table, where Michael carved the lamb and Elizabeth served the vegetables. Over the meal, Michael told Hannah that Hunter's Down was named after the small settlement he came from in the dales of Cumberland.

'People round here often presume the place is named after the Hunter Valley. That's just a coincidence.'

Hannah swallowed some of the delicious lamb before replying. 'Were you a sheep farmer there too?'

'I were a miner. A lead miner. But I used to dream of getting away from't pits and building a new life. I loved the vale where I lived – that's why I named this place for it.' Michael shook his head sadly. 'But there were no future for me back there outside pits, and even they were under threat of closure. Only a few seams left, and nowt very productive. The writing were on't wall, so I came to Australia. It were all the same to me whether it were Australia or America but there were a berth going on a ship about to sail, so Australia it was. And that's how I met yer aunt.' He looked at Elizabeth with an expression that made Hannah envious. 'I'd a yen for sheep farming but ended up mining again. This time for coal.'

Michael hadn't mentioned the death of his brother in his decision to leave Britain. Will had told Hannah that Michael had accidentally shot his brother when they were hunting rabbits. Perhaps, even after all this time, the pain was still raw. She knew how that felt.

She looked across the table at Michael. Now in his fifties, he was still a good-looking man, his features open, his eyes kind. A shock of thick salt and pepper hair fell over his forehead, and he pushed it back.

Just as Michael had avoided talking about past tragedy, so too did Hannah. As Elizabeth had promised, there were no questions about her early life or the circumstances of her mother's death

Michael began to speak of Will again but stopped

suddenly. 'I'm sorry; does it upset you, me blethering on about him?'

'No!' she cried. 'Please go on. Until now, there's been no one to tell me things about Will. I'll never tire of hearing about him' She gave Michael a sad smile. 'We were together for such a short time, and he was at sea for much of that. There's such a lot I didn't know about him. I thought we had all the time in the world.'

'Aye. We all think that when we're young. But the last war cured me of it. Seeing so many friends killed in their prime, I've tried to live every moment of life with relish.' He looked away, clearly remembering the previous war.

'Your Will used to dream about going to sea. We'd talk about it over a beer at the pub.' Michael smiled, thinking about his friend. 'He hated the mine and fought like a demon against going down't pit, but his old man insisted on it. Jack Kidd used to rant about needing to make a man of Will, didn't he, Lizzie?'

'Poor Will. Jack Kidd never took the trouble to understand his son.' Elizabeth gave a sad smile. 'And he wouldn't listen to me.'

'He wouldn't listen to anyone.' Michael shook his head, his face set hard. 'Drove me crazy, when the old devil would have gone nowhere near that mineshaft himself.' He forked a roast potato into his mouth and chewed thoughtfully. 'Will didn't need toughening up. He were already an independent lad, used to working hard on't smallholding out at McDonald's Creek. He were a fish out of water in town, weren't he, Lizzie?'

'Completely. The first time I met him, he told me he planned to run away to sea. I thought it was just a boyish dream, but it seems it wasn't.' Elizabeth put down her knife and fork and smoothed a hand over the tablecloth, flattening a wrinkle. 'His father never troubled to introduce us. He didn't even tell me he had any children. Just dropped me off at McDonald's Creek and drove away. Will came upon me trying to light a fire outdoors. It was the dry season, so he tore me off a strip for risking a bushfire.' She gave a dry chuckle, remembering. 'I don't know whether he was horrified or angry when I explained I was his father's new wife. Certainly shocked.' She smiled, recollecting. 'But by the end of the evening he'd told me the names of the stars of the southern sky and we'd become firm friends.'

Hannah's eyes welled. This was bittersweet. She was hungry to know everything the couple could tell her about Will, but the pain of loss intensified. She swallowed, determined not to give way to tears. 'Will loved the sea. Strange really, having been born in the bush. He went all over the world. First in Australian waters, but later he spent several years working on a tramp steamer, up and down the east coast of Africa. He used to show me on a map all the ports he called at. Such exotic names – Zanzibar, Mombasa, Djibouti, Dar es Salaam.' She took a sip of water before continuing. 'But when we met, he was doing regular runs across the Irish Sea between Liverpool and Dublin. Mainly transporting cattle from Ireland to the slaughterhouses in Birkenhead.'

Michael chuckled. 'Cattle, eh?'

'We talked about coming here after the war. He wanted to show me Australia. He was keen to see the Harbour Bridge completed, and to show me McDonald Falls. He said he was ready to give up the sea, that it wasn't a job for a married man and he wanted us to live on a small farm. I think he had in mind something like the place at McDonald's Creek.'

'That would have been a struggle,' said Michael. 'Soil's poor. Thin and sandy. It's just woodlands and scrub.'

'How did he and his dad get by when they lived there?'

Elizabeth answered. 'Jack Kidd made money as a card-sharp in between doing whatever work he could get. His first wife died in childbirth while he was away working – or gambling. I think the family barely subsisted on the land. When I lived there, he kept a cow and a few hens, and Will used to fish and shoot rabbits. We had a vegetable plot that did fairly well with a lot of love and attention. But it was a pretty barren, scrubby place.'

Hannah took a long breath. 'Maybe it was a rose-coloured memory then. He always told me it was beautiful. And when I went to McDonald Falls, I thought the scenery was stunning.'

'You're right.' Elizabeth gathered up the plates. 'A magical place of mountains and crags and eucalyptus forests, dense ferns and waterfalls... but not farming country. It had been a mining area, but even that's finished now. The Falls is – and always was – a place where Sydneysiders escape the heat of the city for the fresh air and the views.'

Over the apple pie, Hannah tried to draw out her cousin who so far hadn't joined in the conversation. 'Are you at a school nearby, Harry?' she asked.

'I've left school. Didn't like it much. The teacher reckoned I was thick.'

'The teacher needed her head examining,' said Elizabeth. She turned to Hannah. 'Harry hates lessons, but he loves to read. He takes after the two of us in that respect. We're a family of bookworms.'

Hannah grinned. 'Me too. Ever since I was a girl and discovered the library in Crosby, I've had a passion for reading, even though I had to hide the books from my father.'

Elizabeth's lips tightened. 'He didn't approve of reading, then?'

'Only the Bible. And then mostly the Old Testament. Used to make Judith and me learn long tracts and recite them back to him. Heaven help us if we weren't word perfect.' She looked down at her plate.

They'd strayed into unwelcome territory, but fortunately Michael intervened. 'Harry's now working here as roustabout.'

'What?' Hannah had never heard the term.

'General dogsbody,' Harry said. He rolled his eyes, then gave a broad grin. 'I love it though. Ray's promised he'll let me have a go at the shearing this year.'

'We'll see about that,' said his father. 'You have to earn yer place on't board, son.'

'Harry, you'll show Hannah around the farm tomorrow?' Elizabeth put her hands on her son's shoulders. 'I'm sure she'd love to get an idea of what we do here. But don't you dare overtire her. Is that all right with you, Hannah?'

'Yes. I can't wait.'

'We start early, but that doesn't include you,' said Elizabeth. 'Have a lie-in and I'll cook your breakfast when you're ready. You must be exhausted after that long train journey today.'

Hannah's offer to help with the dishes was firmly refused. Grateful for the chance to retire early, she wished the Winterbournes good night and went to bed.

THE DELICIOUS AROMA of frying bacon woke Hannah. It took her a moment to recognise her surroundings and remember she was at Hunter's Down. She threw back the faded patchwork quilt and got out of bed, quickly washing and dressing, before making her way into the kitchen.

Michael and Harry were sitting at the table eating their bacon and eggs, while Elizabeth sipped a cup of tea.

'I told you to have a lie-in, Hannah!' she said, wagging a finger. 'These two have to be up with the lark, but there's no reason for you to be.'

Hannah smiled at her. 'I'm used to early starts. In the WAAAF I worked shifts, and the first one was at six a.m. so I had to get up at five. Once the sun's up, I find it hard to linger in bed.'

'Well, you need to make sure you get plenty of rest.' Elizabeth looked pointedly at Hannah's belly. 'Now let me get some bacon in the pan for you and me.'

Hannah was too quick for her. 'Stay where you are. I'll do it. I haven't done any cooking since I left Victoria. Sal, our landlady, used to let me help in the kitchen, but Dot, my landlady in Sydney, wouldn't let me near her domain. I'd hate to forget how to cook.'

Elizabeth ceded. 'Thank you, Hannah. This is a luxury indeed.'

As Hannah bustled about, frying the bacon and eggs and boiling the water for a fresh pot of tea, the two men got to their feet.

'So, Michael, what's on the list for this morning?' asked Elizabeth.

'Ray and I are doing fencing repairs in the northwest pasture. Harry's going to check on the late lambs and make sure all's well. There are one or two looking sickly. He'll be in the home paddock, so Hannah can find him there when she's ready, and he'll give her the tour.'

Hannah glanced over as she poured boiling water into

the teapot. 'As long as I won't be getting in the way or stopping you working, Harry.'

The lad gave her a broad grin. 'Don't worry, I'm delighted to get out of fencing. You're doing me a favour.'

AFTER SHE'D BREAKFASTED and helped Elizabeth with the dishes, Hannah finished unpacking and then made her way out to the paddock behind the homestead. She found her cousin among a group of ewes with their lambs under the shade of the trees.

Harry told her they would start the weaning process soon. 'I'm checking on the flock to see if there are any lambs struggling. At the moment they're all on milk, so my job is to check that they're taking it in and growing. When they're two or three months old, we wean them by encouraging them to eat grass.'

'They'll have both mother's milk and grass?'

'At first. But we need to get them off milk completely as the grass is more nutritious. When the time's right, we'll be separating them from their mothers to encourage them to eat the grass. We also give them solid supplements to help develop their digestive systems. But it's too soon, so I have to make sure none of them are going hungry because they're not suckling properly. If the ewe's had three lambs, the runt can miss out 'cause the ewes only have two teats.' He folded his arms, looking pleased at the chance to show off his knowledge.

'What happens if one is missing out?'

'We bottle-feed them. That's my job. Come and I'll show you. I'm looking after two at the moment. And I'm going to add this little one.' He bent down and scooped up a scrawny lamb and cradled it in his arms.

Harry led Hannah across the field and into one of the outbuildings where a couple of lambs were lying on a bed of hay, bleating. On a shelf at the side was a basket covered with a dishtowel. He lifted the cloth and took out two bottles of formula. 'Mum gets it ready and disinfects the bottles. We have to feed them every few hours at the moment. You want to do one of them?'

Hannah was taken aback. 'Me?'

'You'll soon get the hang of it.' He handed her a bottle.

Hannah knelt down in the straw and Will carefully placed the lamb he'd been carrying in her arms. She offered up the bottle and teat to the lamb.

'Keep the bottle tilted.' Harry did the same for the other lamb.

'You're very knowledgeable, Harry.'

He grinned. 'I love working on the farm. Glad I'm done with school. This is tons more interesting.' He lifted his hat and pushed his hair back from his forehead. Hannah was struck again by how much he resembled his father.

'We'll be shearing the ewes soon. Getting their coats off before the summer heat.'

'What about the rams?'

'Most of them have been sold for meat. We just keep a small number for breeding. One ram can do thirty ewes. More experienced ones even more. Even up to a hundred.' His face turned pink, suddenly embarrassed.

After a few moments, he looked across at her. 'You're doing a great job, Hannah.'

'Thank you. I'm getting in some practice.'

Harry reddened again and looked the other way. He must be aware she was expecting a baby and, as a boy living on a farm, she thought he'd be more sanguine about such matters – but he was only sixteen, after all. Hannah had no idea what his mother had told him about her condition or her circumstances. She felt herself blushing too and focused her attention on the lamb.

Having completed the feeding, they put the empty bottles back into the basket.

'Mum will collect them. Now I'll show you the shearing shed, and then I'll take you to meet the land girls in the barn.'

The shearing shed was a large building with a tin roof and a wooden floor. There were pens on one side and a large space with electric shears hanging on the walls.

'Nothing to see right now,' said Harry, 'but when we start shearing it's very different. We put the sheep in these holding pens, one pen for each shearer. It's important they're dry, as a wet coat is too hard to shear, We also make them fast overnight when they're in the pens 'cause they're more comfortable on empty stomachs. After they're shorn, they go into the outside pens.' He pointed to the other exit as he led her across the room to a large table. 'We lay each fleece out here on the skirting table and pull away the tatty bits round the edges before it goes in the presser over there.' Hannah looked over at the large box-like structure with a huge lever on one side and a pulley system above.

'What's that for?'

'The fleeces get squashed into woolsacks ready to be shipped to the wool stores in Sydney. You'll soon see it working. Let's find the land girls now.'

As they strolled over to another building, Harry continued to chat to her. 'Dad says I have to wait before he'll teach me how to shear. Wants me to prove myself on all the other tasks first, but I know I'm ready.' He gave Hannah a sly grin. 'Ray's promised to hold one sheep back for me to have a go on after Dad's left the shed.'

'Ray is able to shear?' She thought of the man's missing arm.

'Not as fast as he used to, but he still gives Dad a run for his money.'

'With one arm? That's extraordinary.'

'Ray's an extraordinary man.'

Her curiosity piqued, she asked, 'How did he lose his arm?'

Harry ran a hand through his hair like an echo of his father. 'Dunno exactly. He doesn't like talking 'bout it. But it was at the beginning of the war. He was in the desert.'

Hannah was surprised. She'd assumed it must have been a farming accident. 'So the war must have been over very quickly for him.'

'Too quick, I reckon. Probably why he never mentions it. Dad says he was incredibly brave. I heard he captured ten greasy Eye-ties.'

Hannah flinched. She hated hearing Italians being called Eye-ties, and the greasy epithet was uncalled for. Doubtless there were many conscripts in the Italian army, and she was sure lots of them would hate Mussolini and fascism as much as Paolo, did.

'Actually, Harry, my brother-in-law is Italian. Don't assume they're all fanatical fascists. There are ordinary, decent people on both sides. Italy has conscription, and I'll bet most of them aren't fighting out of choice or principles. They may be the enemy, but there's no need to call them rude names.'

Harry looked contrite, and his face reddened again. 'Sorry, it's just that's what the boys at school call them. Everyone reckons Italians are all cowards and useless fighters. They stick their hands up rather than fight.'

She smiled. 'If you were forced into a war you didn't

believe in, by a dictator you didn't support, you might be reluctant to get yourself killed too.'

'I suppose so.' He looked down, shuffling his feet. 'Sorry.'

She put an arm round him and gave him a squeeze. 'No apologies needed. When you meet Paolo, as I hope you will one day, you'll see he's a lovely chap. He was my husband's best friend and my sister Judith's husband. You'd struggle to find a kinder, funnier, gentler man.'

Harry nodded solemnly. 'I get it. I suppose it's just 'cause Ray's a good bloke, and it's thanks to the Italians he lost his arm.'

'That's the awful thing about war.' She decided to steer the conversation away onto more solid ground. 'Now, what are you going to show me next?'

He whistled and called to a dog who had been lying in the sunshine outside the large barn-like structure where the land girls were working. 'Come and meet my dog. Here, Meggsie!'

The reddish-coloured dog with pointy ears ambled over. Hannah bent to stroke him. His fur was short but soft. 'Hello, Meggsie,' she said.

'His full name's Ginger Meggs. You know – after the boy in the comic books.'

'I've never heard of him, I'm afraid.'

'Ginger Meggs is a larrikin. Always in trouble.'

'A larrikin?' Spending time with Harry was proving to be an education.

'A larrikin's what Dad calls me when he's mad at me.'

'I see.' Hannah grinned at her cousin. 'So Meggsie here's a larrikin too?'

'He's still only a puppy. I'm trying to train him to be a proper sheepdog.'

'He looks different from English sheepdogs.' She laughed. 'Not that I'm an expert. I've never owned a dog.'

'He's a kelpie. They're brilliant. They make perfect sheepdogs as they're really, really good at mustering animals.'

Before she could ask him anything else, they were at the open door of the barn. Inside, two young women were at work, sharpening and disinfecting combs and cutters, ready for the shearing, both wore overalls and had their hair tied up in scarves. Harry introduced them as Sally and Violet. They gave Hannah broad smiles and shook her hand. Sally was tall and solidly built and Violet so small and skinny that Hannah wondered how she had the stamina to be a land-girl. 'Where are Amy and Maxine?' he asked them.

'Fence-mending with the boss and Ray,' said Violet. 'We're almost done here. We're cleaning and disinfecting the shearing shed this arvo.'

Harry winked at Hannah. 'I think we'll skip that part of the tour.'

As he spoke, they heard Elizabeth calling from the back door to tell them their lunch was ready.

Hannah was walking towards her aunt when she felt a sudden cramping that made her clutch her stomach. It passed quickly. She walked on, hoping this was a normal part of pregnancy, but as she reached the veranda, she heard Harry give a little cry and, following the direction of his horrified gaze, she saw there was blood running down her leg.

The next thing she knew, Elizabeth's arms were around her as her aunt helped her up the step and into the house.

'Go and find your father, Harry. Tell him to fetch the doctor.' Elizabeth's voice was calm, but there was an unmistakable stridency in her tone as she called to her son.

22

Inside the house, Elizabeth steered Hannah into her bedroom and helped her onto the bed.

'Am I losing the baby?' Hannah's voice was barely a whisper.

'I'm sure it will be all right. Bleeding can happen. But the doctor will check you over to make sure.' Somehow Elizabeth's voice lacked the conviction of her words.

Hannah's heart was racing. She heard an engine starting up outside, then Harry's voice called out to say his father had left to find the doctor.

'How long will he take?' Hannah clutched her aunt's hand.

'He'll be as quick as he can. Don't worry. It's lunchtime, and if Michael drives fast – which he will – he should catch the doctor before he does his afternoon rounds. Will you be all right if I leave you for a moment?'

Hannah nodded. Fear wrapped itself around her, choking like a vine. She stared at the ceiling, willing the baby to stay inside her. Up until now, she'd been wishing it wasn't there. It had cost her the job at iFSHQ, drastically altered her future and limited her options. Having longed for a child with Will, this baby, so easily conceived, had seemed a mockery.

How often had she castigated herself for sleeping with Eddie, wishing she weren't pregnant? But now that she was at risk of miscarrying, she found she was desperate to hold on to her unborn child.

Elizabeth was gone for about five minutes, returning with hot water, a flannel and a towel. She set about cleaning up the blood, which had already dried on Hannah's legs. 'I've asked one of the land girls to bring us some sanitary towels. They get them provided for free in the land army. But the bleeding appears to have stopped already. Are you in pain?'

Hannah shook her head. 'Not now.'

Elizabeth, still holding her hand, called again to Harry, instructing him to make Hannah a sweet tea. While they were waiting, there was a knock at the bedroom door. Elizabeth went out and Hannah heard whispered voices in the passageway. Her aunt came back holding a plain brown-paper bag.

Hannah opened the packet and slipped a sanitary napkin inside a clean pair of knickers her aunt handed her from the chest of drawers.

Leaning back against the pillows, she closed her eyes. It was her own fault. She'd brought this about by wishing the baby away. But before she could agonise further, tiredness overwhelmed her, and she drifted off to sleep.

Hannah woke to see a man entering the room behind her aunt.

'This is Dr Netherton, Hannah.' Elizabeth slipped away, leaving her alone with the GP.

He was an elderly man with kind eyes and a slight stoop. He examined her, listening to her belly with his stethoscope, then moving it higher to check her heart, before taking her temperature with a thermometer. 'Has there been more bleeding, Mrs Kidd?'

'No.'

'Pain?'

'Just briefly. A cramping sensation when the bleeding happened.'

'Has this happened before?'

Her eyes welled with tears, which she sniffed back. 'I only recently found out I was pregnant. I thought I'd had periods. I've always been light and irregular, but these were just spotting, really. It never occurred to me I was expecting a baby. But this time, there was a gush of blood.'

'Mrs Kidd, I have to warn you this could be a miscarriage. However, the baby's heartbeat is normal.' He packed away his stethoscope. 'A bit of bleeding is not unusual, but I'd like you to stay in bed for a few days until we're sure you're not miscarrying. I'll check on you again tomorrow. In the meantime, if the bleeding starts again and becomes heavy, call me immediately.' He looked around. 'Mr Kidd?'

She swallowed. 'I'm a widow. My husband was killed.' She didn't elaborate.

'I'm sorry, my dear. In the forces?'

'Navy.' Again, she chose not to be more specific.

'I lost a brother in the last one. Gallipoli. My son is serving in Egypt. He's a tank operator with the Ninth Division. Such a worry. War is a terrible thing.' The doctor shook his head.

He picked up his holdall. 'Drink plenty of milk, eat lots

of fruit and lean meat and don't forget the cod liver oil. It doesn't taste nice, but it's a wonderful source of vitamins.' He put on his hat and gave her a gentle smile. 'Most of all, Mrs Kidd, try not to worry.'

After he'd gone, Elizabeth brought her a cup of tea and sat with her while she drank it.

Hannah passed the empty cup and saucer back to her aunt. 'What did the doctor tell you?' Had he been more honest with Elizabeth than with her?

Elizabeth patted the bedcovers. 'Just that you must have complete bed rest until he checks you over again. But he seems to be quite phlegmatic about it. He said bleeding can be due to several factors, only one being the start of a miscarriage. And he said your baby's heartbeat was strong and steady.'

'Can't I even get up for my meals?'

Elizabeth shook her head. 'Maybe tomorrow or the day after. We'll see what the doc says next time he calls.'

THE WINTERBOURNES WERE TREATING her like a china doll. But Hannah knew, since the paralysing fear that she was about to miscarry, that she wanted to keep this baby.

It was three more days before the doctor told Hannah he was happy for her to leave her bed. 'I want you to take it easy for another couple of weeks. My nurse will see you in clinic after that. I'm sure there's nothing to worry about, Mrs Kidd, but we'll keep a close watch on you, just in case.'

Days of doing nothing but read and, when Elizabeth allowed it, chopping a few vegetables or laying the table, were making Hannah frustrated and anxious for activity. Her confinement to the house coincided with a period of heavy rain, contributing to her low spirits.

During the first evening meal together with the family at the dinner table, they initially avoided the topic of Hannah's scare. Michael spoke of how, despite the rain, they'd finished the fencing repairs, which had not been as extensive as he'd feared. 'Fencing is a never-ending task. Otherwise, we'd be overrun with rabbits. Not my favourite animals and a real pest in Australia. If you don't keep them down, they eat all the grass, and there's nothing for the sheep to graze on.'

Hannah glanced up at him, remembering that it had been while shooting rabbits that Michael had accidentally shot dead his own brother: the trigger for his decision to emigrate to Australia.

He told Hannah he was thinking about diversification on the farm. 'I don't like to have all my eggs in one basket. While the war's on, it makes sense to stay focused on sheep. We need as much lamb and mutton as possible since we're supplying Britain too. But once the war's over, I'm considering planting a few acres with vines and seeing how they go. The climate and soil here is perfect for grapes, and there are several wineries doing well. I wouldn't be surprised if that business grows even faster in the future.'

'I'd no idea wine was made in Australia. But I suppose there's the weather for it.'

'The conditions here in the Hunter Valley are perfect. Winemaking is the main activity in this area. That and breeding horses. It's been dominated by a few families of growers who've been established since Victorian times, but I think there's room for some newcomers.'

He glanced at his wife then spoke again to Hannah. 'I hope you're feeling better now, Hannah. Elizabeth and I have been saying we should have given you a couple of days to recover from your journey. I understand Harry had you sitting in the straw on the barn floor feeding the lambs.'

Harry flushed and looked down. It was apparent he'd been reprimanded.

Hannah rushed to the boy's defence. 'It was hardly taxing. The lambs were adorable, and I enjoyed stretching my legs after being stuck on the train for so long. Harry was a terrific guide.' She glanced in the boy's direction. 'Very knowledgeable. I'm just sorry I gave you all a fright.' Harry gave her a grateful smile.

Elizabeth said, 'The doc wants you to get plenty of rest – early nights and a lie down after lunch if you need it.'

Hannah didn't like to be fussed over. 'He gave me a clean bill of health this afternoon. Even said a little light exercise would be beneficial. I expect Michael's right, and the train journey overtired me. And I was working in pretty awful conditions in Sydney, stuck underground with no proper ventilation. All of us got sick and dizzy. I'm used to plenty of exercise – we had to go up and down eighty-seven steep steps on two shifts a day just to get to work. And no lift in the building where we were staying on Macquarie Street. I was on the top floor.'

'No wonder you were unwell. Doing all that while pregnant.' Elizabeth shook her head as she passed a dish of mashed potatoes to Michael. 'The working conditions sound dreadful.'

'Lizzie tells me you were doing the same work in Liverpool.' Michael piled up the potatoes on his plate and covered them in gravy.

'Yes. For the navy. They shared the same building alongside the air force. In Sydney, they're located separately. And although we were in an underground bunker in Liverpool, it was purpose-built and much more spacious.'

Not wanting to sound too critical of Australia, she added, 'Of course Australia's had little time to prepare as Pearl Harbour wasn't exactly expected. And back then it was Britain alone. Here, as well as Australians, the staff are British and American, so there's bound to be some tension.'

She told them about the night of the attacks on Sydney and how she believed poor communications had delayed the Allied response. 'The man in charge was British. An admiral, no less. But he and the American captain of the *USS Chicago* believed the reported submarine sightings were erroneous.' She shook her head. 'Although the rumours were that they were both the worse for drink after dining together.'

Elizabeth shook her head. 'I'd hate having to make life and death decisions like that. All those poor sailors lost.' She began to clear away the plates. 'Enough of war. Tomorrow, you are going to have a restful day, curled up with a book.'

THE NEXT DAY, Hannah was delighted when Elizabeth tried out some sonatas from the collection Hannah had given her. The sweet strains of the violin raised her spirits as she listened.

'You're so talented. It must be wonderful to play like that.'

Elizabeth replaced her fiddle in the case. 'Didn't you learn music?'

Hannah snorted. 'No. Dawson would never have allowed it.'

'Ah, of course. Your mother only let me play when he was out of the house. Back then, when we all lived in the family home in Northport, I took music pupils. It was the only way I could contribute to the housekeeping.'

'I have no memories of living there. What was it like?'

'A tall, elegant townhouse with a large garden at the back. Servants in the attic. A huge basement kitchen. But by the time I left, we were reduced to just a cook and a housekeeper.'

Hannah stared at her, open-mouthed. 'We had servants? You'd have been shocked to see where we ended up: a two-up, two-down terrace near the docks in Bootle with just a tiny yard at the back for the privy.'

'My goodness. My father would have been horrified. When he left the family home to your father, it was with the intention that you and Judith would grow up there.' Elizabeth sighed. Then she nodded towards her violin case. 'Would you like to learn to play? Or perhaps you'd prefer the piano, then we could duet together. I'd be happy to teach you.'

Hannah's face broke into a wide grin. 'Really? I'd love to learn the piano.'

'No time like the present. We'll start right away. I bet you'll prove a more willing and dedicated pupil than Harry ever was!'

AN HOUR LATER, Elizabeth's prediction had proved true. 'You're a natural, Hannah. If you practise for an hour every day, you'll soon master 'Clair de Lune' and 'Für Elise'. Now let's have a cup of tea, then I think you should lie down until dinner.

Over tea, which they drank at the kitchen table, Hannah confessed her fears about losing the baby. 'As soon as I found out I was pregnant, I wished it would end. But when I thought I was losing the baby, I knew I wanted it.' She paused. 'Yet I can't imagine ever loving it as I'd have loved a child that was Will's.'

Elizabeth gave a long sigh. 'When I found out I was pregnant with your fath— sorry, Dawson's child, I begged my landlady to help me get rid of it. I even got so far as going to the house of the woman who was going to do it.'

Hannah gasped.

'I was desperate. I had no means of supporting myself, let alone a child. I'd fallen in love with Michael, but I didn't know where he was. Besides, how could I have told him I was carrying a child? But when I stood in that filthy kitchen and met the woman who was to carry out the procedure, I couldn't go through with it. After that, I had no choice but to marry Will's father. He was much older and I felt nothing for him. That I might come to love that baby seemed impossible. Yet, from the moment I first held little Mikey in my arms, I was besotted. Losing him and his sister was the worst thing that ever happened to me. I still miss them both every day of my life.' A tear ran down her cheek.

Hannah moved around the table and embraced her aunt. 'I'm so sorry.'

Elizabeth wiped her eyes with the corner of her apron. 'All I wanted to say was that I understand what you're going through. If I could love Mikey, you too will love your baby.'

Hannah sat back down. 'I feel ashamed. My situation isn't nearly as bad as yours was. And I'm so grateful to have you and Michael in my life. My baby may not have sprung from love, but I liked Eddie. He was a nice man.' She gave a wistful smile. 'He taught me to swim.'

'Tell me about him. How did you meet?'

'He was a friend of one of the partners at work. We met at the beach. He made it clear from the beginning that he liked me. I tried to keep him at a distance.' She smiled. 'But he was very handsome. He kissed me. I enjoyed it. Then one thing led to another. I made it clear from the start that I didn't want a relationship. We had a one-off weekend together before he went off to war.'

Elizabeth took her hand. 'I'm sure when your baby arrives you'll fall in love with him or her, just as I did with Mikey. Your Eddie sounds a nice chap. Do you have a photograph of him?'

Hannah shook her head, suddenly sad. 'No. That means I'll never be able to show the baby who their father was.'

'Maybe one day, when you feel differently, you'll be able to introduce your child to their grandparents.'

'Perhaps.' But Hannah doubted it. Mark's words to her at Shirley's engagement party still stung. And she remembered how Eddie's mother had banished all the photographs of June from display. Would she have done the same with Eddie? Instinctively, Hannah was far from certain that Mrs Greenbank would want anything to do with her.

23

Two days after the rain stopped and the sheep had dried off, it was time for the mustering. Michael, Harry, Ray Gaffney, and the sheepdogs set off on horseback to round up the flock and shepherd them into the shearing pens.

Doctor Netherton, having satisfied himself that Hannah was not in danger of losing the baby, said she could venture out around the farm again. She watched the men and dogs as they set off, surprised to see Ray mount and manage his horse effortlessly with only one arm.

'Riding is all in the legs,' said Elizabeth, standing beside her, reading her mind. 'Can you ride?'

Hannah raised her eyebrows, smiling. 'Not much chance of acquiring equestrian skills on the Liverpool docks. Can you?'

'After a fashion. It's not my favourite pastime, and you'll rarely see me on a horse these days.'

Hannah was curious about Ray Gaffney. 'Harry mentioned that he lost his arm serving in Egypt at the beginning of the war.'

Elizabeth nodded. 'A grenade I think. Poor Ray. He was devastated to be wounded out of the war when he'd barely got started.'

'Harry said he'd captured ten Italian soldiers.'

'Really? I didn't know that. But I wouldn't be surprised.' Elizabeth stared after the men as they receded into the distance. 'I think being out of the war so soon is why he refuses to acknowledge his disability. Mustering, shearing, repairing fences. He finds a way to do it all.'

'I can't imagine how he can shear with only one arm.'

'Wait and see. He holds his own with all of them.'

Now that the doctor had allowed her to be up and about, Hannah tried to make herself as useful as Elizabeth would allow around the homestead. She collected eggs from the hens each morning, washed dishes, and helped with the cooking and laundry. But Elizabeth was insistent on Hannah getting lots of rest.

'I managed all this on my own before you arrived, and I can manage it still. The most important thing you can do is take it easy. And keep practising the piano!'

But Hannah wasn't the kind to willingly put her feet up while someone else worked.

Hannah leant against a fence, watching as the sheep were herded into the holding pens. They were funnelled by the dogs into a long run between fences with a swing gate in the middle. As the sheep rushed through, Michael swung the gate, directing them either to the left or the right.

'What's he doing?' she asked Harry.

'Drafting. We do it to divide the flock.'

The speed with which Michael swung the gate, making the split-second decision, impressed her. Curious, she asked Harry, 'How old are the lambs when they're slaughtered?'

'Under twelve months. After that, they're classified as mutton. Dad specialises in wool production, and the flock is mostly Merino. They make the best wool. But since the war started, we've been doing more meat production. Some of the flock now is a dual-purpose crossbreed.'

'You really are the expert, Harry.'

He glowed with pleasure. 'Not really. One day the farm will be mine, so I have to learn everything. Before Mum and I came to Hunter's Down, we lived in Sydney, so I've got tons of catching up to do compared with kids who grew up on a farm.'

It was late afternoon by the time the flock was in the large outdoor corrals which fed into smaller holding pens next to the shearing shed.

'Done,' said Harry as his father swung the gate for the last time. He grinned at Hannah. 'Tonight they have to fast, ready for shearing.'

'Fast?' For a moment she thought she'd misheard.

'It's to make the sheep comfortable when they're sheared. We take them off the grass, and they fast overnight so their stomachs aren't full when they're sheared. I bet you didn't know that sheep have four stomachs.'

She acknowledged she didn't.

'We get them to empty their stomachs before they reach the shearing floor. That way they don't get distressed and are lighter for the shearer to handle.' He grinned. 'We also want to make sure they don't do their business all over the board and the fleece. The board gets slippy enough anyway during shearing from all the lanolin.'

'Gosh. It's fascinating. I'm looking forward to watching tomorrow.'

'When the shearing's finished we have a feast. It's a tradition. Loads of tucker and the shearers drink beer and sing songs.'

Hannah asked if the land girls sheared too.

Harry looked at her askance, arms folded. 'It's men's work. They'll be in the shed doing other things. Dad only lets Ray and a couple of neighbours do the shearing. Tomorrow, the girls will keep the board clean and assist me.' He puffed his chest out and Hannah suppressed a smile. She wondered whether the land girls saw themselves as the sixteen-year-old's assistants. Somehow, she doubted it.

'When we do the drenching and dipping, we may let them help with that.'

She asked what drenching was.

'It's when we pour stuff down the sheep's throats to kill off the worms in their stomachs,' Harry explained. 'Otherwise, they won't gain weight.'

'I hadn't a clue so much was involved in rearing sheep.'

'A different job every day. We also dip them to stop blowfly strikes and ticks and lice.' Harry was clearly enjoying his role as ambassador and showing off his knowledge. The more she knew him, the fonder Hannah became of her young cousin.

AFTER SUPPER THAT EVENING, Hannah heard the distant sound of bullfrogs coming from the creek that bordered one side of the land. Closer, in the shearing pens, she could hear the occasional bleating from the fasting sheep.

Elizabeth and Michael lingered at the table after dinner, and Hannah decided to give them some privacy. Harry was on the veranda, happily whittling a stick, illuminated by a storm lantern.

Hannah wandered towards the glow of a small fire in a dugout pit on the far side of the shearing sheds. It was an area she hadn't been to before. She settled on the grass, enjoying her solitude and the warmth of the fire. The logs crackled, a few random sparks snapping out of the wood to dance in the air for a moment then die. Propped on her elbows, she stared up at the vastness of the night sky. Tiny pinpricks of stars; great, sweeping, clustering galaxies of them; the brighter lights of planets; the swollen gibbous moon. She hadn't a clue how to identify the constellations. Will had known them all – had observed them from both hemispheres, able to navigate by them – and he had promised to teach her. The war had stopped that. When she'd looked at the night sky back in Liverpool, it was in terror at the dark shapes of Heinkel and Junkers bombers, the slow sweep of searchlight beams raking the heavens, the brilliant yellow and orange flames of burning buildings or the clouds of dust and smoke rising from the rubble.

Hannah sighed, staring up at the vast firmament. Was Will up there somewhere? On a distant planet? In some alternative universe? If he were, she doubted it would be in the traditional idea of heaven. She no more believed in that than she did in the agonising eternal fires of hell. She'd been brought up haunted by the visions of fire and brimstone that her father had thundered about. If his proclamations had been correct and hell existed, then Charles Dawson would be experiencing it for himself now, having done so much evil in the name of his vengeful God.

She thought of the baby growing inside her. Most of the time she tried to put the fatherless child-to-be out of her mind. If Will was looking down on her, would he understand why she'd slept with Eddie Greenbank? Would he forgive her for bringing another man's child into the world? Hannah decided he probably would. He wouldn't have expected her to live as a nun. He'd had a colourful past himself before meeting her.

But why was she thinking like this on such a beautiful clear night? She tried to redirect her thoughts back to the beauty of the sky. Thinking of Will filled her with an existential loneliness. He should be here beside her now. Here, in his native country, telling her stories about his childhood in the Blue Mountains, recounting the legends as old as time that he'd learned from the old Aboriginal man he used to talk to when a boy. If only she could recapture and reclaim those conversations, play them in her head like a gramophone record, savouring them whenever needed. They'd had so little time in their brief marriage. She'd believed they'd have the rest of their lives together after the war was over, that their short-term sacrifices would reap long-term rewards. But here she was, the war raging on and now engulfing the entire planet, alone without Will. The rest of her life, maybe sixty or more years, stretched ahead of her in an empty continuum.

Something moved beside her, and she dropped her gaze back to earth. A sheepdog settled close to her to enjoy the warmth of the fire. Hannah stretched out a hand and stroked his fur, which felt rough to the touch. A dog with a purpose – no overindulged house pet. The animal turned its head slightly and looked at her, perhaps unused to physical affection, but didn't demur.

The dark bulk of a man, presumably one of the shearers, came and squatted beside the dog. 'Is he bothering you?'

'Not at all.'

The man eased himself down on the other side of the dog. 'Name's Rocky.' His voice was deep but quiet.

'Pleased to meet you, Rocky,' Hannah said, although she wasn't really, preferring to be alone.

The man gave a low chuckle. 'Not me. The dog.' He stretched his legs out in front of him towards the fire pit, mirroring her position. 'My name's Ray – Ray Gaffney. We met the other day.'

Hannah, mortified, instinctively corrected her own posture, sitting upright and tucking her legs neatly to one side. 'I didn't recognise you in the dark, Ray. I'm sorry. You must think me an idiot.'

In the soft glow of the fire, she could see his outline but not his features or expression. The missing arm was farthest from her; otherwise, she'd have noticed its absence and realised it was him. His head tipped to one side as though to brush off her comment. 'Easily done. And I'm sure you're no fool. Not if you're anything like your aunty.'

With no choice but to accept his company, Hannah tried to make conversation. 'Elizabeth says you've worked with Michael for a long time.'

'We met in New Zealand. I'm a Kiwi. We used to shear together there. Became mates. When he moved back to Australia, he talked me into coming with him.'

'I thought your accent was different. But I didn't realise you were a New Zealander.'

After a few moments of silence, he spoke again, sending his words in the direction of the fire. 'What brings someone like you to a place like this?'

'Someone like me?' Her initial reaction was defensive, although his tone implied he'd intended no offence. She had to stop being so prickly.

'I meant you're not from around here, not even an

Aussie. I imagine you're getting away from the war back in England. Gather it's been bad there.'

At least he hadn't called her a Pom. Maybe New Zealanders were more polite. 'I'm from Liverpool. Yes, it was bad.' She wasn't going to tell a stranger about her home being bombed and her husband being killed by a German plane in the North Atlantic.

'Don't say much, do you?'

'I came to Australia nearly a year ago. I moved to Sydney, and then my aunt, Mrs Winterbourne, invited me here.' She realised she was using Elizabeth's formal name to create more distance between them.

It didn't work. He leant forward to look at her, studying her in the half light from the fire. 'You're the dead spit of her. Didn't know Lizzie had family in England.'

'Only my younger sister and me. We'd lost touch with my aunt, and it took me a while to find her.' She paused, then anticipating his question, added, 'My sister's name's Judith. Her husband is called Paolo; they have a baby called Sarah and now live in Victoria.' It was all spoken in a breathless rush that made clear she resented being questioned.

'Sorry, I didn't mean to be a stickybeak.'

Hannah was immediately contrite. She smiled at him across the shadows. 'No apology needed. You weren't being nosy. It's just that the war's been hard, and I don't enjoy talking about it.'

'Fair enough.'

In the distance, behind her, on the steps up to the veranda, she could see the dark outline that was Harry, still whittling a stick. No one else was around. She was trapped for at least a few more minutes. Leaving now would be justifiably viewed by the man as rudeness.

'Is this your fire?' she asked. 'Have I intruded? Only I came out for some air after dinner and was drawn to it.'

'It's a free country. Before the war, the shearers would have a few beers round a fire the night before shearing. I thought the land girls might be here tonight, but turns out there's a dance in Hazelton.'

They sat motionless as the fire crackled. Ray squatted on his haunches and picked up a hooked metal bar. He leant forward, and Hannah noticed there was a large black pot standing in the embers, its lid covered with embers too. It was only then that she realised she'd interrupted his cooking.

'I'm sorry. You were cooking your supper.' Mortified, she scrambled to her feet. Ray put down the bar and reached up, grasping her by the wrist to stop her from leaving. 'Don't run off. I've already eaten. This is just some damper I'm making.'

'Damper?' She eased herself back down, curious.

'Bush tucker. Basic bread. Should be ready now.' He picked up the bar, hooked it under the handle and lifted the blackened pot off the coals. Using the hook again, he raised the pot lid, and they were greeted by the delicious smell of the cooked dough. He tapped the crust. 'Nice and firm. You never tried damper?'

Hannah shook her head.

'We'll put that right. I made this for tomorrow morning, but it tastes better hot from the camp oven.'

'I can't take your food.'

He laughed. 'Don't be a goose. It's just flour and milk. Only took a few minutes to mix up. Wait here.'

He got to his feet and went into the lean-to where he lived, next to the shearing shed, returning with a butter dish, a plate, a knife and a pot of jam. 'It's good when it's warm enough to melt the butter and with some jam on top. Go on, try some.'

'Just a little. It smells delicious.' She accepted a piece of the warm bread, spread it with butter and jam, and took a bite. 'That *is* good,' she said, licking melted butter from her fingers. 'It tastes like a scone. Delicious.'

'Food always tastes better when it's cooked in the open.' He fixed his eyes on her and she looked away, disturbed by the intensity of his gaze.

After they'd finished eating, Ray reached under the rolled-up cuff of the shirtsleeve above his missing lower arm and pulled out a packet of cigarettes, silently offering her one, which Hannah declined. He flicked one out of the pack with a practised flourish and lit it with a twig he stuck into the fire. Squatting on his haunches, he drew on the cigarette, savouring it, before slowly expelling the smoke. Hannah studied his profile in the firelight as he smoked. His hair was cropped short under his ubiquitous sweat-stained canvas bush hat. He looked as though he hadn't shaved for a few days, his chin dark with stubble.

Perhaps sensing she was looking at him, he turned his head and stared straight back, causing Hannah to drop her eyes guiltily. She cursed her own curiosity. Now he'd think she was interested in him when she was anything but. She scrambled to her feet. 'I'm going to see what Harry is up to. Goodnight, Mr Gaffney. Thanks again for the damper!'

Without waiting for his reply, she hurried away towards the homestead.

Harry looked up from his whittling as she arrived on the steps of the veranda. 'Ray scare you off?' He gave a little chuckle. 'He can be a bit full-on.' Seeing her frown, he added, 'Serious. Intense. But he's a good bloke, is Ray. He lets me do stuff that Dad won't. Dad gives me all the dull jobs even though I know I could do much more.'

Hannah smiled. 'Better than being at school though?'

'Deffo.'

'My late husband had it far worse. His dad made him work in a coal mine. Will hated every minute. Being underground in the dark. He only got through it, thanks to your dad.'

'Sorry about your husband. Mum said he was killed at sea by a German dive-bomber.' Harry looked impressed. 'He must have been really brave.'

Hannah gave him a sad smile. 'He was. He died trying to help another man.' She bit her lip.

'Mum used to be married to his dad.' He thought for a moment. 'Does that make you my stepsister-in-law or my cousin?'

'Probably both, but let's settle for cousin. My *only* cousin. Very special.'

She pointed at the wood he was chipping at with his penknife. 'Will used to do that too when he lived in Australia. Someone gave me a little kangaroo he carved.' She reached into her pocket and pulled the figure out to show him.

Harry whistled. 'Wow! That's bonzer. I wish I was as good as that.'

'You will be if you keep practising.' She chuckled. 'As your mum keeps saying to me about the piano.'

'You're much better than I ever was. Mum gave up on me in the end!' He got to his feet. 'I'd better keep old Ray company. I'm hoping he might sneak me a beer while Dad isn't around. You coming?'

'Thanks, but I'm going to have an early night. All this country air makes me sleepy. I'll see you tomorrow.'

'Don't forget about the shearing. You must come and watch.'

'I wouldn't miss it for the world.'

As she spoke, her aunt and uncle emerged from the house, hand-in-hand. 'You not coming to join us?' asked Michael. 'We're going to have a beer by the fire with Ray.'

'I'm a little chilly. I've decided to turn in early. Want to be up bright and early for the shearing. See you in the morning.'

Back in her room, Hannah asked herself why she'd fled. Ray Gaffney had been perfectly civil and yet she'd been nervous in his presence. Perhaps it was a reluctance to be alone with a man again after her experience with Eddie. And if she were honest, she'd resented his intrusion into her solitary wallowing in her memories of Will.

NEXT MORNING, Hannah went with Elizabeth to the shearing shed, each carrying baskets with flasks of coffee and enamel mugs.

It was a different atmosphere from when Harry had shown her around the day after she arrived. The holding pens were full of hungry sheep, bleating in a noisy chorus, and the air buzzed with the hum of electric shears. On the board, Michael and Ray, together with two men Hannah hadn't seen before, were shearing. Harry moved between them, gathering up the fleeces and tossing them deftly onto a table, where one of the land girls removed the outer edges of what Hannah now knew was called 'the skirt' and crammed these scraps into bales for sale as low grade wool. After this trimming operation, the girls moved the fleeces into the wool press, where one of them climbed on top and stamped them down. When full, they pulled a lever and the pressing machine compressed the wool into bales, a third of their original size, ready for transportation.

There was a distinctive smell in the shed: the odour of the sheep themselves and their manure, the strong waxy scent of lanolin, and the sweat from the men.

Hannah watched, fascinated, as the shears swept over each sheep, starting at the belly, meticulously removing the wool in one complete piece. She couldn't help watching Ray Gaffney. He entered the pen, grabbed a sheep by a leg with his one arm and dragged it on its back onto the board. Clamping the struggling ewe between his knees, he began to shear with his right arm, one leg under the left armpit held in place with his stump. Hannah gazed, transfixed, as the shearing comb swept up through the wool, detaching the fleece from the body with long strokes – or as Harry corrected her, 'blows'. Beads of sweat formed on his forehead and his face was a grim mask of concentration. His leg muscles must have been like rocks as he kept the sheep firmly in place, lifting the shears momentarily so he could use his arm to manoeuvre the sheep into a different position. Hannah was incredulous. Despite his handicap, Ray managed to shear a sheep as fast or faster than the other men – in just a few minutes. She stood beside Elizabeth, awestruck, as the shears buzzed and the pile of fleeces grew larger.

One of the land girls exchanged and sharpened the shearing combs, each needing to be sharpened several times over the course of the day. In between gathering the fleeces, Harry ran between the shearers, responding to the occasional call of, 'Tar!' and applied a brushstroke of tar from a jar onto any wounds or nicks made by the shears. The pot was rarely required, as once the men wrangled their sheep

into position, most of the animals were calm and coop-
erative.

Hannah and Elizabeth poured coffee and moved around
the shed, handing out mugs to each of the workers. The
men paused to drink after finishing the sheep they were
working on. Hannah held out a mug to Ray Gaffney, who
pulled off his hat first and wiped the sweat from his brow
before taking the mug with a muttered thanks and an appre-
ciative nod.

'Who are the other shearers?' she asked Elizabeth.

'Local farmers. Grant Johnson and Dave Carmichael.
Michael and Ray did the same for them a couple of weeks
back. Before the war, we had several local shearers who
worked their way around the Hunter Valley and then did
odd jobs out of season. But most of them have either joined
up or have moved south or to the Tablelands to the big
stations where there's more shearing work.'

When the work was complete, there was a supper for the
shearers and land girls, prepared by Elizabeth with
Hannah's help and with the wives of the two other farmers
bringing more dishes.

'We do this every year after the last shearing, and it's our
turn to host this time.'

The weather being mild, a long trestle table was set up
on the grass between the house and the shearing shed and
they all gathered around it. A piece of beef had been
roasting on a spit, its aroma making everyone salivate with
hunger all afternoon.

After laying the table, Hannah heard voices in the
shearing shed. Curious, as the work had finished, she went
across and stood in the doorway. Ray Gaffney was squatting
on his haunches next to Harry who was standing beside a
sheep. She watched, unseen by the two who were both

concentrating on the task in hand, as Ray gently coached Harry in his efforts.

'Even with two hands and arms, the most important and hardest part to master is your legs. Unless I'm sure you can safely control the sheep with them I won't let you have a shearing comb in your hands.' He nodded to Harry. 'Ready? Turn her head round now and get her on her back and into your first position.'

Harry's face was a mask of concentration as he manipulated the sheep until it was sitting upright on the board, its back wedged between his legs.

'That's it, nice and easy. Don't distress her. Talk to her. She'll stay still as long as she knows you're in control.' Ray's tone was gentle and reassuring. 'Now, get her fleece off as quickly and smoothly as possible and in the right order. No rushing. Pick up the shears. Gently, lad. Use your left hand to pull the skin tight as you shear so you won't catch the skin folds and nick her.'

Hannah continued to watch, impressed by Ray's quiet and supportive tone. 'Right. Change position now. Exactly as we've practised it. Remember the direction of the blows. We've been over this so many times, I'll bet you can do it in your sleep.'

Hannah was fascinated as Ray broke down each stage and she understood the complex choreography of the operation as Harry manoeuvred the animal and his own body into different positions to accommodate each part of the sheep's anatomy. The longer she watched, the more impressed she was with Ray Gaffney's own performance when shearing, as she now understood how the left hand played as important a role as the right. This had been something Ray had achieved by lifting his shearing hand off to stretch the skin, clamping it with his legs, before lowering the shears again. She hadn't appreciated that when she'd seen him that afternoon.

'Nearer you get to the end, more likely she is to struggle. The weight of the detached part of the fleece drags on her skin.'

Harry reached the end of the shearing, stepped back and let the newly shorn sheep scamper away. Hannah spontaneously applauded. Ray turned around and his face lit up.

'Well done, Harry!' Hannah said. But she had also been impressed with the skill, kindness and patience of Ray Gaffney.

WHEN HANNAH and her aunt finished ferrying the side dishes from the homestead kitchen, the only available space for Hannah to sit was next to Sally, one of the land girls, a big rather loud-voiced woman with a wide smile and a friendly open manner. She was about Hannah's age and told her she was from Queensland, where she'd been working in a hotel kitchen before joining the land army. On Hannah's other side was Ray Gaffney. Opposite them was the other landgirl, Violet, whom Hannah had also met on that first morning before her threatened miscarriage. She gave Hannah a shy smile.

Conscious of Ray's missing arm, Hannah passed bowls of vegetables to him, holding them while he served himself. She wondered whether she ought to offer to cut his meat for him but, like the shearing, Ray had mastered a one-handed technique. She sensed he wouldn't appreciate anything that drew attention to his handicap.

For most of the meal she chatted to Sally, asking her about Queensland and her family, hearing about her boyfriend who was serving in Europe, and their plans to marry after the war. Not for the first time, Hannah mused about how often conversations were peppered with the words 'after the war'. Who knew when that might be? She remembered how Eddie had said it was certain the Allies would prevail, but it would be a long, hard haul to victory.

When Sally started chatting to the wife of one of the shearers, Hannah turned to Ray. 'You were so kind and patient with Harry today.'

'He's a good lad.'

There was a protracted silence then Ray said, 'First time seeing a shearing? What ya think?'

'Impressive. You all work so fast...' She felt herself colouring. What was obviously unsaid was his handling an already tough job with only his right arm.

Ray looked at her steadily. 'I'm slower than I used to be. Two and a half minutes a sheep when it used to be two. I'm working on it.'

'It must have taken such effort. What even made you try? Most people wouldn't.'

He stared at her, his gaze rather unnerving. 'Everyone said it couldn't be done. Nothing makes me more determined than someone telling me I can't do something. I have to work out a way to do it. Nothing in this world that can't be done if you've a mind to do it and a belief in yourself.'

'Harry said you were injured in the fighting in the desert.'

He was silent for a moment, and she wondered if she'd been insensitive in bringing it up.

Ray swigged some beer from the bottle. 'Didn't get to see much of it. The desert. Or the fighting.' He took another gulp of beer. 'Copped a stray grenade on the first day in combat. I was driving a lorry loaded with prisoners. Most of the buggers carked it when the grenade hit us. Poor devils had been relieved when we captured them. Looking forward to getting away from the front. Five minutes later, all but one of them blown to bits.'

'I'm sorry that happened to you.'

He shrugged. 'Life goes on. Better than the alternative.'

She swallowed, staring at her plate.

'Sorry,' he said. 'Thoughtless of me. You lost your man at sea, I heard.'

Hannah nodded.

'How long you married?'

'Only fifteen months.'

'Jeez. Rough. Still, you'll have the bub soon.'

She squeezed her hand into a fist, the nails biting into her palm. 'It's not his. He died almost two years ago.' As soon as she'd said it she cursed herself for sharing such a confidence. It had just spilled out.

Around them, the conversation at the table continued. Ray said nothing for a few moments. 'I'm not doing well tonight. Tactless is my middle name.' He smiled in apology, but the smile didn't reach his eyes.

'You couldn't be expected to know.'

'You mean it's none of my business.'

She said nothing.

'Life's tough for a single mother.' He put his fork down and pushed his plate away. 'My old man died when I was thirteen. Tuberculosis. We had to sell the family farm. My mother took in washing and cleaned houses. What do you plan to do?'

She gave a long sigh. 'I don't know. I try not to think about it. Elizabeth and Michael say I can stay here. To be honest, I have no one else. My sister has a husband and a baby and can't take me in – even if I wanted to live with her, which I don't.'

'What about the father?'

'He's dead too.'

'Jeez, you have had it bad.' He pulled a cigarette out of his sleeve and lit it, blowing the smoke upwards.

Keen to steer the conversation away from herself and not wanting his pity, Hannah changed the subject. 'Do you think you'll ever go back to New Zealand?'

'Nothing to go back for. I threw my lot in with Mick Winterbourne long ago, and I owe him everything.' He drew deeply on his cigarette. 'When's the bub due?'

'Late November.'

He looked thoughtful but said nothing. At the other end of the table, Harry was speaking, urging his parents about something. Hannah couldn't hear what he was saying above the hum of conversation and Sally's loud laughter. Hannah looked across the table at Violet, who immediately looked away. Elizabeth went inside the house and emerged carrying her violin.

'Come on, Ray!' called Harry. 'You can't leave Dad to sing on his own.'

As the notes from the violin filled the air, the talking stopped, and one of the neighbouring farmers pulled out a guitar and joined in with Elizabeth's fiddle. Michael's tenor voice began to sing, soon joined by Ray harmonising with a rich baritone. The song was an old Australian shearing song, 'Click Go the Shears', and everyone, including the land girls, joined in on the chorus.

> Click go the shears, boys, click, click, click,
> Wide is his blow and his hands move
> quick,
> The ringer looks around and is beaten
> by a blow,

And curses the old snagger with the
bare-bellied yoe.

Hannah listened with delight, the awkwardness of her conversation with Ray forgotten.

When the song ended, they went straight into a rendition of 'The Wild Colonial Boy'. Then the land girls got to their feet and launched into 'Along the Road to Gundagai'. Michael took up the challenge of singing a song from where he came from and gave a spirited version of 'D'ye Ken John Peel.'

Hannah let the music wash over her, a warm glow inside. She began to feel drowsy and slipped away from the table as they started on 'Waltzing Matilda'.

Soon in bed, Hannah drifted off to sleep to the sounds of 'The Wild Rover', while breathing in the scent of the mock-orange plants outside her open window.

24

The following morning, Hannah awoke feeling guilty at having left Elizabeth to clear up after the party. Since giving up shift work and discovering her pregnancy, she no longer had the stamina for late nights. She hoped her aunt would have left everything until morning, but when she went into the kitchen, it was pristine. A glance through the window showed the trestle table had gone from the lawn, leaving no evidence of the large gathering the previous evening.

Elizabeth was already in the kitchen, apron on, ready for another day. She dropped a kiss on Hannah's cheek. 'Good morning, Hannah. I hope we didn't keep you awake last night?'

'I went out like a light as soon as my head touched the pillow. How late did you stay up?' Hannah suppressed a yawn.

'Not long. We had a few more songs after you went to bed, then the van collected the girls and the party broke up.'

'You were left alone to do the dishes?' Hannah was mortified.

Elizabeth smiled, reached out a hand and stroked her niece's hair. 'Don't worry. Thelma and Audrey gave me a hand,' she said, referring to the wives of the other farmers. 'We always pitch in and help each other.'

Hannah thought about the previous evening – the camaraderie around the table, the hearty food and the singing. She felt a contentment and sense of belonging she hadn't experienced since arriving in Australia. 'It was a wonderful evening. I really enjoyed it.'

Elizabeth beamed as she took down a frying pan from a hook above the stove, ready to cook their breakfast.

Hannah put on an apron, moved behind her aunt and took hold of the pan. 'I'm doing this. Otherwise, I'll forget how. You've already cooked breakfast for Michael and Harry. It's my turn now.'

'The doc said you need to rest.'

'The doc also said a little light exercise will do me good.'

Elizabeth frowned, shaking her head. 'I don't think he meant standing up in front of a hot stove, young lady.' She put her hands on her niece's shoulders and steered her into a chair. 'Let me look after you. It's what I want to do.'

Hannah grimaced. 'I feel useless.'

'Don't. I'm doing nothing I don't normally do. Your priority is to take care of yourself and your baby. Now, no more discussion.' Elizabeth narrowed her eyes and pulled a mock-angry face.

After breakfast, Hannah went off to do the egg gathering. What was she going to do once the baby was here? She loved being at Hunter's Down, and it was a huge relief to have a place to stay when she gave birth, but despite Elizabeth's insistence that she would always have a home here, she didn't consider that to be an option. How could she expect the Winterbournes to house and care for her and her baby for the indefinite future when she had no means of supporting herself? Her vague plan of offering the baby for adoption was less appealing since her miscarriage scare – and she dreaded the child ending up unwanted in an orphanage, mindful of what Betty had said about her terrible childhood experiences in one.

The previous night, Ray Gaffney had spoken of his mother's hardship as a widow with a child – but Ray had been thirteen, not a helpless baby. In a rush of annoyance with herself, Hannah remembered she'd told Ray the baby wasn't Will's. The entire district would assume she was a woman of low morals. While Ray didn't seem the kind of man to share idle gossip, she didn't know the fellow well and shouldn't have entrusted him with such a confidence. There had been something about the evening: the genial atmosphere around the table; the singing. And Ray had been open about what had happened to him in the desert, even though Harry had said he didn't like to talk about it. She'd been lulled into a false sense of security and said things she now regretted.

Setting aside the egg basket, she sat down on a wooden bench at the side of the barn and thought about her future. The only practical solution was to have the baby here at Hunter's Down and stay until it was weaned, making herself as useful as possible to earn her keep. After that, could she return to Sydney and find work, paying Dot to mind the baby? A job paying enough to cover rent and child-minding sounded unlikely. Her salary at the solicitors' had covered her rent and a little spending money but wouldn't go far with a child to clothe and feed – even were a vacancy to arise, which would only happen after the war, if at all. There it was again. That refrain – *after the war*. Now she was adding another line to the chorus – *after the baby comes*.

She stood up with a sigh and made her way back to the house.

'What a glum face,' said Elizabeth as Hannah entered the kitchen. 'What's wrong?'

Hannah slumped down onto a chair. 'I can't help worrying about the future. How I'll cope with a baby.'

'You'll be a wonderful mother.'

'I didn't mean caring for the baby but supporting it. I can't stay here indefinitely.'

'Yes, you can. I love having you here. Michael and Harry feel that way too. You're company for me. And most of all, you're family.' Elizabeth sat down at the kitchen table, reached for Hannah's hand and held it between both of hers. 'Stop trying to manage the future. You'll feel different when the baby's born. There's no point in overthinking at this stage. It'll make you anxious, and you know what the doc said about relaxing.'

Hannah looked away. 'I can't help it. I spent my life looking after Judith, and I'm not used to anyone looking after me.'

'What about Will?'

'Of course, he did. But you know what I mean. Besides, he was away at sea so much.' She looked through the window over the green meadows where the newly shorn sheep were grazing. 'I always knew he was there for me though. Until he wasn't anymore. Now I feel helpless. Dependent. And I hate feeling like that.' She compressed her lips. 'I've been thinking maybe I could get a job in Sydney and pay Dot, my old landlady, to look after the baby.'

'You could, I suppose.' Elizabeth frowned. 'But it doesn't sound like much of a life. What about Eddie's parents? Have you thought any more about asking them for help? I'm sure once they know they have a grandchild, they'll want you and the baby in their lives.'

Hannah didn't think they would. The mention of them reminded her that returning to Sydney would risk her running into the old gang again. After falling out with Mark, she couldn't face that. It would be going backwards rather than moving ahead.

'I'll put on some coffee.' Elizabeth got up and bustled about, putting the kettle onto boil. Brew made, she sat down again and looked Hannah in the eye. 'Don't rule out the possibility of meeting someone and marrying again.'

Hannah bristled, glaring at her aunt.

'Hear me out. I realise Will was the love of your life, just as Michael is mine. But it is possible to build a future and achieve contentment, even without love. I loathed Jack Kidd when I was forced to marry him, and nothing he did at first gave me any reason to change my mind. He was taciturn, rude, and secretive. Much older than me. Unattractive. We had nothing in common. Yet he gave a home to me and Mikey, accepting him as his own. We had Susanna together, grieved the loss of the children together. I never loved him, couldn't love him. But over time I grew to understand and respect him. By the end, I'd even become fond of him. Honestly, Hannah, when I was forced into marrying him, I thought it was the end of the world. It wasn't.'

Hannah frowned. 'What are you saying? How is this relevant to me? No one's forcing me to marry anyone.'

'I'm just saying that even without that all-consuming, head-over-heels love you had with Will, don't rule out the possibility of finding a good kind man and over time building a happy life with him.'

Hannah stared at her before answering. 'When I came to Australia, I decided I'd build a life for myself on my own. I didn't imagine then there'd be a baby. And I still think my best option may well be to give it up for adoption. But whatever I do, I'd rather build a life for myself than with some man I feel nothing for.' She rose from the table, leaving her coffee untouched. 'I need some fresh air. I'm going for a walk. See you later.'

She left the house, fighting back tears. Elizabeth meant well but why did she assume Hannah must be like her? She strode along, heading away from the house, not thinking where she was going, desperate to put some distance between herself and her aunt.

After several minutes, she saw a cluster of gum trees ahead on a steep grassy slope. The sun was warm, and the trees would offer some shade, as she'd come out without a hat. As she walked, she replayed the conversation, growing angry. Then, with a sharp intake of breath, she realised her anger should be directed at herself for getting into this situation – not at Elizabeth. Her aunt was offering her a home. What was the point of taking umbrage at the suggestion of remarriage when it wasn't even a remote possibility?

She'd been walking briskly and was hot and perspiring, so the shade of the trees, once she reached them, were a welcome respite. The ground sloped away more steeply than she'd expected, so she had to grab onto a tree trunk to avoid slipping and falling. Slowly, she worked her way down the slope from tree to tree until, at the bottom, she came upon a large rock formation. Following its perimeter, she reached a pool of water surrounded by casuarina and gum trees with a waterfall cascading from the rocky outcrop.

Hannah gasped with pleasure. Bending down, she dipped a hand in the water. It was cold and crystal clear. This could be a perfect place for a cooling dip in summer – even now on a warm day in early spring it was tempting.

She sat on a flat slab of rock at the edge of the pool, shaded by the casuarinas, her anger after the conversation with Elizabeth forgotten.

She took off her shoes and, with her feet in the pool, listened to the sound of the birds. High-pitched squawks were repeated by the same sound from a different location, in a perfect echo. Looking up, she saw a flash of vivid colours. Rainbow lorikeets. After almost a year in Australia, she still took delight in the brilliance of the exotic wild birds.

After a while, Hannah got up, slipped her wet feet into her sandals and made her way around the pool to where a stream flowed out. Following a narrow path beside the stream, she eventually emerged from the trees. The ground rose gently above her with a clear pathway. Less steep than the route she'd taken to get here, it took her back to the same starting point. Slightly longer but much easier than clinging from tree to tree, and firmer underfoot.

Arriving back at the farmyard, she found Harry sawing planks of wood. He paused as she approached, wiping the sweat from his brow. 'G'day Hannah! How you going?'

'I've been for a walk. I discovered a beautiful pool with a waterfall.'

Harry grinned. 'The little billabong. You had a dip?'

'Just my feet. Is it deep?'

'Only the part closest to the waterfall. Me and my pal Bob used to jump off it, but the rest of it's only four or five feet deep.'

'Do you often swim there?'

'Nah. There's another natural pool much closer – just beyond the home paddock. We've got a diving board there and a jetty. Dad built them as Mum didn't like me jumping off the top of the waterfall. It's a much bigger pool, and better for swimming. I'll show you sometime.'

Hannah thanked him but knew she'd prefer the quiet isolation of the pool she'd found herself.

'What are you making?'

'Fence panels.'

'Then I'll let you get on. See you at lunchtime – which is probably soon.'

She walked back to the house, ready to make her peace with her aunt.

THAT NIGHT AFTER DINNER, Hannah went to her room and found her swimming costume at the bottom of a drawer. The gift from Shirley now fitted tightly, stretching at the seams. She'd have to let it out. Skirted bathing costumes were in fashion, according to a women's magazine she'd glanced through at Dot's. Perhaps she could insert a panel at the front and disguise it with an overskirt made from a slip. Not that she needed to bother. No one was going to see her in it if she used the little billabong to swim.

She'd make the adjustments tomorrow when the light was better. Hannah wished she had half the talent for sewing that Judith, who'd once been a seamstress, had. Yesterday, she'd finally plucked up the courage to write to her sister and tell her about the pregnancy. She was sure Judith, who had conceived Sarah before marrying, would be sympathetic to her plight. Yet it had been a hard letter to write. Judith looked up to her and Hannah had always been the sensible adult in their relationship.

. . .

THE FOLLOWING AFTERNOON, Elizabeth, armed with her ration coupons, planned to go into Hazelton to do some grocery shopping. She asked Hannah if she wanted to come too, but Hannah said she'd prefer to go for a walk.

'Of course. Bouncing about in the cart on rough tracks isn't a good idea. I can take the ute instead if you'd like to come.'

'Thanks, but I'll leave it till next week when I have the appointment with the nurse.'

'I forgot to mention. It won't be me taking you that day as I've promised Audrey I'll help with her bake sale for the war effort. Michael or Ray will run you into town in the ute.'

Hannah put her hands up in protest. 'I don't want to interrupt their work. I can change the appointment.'

'No, you can't. Anyway, they always have stuff to pick up at the hardware store. It's no trouble. And it gives them an excuse for a beer and a catch-up with other farmers in the pub.'

Hannah asked her aunt if she'd mind posting the letter to Judith.

Once Elizabeth had gone, Hannah undressed and slipped into the swimsuit she'd altered that morning, pulling on a loose cotton dress over the top.

Half an hour later, she was standing beside the rock pool. She slipped off her dress, laid it beside her towel and sat on the edge of the flat boulder where she'd been yesterday, dangling her legs in the water. The cold water on her skin after the warmth of the afternoon was bracing. The thermometer attached to the barn wall had been showing the high seventies when she looked that morning whereas the previous week it had been in the sixties. This was the Australian springtime – by the time the baby was due in late November, it would likely be extremely hot. She shuddered at the prospect of carrying all that extra weight as the mercury rose and going through labour in the appalling heat.

Just as she was about to ease herself into the water, the thought of the baby made her hesitate. Her recent miscarriage scare made her extra cautious, despite Harry's assertion that the pool wasn't terribly deep. She lacked confidence in water, despite Eddie's efforts. Perhaps she ought to consult the doctor first. Might cold water be harmful to the baby? She didn't want to risk another episode. Next time she might not be so lucky.

Yet a miscarriage would solve her dilemma. She'd be free to find a job. She could earn her keep here on the farm, return to Sydney – or even move to Melbourne.

Her hands went to her stomach. As she did, she felt the baby move inside her. How could she put this child at risk? Without further thought, she swung her legs out of the water and dried them off with a towel. Sliding further up the boulder, into the shade, she picked up her book and began to read.

It was Somerset Maugham's *Cakes and Ale.* She'd found it on the bookshelf in her bedroom. She was finding the book irritating, with the supercilious narrator's tedious observations on literary London. It felt old-fashioned and irrelevant. The world had changed radically since it was published. She did take some comfort regarding her own morals, in the light of Maugham's character, Rosie Driffield, who, if she liked someone, had no hesitation whatsoever about hopping into bed with them. Charming as Rosie was, she was a character on the pages of a book and Hannah didn't want to behave that way. She could forgive herself for what had happened with Eddie, but she wouldn't ever repeat that mistake. Nor would she be giving further thought to what Elizabeth had said about marrying again.

There was one thing that her aunt had raised that perhaps she oughtn't brush aside. Having lost a daughter and a son, wouldn't Eddie's parents want to know they had a grandchild? Her baby would grow up without a father – was she justified in insisting they grew up without grandparents too? And might the existence of a child help mitigate the pain of Eddie's loss? It ought to – yet she had serious doubts.

Hannah pulled her frock and shoes back on and made her way slowly back to the house.

WRITING to Eddie's parents was one of the hardest things Hannah had ever had to do. She had never met the Greenbanks and instinctively sensed they wouldn't welcome her approach.

Unaware of the judge's name or initials, she addressed the envelope to The Honourable Mr and Mrs Greenbank. The letter took several drafts before she was satisfied with the wording.

Dear Judge and Mrs Greenbank,

We have never been introduced. I was a friend of your late son, Eddie. Please accept my sincere condolences for his loss, which I heard about only recently.

Eddie and I had a brief relationship – lasting little more than a few weeks and culminating in a weekend spent together before he went to join his regiment.

It is hard for me to tell you this and I have struggled whether to tell you at all, as the last thing I want to do is cause you more pain at such a difficult time, but I am expecting to give birth to Eddie's child in late November. I realise this will come as a shock, and I want you to know that I will respect your decision as to how much – if any – involvement or contact you wish to have with me and your grandchild.

I am staying with relatives and cannot be in Sydney at present, but you can write to me at this address, and I will endeavour to answer any questions you may have. Once the baby is born and we can travel, I am of course willing to meet with you at your convenience, should you so wish.

Once again, my deepest sympathies.

Yours sincerely,

Hannah Kidd.

After reading it through, she decided not to use the judge's title since this was a personal and not a professional matter, and it might make matters worse if she used the wrong form of address because she didn't know what type of judge he was. Better to assume she wasn't aware he was a judge at all. She rewrote it as Dear Mr and Mrs Greenbank. If she'd committed a dreadful faux pas, so be it.

Palms sweating, she folded the letter and sealed it in the envelope. She would post it when she went into Hazelton to visit the clinic.

BEFORE SENDING the letter to the Greenbanks, Hannah received a reply from Judith – the only time she'd ever replied by return. Elizabeth was outside working in the vegetable plot she cared for with skill and relish. Hannah went into her bedroom, where she read the letter with dismay and disbelief. She'd expected Judith to show some empathy, having herself fallen pregnant before Paolo was rounded up and interned as an enemy alien. She, of all people should have understood her situation.

Dear Hannah,

I am still reeling from the shock of reading your letter.

How could you sleep with a man you barely knew and didn't care for? What a thing to do, and so soon after the death of poor Will. I am so disappointed in you. I don't know how I am going to tell Paolo. He will be horrified that you could betray his dear friend's memory in such a way.

How can you possibly expect to bring up a baby on your own? I suppose you will have it adopted? Since the father is dead, have you spoken to his family? Maybe they can bring up the child. It's the least they can do when their son has been so irresponsible.

I suppose you'll say I had Sarah before being married, but it was completely different. I <u>loved</u> Paolo and had every expectation of marrying him. You slept with a man you had already decided you didn't want to marry.

I never expected this from you, Hannah. I've always looked up to you and put you on a pedestal. I thought you were a responsible person with strong morals. My sensible sister. I don't know how I will ever get over this disappointment in you. But I suppose I must.

I hope you realise it is out of the question for you to come here with a baby. The Clancys can't be expected to have a newborn in the house. But once it's adopted, it would probably be a good idea for you to come back to Tatura. I don't think Sydney is a suitable place for you on your own. I still don't understand why you abandoned us to go there in the first place.

Sarah has cut another tooth.

Judith

Hannah screwed the letter up into a tight ball and threw it across the room. How many times had she overlooked Judith's selfishness? How many times had she protected her sister from their father's wrath? Hannah had given up the job she loved and everything she'd known in Liverpool to accompany her sister to Australia and support her in her efforts to be reunited with Paolo. She had held Judith's hand when she gave birth to Sarah and never once lectured her about morality. Now she had no choice but to face up to her instincts and acknowledge that her sister was not only immature and unsympathetic but was a narcissist. She took out the small folder in which she kept Judith's infrequent letters. Reading through them again, a pattern emerged. Her sister never showed any interest in Hannah's life or her well-being. Nor had she expressed the slightest interest in hearing about their aunt. For the first time, Hannah felt sorry for Paolo and hoped he would fare better.

Taking the folder of letters, along with the most recent one, she went into the kitchen, lifted the lid of the firebox on the range and stuffed the papers inside to burn.

25

Hannah didn't mention Judith's snub, nor tell her aunt that she had written to the Greenbanks, preferring to wait and see what response it elicited first.

The following day, Ray Gaffney drew up in front of the house forty minutes before her scheduled appointment at the clinic and told Hannah he would be driving her into Hazelton. As she eased herself into the seat next to him in the small utility truck, Hannah wondered how he managed to drive with only one hand. She found out that he simply took his hand off the steering wheel when he needed to change gear and reached across it to reach the gear stick. Unnerved at first, Hannah relaxed as he was so calm and confident.

After some minutes' silence, he said, 'You thought anymore about what you'll do when the bub's here? Maybe I'm wrong, but you don't seem to be a woman who's willing to depend on others.' He kept his eyes fixed straight ahead on the road.

'Probably go back to Sydney and look for a job.'

He raised an eyebrow. 'With a baby?'

'My former landlady may agree to mind it while I'm working. Or there's always adoption.' As Hannah uttered the words, she knew she no longer considered adoption an option. She was tempted to tell him to mind his own business, but Ray Gaffney appeared to be genuinely concerned. She sensed that it was unusual for him to ask questions like this. 'I suppose I'll cross that bridge when I come to it,' she added.

They drove on in silence. Eventually, she turned to him. 'Mind if I ask *you* a question?'

He shrugged, which she took that as a sign to press on.

'Why don't you eat with the family? I mean, you're on your own since the land girls go back to camp each night.'

Ray gave a little grunt. 'They've asked me often enough, but I learnt to look after myself when I was a kid. My mother was working, so I used to get the tea ready when I got home from school. As a stockman, you get used to camping out, to preparing your own tucker over a campfire – there's a kitchen of sorts in the shearers' block where I live.'

'Doesn't it get lonely?'

Another grunt. 'I spend all day with Mick and the lad, so I'm happy enough to be on my own the rest of the time. And there's Rocky for company.' He jerked his head towards the open truck bed behind them, where the dog was settled on an old blanket.

'What do you do in the evenings?' She was genuinely curious now.

'Sometimes go into Hazelton for a couple of beers and a game of cards. Sleep. By the time I've cooked and eaten my meal, I'm ready for bed most nights. Suits me.'

Hannah turned away to gaze out of the window. It all

sounded rather sad. Lonely. She couldn't help but feel sorry for him.

After a few moments, Ray spoke again. 'Sometimes I sit and dream. Make plans. One day, I'll have my own place. Find a wife. Start a family. If I can find a woman who isn't put off by a one-armed man.'

Hannah twisted round to look at him, indignant on his behalf. 'Why should anyone mind? You lost your arm serving your country.'

'You'd be surprised.' He gave a humourless chuckle. 'I was seeing a woman before I shipped out to Egypt. We'd not made any promises, but we had an understanding. When I came back like this, she was gone in a flash. Married a schoolmaster in Newcastle. That was that.' He kept his gaze on the road ahead.

'I'm sorry.' Hannah wished she hadn't embarked on this conversation. They lapsed into silence until they reached the small town, where he dropped her off at the doctor's surgery.

AT THE CLINIC, when the routine tests were complete, Hannah asked whether it would be safe for her to go swimming and was reassured that she could. The nurse said it wouldn't be harmful for the baby and was a good way to get some gentle exercise. 'No jumping or diving though, and don't overdo it!'

Afterwards, Hannah strolled up the street to post the letter to the Greenbanks. As she handed it over, she felt a jolt of anxiety about how it would be received. Too late to change her mind now.

When she emerged from the post office, Ray Gaffney

was outside, leaning against the ute, smoking. 'You done?' he asked.

She nodded. 'How about you?'

'Yep.' He moved his head towards the open back of the vehicle, where a pile of wooden planks were now stashed. 'That'll keep Harry busy for a while.' He ground his cigarette under his heel. 'You don't mind if Rocky's up front with us?'

She said she didn't, and the dog settled in the space between them.

'Let's go then.'

It was hot in the vehicle, so they opened the windows and let the air rush in.

Hannah raised her voice to be heard above the engine noise. 'I enjoyed the shearers' supper the other night. You have a lovely singing voice.'

Ray continued to gaze at the road ahead, gave a shrug but said nothing.

Persisting, she added, 'You should join a choir. You and Michael both.'

A hint of a smile played around his mouth but quickly vanished. 'Not the joining type.'

Not one for small talk either, she thought.

The rest of the drive back to Hunter's Down was spent without conversation. Ray kept his eyes fixed on the road, a cigarette dangling from his lips. They were almost back at the farm when he spoke.

'Go all right, did it? The check-up?'

Surprised, she told him it was just routine.

'Nothing to worry about then?'

'I hope not.'

'So whatever they had to call the doc for is sorted out now?' He continued staring ahead, avoiding eye contact.

Hannah's cheeks were burning and she looked down at her lap and the swelling above it. 'Yes, everything is in order. The baby's fine.'

He made no reply.

They drove on, and Hannah was relieved when Ray pulled into the driveway and stopped to drop her off in front of the house.

'G'day,' he said. Without waiting for her to respond, he released the handbrake and drove off towards the outbuildings where the ute was kept.

As SHE WENT UP into the house, Hannah heard the strains of the violin. She found her aunt in the drawing room, standing in front of her music stand. As Hannah entered, Elizabeth broke off at once.

'No! Don't stop!'

'I was about to call a halt anyway. It's time to get the dinner ready. How did you get on, my love?'

'All good. The nurse was very kind. She said everything appears to be in order – blood pressure, baby's heartbeat, temperature and pulse – and my weight's on track too.' She didn't mention the swimming, as something told her Elizabeth might not be so sanguine about it. Hannah was relishing the prospect of spending time in what she now thought of as her own special place.

She followed her aunt into the kitchen and set about cleaning and chopping the vegetables for the evening meal.

'How did you get along with Ray?' Elizabeth studied her intently.

Hannah felt herself blushing, annoyed at the question. 'It's extraordinary how he drives with only one arm.'

Elizabeth tilted her head in agreement. 'It is. Nothing

defeats that man. What did you talk about?' The tone of her voice was casual, but her eyes, as she fixed them on Hannah's, were alert.

'This and that. Not much, to be honest.' Was Elizabeth intent on nurturing a relationship between her and Ray? Hannah hoped not.

'Ray's not much of a talker, but he seemed to get along well with you at the shearers' supper.'

Hannah's shoulders tensed. So, her aunt had been watching them!

'Come on, what did you talk about?'

Conceding she'd need to offer something to satisfy her aunt's curiosity, she said, 'He asked what my plans are for after the baby comes.'

The grin widened. 'What did you tell him?'

Hannah frowned. 'That I haven't any yet. I'm taking each day as it comes.'

'Good. That's the best thing to do.'

They busied themselves preparing the evening meal, but Elizabeth began her questioning again as she made pastry. It felt like an interrogation, even though she spoke with a light, chatty tone.

'Did Ray mention his arm?'

'He told me how it happened at the supper. It's marvellous that he doesn't let it hold him back. I was nervous about him driving at first, but he's so competent and confident.'

Elizabeth smiled. 'He is, isn't he?'

'He did mention that he thought it put some people off.' She hesitated for a moment. 'He said his girlfriend broke up with him because of it.' She picked up a carrot and started to peel it. 'I can't believe it was because of the arm though.

That would be awfully heartless since he lost it defending King and country.'

Elizabeth nodded. 'Pam Jennings.'

'Did you know her?' Hannah's curiosity was piqued.

'Not well. She's the daughter of the auctioneer at the sheep market. I gather she started seeing the man she's now married to soon after Ray went to the Middle East. Everyone assumed it was a flirtation and nothing serious. Sure enough, she was waiting to meet Ray when he arrived back in Australia. Travelled to Sydney to see him in hospital.'

Elizabeth laid a rolled-out sheet of pastry dough over the top of the pie, trimmed the edges and put it in the oven. 'As soon as it was clear they couldn't save his arm, Pam was off. She took up again with the schoolteacher and married him not long after Ray was discharged.'

'Poor chap. You really think it was because of his missing arm?'

Elizabeth shrugged. 'Ray certainly thinks so, and he should know.'

'It was heartless of her if that was truly the only reason. But perhaps if she'd been seeing the other man, she realised he was "the one" when she saw Ray again. It might have had nothing to do with the missing arm.'

'Whatever the reason, it knocked Ray for six.'

The discussion about Ray Gaffney ended when Harry burst into the kitchen. 'Mum, can I cycle over to see Bob after we've eaten? His uncle's up from Sydney and brought Bob a load of American comic books. Please?'

'As long as that uncle of his doesn't go giving you beer.'

'No beer. Promise, Mum.'

'Very well.'

'You beaut!' Harry waved his fist in the air.

· · ·

THE FOLLOWING AFTERNOON, Hannah stuffed the copy of *Cakes and Ale* into her straw bag, along with a towel and a flask of water, and headed for the little billabong. She sat in the sunshine, the book untouched, as she tried to summon the courage to enter the water. Eventually, telling herself she didn't have to swim, she eased herself off the flat rock and into the cool clear water. She stood there, comfortably within her depth, acclimatising herself, listening to the bird-song and breathing in the medicinal scent from the eucalyptus trees. The water dappled and shimmered in the sunlight, and she bent her knees until her body was submerged. Letting her head fall back and her legs lift until she was floating on her back, she gazed up at the blue sky and the few light scudding clouds. Eddie had taught her well. She let the water support her, enjoying the sensation of weightlessness, allowing her mind to go blank and her senses to take over.

After a while, she moved onto her front and performed a few strokes, proving to herself that she could still swim – even if at a novice level. Deciding that was enough for today, she realised that getting out was going to prove a greater challenge than getting in had been. Telling herself not to panic, she worked her way around the edge of the pool until she found a rocky shelf. She scrambled up and used it as a platform to clamber out.

Back on her rock, she lay in the sunshine, reading her book.

The tranquillity was broken by a loud splash. Hannah looked up, thinking it must be an animal or – more likely – Harry defying his mother and jumping off the high rock. It took her a moment to see it was a man and another moment to recognise him as Ray Gaffney.

Hannah froze. She didn't want him to know she was

there; to think she was watching him, or to have to talk to him. The flat boulder she was on was higher than the surface of the water, so she was likely out of his sight range. She squinted into the sun, trying to establish if he'd seen her. Ray splashed about, presumably cooling off after working. She watched him duck completely under the water and then bounce back upwards, shaking his head and sending drops spinning onto the surface of the pool, as if he were a playful dog. Witnessing him like this seemed wrong, as though she were spying on him.

Steadying himself on the edge with his arm, he climbed out of the water on the far side, and she saw he was naked. It was now out of the question for her to make her presence known. Hannah wanted to shrink into herself; her face was burning; she wanted to be anywhere but here. She closed her eyes. If he spotted her, she'd pretend to be asleep.

When she dared to open her eyes again, he was gone. Relieved, she looked around, making sure he wasn't about to reappear. But the billabong was quiet now, the silence broken only by birdsong. It was as though she had imagined his brief appearance. Unfortunately, she hadn't.

It wasn't as though she'd never seen a naked man before. But both Will and Eddy had been tall and athletic in build. Ray was short, stocky, thick-thighed and muscular, with a forest of matted dark hair on his chest, and around his groin. She wished she could unsee him. It wasn't the stump of his left arm that she found repellent, but the ape-like shape of his body and the dense dark hair covering so much of it. She shuddered. He was like a primeval being.

His presence there felt like an invasion of her privacy. A desecration of her special place.

26

Over dinner that evening, Harry grinned at Hannah. 'Saw your cozzie hanging on the line. Did you get a swim at the little billabong?'

Elizabeth looked up. 'You've been swimming? Oh, Hannah, do you think that's wise?'

The blood rushed to Hannah's face. 'It was only a quick dip, and I asked the nurse if it would be okay. She said it wouldn't harm the baby and it's a good way to get some gentle exercise.'

'I don't like to think of you there on your own. What if something happened? There'd be no one around to help. If you want to swim, I'll come with you. And it's better to use the large billabong close to the house. Have you tried it?'

Hannah admitted she hadn't. She glanced at Harry who gave her an apologetic smile and mouthed that he was sorry.

She agreed to try the other pool next time. The little billabong was spoilt for her anyway since Ray's appearance.

They carried on eating, discussing the progress of the war. As they were about to tuck into the apple crumble Elizabeth had made, Harry looked over. 'I reckon Ray has a crush on you, Hannah. He's always asking me about you.'

'Don't be daft,' she snapped. 'Of course he doesn't.'

'That's enough, Harry,' said his father, but Elizabeth was smiling.

Surely not, Hannah thought. But it was looking increasingly likely that Elizabeth wanted to encourage something between her and Ray. Her mind was filled with a picture of his short, stocky body, the thick thighs and his cold water shrivelled penis, nesting in a dense forest of dark hair.

OVER THE FOLLOWING DAYS, Hannah forgot about swimming and kept close to the house to avoid bumping into Ray Gaffney.

She hoped the supposed infatuation was a figment of Harry's imagination. Ray had shown no obvious signs of being attracted to her – he had merely been polite and friendly. But Hannah had a definite sense that Elizabeth hoped that there was a possibility of a romance blossoming. Her aunt had Hannah's best interests at heart, but she wished she would stop commenting on what a good man Ray was.

It was inevitable that she would run into Ray at some point. Looking for Harry one afternoon, she wandered into the lean-to at the side of the barn. Inside, she found Ray, working on a piece of wood held in a vice. When he looked up and saw her, he moved in front of whatever he was working on, as though trying to conceal it, his expression furtive.

Hannah couldn't imagine what could be secret about carrying out a routine job on the farm, but rather than ask questions, she mumbled something and backed away.

Later that day, she passed the lean-to again when she was gathering eggs. The sound of sawing had been replaced by hammering. What was Ray doing, and why was he so cagey about it?

She asked Harry, who shrugged, saying Ray was practising his carpentry skills.

'Why in secret though?'

'Doesn't want anyone to see him struggling, I reckon. He likes to get it right first.'

She had to admire Ray's tenacity. At the shearers' supper, he'd said that anything was possible if you put your mind to it. He was living up to this maxim. His refusal to be limited by his missing limb was a sign of courage and character. But she still wanted to avoid any interest in herself. The best way to stop him from getting any romantic notions was to stay out of his way.

A couple of days later, when Michael and Elizabeth went into Tamworth, Ray was leading a sheep-dipping operation, helped by Harry and the land girls, marshalling the sheep from a large holding pen, through a run into the dipping tank.

Knowing Ray would be occupied for the rest of the day, Hannah went with a book to the little billabong. She wouldn't swim, having promised her aunt she wouldn't do so alone, but at least she'd be safe from an unannounced appearance by Ray Gaffney.

Rather than read a novel, she'd brought an anthology of English poems she'd found in the sitting room. Poetry suited her mood today: perfect to dip in and out of.

Drowsy, she must have nodded off. When she woke, the sky had clouded over and it had become chilly. Something felt amiss, but she couldn't say what at first.

Plaintive wailing reached her from somewhere on the

far side of the waterfall and grew in volume, but she couldn't determine its source.

She scrabbled about, gathering up her things and cramming them into her straw bag, and got down from the rock. She didn't have a clear view of the other side of the waterfall, so she walked towards the stream, hoping for a better vantage point from there. The far side of the rocky outcrop was covered with scrub growth, and she strained to see the person or creature that was clearly in distress.

Nothing. Hannah stood, staring up at the rock face, at the tumbling cascade of water, at the vegetation that clung to fissures in the rock surface.

The cries got louder, and she realised it was the bleating of a sheep or a lamb, the sound distorted by pain, fear or both. Then she saw it. Two dark eyes stared out from a thorn bush about halfway up the rock face on the left-hand side. Out of reach. Hannah couldn't even work out how to get over there without swimming across the billabong. There must be a route from above as how else had Harry and his friend jumped off the top of the waterfall?

The cries were reaching a crescendo, so without further thought, she raced back up the path through the trees towards the farm.

She must have been sleeping for longer than she'd thought. When she got to the place where the sheep-dipping had been taking place, the operation was over and there was no one about. Hannah heard movement from inside the nearby barn so hurried over, and found Ray Gaffney stacking empty cans of sheep dip. He turned when she burst in.

'You looking for me?' He looked pleased to see her.

'No. I mean, yes.' She struggled to catch her breath after the rush back up the slope from the billabong. 'Anyone, actually. There's a sheep – or maybe a lamb – at the little billabong. I think it's hurt. It's fallen off the rocks by the waterfall and is trapped. Stuck in a crevice, I think. It's in a lot of distress.'

Ray dropped the can he was holding and, followed by Rocky, ran out of the barn. He shouted back over his shoulder to Hannah. 'Get that rope.' Then yelled, 'Harry!'

Hannah looked about her and saw a coil of narrow rope lying on the floor, presumably ready to tie up the empty cans for transportation. She grabbed it and, half stumbling, went after Ray towards the little billabong. A moment later, Harry appeared. He overtook Hannah, grabbing the rope from her as he ran past.

She lost sight of the two of them as they entered the trees – presumably they'd taken a different route – one that led to the top of the waterfall. Sure enough, as she reached the billabong, Ray and Harry emerged at the top of the rocky ledge next to the waterfall.

Hannah stood at the point where the water drained into the creek. She called up to Ray and Harry, guiding them towards the place where the injured sheep was trapped.

Transfixed, she watched as Ray climbed down the rock face towards the sheep. Yet again, his courage confounded her. Steadying himself with his only arm, his legs searched for purchase on the rock face, then finding it, his arm moved lower, gripped, and his feet swung out again, seeking another placement. Hannah gasped each time he let go and swung his body towards the next holding place, scarcely able to breathe. In trying to rescue one lost sheep, had she put a man's life at risk?

Above Ray, Harry was crouched on the rock edge, the coiled rope in his hands. She couldn't make out the words that passed between the two of them, but she watched, breathless, as Harry, lying on his stomach, paid out the rope. Ray balanced on the rock beside the sheep and pulled off his shirt. He wrapped it around the middle of the animal to provide some cushioning before tying the rope behind its front legs. All the while, the sheep continued its desperate bleating. Ray leant towards it and appeared to be talking to the creature, and to Hannah's surprise, it quietened. Ray called up to Harry, then scrambled back up the rock face to join him. Hannah watched, her heart in her mouth as he negotiated the almost sheer rock surface, using his good arm to grip and his stump to steady himself. Once he was at the top, she breathed again. Together, Ray and Harry hauled on the rope and brought the sheep up to safety.

Hannah had to acknowledge that Ray Gaffney was intrepid, brave and determined.

She went back up the path, more slowly than the previous time, and found Ray, Harry, the sheep – a yearling – and Rocky, slowly making their way back towards the home paddock. Hannah fell in behind them.

Once the sheep was reunited with the flock, she turned to Ray Gaffney. 'That was an amazing rescue.' She was still in disbelief at the scale of his achievement.

He looked at her, his face expressionless. 'It's my job. Thank you for finding the sheep. It would have died if you hadn't spotted it and raised the alarm.'

Hannah wanted no credit. Ray Gaffney had risen in her estimation, but she still couldn't eradicate the image of him coming naked out of the water. Nor did she feel comfortable when he looked at her. It was as if his eyes seared through her skin.

.   .   .

WHEN MICHAEL AND ELIZABETH RETURNED, Elizabeth insisted on Ray joining the family for supper to celebrate the rescue of the hogget, as Hannah discovered a yearling sheep was called.

To Hannah's dismay, Ray was placed next to her at the table – in the more formal dining room rather than as usual in the kitchen. She tried her hardest to make conversation with him, but his answers were mostly monosyllabic and he initiated little himself, putting the burden on her.

Fortunately, Michael and Harry filled the void, Michael talking of the sale he'd been to in Tamworth, and Harry delivering a blow-by-blow account of the rescue that afternoon. To Hannah's horror, after the pudding was cleared away, her aunt announced Hannah should give a rendition of 'Clair de Lune' on the piano.

Consumed by nerves, and furious with Elizabeth, she stumbled her way through it, making no serious errors, and was greeted by enthusiastic applause from the men.

As she stepped away from the piano afterwards, the look Ray gave her left her in no doubt that Harry had been right. He had a crush on her.

HANNAH'S worst fears were confirmed when, one afternoon, a few days after the sheep rescue, she was reading in the shade on the veranda. Ray returned from a trip into Hazelton on horseback, bearing a bunch of flowers, his bush hat clamped under the stump of his missing arm. 'I haven't seen you about, so I brought these for you. I hope you're not feeling crook.'

'Crook?' she echoed.

'Unwell.'

'No, I'm fine. Why wouldn't I be?'

'I was concerned you might have overtired yourself running around after the stray sheep.' He looked her square in the eye and held out the flowers.

'For me?' she said feebly, accepting them and placing them behind her on the chair. 'That's awfully kind, but—'

He cut in. 'Please let me speak. I've come here today to ask you to marry me.'

Hannah's insides clenched. Had she heard right? Her mind scrambled. This couldn't be happening.

'I know a one-armed man isn't exactly...er... well... I promise to take care of you and the bub too when it comes. It isn't right for a girl like you to have to raise a child on your own.'

She tried to answer, but he lifted a hand to stop her. 'Let me finish. I don't expect an answer right away. Think it over. I'm a hard worker. Dependable. I've built up some savings. In a few years, there'll be enough for the down payment on a place of our own. Nothing fancy. A start.' He paused, watching her. 'You're surprised, but when you give it some thought, you'll see it makes sense.'

Hannah stared at him, aghast. She lowered her gaze, uncomfortable when he met her eyes.

'I'm ready to marry you right away, but if you want time to get to know me better, we can court for a while.' He lifted his hat and put it on his head, turned and led the horse away towards the stables.

Hannah stared at the flowers. Pink carnations. She wanted to throw them away, but she went inside and put them on the kitchen table. Elizabeth was standing at the stove, stirring a pot. 'Where did they come from?'

Hannah swallowed. Her legs were jelly under her, so she pulled out a chair and sat down at the table. 'Ray Gaffney just proposed to me.'

Elizabeth spun around, with a wide smile across her face. 'Have you accepted?'

'Of course I haven't.'

Elizabeth edged the pan off the burner and sat down opposite her niece. 'Tell me everything.'

'There's not much to tell. Completely out of the blue just now he asked me to marry him. Says he has some savings and wants to take care of me and the baby. Said he'll give me time to think about it.' She closed her eyes, fighting for breath. 'But I don't need to think about it.'

'You'll say yes?' Elizabeth's expression was full of hope

'No! I'll never marry again, and certainly not to him.'

'Oh, Hannah, don't rule it out.' Elizabeth clutched at her niece's hand. 'I don't think you've grasped how hard it will be as a single woman with a baby. You're young, with your life ahead of you. I know you don't love Ray, but you could come to do so. To build a family together.' Her brow furrowed, and she let go of Hannah's hand. 'You seem to get on well with him, and he's awfully keen on you. He could barely take his eyes off you the other night.'

Hannah glared at her. 'You've been talking about this with him, haven't you? You knew he was going to propose.' She jumped up from the table. 'How could you? I trusted you.'

'Calm down, Hannah. Please! I want the best for you. I'm not pushing you into anything. All I'm asking is for you to consider it. Get to know him better. Give him a chance.' Elizabeth looked down, then directed her gaze back to Hannah. 'Is it because of his missing arm?'

Hannah was scornful. 'Of course, it isn't. It's incredible how he copes. Admirable. No. I simply don't find him attractive. We've nothing in common. We've exhausted all topics of conversation.' She didn't want to mention that his hirsute body and muscular thighs repelled her.

Elizabeth sighed.

Hannah clasped her hands together. 'I can't believe you and he discussed this.'

Elizabeth dismissed the comment with a wave of her hand. 'Think of the baby, Hannah. Don't you think it deserves a father? I know how much I worried about Harry not having one in his life. I feel bad admitting this – but it made me fuss too much over him. Having Michael in our lives made such a difference – more than I ever imagined.' Elizabeth's face was a picture of concern. 'Obviously, you have us. And your sister and her family, but a father is important. When I think of those lonely years when it was just me and Harry—'

Hannah burst out angrily. 'But you did it! And so can I. You didn't settle for just anybody in order to give Harry a father.'

Hannah couldn't take any more. Saying she was going to lie down until dinner, she went into her bedroom and flung herself on the bed. First Judith had disowned her, and now Elizabeth was trying to press her into marriage with a man she barely knew and found physically unattractive. The thought of sharing a bed with Ray Gaffney made her shudder. She didn't need a man. Why couldn't she be allowed to manage on her own?

In a turmoil, she lost track of time until a knock on the door, when she realised it was already dusk. The door opened and Michael put his head around it. 'Can I come in for a minute?'

Hannah nodded.

He sat on the only seat, a stool in front of the dressing

table. Hannah positioned herself on the edge of the bed opposite him.

'Lizzie told me Ray proposed to you.'

'I suppose you were in on it too?'

He shook his head. 'Ray said nowt to me. I had the impression he were soft on yer, but I'd no clue he were about to pop 't question. You aren't happy about it, I gather.'

'I'm sure he's a decent man, but that doesn't mean I want to throw in my lot and my baby's with him for the rest of my life.' She tried to read his expression. 'Elizabeth thinks I should marry for security, even though I feel nothing for Ray. She says even though it's not there now, love will come. I imagine you're going to tell me the same thing.'

'Don't yer think I've a mind of me own, lass?' His voice was calm and measured.

'Sorry,' she said glumly.

'Lizzie and I have different views on this. She made 't best of a bad lot when she wed Will's father, whereas I made 't worst mistake of my life when I married Will's sister – for all't wrong reasons.'

Curious, she asked why.

'I were jealous. Angry. Pigheaded. An honest conversation could've sorted it out, but I were too proud and thought I knew better. Looking back, I only married Hattie Kidd to punish Lizzie, God forgive me.'

'What happened?'

'It were a disaster from the word go. I won't rake over the details, but I woke up't day after we wed knowing I should-na've done it. Hattie did too.' His mouth formed a hard line as he remembered. 'Later, when I were in New Zealand, I almost married again. But I didn't love her either, and even though she were a good woman and would've made a good wife, I couldn't go through with it. There's only ever bin one woman for me, and that's your aunt. So yes, Hannah, I understand yer.'

Relief swept over her, but she could see he hadn't finished. There was a but coming.

'Thing is though, it's not just yerself, there's 't bairn to think about. A child needs a father. Give it some thought, lass. Mebbe get to know Ray better before you decide.'

She looked down, twisting her fingers together. 'I want to make my own way and not rely on you both. I'm enormously grateful, but staying here indefinitely isn't an option. I haven't told Elizabeth yet, but I've taken her advice and written to Eddie's parents.'

Michael's eyes lit up. 'I'm glad you've written to them. I'm sure they'll want to help. At least 't bairn'll have grandparents. Apart from me and Lizzie, of course.' Michael smiled, his eyes sad. 'There's no rush. Yer in no trouble, lass. But you'll find life a lot easier if you've a man by your side.'

After he'd left, Hannah got up and stared through the window at the sheep grazing in the meadow. She watched the sun go down over the distant hills, bathing them in a rosy aura. Why was life so complicated? Whatever her aunt and uncle said, Hannah knew she wanted to do this on her own. Surely there was a way?

27

Several days passed while Hannah continued to avoid Ray Gaffney. To her relief, Elizabeth and Michael didn't broach the subject again, but Hannah knew she'd have to confront it before long. Ray would no doubt soon materialise on the veranda to ask for her answer.

She tried to give his offer some proper thought, although every instinct made her want to make it clear she wouldn't marry him. She remembered what her aunt had said about her marriage to Jack Kidd and how she had moved from loathing to affection for him. Then Jack Kidd was Will's father, so he must have had many redeeming qualities. But so did Ray Gaffney, didn't he?

Ray was hero-worshipped by Harry and treated the lad with more patience than even Michael managed. His painstaking tutoring of the boy in shearing technique testified to his kindness and his suitability as a father. She ought to look at such things dispassionately, not emotionally. His strength of character also shifted the balance in his favour – he was indomitable, brave, determined, and hardworking. All desirable qualities.

Yet she couldn't get past the fact that he had made his proposal even though he barely knew her, which smacked of desperation. And most of all, after seeing him naked at the billabong, she couldn't help shuddering at the thought of ever being intimate with him.

ONE MORNING, two letters with Sydney postmarks arrived for Hannah. She sat at the kitchen table where Elizabeth, sitting opposite, was frowning as she pored over the farm accounts.

Hannah opened the first envelope. To her delight, it was from her WAAAF friend, Betty, but the contents soon dispelled her joy. News had at last reached Betty that her husband, Jimmie, was in a Japanese prisoner of war camp. Betty had been given no details other than that he had been in captivity since soon after the Japanese had invaded New Guinea. The rest of the letter showed her friend's stoicism – news of the other girls they'd worked with, as well as an update on the move to Bankstown, how awful the barracks were but how they were making the best of it.

Hannah put the letter back in the envelope. This bloody awful war. Still, it was better that Jimmie was in a prison camp than starving to death in a hostile jungle or dead. She hoped the Axis powers would treat prisoners of war in line with the Geneva Convention, but remembered her friend's scepticism about that, based on the atrocities committed by the Japanese in China.

She turned to the other letter. The handwriting on the envelope was unfamiliar. She froze. It must be a reply from the Greenbanks. Hands shaking, she slit open the envelope and took out the single sheet.

Dear Miss Kidd,

We read your letter with pain and dismay. It was an unwanted intrusion by a stranger into this family's grief. Our beloved son would never have had a liaison with a woman unknown to his family.

No doubt you read the announcement of our son's loss in the newspaper and thought you would try to profit from our grief.

The enclosed is sent without prejudice and on condition we hear no more from you. Please do not contact us again.

The Honourable Mr Justice Greenbank and Mrs Greenbank

A cheque for one hundred pounds accompanied the letter.

Hannah let the letter and cheque fall from her hands onto the table.

Elizabeth looked up, peering at her niece over the top of her reading glasses. 'Bad news?'

Humiliated, Hannah fought back tears. 'I took your advice and contacted Eddie's parents. Not for help but because of what you said about them needing to know they were going to have a grandchild. As I suspected, they don't want to know.'

'Let me see.' Elizabeth took the letter and scanned it quickly, her face contorting. 'Oh, my poor darling. What a vile thing for you to have to read.' She picked up the cheque. 'And this is intended to buy you off? What horrible people!'

Hannah stood up and went to her room, returning with an envelope. She tore the cheque in half and put it in the envelope, which she addressed to the judge and his wife.

Elizabeth got up and wrapped Hannah in her arms. 'Was that wise, Hannah? It was a substantial sum of money. You're entitled to some support from them. It's the least they can do.'

Hannah shook her head. 'I'd die rather than cash that cheque.'

Elizabeth hugged her again. 'I'm proud of you. But perhaps it was rather foolish.'

Drawing a deep breath, Hannah sat down at the table again. 'How could I possibly have accepted their money? It would have been tantamount to admitting they're right. At least now I have the satisfaction of proving them wrong. They can live with the shame of what they've done.' But she knew the Greenbanks wouldn't be feeling any shame.

As THE DAYS PASSED, Hannah was no clearer about what to do. Lacking the financial wherewithal to contribute to the household, she tried to make herself as useful as possible. It was a constant battle of wills with her aunt, who wanted to fuss over her and spoil her.

She was conscious that she needed to talk to Ray Gaffney – she couldn't delay giving him her answer indefinitely. But every time she made up her mind to tell him her answer was no, Elizabeth urged her to give it more thought.

Was she being selfish in depriving her unborn child of a father? Was Elizabeth right that, given time and effort, she would come to like and respect Ray, even if she couldn't love him? But Michael's words – that there could only ever be one woman in his life – had struck a stronger chord in her. Will was gone, but she still held him in her heart and wasn't willing to share her life with anyone else.

Failing to fall asleep one night, and with her throat dry, she padded into the kitchen to fetch a glass of water. As she stood at the sink filling the glass, she heard voices from the veranda through the open kitchen window. She didn't intend to eavesdrop but couldn't help herself. Michael and Elizabeth were discussing the farm accounts. Frozen to the spot, Hannah heard terms that made only vague sense to her, but she got the picture: the farm's finances were stretched. Low wool prices, disappointing yields, and an outbreak of fly strike the previous year were mentioned, but it was the anxiety in their voices that most alerted Hannah that all was not well.

'The war's made it worse,' said Michael. 'With the government controlling prices and setting production targets, there's little room for manoeuvre.'

She couldn't hear Elizabeth's reply, her voice being softer.

Michael's words when he spoke again chilled Hannah to the bone. 'If, as is likely, Hannah turns Ray down, he'll probably leave. Ray's too proud to stick around. I doubt we can replace him until after the war. And finding someone who knows as much about sheep as Ray, well...'

Unable to bear listening anymore, Hannah went back to her room and lay in bed, sleepless, thinking. It wasn't just feeding and housing her and the baby; the birth would bring with it a host of other expenses. She'd be a further drain on the Winterbournes' strained resources and could cost them their most-valued worker.

The following morning, Hannah rose early and left the house before Michael and Harry breakfasted. She walked over to the annexe behind the shearing shed and waited until Ray emerged, carrying a plate of fry-up. He sat on the wooden step and was spearing a piece of sausage when he looked up and saw her and put the plate aside.

'Don't let me interrupt your breakfast,' said Hannah. 'I'll walk around the paddock for fifteen minutes.'

He fixed his gaze on her, chewing slowly, then spoke again. 'No. Stay. You've come to give me an answer, Hannah?'

His eyes on her made her feel like a specimen. She almost turned and ran back to the house. But she had to go through with this and reminded herself that she'd liked Ray well enough until the afternoon she'd seen him at the billabong. They'd got along well at the shearers' supper and when they drove together into Hazelton. She'd witnessed his kindness to Harry and the courage and gentleness with which he'd rescued the stricken sheep. Running out of conversation topics was an insufficient reason to reject him – as were his stocky build and his profuse body hair. Yet the way he was looking at her now made her uncomfortable – it was like an appraisal. Checking the goods.

Hannah swallowed. At least, unlike Jack Kidd when her aunt had married him, Ray was a relatively young man – she'd established from Elizabeth that he was thirty-three, although he looked older.

She cleared her throat and in a faltering voice said, 'Do you still want to marry me?'

He nodded, eyebrows knitted in a frown, expression grave.

'You're prepared to accept the baby as if it were your own?'

Without a moment's hesitation he said, 'I meant what I said.'

'Then my answer is yes.' She looked down at her feet, noticing how scuffed her shoes were.

Ray stood up, stretched out his hand and drew her towards him. 'You won't regret it, Hannah, I promise you. I'll be a good husband. And I'll care for the child as if it were my own.' He held her by the shoulder with his single arm, looking into her eyes. 'No point waiting. Better sooner than later.'

She swallowed. She hadn't expected this. 'You want us to marry right away?'

'As soon as we can get the banns read.'

Hannah looked past him, fixing her eyes on the hills as the sun rose. 'I'd prefer to wait till after the baby's born. I want to be sure you won't change your mind. The idea of a baby differs from the reality. When you see it, you may not accept it.' She looked away, avoiding the intensity of his gaze.

'It's due late November, you said?'

She nodded.

'Now you've said you'll have me, I can't wait that long.'

Hannah bit her lip. She spoke quickly. 'Well, you'll have to. That's my condition. I won't marry you until the baby's born.' She looked down at his breakfast plate. 'You'd better eat that before it goes cold.' She turned on her heels and hurried back to the house.

Hannah saw the relief in her aunt's eyes when she told her the news. Elizabeth rushed across the kitchen and hugged her. 'You've done the right thing, Hannah. I'm sure of it.'

Hannah herself was far from sure. Logically, she understood the reasons for throwing in her lot with Ray Gaffney, but her heart refused to play along. She hadn't loved Eddie Greenbank, yet she'd happily slept with him. The thought of doing the same with Ray filled her with revulsion. And it would be for the rest of their lives. She didn't want to contemplate that.

Elizabeth clasped her hands together, her eyes shining. 'I'll cook a joint of beef and invite Ray to join us this evening. Thank heavens there's no meat rationing yet. It's going to be a glorious day, so we can eat outside.'

Before Hannah could protest that she didn't want a fuss, Michael came into the kitchen, Harry behind him, and Elizabeth lost no time in sharing the news.

Michael embraced Hannah, his eyes silently asking if she was sure. Remembering the conversation she'd overheard, she forced her mouth into a smile.

'That's good news,' he said.

'Bonzer!' said Harry. 'I knew Ray fancied you. Didn't I say so, Dad? I bloody well knew it!'

'Less of the language, Harry,' his mother said, but she was smiling too.

'I've told him it's on condition that we wait till after the baby comes.'

'Elizabeth frowned. 'Why?'

'I want to be sure he'll accept the baby. It's all very well to say he will, but it's a different thing to face the reality of another man's child. Besides, it gives us time to get to know each other better.'

'That makes sense,' said Michael before Elizabeth could answer. 'For both of you. No need to rush things.'

Hannah felt a surge of relief. She'd bought herself some time.

Elizabeth went to great lengths to prepare a delicious meal. She gathered flowers for the table and cooked up a feast. To Hannah's dismay, she invited the land girls too, determined it would be a proper engagement party. 'There's been little enough cause for celebration with this war raging.'

Hannah watched the preparations with a sense of powerlessness. She hated the fuss and felt boxed in by the public celebration.

At the table, she was seated beside Ray. As she took her seat, he placed his hand on her thigh. She stiffened. He was claiming her as his own. She edged her chair towards Harry's on her other side, but the hand remained until, mercifully, Elizabeth served the food.

Sally from Queensland, sitting opposite, said, 'You two kept that quiet. A bit of a whirlwind romance, eh? I should have guessed at the shearers' supper when you were chin-wagging.' She laughed loudly. 'At least one broken heart round this table, eh, Violet?'

Violet, the small, quiet girl from Tamworth, blushed to the roots of her hair and elbowed Sally. 'Leave off, Sal.'

'Only teasing.'

Hannah couldn't help wishing Violet, not her, was the object of Ray's affections. With his hand now occupied with eating his food, it was replaced by the pressure of his thigh against hers.

She spent most of the meal chatting to Harry, who was keen to tell her about the comic books his friend Bob had lent him. Feigning fascination with Captain America and Archie Andrews, she listened as he needed no encourage-ment to recount their adventures. Across the table, Eliza-beth was frowning until eventually she called her son and instructed him to help her clear the table, leaving Hannah with no escape.

Ray immediately spoke to her, his voice low enough to exclude the others at the table. 'You seem to have been avoiding me for a while, Hannah. I was glad to see you this morning and even gladder to hear what you had to say.'

'Elizabeth worries about my being out of her sight.' She forced a smile.

'Well, maybe we can go to the Little Billabong together. I promise I'll have some shorts on.'

Hannah shivered. So he had seen her that afternoon when he was naked. But she wanted to give him the benefit of the doubt. Until that incident, she'd found him open and friendly, and there was no reason to assume he had been creeping up on her or deliberately parading his naked body.

The land girls left as soon as the meal ended, but everyone else lingered on the veranda apart from Elizabeth, who was in the kitchen. Michael stood and beckoned to his son. 'Come on, Harry, let's give your ma a hand.' Before Hannah could protest, they had disappeared inside, leaving her alone with Ray.

He hooked his arm around her, drawing her close, and kissed her, tentatively at first, then his tongue probing and darting. Hannah tried to push him away, but his grip was strong, even with just the one arm, and she was trapped in the narrow space between the table and the veranda rails. She tried to force her mouth shut, and he sensed the tension in her and pulled back.

'What's wrong?' he said.

'Nothing. I just wasn't expecting it.'

He smiled. 'We're engaged now.' He bent forward and kissed her again. This time she didn't resist but held herself rigid, wishing it over.

When he released his hold, she got to her feet.

'You're not bailing on me already? You bushed?' He looked up at her.

'It's been a long day, and I'm tired.'

'A special day,' he said, but his voice was flat.

IN THE HOUR before the evening meal the next day, Ray presented himself at the door and asked for her. He'd clearly just taken a shower and changed his clothes and was without his ubiquitous canvas bush hat, his still damp hair plastered flat to his skull.

She emerged onto the veranda. Her situation wasn't going to change. The least she could do was try to find some common ground.

They walked into the paddock behind the house. It was a cloudless night, with a myriad of stars, like the night they had first talked in front of his fire when he'd cooked the damper. He reached for her hand, and she didn't resist, letting his warm hand hold hers.

Eventually, they arrived at the grassy slope in front of the shearers' quarters where he lived. They sat on the steps, and he continued to hold her hand. She had a feeling he was going to kiss her again, so she cast about for a topic of conversation in order to delay the moment.

'I've been wondering. Will we live here after we're married?' She was curious about what the place was like, having never been inside.

'Until I can get us a place of our own. A proper home for you and the bub.' He got up and pulled her to her feet. 'Come and have a look. It needs a woman's touch to make it more homely.'

Inside he pulled on a light cord. The room was illuminated by the dim glow from a naked bulb. The concrete floor was mostly covered by an oilcloth, the beige of the tarpaulin decorated with faded blue diamonds. One wall was lined with three sets of bunk beds – one of the lower bunks was neatly made up, so must be Ray's. There were a few old, upholstered chairs, an upturned wooden orange crate on which there was a beer bottle. The walls were unadorned apart from an old calendar for the year 1938, with a picture of a sheep. The place looked spotlessly clean, which was about its only positive. There was a doorway leading into a galley kitchen. Some lamb chops and a piece of liver sat on a plate under a mesh fly cover, next to a bowl of eggs.

'What do you reckon?' he asked. 'Place could do with a spruce up. Mike says I can store the bunks in the barn and put in a proper bed for us.'

She gazed around, struggling to imagine living here herself. 'What about the baby?'

He grinned. 'It was meant to be a surprise. Come with me.' He led her out of the building and into the lean-to next door, where a wooden cradle stood in the centre on sheets of newspaper, a pot of white paint and a pair of brushes beside it. 'Finished making it yesterday. Just got to give it a coat of paint.'

So that was what he'd tried to conceal from her when she'd come upon him there before. 'You did this yourself?' She ran a hand along the smoothly planed wood.

'Had a bit of help from Harry to hold the wood in place while I worked it. But then I found a vise. There's usually a way to get most things done.'

'Thank you,' she said. When she went to give him a quick kiss on his cheek he moved his head and met her mouth. She pulled away quickly. Ray's eyes narrowed, but he made no comment. She'd hurt his feelings.

Feeling trapped, Hannah cast about for something to say to break the tension between them.

'Tell me about New Zealand. Is it similar to this? She looked about her, sweeping her arms out.

His bottom lip jutted, and he shrugged. 'Cooler. More rain. Better grass,' he said after a pause, apparently indifferent to the landscape of his old home. He kept his eyes on her as he reached for the cigarettes he carried in his sleeve and lit one. They went to sit again on the step.

'I grew up in Liverpool,' she said to fill the silence. 'It's a huge port on the estuary of the River Mersey, dominated by the docks, the buildings all blackened with smoke. There are some fine buildings – assuming they survive the war. Being a big port and the gateway to the Atlantic, it's a target for German bombers.'

He said nothing. Did he have no curiosity? Hannah didn't know how to draw him out. At the shearers' supper he'd been more talkative. Uncomfortable with the tension between them, Hannah said her dinner would be ready. She stood up, and he grasped her hand.

'I'd like to cook your tea for you tomorrow,' he said. 'It's always the same. Mixed grill. With or without eggs. Up to you.'

What a miserable prospect. A plate of fried meat in a gloomy room or here on the step with no conversation. She didn't respond other than to wish him goodnight. He pulled her into another kiss. Hannah stiffened at the smell of tobacco on his breath, wanting to push him away but forcing herself to endure it.

As she walked back towards the glowing light of the homestead, she couldn't wait to be sitting at the big kitchen table with Elizabeth, Michael and Harry, eating a well-cooked meal with plenty of vegetables from the kitchen garden. It was wonderful to be in a room where the conversation flowed. How was she going to endure spending the rest of her life with such a taciturn man? But it was too late to back out now.

28

NOVEMBER 1942

As Hannah drew nearer to her confinement, she welcomed spending time each day with her aunt at the large billabong. It was a refuge from the heat and a relief from the bulk she was now carrying. Floating on her back in the cool water was a tonic and helped her forget about the worries weighing her down.

As the weeks went by, the relationship with Ray remained strained. She tried to get him to open up – to talk of his childhood, of his brief time in the army. Even when she asked about sheep rearing, he was reticent, unlike Harry, who needed no encouragement to share his growing knowledge. Over and over, Hannah asked herself what she was doing wrong. If only she could communicate with him verbally, she might eventually get over her lack of physical attraction to him.

Eventually, she spoke to Elizabeth about it. They were walking to the billabong – her aunt always insisted on accompanying her, even though she rarely swam herself.

'What's wrong with me? No matter how hard I try, I can't

get Ray to talk to me. It's all monosyllables. I'm doing my best, but nothing works.'

Her aunt looked at her sadly. 'I know how that feels. When I married Jack Kidd, I barely got more than a grunt out of him.'

'But you said it got better. What did you do?'

Elizabeth gave her a rueful smile. 'Jack was never a great talker. Not unlike Ray.' She looked away. 'How shall I put this? I think you'll find things improve between you once you're sharing a bed.'

Hannah stopped in her tracks. 'That's what I'm dreading most.' She bit her lip, fighting back tears. 'I think he knows I feel that way. It's making matters worse. When he goes to kiss me, I try to relax but I can't.'

Elizabeth took her hand. 'I'm so sorry, my love. I did rather push you into this. You know it's not too late to change your mind.'

'It's not just the physical thing. It's also his way of life. He doesn't talk, he doesn't read. He eats the same thing every day of his life and he seems oblivious to his surroundings. Have you seen inside the shearers' quarters? There's nothing personal there.'

Elizabeth rolled her eyes. 'He used to be a drover. They often live that way. Used to being on the move in the outback. The place is spartan as it's intended for shearers to bunk down for a few nights. He's never thought it worthwhile making it more homely. Look, I'm not supposed to mention this as he wants it to be a surprise, but he's talking of renting a cottage between here and Hazelton. Just a couple of miles down the road.' She smiled. 'I'm sure once you're settled in there you can make it a comfortable, welcoming home. And we'll be close by. I'll come and visit, and there'll always be a welcome for you and the baby at Hunter's Down.'

Hannah imagined a future in a pretty cottage close to the Winterbournes. If her aunt had adapted to a loveless marriage, then surely, she could too for the sake of her baby.

HANNAH WAS SITTING on the step beside Ray as he smoked a cigarette, and they watched the sun go down. Rocky was curled up at his master's feet. The sky was beautiful – the blood red of the sinking sun mixed with dark grey clouds – red hot fire and grey-black ash. As usual, they sat in silence. Hannah had made a ritual of joining her husband-to-be every evening for half an hour before dinner. She had stopped trying to get him to talk and settled for silent companionship until he kissed her and she went back to the house. Lately, the kisses had been accompanied by his fondling her breasts – something she tolerated, though it gave her no pleasure and made her feel pawed.

Every evening as she walked over to meet him, she determined that this time she'd relax and try to enjoy his caresses. But each evening as she felt his mouth on hers and his hard body pressed against her, she stiffened. It was a Pavlovian reaction, and no matter how hard she tried, she couldn't relax and let go. What was it going to be like when she had to sleep with him?

But on this occasion he didn't make any advances. He ground out the butt of his cigarette under his shoe and looked away towards the dying sun as he spoke. 'I think we should call it a day.' His heel scraped the bare ground as he attempted to bury the stub.

It took her a moment to grasp his meaning.

'Call it a day? she echoed.

'Call off the marriage.'

Hannah hadn't expected that. So many times, she'd considered breaking up with him but had restrained herself with the mantra: *Put the baby first.*

Before she could respond, he carried on. 'Sorry to do this to you, but I can't marry a woman who shrinks from me whenever I touch her.'

Hannah gulped.

'I won't force myself on you, and it feels like that's what I'm doing.' Still with his gaze on the horizon, he said, 'I want a woman who wants me. And that isn't you, is it, Hannah?'

She could almost hear her heart pounding inside her chest.

'I don't have much, but I have my pride. Without that, I've nothing.' He lit another cigarette. She had a sense that he'd prepared this speech. 'You're a good-looking woman, but you might as well be a block of wood. It's better for us to call it off now than make each other miserable for the rest of our lives.'

Protectively, her hands went to her belly, cradling the large bump as she processed what he was saying, trying not to let the relief show on her face. Then she remembered Michael's fear that Ray would leave the farm. If he did, it would be her fault.

'I reckon you'll get by just fine on your own,' he said, still avoiding her eyes.

She nodded. 'I'll have to.'

'Will you stay here?'

'No. I'll go back to Sydney. As soon as the baby's born.'

'That's good.'

'You?'

'Suits me here. Mick and I get along.' He drew on his cigarette and turned to look at her for the first time. 'We gave it a fair go, you and me, I reckon. No point in flogging a dead horse.' He stretched out a hand and shook hers. 'I'll drop that cradle by the house tomorrow. Night, Hannah.' It sounded like goodbye.

She got to her feet, thanked him again for making the cradle, wished him goodnight and walked towards the house. It had been the longest conversation they'd had since they'd agreed to marry – and Ray had done most of the talking.

ELIZABETH INSISTED on Hannah staying at Hunter's Down to have the baby. 'Better to stick with the same doctor and midwife. And I want to be here for you, my love.'

Now that the birth was imminent, Hannah was afraid. The reality of being responsible for a living, breathing child was dawning on her. Yet she had no regrets about not marrying Ray Gaffney.

Her aunt and uncle took the news better than she expected – Hannah had been afraid Elizabeth would be disappointed in her, but she merely said, 'You're strong. You'll manage. When I think of everything you've been through in life already, bringing up a baby should be a doddle for you.' She gave a sad smile. 'I'd rather you weren't doing it alone, but you'll be a wonderful mother. Lord knows how. But you will.'

Hannah didn't know either, but she was buoyed up by a sense of freedom, knowing that she'd never again have to sit in silence with Ray, and would never be obliged to share his bed.

. . .

HANNAH'S due date came and went. As November moved into December, the mercury rose in the thermometer, and she was impatient now for the baby to be born. The hot weather made her substantial bulk even more uncomfortable: sweat pooled between her breasts, her back ached and her clothing chafed at her stretched skin.

If only it were over. She longed to get on with the birth, while dreading what she knew was the inevitability of a long and painful labour. Despite the warmth and kindness of her aunt and Michael, the realisation that she was now facing an uncertain and financially precarious future alone hit home with force. None of the men who had been in her life would be there to support her through this.

About to wallow in self-pity, she pulled herself up. Nothing she was about to face could be worse than the loss of Will, so she gritted her teeth and told herself to get on with it. She'd coped with so much in her past, she could do so again.

Elizabeth was working in her vegetable garden, so Hannah took advantage of an unexpected burst of energy to scrub every surface of the already spotlessly clean kitchen. Drenched with sweat from her efforts, she leant against the kitchen sink when the back pains intensified, and her waters broke.

The nagging discomfort in her back sharpened into sudden flashes of pain. She was restless and couldn't get comfortable, no matter what she did.

Elizabeth appeared at the kitchen door. She glanced at the puddle on the floor. 'It's started? How often are the contractions?'

Hannah tilted her head back and took a gulp of air. 'There's no pattern. Some come in a rush then nothing for ages.'

'Right. I'm going to warn Michael now so he's at the ready.' Elizabeth smoothed a lock of Hannah's hair back from her forehead. 'Go and lie down. I'm going to bring you a cup of tea. Since this is your first baby and bearing in mind the scare you had, I imagine the midwife will want to be here sooner rather than later.' She took Hannah's hand and gave it a gentle squeeze. 'Don't worry, my love. Everything's going to be fine.'

Hannah lost track of time as the day wore on and the contractions intensified and grew in frequency. The midwife appeared in the early afternoon, examined her and told her she'd be back again that evening.

Things didn't get going properly until late the following day. Elizabeth sat patiently beside Hannah, applying damp cloths to cool her, propping pillows behind her and whispering words of encouragement. Hannah herself was in a daze, crushed by the pain that came in agonising waves. She was aware of the midwife's presence but was past caring about anything.

As her labour continued, Hannah experienced a rising panic. No going back now. Her life was going to change forever. Pain engulfed her, and her ever-present longing for Will intensified. It was hard to bear that she was going through all this without him. This should have been *their* baby. Will should have been pacing up and down outside her room, anxious for news. She had never felt so utterly alone, despite the constant soothing presence of Elizabeth. Cursing poor dead Eddie, her own folly in sleeping with him – and even her unborn child, Hannah prayed for it all to be over – or to die. She no longer cared which.

By the time she entered the final stage of labour, she was so weak that she struggled to find the strength to push. The pain was indescribable, tearing her apart. She clutched Elizabeth's hand, gripping it as though hanging on for her life. With a last supreme effort, the baby was delivered.

Hannah lay back, spent, waiting to hear her baby's cry. The room was silent apart from whispered words between the midwife and Elizabeth. Hannah's heart contracted inside her chest, and a shiver of terror ran through her body. She wanted to scream out, to call to Will, to God, to anyone who would hear her. Had she gone through all this only for her baby to die?

Just as she was about to be swallowed by a tidal wave of grief and despair, a piercing yell cut the air.

Elizabeth's face bent over her. 'You have a beautiful son, Hannah. A beautiful healthy boy.' Next thing Hannah knew, her son was in her arms and the midwife was guiding him onto her breast. Hannah felt a surge of euphoria and blinding love as she looked down at the tiny mite she was cradling. In that moment she knew she'd walk through fire and flood for her child.

'Hello, David,' she said.

HANNAH HAD PLANNED to return to Sydney almost immediately after the delivery but was soon disabused of that notion when she discovered – painfully – that giving birth was not something one recovered from in a day or two. She felt guilty about the intrusion of a crying baby into the otherwise tranquil homestead, but no one complained. The whole family made a fuss of David. Harry treated him like a precious jewel, always ready to sit in the rocking chair on the veranda and rock the baby to sleep.

During the two months between giving birth and her intended departure for Sydney, Hannah had no contact with Ray Gaffney, other than seeing him riding out with Michael and Harry to muster sheep, or loading and unloading the utility truck by the barn. One afternoon, however, she was sitting on the veranda while David slept in her arms, when Ray appeared.

He stood at the foot of the steps in front of her, his bush hat in his hand, his face expressionless. 'Harry says you've asked him to stand along with his father as the boy's godfather.'

She looked at him in surprise. 'Yes. And Elizabeth has agreed to be David's godmother.'

He nodded solemnly. 'David. A good simple name. Christening's tomorrow?'

Hannah told him it was.

'I've got a present for him. I don't hold with religion, so it's nothing in that line.' He handed her a small lacquered wooden box. 'It's a music box. Plays a tune when you open it. "Waltzing Matilda".'

Hannah was touched. Tears pricked the back of her eyes. 'That's so kind of you, Ray. We'll treasure it. Thank you.'

'Can I look at him?'

'Of course.'

He squatted on his broad haunches beside the makeshift crib and looked down at the sleeping baby. 'Can't tell if he looks like you,' he said, with the ghost of a chuckle. He stood up and put his hat on. 'Righto. I'll be getting on then. Going into Hazelton. Goodbye, Hannah.' He turned to look back at her as he reached the bottom of the steps. 'No hard feelings.'

Then he was gone.

29

FEBRUARY 1943

Hannah said a tearful goodbye to Harry and Elizabeth and returned to Sydney in early February, this time with a baby. Rather than undertaking the hundred-mile journey by train – a long trip since the train stopped at many small stations – they were driven in the ute by Michael, who wanted to conduct some business at the wool brokerage.

She had written to ask Dot Hodges if she'd be willing to take in her and David and – tentatively – whether Dot would be prepared to look after the baby should Hannah be able to find a job. The answer was overwhelmingly affirmative, with Dot offering to be the baby's surrogate grandmother as it was unlikely she'd get to be a real one until after the war.

Dot insisted Michael have a cup of tea with them before leaving. 'I'm afraid the sugar rationing is getting in the way of my baking, but honey's not on the rations so I've made a honey cake.'

After the tea and cake – which Michael declared to be delicious – he took his leave. As he hugged his niece, he gazed at her intently. 'There's always a place for you at Hunter's Down if you change your mind.'

'Thank you, Michael. I'll never be able to repay your kindness.' Her eyes welled with tears as she spoke.

As he was going out of the front door, he turned back. 'You did the right thing about Ray. It would never have worked.' He gave her a wink. 'I'm sure you'll be glad to hear that he's asked Violet for a drink in the pub in Hazelton and she's said yes. Apparently, she was broken-hearted when he was going to marry you.'

Another load off Hannah's mind. She grinned. 'I'm very happy for both of them. I hope it hope it works out for Ray this time.' And she did.

After Michael had driven away, Hannah nursed the baby, while Dot bustled about the kitchen preparing their dinner. 'I've got us both a nice piece of fish, darl, and I've made a rice pudding for afters.'

As they ate the simple meal, Dot eulogised about Michael. 'That uncle of yours is a good-looking fellow. Reminds me of Cary Grant. All dark and handsome with gorgeous eyes. What I call "come-to-bed-eyes". Your aunty's a lucky woman.' She winked at Hannah. 'Now, talking of handsome men, I know you didn't want to tell that nice Eddie about the baby, but maybe the time's right now, what do you reckon?'

She'd forgotten that she hadn't told Dot. 'Eddie died, Dot. Killed in action in Papua.'

Dot clasped her hands together as if in prayer. 'Oh no! That lovely young man. What a crying shame.' She looked at David, sleeping in his bassinet. 'Poor lamb. To think he'll never know his father.'

· · ·

HANNAH'S SEARCH for a job wasn't proving fruitful. Clerical vacancies were thin on the ground and much in demand. She came to the conclusion she'd have to cast the net wider.

'Go easy on yourself, Hannah,' said Dot when Hannah came home tired and dispirited from another fruitless search. 'No need to rush into things.'

'I have to pay my way.'

'You will. All in good time. Something will turn up. Meanwhile, don't worry. I had a little windfall at the bingo the other night and I've nothing else to spend it on these days. Remember what they say about winning the war. We all have to pull together. So that's what we'll do.'

Hannah flung her arms around her, wondering why she'd once found her landlady annoying.

Eventually, she landed a part-time job, working mornings as a clerical assistant in the accounts office at the David Jones department store. The work was dull and undemanding compared with her time in the WAAAF, but returning to her old job was out of the question because of the relocation to Bankstown, several miles outside the city, as well as the antisocial hours, even supposing they'd be willing to re-employ her. The accounts job was relatively well paid for part-time work, and she calculated she could just about cover the rent.

Dot refused flat out to be paid to look after David. 'I'm his honorary grandmother, aren't I, pet?' she said, tickling him under the chin.

Hannah soon got into a routine of going to work each morning and then spending her afternoons walking the baby in his pram – a hand-me-down from one of Dot's neighbours. They strolled in Hyde Park, the Domain or down at Circular Quay, where she sat on a bench, watching the ferries come and go. She visited the library and would sit on the grass reading while David slept in his pram.

As the weeks passed, she thought more about the two men she'd taken up with since arriving in Australia.

Her feelings towards Eddie had softened since her brief and wounding exchange with his parents. How must it have been for him growing up with parents as cold and unfeeling as his? Given her own parentage – her father's brutality and cruelty and her mother's subjugation – she had to sympathise with Eddie. Might things have turned out differently between them had she given him more encouragement? Perhaps he wouldn't have joined up and lost his life. A future with him would have been a much more appealing prospect than the one she'd almost settled for with Ray Gaffney. But now she had experienced the coldness and snobbery of Eddie's parents, she knew they'd have moved heaven and earth to prevent them marrying.

At least Ray had found some well-deserved happiness. A recent letter from Elizabeth had mentioned that he and Violet had married quietly. She had left the land army and was happily settled with him in the cottage he'd intended to live in with Hannah on the way to Hazelton.

Australia had represented hope and a new beginning for Hannah. Now she knew for certain it didn't have to involve a man. It was hard to regret her brief affair with Eddie when it had resulted in David, but she'd been wrong to let things go so far with Ray. She'd fallen into the trap of accepting that a woman was incomplete without a man, whereas she knew that wasn't the case. Never again would she let herself be talked into settling for second best. She'd loved Will with her heart and soul and now that he was gone, she would pour her love into her son and draw on the strength that had already enabled her to survive her father's abuse, her sister's dependence and her relocation to the other side of the world. Far from being lonely in her unmarried state, Hannah felt content. David had brought much-needed joy into her life. She relished her independence – apart from her reliance on Dot, of course. The job at David Jones was dull, but her colleagues were friendly, and for the first time since leaving Liverpool, she felt settled and in control of her life.

The relationships with Eddie and with Ray had taught her a lot about herself, and she felt more confident as a result.

ONE AFTERNOON IN LATE FEBRUARY, Hannah went with the baby to her favourite spot by the Archibald Memorial fountain in Hyde Park. Sitting on a bench, she tried to read but couldn't help gazing at her sleeping child. She'd never imagined it would be possible to love a child so much – particularly one she hadn't wanted to have.

David's face was a picture of contentment. It was too soon to tell whether David would resemble her or Eddie. Hannah wondered whether babies dreamed. How could she ever have contemplated giving him up? From the moment he was placed in her arms, a fierce protective love had burgeoned inside her. She had all she needed now. Times would be hard. The war would add to the struggle. Yet she had the strength to prevail.

The heat was stifling, and she thought about heading back to Dot's. She looked towards the fountain. The heat of the day – it must have been in the low nineties – and the brilliance of the sunshine made the splashing water particles from the fountain refract and distort into a fine mist.

She sat bolt upright on the bench. A shiver ran through her body like an electric charge.

Through the haze, someone was walking towards her, his features invisible in the refracting sunbeams. Hannah froze, unable to move. No, it wasn't possible. Her thoughts fractured, incoherent. She had to be dreaming. Hallucinating, maybe, due to the intense heat.

A cry emerged from her throat without her consciously shaping it, then she was up, hurling herself forward, running towards the mirage.

Arms wrapped around her, enclosing her, anchoring her, crushing her against his body until she thought she couldn't breathe. She inhaled the familiar smell of him and knew then it was real. She clutched at him, her fingers running over his face as if she were a blind woman feeling her way, unable to comprehend or believe what was happening. She couldn't speak, couldn't move, rooted to the spot as the world went on around her and she remained oblivious, locked in the haven of his arms.

After a few moments, she eased herself away to step back and look at the face she'd thought she'd never see again. More haggard and weary, but his eyes, locked on hers, shone with love. She realised she was crying. Great gushing tears of joy and shock and amazement.

As she struggled to get her mouth to form his name, he spoke first. His voice was choked with emotion, and she realised he was crying too. 'Is it really you? At last! I've found you.' His voice broke, and she clung to him. Time seemed to stand still as they held each other, hugging as though they were the last survivors on an empty planet.

'You've led me a dance, my darling girl,' he said, at last. 'I thought I'd never find you.'

Through her tears, she hung onto him, her head on his chest, dampening his shirt.

'They said you were dead, Will. I have the death certificate.' The enormity of what was happening hit her, and her legs buckled. He held her up, stroking her hair and gazing into her eyes as though he were looking straight into her very soul.

'By rights, I should be dead. I went down with the ship. Lost consciousness. They told me my leg was caught in the rope on a lifebuoy and it must have dragged me back to the surface. No idea how long I was floating there, unconscious, but I was picked up by a Portuguese merchant ship and taken to the Azores. I was in hospital there for three months with hypothermia and pneumonia. I was extremely lucky to survive.'

Hannah squeezed her eyes closed tightly, imagining that when she opened them again, she'd find she was dreaming. But she wasn't. The man holding her in his arms was flesh and blood and unmistakably Will.

As they stood together, lost to the rest of the world, David, several feet away in his pram, began a soft mewling. Hannah gasped. How could she explain to Will what she'd done?

But he anticipated her. 'Don't worry. I know about the baby. The Winterbournes told me everything.'

'You've seen them?'

'I went to Hunter's Down to find you.' He grinned. 'It was bonzer seeing Lizzie and Michael again and meeting their lad. I'm so happy you found them.'

'But how did you know where they were?'

'Back in Liverpool Sam gave me the only address he had for you— in Tatura with Judith. So I went there first. Judith said she hadn't heard from you for a while but gave me the Winterbournes' address. They told me you'd had a child.'

She gave a little gasp. 'Can you forgive me? Because I can't give David up.'

'I'd never ask you to. Things happen in war. How could I blame you when I was supposed to be dead?' He stroked her hair again then kissed her, a long slow lingering kiss that made her body shiver. 'Over these past two years, sometimes I despaired of ever finding you again. Now that I have you back, each day for the rest of my life is going to feel like a miracle.'

The baby's cries grew louder. Hannah turned and, still holding her husband's hand, went to the pram. She picked her son up and tried to soothe him.

'May I hold him?'

She put the baby into his arms.

Will cradled the child, holding out a finger which the baby gripped in his tiny fist. 'Hello, David, I'm your new dad.' He rocked the child gently in his arms, calming him. The crying muted to a soft murmur.

Hannah beamed. 'He likes you.'

They sat together on the bench under a spreading fig tree. Hannah laid her head on her husband's shoulders as he held the baby. Her happiness was complete.

He told her everything that had happened. How after leaving the Azores, he'd returned to Liverpool to find a heap of rubble where the house in Orrell Park had stood. He'd tracked down Sam, their friend and former landlord, who'd explained about Paolo and the sisters' journey to Australia. After several attempts and with some help from the commodore, he'd found a place on a ship bound for Cape Town, from where he'd made his way to Melbourne on another.

Hannah listened, spellbound. 'I owe Sam a letter,' she said. 'Not to mention my eternal gratitude.' She bit her lip. 'You saw Judith then?'

'And her little girl. She took me to the camp to see Paolo. It's a bloody disgrace that he's under lock and key.' He paused. 'Judith said she'd fallen out with you, and it was all her fault but she'd leave it to you to explain why.'

Hannah bent down and kissed the top of David's head. 'He's why. Judith was angry that I slept with someone else. You know she's always adored you. She told me it was a betrayal of your memory.'

He smiled. 'She's young and a bit naive.' He leant in and kissed her again. 'I don't see it that way. How could I begrudge you wanting some pleasure in this war-torn world. And you thought I was dead. Lizzie said the poor chap was killed.' He hesitated. 'Did you love him?'

Her answer was immediate. 'No.' Then she added, 'But I liked him very much.' She smiled. 'I'm incapable of loving anyone except you, Will.

THEY WALKED BACK to Dot's, arm-in-arm, pushing the pram, stopping every now and again to touch each other, reassuring themselves that this other person wasn't a figment of their imagination.

'You found her then?' Dot grinned from ear to ear when she opened the front door. She fussed over Will and led him to the table that was set with her finest Irish linen cloth. 'While you were looking for Hannah, I made up my bed fresh for you both. I'm going in the other room with the bub. No arguments. I don't want you two squashed up in a single bed with a crying baby when you've not seen each other for over two years and he's come back from the dead.'

. . .

THAT EVENING, when they were at last alone in the privacy of Dot's bedroom, with its lace doily-covered dressing table and collection of little china figurines of ballet dancers and baby deer, Hannah felt suddenly nervous. It had been so long since they'd been together. So long since they'd last made love.

Will was sitting on the side of the bed watching her, then he bent forward, his head in his hands. She sat down beside him, anxious. Didn't he want her anymore? Was it because of David? He lifted his face, and she saw he was crying.

'I'm sorry,' he said, his voice breaking. 'It's just that I thought I'd never find you. And you need to know I'm not the same man I was when I last saw you.'

She wrapped her arms around him and laid her head on his shoulder. 'Nothing matters other than that you're here and we're together.'

'In the hospital they told me I may never get over the trauma of what happened to me. I have nightmares every night. Sometimes I wake myself up, calling out, screaming. Something inside me is broken.' He gave another choked sob. 'I'm so afraid, Hannah, afraid that you won't want me anymore.'

Hannah cradled him in her arms. 'Oh, I want you. I want you so much. Nothing else matters, Will. Nothing at all – other than that you and I are together again. We'll face everything together – as long as you promise me you'll never go back to sea.'

He looked up at her and smiled. 'I'll never let you out of my sight again, Hannah.'

She got up and stood in front of him. Reaching behind her, she unfastened her dress and let it fall to the floor. Stepping out of it, she moved towards him to stand between his legs in her underslip. Will ran his hands over the flimsy fabric, tracing the curves of her body and gave a low groan. Hannah bent forward and undid the buttons on his shirt, which he shook off impatiently, then stood and took off his trousers. They fell onto the bed and each other.

For Hannah, it was like coming home.

LATER, as they lay in each other's arms, Will looked deep into her eyes. 'If I can't go back to sea, I don't know what I can do.' His brow formed deep furrows, and she smoothed her fingers over it.

'What about that farm you wanted in the Blue Mountains?' she said.

He shook his head. 'I've no money. Not to mention no strength. Since the sinking, I have problems breathing. I'm sorry. I told you, I'm not the man I once was.'

'You're still the man I love. Whatever's changed, that never will. And whatever scars you carry and problems you face, we'll face them together. I'm not the same woman you left behind either.'

'No,' he said, smiling. 'You're much stronger. More independent. I can see that clearly.'

'Don't you like it?' She felt nervous again.

'I love it. Even though I'm rather in awe of you, Hannah Kidd.' He kissed her again.

'You may have changed, but you're still the best kisser on the entire planet,' she said.

'I hope that doesn't mean you're able to quantify that extravagant claim.' He gave her a cheeky grin. 'But, seriously, what am I going to do? I have to find work. I won't be able to volunteer for the forces as I wouldn't pass the health and fitness test. I'm not qualified for anything.'

Hannah thought for a moment and was about to suggest a job on the harbour ferries but knew Will would find it boring and it might reignite a wish to return to the sea – or worse, feed the trauma caused by his experience when the *Shelbourne* went down. Then it struck her.

'I don't know whether you know this, but when we thought you'd been killed, the commodore gave me a job at Western Approaches Command.'

'I didn't know.' He looked at her in astonishment. 'Doing what?'

'Working in the plotting room.'

He gave a long whistle of admiration.

'Then, until I found out I was expecting David, I did a similar job here in Sydney for the air force.'

'I don't know why I should be surprised. I've always thought of you as the most exceptional woman.'

'Not when I first met you. I was just a slip of a girl, living in fear of her father.'

'With justification. But you were always resilient, Hannah. One of the many reasons I fell in love with you.'

She dropped a kiss on his brow. 'I happen to know a few of the bigwigs in air force intelligence. Not the naval ones – they handle them separately here – which is not a good idea in my opinion – not that anyone is the least bit interested in my opinion. But to return to the point, I know there's a need for men to work at the observation posts that feed into North Fort in Manly. That's where they plot ship and submarine movements for this section of coast. The triangulation and plotting is done by women like me, but most of the observation posts and all the batteries are operated by men. There's radar too, but it's very limited – not as extensive as the home chain system back in Britain.

Will was looking at her, open-mouthed. 'I'm in awe of you, Hannah. You've come so far. You know so much.'

'So, why don't I find out if there are any suitable vacancies and you can apply? You'd be perfect. You've got keen eyesight. You're used to looking through telescopes for submarines. And you can identify all the various types of shipping vessel.'

'It's strange,' he said, his voice sad. 'I'd always imagined introducing Australia to you, but it turns out you've found it all out on your own and are reintroducing it to me. You've left me behind, Hannah Kidd.'

'Never!' she said, her voice fierce. 'Now that I've found you again, I'll never leave you. You're stuck with me forever. Me and David,' she added.

'You and David.' He bent his head and kissed her.

Before you go! And

For Elizabeth and Michael's story read A GREATER WORLD

For Hannah and Will's story read STORMS GATHER BETWEEN US

For Hannah's and Judith's stories read SISTERS AT WAR

These four books form one series, ACROSS THE SEAS, but because the first two have a different publisher they appear on retailers as two separate series. Sorry! While it's obviously better to read them in order I hope I've made them each work as stand-alones too.

SUBSCRIBE TO CLARE'S MONTHLY NEWSLETTER

Sign up to Clare's monthly newsletter. As a thank you Clare will send you a free download of her short story collection, A Fine Pair of Shoes and Other Stories.

The newsletter will update you on Clare's writing and travels, special offers, and all sorts of nonsense that happens to be on her mind.

To subscribe go to Clare's website - https://clare flynn.co.uk to sign up

Follow clare on Facebook - /authorclareflynn

On X where she's @clarefly

ACKNOWLEDGEMENTS

Thanks to my friend and critique partner Margaret Kaine for her perceptive comments, support and encouragement.

To Debi Alper, my editor – it's been wonderful to work with Debi again on what was our twelfth book! You are a legend!

To Jane Dixon-Smith for the gorgeous cover design – I've lost count of how many fabulous covers Jane has designed for me over the years.

Thanks to Liza Perrat for making sure there were no Aussie-related bloomers! If any are present they will have crept in thanks to my incompetence in the final editing.

To my fellow Sanctuaryites for support and advice via our Facebook group and get togethers. We are overdue for another retreat!

Last but not least, to all my faithful readers. I so appreciate the support and enthusiasm you have shown for my books over the eleven years I've been published. Thank you!

ALSO BY CLARE FLYNN

THE PENANG COLLECTION

The Pearl of Penang

Prisoner from Penang

A Painter in Penang

Jasmine in Paris

HEARTS OF GLASS

The Artist's Apprentice

The Artist's Wife

The Artist's War

THE CANADIANS

The Chalky Sea

The Alien Corn

The Frozen River

THE SEPARATION COLLECTION

Kurinji Flowers

The Gamekeeper's Wife

Letters from a Patchwork Quilt

The Green Ribbons

ACROSS THE SEAS

A Greater World

Storms Gather Between Us

Sisters at War

Under a Southern Sky

THE CEYLON COLLECTION

The Star of Ceylon

The Tea Planter's Secret (coming soon)

The Monsoons's Gift

SHORT STORIES

A Fine Pair of Shoes and Other Stories

ABOUT THE AUTHOR

Clare Flynn was born in Liverpool and has lived all over the UK with spells abroad in Paris, Brussels, Milan and Sydney. After eighteen years living in West London she decamped to the seaside in Sussex, where she can see the sea from her windows.

Clare is the winner of the 2020 Bookbrunch Selfies Adult Fiction Prize for *The Pearl of Penang* and was the 2022 Indie Champion for the Romantic Novelists Association.

For more about Clare's books www.clareflynn.co.uk

If you enjoyed *Under a Southern Sky,* please leave a review. Authors rely on reviews and welcome them – even just a few words – and readers depend on them to find interesting books to read.

You'll find regular news and updates on Clare's Facebook page – AuthorClareFlynn

www.ingramcontent.com/pod-product-compliance
Lightning Source LLC
Chambersburg PA
CBHW030533190726
48283CB00006B/1896